R. M. Ballantyne

# Man on the Ocean

A book for boys

R. M. Ballantyne

**Man on the Ocean**
*A book for boys*

ISBN/EAN: 9783337319748

Printed in Europe, USA, Canada, Australia, Japan

Cover: Foto ©Andreas Hilbeck / pixelio.de

More available books at **www.hansebooks.com**

# MAN ON THE OCEAN.

## A Book for Boys.

### BY R. M. BALLANTYNE,

AUTHOR OF " YOUNG FUR TRADERS," " THE GORILLA HUNTERS," ETC., ETC.

LONDON:

T. NELSON AND SONS, PATERNOSTER ROW;

EDINBURGH; AND NEW YORK.

MDCCCLXIII.

# Preface.

THE wonders of the Ocean, and all connected therewith, need no preface, either by way of explanation or apology. They are of themselves sufficiently attractive to most minds to warrant the launching of this book without a preface. But we think it right, in justice to ourself, to say that the information contained in the following pages is by no means meant to be regarded as a complete account of Ocean and its concerns. It is simply such a desultory narration and explanation of things maritime—historically and otherwise—as, it is hoped, will imbue the reader's mind with a just conception of the nature of man's doings upon the Great Deep from the earliest ages to the present time.

R. M. B.

EDINBURGH, 1862.

# Contents.

# MAN ON THE OCEAN.

## CHAPTER I.

### TREATING OF SHIPS IN GENERAL.

THERE is, perhaps, no contrivance in the wide world more wonderful than a ship,—a full-rigged, well manned, gigantic ship !

Those who regard familiar objects in art and nature as mere matters of course, and do not trouble themselves to wander out of the beaten track of every-day thought, may not at first feel the force or admit the truth of this statement. Let us entreat such folk to shake themselves vigorously out of this beaten track of every-day thought. Let them knit their brows and clench their teeth, and gaze steadfastly into the fire, or up at the sky, and endeavour to realize what is involved in the idea of a ship.

What would the men of old have said if you had told them that you intended to take yon large wooden house and launch it upon the sea, and proceed in it out of sight of land for a few days? "Poor fellow," they would have replied, "you are mad." Ah, many a wise philosopher has been deemed mad, not only by men of old, but by men of later days. This "mad" idea has long since been fulfilled, for what is a ship but a wooden house made to float upon the sea, and sail with its inmates hither and thither, at the will of the guiding spirit, over a trackless unstable ocean for months together? It is a self-sustaining moveable hotel upon the sea. It is an oasis in the desert of waters, so skilfully contrived as to be capable of advancing against wind and tide, and of outliving the wildest storms—the bitterest fury of wind and waves. It is the residence of a community, whose country for the time being is the ocean; or, as in the case of the *Great Eastern* steamship, it is a *town* with some thousands of inhabitants launched upon the deep.

Ships are the electric sparks of the world, as it were, by means of which the superabundance of different countries is carried forth to fill, reciprocally, the voids in each. They are not only the media of intercourse between the various families of the human race, whereby our shores are enriched with the produce of other lands, but they are the bearers of inestimable treasures of knowledge from clime to clime, and of gospel light to the uttermost ends of the earth.

But for ships we should never have heard of the wonders of the coral isles and the beauties of the golden south, or the phenomena and tempests of the icy north. But for ships the stirring adventures and perils of Magellan, Drake, Cook, &c., had never been encountered, and even the far-famed Robinson Crusoe himself had never gladdened, and saddened, and romantically maddened the heart of youth with his escapes, his fights, his parrots, and his philosophy, as he now does, and as he will continue to do till the end of time. Some account then of ships, with anecdotes illustrative of the perils to which they are frequently exposed, cannot fail, we think, to prove interesting to all, especially to boys, for whose particular edification we now write. Boys, of all creatures in this world, are passionately fond of boats and ships; they make them of every shape and size, with every sort of tool, and hack and cut their fingers in the operation, as *we* know from early personal experience. They sail them, and wet their garments in so doing, to the well-known sorrow of all right-minded mammas. They lose them, too, and break their hearts, almost, at the calamity. They make little ones when they are little, and big ones when they grow big ; and when they grow bigger they not unfrequently forsake the toy for the reality, embark in some noble craft, and wed the stormy sea.

A word in your ear at this point. Do not think that because you fall in love with a *ship* you will naturally and necessarily fall in love with the *sea !* Some do, and some don't; with those who do, it is well—with those who don't, and yet go to sea, it is remarkably ill. Think *philosophically* about " going to sea," my lads. Try honestly to resist

your own inclination as *long as possible*, and only go if you
find that *you can't help it !*   In such a case you will probably
find that you are cut out for it—not otherwise.   *We* love the
sea with a true and deep affection, and often have we tossed
upon her foam-topt waves, but we don't wish to be a sailor
—by no manner of means !

And now, boys, come along and we will conduct you as
pleasantly and profitably as we can from a ship's cradle,
through all her stormy existence to her grave.

# CHAPTER II.

## THE EARLIEST DAYS OF WATER TRAVELLING.

ONCE upon a time there were no ships. Men did not know the meaning of the word; they did not want them, and, for many many centuries, the sea-gulls had the ocean all to themselves. But *boats* are of very ancient date. Doubtless the *first* boats must have been constructed by the *first* men who dwelt on the earth. They consisted, probably,— for we are now in the land of Conjecture,—of stumps of fallen trees, seated astride of which the immediate descendants of our first parents ferried themselves over small lakes and across rivers.

Wet feet are not agreeable under any circumstances. We can conceive that prolonged voyages performed in this fashion—say several hundred yards or a mile—rendered those primitive mariners so uncomfortable that they resolved to improve their condition, and, after much earnest thought, hit upon the plan of fastening several logs together by means of twigs, and thus they formed *rafts*.

As time progressed, and men began to display wisdom in the moulding of brass and iron, we can imagine that they soon bethought them of flattening the surface of their rafts, and then finding them unwieldy and difficult to manage, no doubt, they hit upon the idea of hollowing out the logs. Adzes were probably not invented at that time, so they betook themselves to the element of fire—which is at the present day used by savage nations for the same purpose—and burned out the insides of their logs. Thus *canoes* sprang into being.

But such canoes were clumsy and heavy, besides being liable to split; so men bethought themselves of constructing a light framework of wood, and covering it with bark or skin. Then artificers in iron invented saws; logs were ripped up; planks were formed; pitch oozed ready to hand from the trees; with grass, perchance, they caulked the seams;—and soon the first *boat* floated on the water,—clumsy and tub-like, no doubt, but serviceable withal,—and youths of a hundred years old, and full-grown men of two or three hundred, capered and shouted on the shore with delight at the great invention, while venerable patriarchs of seven or eight hundred summers gazed in wonder, with almost prophetic solemnity, and exclaimed that they had never before seen the like of *that* in all the course of their long long lives!

These times are old now—so old that men can scarcely get their minds to realize how old they are; but the things that were used then are used even now, and that not only among the savages of distant lands, but by men living at our very doors.

*The coracle*, a basket boat, of the most primitive descrip-tion, is still occasionally met with in South Wales. It is neither more nor less than a large wicker basket covered with a hide, and is tub-shaped and clumsy to a degree. When the Romans invaded Britain this species of boat was in common use. Like the canoe of the North American Indians, it is easily upset, and we should think must be rather unmanageable, but as we are not likely ever again to be reduced to it in this country, we can afford to regard this fact with indifference.

From little boats to big boats there is but a step, and no

THE CORACLE.

doubt rivers were soon navigated, and new countries ex-
plored, while those who lived near the sea-coast dared even
to launch their boats upon the ocean ; but they "hugged
the shore," undoubtedly, and seldom ventured to proceed at
night unless the stars shone brightly in the sky.   Years
rolled on, and dwellers on the sea-coast became more and

more venturous in their voyages along the shore; and it behoved them to have larger boats, or barges, with numerous rowers.   War-galleys sprang into being.   Strong winds sometimes carried them off shore, and out of sight of land. Ah, reader! who can conceive the feelings of the first mariners who saw the solid land sink on the horizon, and beheld nothing in all the waste of waters save their own tiny bark that reeled beneath them on the heaving billows?   Perchance these first adventurers on the deep found their way back to land, and tried the bold experiment of steering by the stars.   Perhaps not; but at length it did come about that ships were built, and men were found bold enough to put to sea in them for days and weeks together.

The ark is the first ship of which we have any authentic account.   We now leave conjecture, for the ark was built by Noah under the immediate direction of the Almighty, and we have a minute account of it in the Bible.

More than two thousand three hundred years before our Lord and Saviour Jesus Christ came to earth, man's wickedness had attained to such a height that God resolved to destroy the inhabitants of the world by a deluge.   But in the midst of wrath God remembered mercy.   He spared Noah and his family, and saved them from destruction by placing them in the ark along with pairs of the lower animals.

Every reader of the Bible knows the story of the deluge, but every one may not be aware that traditions of this deluge are found in every nation of the earth.   East, west, north, and south—civilized and savage—all men tell us of a great flood which once covered the world, and from which only one family was saved, in a boat, or a canoe, or an ark. This is one proof of the universality of the flood; but another and stronger proof is, that shells and petrifactions of marine animals are found on the tops of the highest hills all over the world.

What the barbarous and savage nations know dimly from tradition, we know certainly and fully from the inspired word of God. The ark was built; the flood came; Noah with his family and two of every living creature entered into it, and for months the *first ship* floated on a sea whose shoreless waves flowed round and round the world.

What the ark's form was we cannot tell precisely; but we know its dimensions pretty accurately.

Although it was not intended for voyaging, the ark must necessarily have been a perfect model of a vessel meant to float upon the waters. To some extent, too, it must have been fitted to ride upon turbulent billows, for it " went upon the face of the waters " for upwards of seven months; and before it rested finally on the top of Mount Ararat, " God made a wind to pass over the earth, and the waters asswaged."

In regard to its size the most interesting way to consider it, perhaps, will be to compare it with the *Great Eastern*— the largest ship that has yet been built by man. Assuming a cubit to be about 18 inches, the length of the ark was about 450 feet, its breadth about 75 feet, and its depth about 45 feet.

The *Great Eastern's* length is 680 feet, its breadth 83 feet, and its depth from deck to keel 60 feet.

The ark was built of gopher-wood, which is thought by some to be pine, by others cedar. It consisted of three stories, and had a window and a door, and was pitched within and without; but it had neither masts nor rudder, and it is evident that although it was man's refuge, the ark was not designed to be managed by man, for after Noah and his family had entered in, God took on himself the guidance and preservation of their vessel. Thus our Saviour—of whom the ark was a type—specially guides and protects those who fly to him for refuge.

But although we have noticed the ark as being the first ship, we cannot with propriety place it in the front of the history of navigation. After the flood the ark seems to have been soon forgotten, or at least imperfectly remembered, and men reverted to their little canoes, and clumsy boats, which sufficed for all their limited wants. It was not until about a thousand years later in the world's history that men began to build ships of considerable size, and venture on prolonged *coasting*-voyages for the purposes of discovery and commerce. Navigation had been practised, and the art of ship-building had made very considerable progress, long before men dared to lose sight of the shore and venture out upon the mysterious bosom of the great unknown sea.

# CHAPTER III.

## RAFTS AND CANOES.

To the ancients the Mediterranean was the ocean, and among its bays, and creeks, and islands, maritime enterprise sprang into being and rose into celebrity. Among the Phœnicians, the Egyptians, and Hebrews, we find the earliest traces of navigation and commerce. The first of these nations, occupying the narrow slip of land between mount Lebanon and the Mediterranean, rose into fame as mariners between the years 1700 and 1100 before Christ—the renowned city of Sidon being their great sea-port, whence their ships put forth to trade with Cyprus and Rhodes, Greece, Sardinia, Sicily, Gaul, and Spain. Little is known of the state of trade in those days, or of the form or size of ancient vessels. Homer tells us, in his account of the Trojan war, that the Phœnicians supplied the combatants with many articles of luxury, and from Scripture we learn that the same enterprising navigators brought gold to Solomon from Ophir in the year 1000 B.C.

A short time previous to this the Phœnicians ventured to pass through the Straits of Gibraltar, and for the first time beheld the great Atlantic Ocean. Proceeding along the coast of Spain they founded Cadiz, and, not long after, creeping down the western coasts of Africa, established colonies there. But their grandest feat was achieved about 600 years B.C., when they sailed down the Red Sea and the eastern coast of Africa, doubled the Cape of Good Hope, sailed up the western coast, and returned home by the Straits of Gibraltar. Bartholomew Diaz must hide his diminished head before this fact, for, although he gets all the credit, the Phœnicians of old "doubled the Cape" at least twenty centuries before him!

That long voyages were made by the men of old, before authentic history began, seems highly probable. The expedition of the *Argonauts* to Colchis in the year 1250 B.C. in search of the "Golden Fleece," is the first ancient voyage that lays claim to authenticity. What the Golden Fleece was is uncertain; some think it was a term used to symbolize the mines of precious metals near the Black Sea. Whatever it was, the *Argonauts* went in search of it; whether or not they found it is unrecorded in history. Jason, son of the King of Thessaly, was the leader of this expedition, which consisted of one ship and fifty men. A man named Argus built the ship, which from him was named the *Argo*, hence the name of *Argonauts*.

In treating of ancient vessels, we may as well proceed on the principle suggested by a sagacious child who, when his mother was about to tell him a story, usually begged of her to "bedin at the bedinning." We shall begin at the beginning.

RAFTS, as we have already remarked, must undoubtedly have been the beginning of navigation. But they have not, like many other species of ancient craft, been altogether superseded by modern inventions. True, we do not now-a-days carry on war on rafts, but we still carry on trade with them in many parts of the world. How the rafts of ancient times were formed we cannot tell precisely, though we can easily guess; but one thing we know, and that is, that the first improvement made in such craft, was the thrusting of a few thick planks down into the water to the depth of three or four feet between the logs which compose the raft. These acted the part of a keel, and by pressing against the water *side-ways* when a *side* wind blew, prevented the raft from making much of what is called *lee-way*,—that is, drifting in the direction in which the wind happened to be blowing. Some sorts of Dutch vessels use *lee-boards* for this purpose at the present day.

The rafts now in use on the great rivers of America are exceedingly curious in many respects. One peculiarity of many of them is this, that they float *themselves*, not goods, to market—the pine logs of which they are constructed being the marketable commodity. Some of these lumber-rafts, as they are called, are of great size, and as their navigators have often to spend many weeks on them, slowly floating down the rivers, they build huts, or little cottages, on them, cook their provisions on board, and in short, spend night and day in their temporary floating homes, as comfortably as if they were on the land.

When these rafts approach a water-fall or a rapid, they unfasten the lashings and allow several logs tied together to run down at a time. After the rapid is passed the loose logs are collected together, the raft is reconstructed, and the voyage down to the sea continued. Of course huts are built only on rafts which navigate the largest rivers, and are not thus liable to be taken to pieces.

When the logs reach the sea they are shipped to various parts of the world where timber is scarce. Large quantities are imported into Great Britain from Canada and other parts of America. A bold thing has once or twice been done. Instead of shipping the logs in vessels, enterprising and ingenious men built them into a *solid ship*, leaving a small space to serve as a cabin and a hold for provisions; then erecting masts they hoisted sail, and in this singular craft crossed the Atlantic.   On arriving at port they broke up their raft-ship and sold it.

RAFT.

Rafts, however, have not been confined to the purposes of traffic.   They have frequently been the means of saving the lives of shipwrecked mariners, and too often they have been the means only of prolonging the wretched existence of those who have ultimately perished at sea, as the following sad anecdote will show :—

### WRECK OF THE MEDUSA.

The *Medusa* was a French frigate which was wrecked in

the year 1816 in consequence of mismanagement. On her voyage to the coast of Africa she was carelessly run on a sand-bank, and all efforts to get her off failed, so that the passengers nd crew were obliged to take to the boats. As the vessel's object was colonization, there were men of various ranks, professions, and trades on board, amounting to more than four hundred souls; the boats were, therefore, insufficient to convey them all off, and a raft was constructed, on which one hundred and fifty persons, soldiers, and sailors, embarked. Wine, biscuit, and other provisions, were put on board of the boats and raft, and it was agreed that the former—five in number—were to tow the latter. Discipline, however, without which no body of men can work success-fully, was not maintained by the incompetent commander. One by one the crews of the boats basely and selfishly cut the tow ropes, and left the raft to the mercy of the waves.

At first the poor creatures on it could scarcely credit their senses, but when the boats disappeared the full horrors of their situation burst upon them. In the haste of departure from the wreck chart and compass had been forgotten, and worse than all, only a small quantity of biscuit had been put on board, and no other provision, except wine, of which they had more than enough. But wine without food was worse than useless. Having taken no food for some time before they left the wreck, they were hungry, and mixed all their biscuit with wine and distributed a portion to each. Then they succeeded in setting up a mast and hoisting a sail, but the raft sank so deep in the water that they were huddled together, scarce able to move, on the part left dry. Soon the wind began to rise, and the sea broke over them furiously, and now the night came on, shrouding in a scene of darkness and horror that our minds cannot possibly realize. But the dawn of the following day revealed still more appalling features of their situation. During the night nearly a dozen of their number had slipped between the spars of the raft and been jammed to death.

The wind moderated during the day, and hope began to rise, perhap a little, as they scanned the horizon earnestly in search of a passing ship, or one of their own returning boats. But neither ship nor boat appeared. The day passed—how wearily none can tell—and the second night came on. With it also came the wind, and before morning many of the famishing crew of the raft were swept off and drowned, while the weaker among them were killed by the pressure of their companions.

Hope now left them, and in the despair that followed, the wretched men resolved to relieve the sufferings of their last hour by drinking! Unaccountable madness! one is tempted to exclaim. God was present there. He has told men to call upon him "in the time of trouble," and has promised to deliver them. He was able, if need were, to work a miracle for the deliverance of these poor men, yet they preferred to end their days in a state of intoxication! This is not uncommon, as the history of wrecks too clearly proves. They carried out their resolve by boring a hole in one of the casks, and continued to drink until the sea-water mixed with the wine and rendered it useless. Rendered mad by drink, the men now determined to murder their officers and cut the ropes that bound the raft together, and one of them even began the work of destruction with a hatchet, when the officers and passengers rushed upon the men in a body, and seizing the fellow who had the axe, threw him into the sea. The other mutineers immediately fell on their knees and cried for mercy, which was granted; but only an hour passed when they made another attempt to carry out their threat; a general fight instantly ensued, and the raft was quickly strewn with slaughtered men. Upwards of sixty of the hapless crew perished in this disastrous affair.

But the survivors had not yet reached the extremity of horror. One cask of wine remained, but this could not allay the pangs of hunger, so they were compelled at last to devour the flesh of their dead companions.

On the fourth day a shoal of flying fish fell upon the raft and were captured. These curious fish have two fins, which are so long and powerful as to enable them to leap out of the water and fly for a short distance through the air. They are thus enabled to escape from their inveterate enemy the dolphin. Collecting these flying fish, the starving crew cooked them over a fire made in an empty cask. On the fourth night the mutineers again attempted to effect their mad purpose, but were quickly overcome, though not without the shedding of more blood.

The crew was by this time reduced to thirty men, most of whom were partially disabled by wounds and bruises, while some of them had all the skin chafed off their legs. In order to allay their sufferings two unhappy soldiers attempted to drink the remaining wine by stealth, but were discovered and instantly thrown into the sea. Of the men who remained only half seemed capable of surviving, even for a few days, the sufferings they had undergone. Perceiving this, the remaining half formed the terrible resolution of throwing their dying comrades into the sea in order to make their scanty provision last longer. The horrible resolve was carried into effect, and the fifteen remaining men spent two more days of suffering on the raft, when a vessel hove in sight and rescued them; but six of

these died soon after, and of the hundred and fifty human

beings who embarked on the raft only nine survived to tell their tale of suffering.

In the account of the travels of the great scientific explorer, Baron von Humboldt, we are told of rafts which are used at the present day on the rivers of South America. Our annexed Woodcut represents one of those that are used near the mouth of the river Guayaquil. It is laden with the fruit of those tropical regions, and is on its way to market. It has a mast and sail, and covered sheds to protect the goods and crew, and it can stand a considerable sea. It sails well too, and can veer, and tack, and sail pretty close to the wind by means of lowering logs or planks into the water as before described. Such rafts, or "*balzas*," vary from 40 to 80 feet in length, and they have been used by the inhabitants of Peru from the most remote periods of the history of that country.

Turning now from the consideration of rafts, we shall consider the canoes which succeeded them.

SMALL CANOE.

CANOES must, we think, have been invented after rafts, and were formed, as we have said, out of logs, of bark, and of skins stretched upon frames of wood. Of ancient canoes we can say little ; but it is probable that they were similar in most respects to the canoes used by savage nations at the present time, for man, in his lowest or most savage condition, is necessarily the same now that he was in ancient times. We shall, therefore, take a glance at the canoes of savage nations now existing, and thus shall form a good idea, we doubt not, of what canoes were in days of old.

Simplest among them all, perhaps, are the canoes of the North American Indians. They are built of thin laths and ribs of wood, and are covered with the bark of the birch-tree. The sheets of bark are not a quarter of an inch thick; several sheets are used in the covering of one canoe;

SMALL CANOE.

they are sewed together with the long pliant roots of the pine, and the seams are rendered tight with gum, procured from the same tree. So light are these canoes, that two men can carry on their shoulders one capable of holding eight or ten men with their provisions, &c., for a voyage of many months. They are of various sizes: from the hunting canoe which holds one Indian, to the large canoe that carries fourteen. They are propelled by short paddles instead of oars.

Many and terrible are the risks run by *voyageurs* who travel through the lakes and rivers of North America in these canoes.

The following anecdote is related of a narrow escape made by some fur-traders while descending one of the rivers in the backwoods of the Hudson's Bay Territory: One fine evening in autumn a north canoe was gliding swiftly down one of the noble bends in the river referred to. New, beautiful, and ever-changing scenes were being constantly opened up to the view of the *voyageurs*, whose plaintive and beautiful canoe songs were rolling over the waters. Suddenly the song ceased as the distant roar of a waterfall struck their ears, and the steersmen—for there are usually two, one in the bow and one in the stern—prepared to land and "*make a portage*,"—that is, to carry the canoe and lading past the falls by land, and re-launch in the smooth water below.

The approach to the landing-place at the head of the fall was somewhat difficult, owing to a point of rock which projected into the stream in the direction of the fall, and round which point it was necessary to steer with some dexterity in order to avoid being drawn into the strong current. The fearless guides, however, had often passed the place in former years in safety, and, accordingly, dashed at the point with reckless indifference, their paddles flinging a circle of spray over their heads as they changed from side to side with graceful but vigorous rapidity. The swift stream carried them quickly round the point of danger, and they had almost reached the quiet eddy near the landing-place when the stem of the canoe was caught by the stream, which instantly whirled it out from the shore and carried it down stream like an arrow. Another moment and the gushing water dragged them to the verge of the fall, which thundered and foamed among frightful chasms and rocks many feet below. The stern of the canoe overhung the abyss, and now the *voyageurs* plied their paddles with the desperation of men who felt that their lives depended on the exertions of the next awful minute. For a second the canoe remained stationary, and seemed to tremble on the brink of destruction—the strength of the water and the power of the men being almost equally balanced—then, inch by inch, it began slowly to ascend the stream. The danger was past! A few nervous strokes and the canoe shot out of the current like an arrow, and floated in safety in the still water below the point.

CANOE ON EDGE OF FALLS.

The whole thing, from beginning to end, was the work of

a few seconds; yet who can describe or comprehend the tumultuous gush of feeling aroused during these brief seconds in the bosoms of the *voyageurs?* The sudden, electric change from tranquil safety to the verge of what appeared certain destruction—and then, deliverance! It was one of those thrilling incidents which frequently occur to those who thread the wildernesses of this world, and was little thought of by those to whom it occurred, beyond the moment of danger; yet it was one of those solemn seasons, more or less numerous in the history of all men, when the

ESQUIMAUX CANOE.

Almighty speaks to his careless creatures in a way that cannot be mistaken, however much it may be slighted, awakening them, with a rough grasp, to behold the slender cord that suspends them over the abyss of eternity.

The canoes used by the Esquimaux who inhabit the Polar regions are made of a light framework of wood, which is covered entirely over with seal-skin, a round hole being left in the centre, in which the Esquimaux sits. Round this hole there is a loose piece of skin, which is drawn up by the man and fastened round his waist. The machine is thus completely water-tight. No waves can dash into, although they can sweep over it ; and if by chance it should upset, the Esquimaux can turn it and himself up into the proper position by one dexterous sweep of his long, double-bladed paddle. The paddle, which varies from 10 to 15 feet, is simply a pole with a blade at each end. It is grasped in the centre, and each end dipped alternately on either side of the *kayak*, as these canoes are called. Esquimaux kayaks are first-rate sea-boats. They can face almost any sort of weather. They are easily upset, however, and those who are unaccustomed to them are pretty sure of a ducking on their first attempt to paddle in them. They are extremely light, and are propelled by the natives very swiftly. In these frail canoes the natives of Polar regions pursue seals and whales, and even venture to attack the walrus in his native element. The kayak is used exclusively by the men. The oomiak, or women's canoe, is of much larger and clumsier construction, somewhat like a boat. It is open above, and can hold a large family of women and children. Like the kayak, it is a framework of wood covered with seal-skin, and it is propelled by means of short paddles of the spoon form.

In order to show that the paddle of the canoe is more natural to man than the oar, we present a picture of the

canoe used by the Indians of the Amazon in South America.
Here we see that the savages of the south, like their breth-

INDIANS OF THE AMAZON.

ren of the north, sit with their faces to the bow and urge
their bark forward by means of short paddles, without using
the gunwale as a fulcrum. The oar is decidedly a more
modern and a more scientific instrument than the paddle,

but the latter is better suited to some kinds of navigation than the former.

Very different indeed from the light canoes just described are the canoes of the South Sea islanders.   Some are large and some are small; some long, some short; a few elegant, a few clumsy, and one or two peculiarly remarkable.  Most of them are narrow and liable to upset, in order to prevent which catastrophe the natives have ingeniously, though clumsily, contrived a sort of " *out-rigger*," or plank, which they attach to the side of the canoe to keep it upright. They also fasten two canoes together to steady them.

One of these *double canoes* is thus described by Cheever in his " Island World of the Pacific:"—" A double canoe is composed of two single ones of the same size placed parallel to each other, three or four feet apart, and secured in their places by four or five pieces of wood, curved just in the shape of a bit-stock.   These are lashed to both canoes with the strongest cinet, made of cocoa-nut fibre, so as to make the two almost as much one as some of the double ferry-boats that ply between Brooklyn and New York.  A flattened arch is thus made by the bow-like cross-pieces over the space between the canoes, upon which a board or a couple of stout poles laid lengthwise constitute an elevated platform for passenger and freight, while those who paddle and steer sit in the bodies of the canoes at the sides.  A slender mast, which may be unstepped in a minute, rises from about the centre of this platform, to give support to a very simple sail, now universally made of white cotton cloth, but formerly of mats."

The double canoes belonging to the chiefs of the South Sea islanders are the largest,—some of them being nearly 70 feet long, yet they are each only about 2 feet wide

and 3 or 4 feet deep. The sterns are remarkably high—
15 or 18 feet above the water.

The war canoes are also large and compactly built; the
stern being low and covered, so as to afford shelter from
stones and darts. A rude imitation of a head or some
grotesque figure is usually carved on the stern while the
stem is elevated, curved like the neck of a swan, and terminates frequently in the carved figure of a bird's head.
These canoes are capable of holding fifty warriors. Captain
Cook describes some as being 108 feet long. All of them,
—whether single or double, mercantile or war canoes—are
propelled by paddles, the men sitting with their faces in
the direction in which they are going.

As may be supposed, these canoes are often upset in
rough weather, but as the South Sea islanders are expert
swimmers, they generally manage to right their canoes and
scramble into them again. Their only fear on such occasions is being attacked by sharks. Ellis, in his fascinating
book called " Polynesian Researches," relates an instance of
this kind of attack which was made upon a number of
chiefs and people—about thirty-two—who were passing
from one island to another in a large double canoe : " They
were overtaken by a tempest, the violence of which tore
their canoes from the horizontal spars by which they were
united. It was in vain for them to endeavour to place
them upright or empty out the water, for they could not
prevent their incessant overturning. As their only resource
they collected the scattered spars and boards, and constructed a raft, on which they hoped they might drift to
land. The weight of the whole number who were collected
on the raft was so great as to sink it so far below the surface, that they stood above their knees in water. They

made very little progress, and soon became exhausted by fatigue and hunger. In this condition they were attacked by a number of sharks. Destitute of a knife or any other weapon of defence, they fell an easy prey to these rapacious monsters. One after another was seized and devoured, or carried away by them, and the survivors, who, with dreadful anguish beheld their companions thus destroyed, saw the number of their assailants apparently increasing, as each body was carried away, until only two or three remained.

"The raft, thus lightened of its load, rose to the surface of the water and placed them beyond the reach of the voracious jaws of their relentless destroyers. The tide and current soon carried them to the shore, where they landed to tell the melancholy fate of their fellow-voyagers."

The South Sea islanders, of whose canoes we have been writing, are—some of them at least—the fiercest savages on the face of the earth. They wear little or no clothing, and practise cannibalism,—that is, *man eating*, from choice. They actually prefer human flesh to any other. Of this we are informed on most unquestionable authority.

Doubtless the canoes which we have just described are much the same now as they were a thousand years ago; so that, by visiting those parts of the earth where the natives are still savage, we may, as it were, leap backward into ancient times, and behold with our own eyes the state of marine architecture as it existed when our own forefathers were savages, and paddled about the Thames and the Clyde on logs, and rafts, and wicker-work canoes.

OCEAN, BOAT, AND SHIP.

# CHAPTER IV.

## THE SEA.

"I love, oh, how I love to ride
On the fierce foaming bursting tide!"

So goes the song, and thousands in all ages act as if that song were their creed. And yet how varied are the feelings with which men regard the sea! Our own early reminiscences of it are tinged with horror. Even to this day do we remember the cold clammy feel and the salt fishy smell of the flannel garment in which our trembling infant form was wrapt, preparatory to being carried to the sea beach and bathed! Oh, it was a hateful operation! Who can describe the gushing horror of the moment when the flannel garment was removed and our panting body was exposed to the fresh cold air. But worse, ten thousand fold, the moment when our frantic yells were stifled in a bubbling gasp beneath the brine ! Ah, mothers, nurses, we doubt the tenderness of your hearts, when we behold your ruthless conduct to the sprawling, squalling, helpless little ones, who are partially drowned by you, daily, in the summer of the year ! We are inclined to think that many a gallant sailor is nipped in the bud thus. Were we in power we would add a clause to Martin's Act, and constitute bathing babies *against their will* cruelty to animals.

Fortunately, the natural love of many for the great sea cannot be cooled even by the strong measures above referred to. Babies get used to bathing as eels do (it is said !) to being skinned, and when they become little boys, their delight in wading in the sea and tumbling on the shore is inexpressible as it is unquenchable.

Do you see yonder urchin with the flowing yellow hair, and the short frock, and the fat legs, and the little pair of shoes and socks, scampering over the sands ? That fellow *adores* the sea; moreover, he revels in it, mentally and physically. Down he flies to its margin where the wavelets fall with a little hiss-s-s upon the sand, and in goes one foot, right over the shoe ! He didn't intend that. Nurse, no doubt, told him he should be whipped if he wet his feet, and he had half promised to be very careful, but he ran down so fast that when he came to the edge of the water he could not pull up, and so the thing is done and can't be helped. What process of reasoning goes on in the brain of that child we cannot tell ; perhaps he thinks that having wet one foot, common justice to the other requires that it should be wet too ; at any rate, in it goes and away he scampers knee-deep, dashing up the water and yelling with delight. He'll catch it, he knows, on returning home,

—no matter, he is happy *now*. Presently he turns his face sea-ward and becomes grave. The little wretch is "outward bound!" The water is up to his knees now, and it is rather cold,—no matter, he *loves it*, and that keeps him warm. Deeper still, and the edge of his frock is wet, —no matter, he gathers his garments in a bundle under his armpits. Hah! he gave a gasp there, for the water swelled up to his waist and sent his heart into his mouth. Presently he turns in considerable trepidation to regain the shore; but the bed of the ocean is proverbially unequal; he staggers into a hole, up to the armpits—the frock is let go—a wild scramble, and he is down, over head and ears. Next instant he is up; the hole is but a small one, and he recovers his footing—but oh, reader, *such* a pair of eyes! Saucers? no, that's not the idea, if you mean white saucers with a large round black spot in the centre of each, you are not far wrong in your conception.

He goes home in a subdued condition, and probably he does "catch it," but his love for the sea is not abated one jot. His passion for little boats and dockyards, for ropes and spars, and blocks and tar, goes on increasing with his growth, and, ten to one, you will see him some day in a blue jacket, white ducks, and a straw hat.

Most people love the sea; some delight in its foam-specked margin, where its waters kiss the land—others rejoice in its far-off solitudes, where its great billows heave, even in the deepest calm, or rage in the wildest storms. And well is it worthy of our admiration, for here the power, and majesty, and terrors of God are seen more forcibly and frequently than on the land. Here, too, his tender care of the smallest and apparently most insignificant of his creatures is exhibited in a wonderful degree.

Much has been written about the sea—many thick volumes treat of it; but of all the works we ever read, none equal the fascinating volume written by Captain Maury of the United States Navy, called "The Physical Geography of the Sea." Maury is a man among a thousand. He makes the mysteries of science plain and comprehensible to the weakest and most unscientific minds. Here is the poetical commencement of his work, in which he treats of that mysterious current known as the "Gulf Stream:"—

"There is a river in the ocean. In the severest droughts it never fails, and in the mightiest floods it never overflows. Its banks and its bottoms are of cold water, while its current is of warm. The Gulf of Mexico is its fountain (hence the name), and its mouth is in the Arctic seas. It is the Gulf Stream. There is in the world no other such majestic flow of waters. Its current is more rapid than the Mississippi or the Amazon, and its volume more than a thousand times greater.

"Its waters, as far out from the gulf as the Carolina coasts, are of an indigo blue. They are so distinctly marked that their line of junction with the common sea-water may be traced with the eye. Often one half of a vessel may be perceived floating in Gulf Stream water, while the other half is in common water of the sea,—so sharp is the line, and such the want of affinity between those waters, and such, too, the reluctance, so to speak, on the part of those of the Gulf Stream to mingle with the common water of the sea.

"At the salt-works in France, and along the shores of the Adriatic, where the 'salines' are carried on by the process of solar evaporation, there is a series of vats or pools through which the water is passed as it comes from the sea, and is reduced to the briny state. The longer it is exposed to evaporation the salter it grows, and the deeper is the hue of its blue, until crystallization is about to commence, when the now deep blue water puts on a reddish tint. Now, the waters of the Gulf Stream are salter than the waters of the sea through which they flow, and hence we can account for the deep indigo blue which all navigators observe off the Carolina coasts.

"These saltmakers are in the habit of judging of the richness of the sea-water in salt by its colour—the greener the hue the fresher the water. We have in this, perhaps, an explanation of the contrasts which the waters of the Gulf Stream present with those of the Atlantic, as well as of the light green of the North Sea and other Polar waters; also of the dark blue of the trade-wind regions, and especially of the Indian Ocean, which poets have described as the 'black waters.'" Much curious and useful information may be gathered from this capital book.

The cause of this Gulf Stream, we are told, has always puzzled philosophers.

Early writers imagined that it was caused by the floods poured into the Gulf of Mexico by the Mississippi River; but this has been shown to be impossible, as the volume of water discharged by that river is not equal to the three thousandth part of that which escapes through the Mexican Gulf into the ocean,—moreover, the Gulf Stream is exceedingly salt, while the Mississippi is fresh. More recent philosophers attributed the stream to the motion of the sun in the ecliptic, or to the escape of the waters that had been forced into the Caribbean Sea by the trade winds. It has been proved, however, that the latter of these influences is insufficient to cause it. The true cause is still a matter of uncertainty; but the theory most worthy of reception is that which attributes the Gulf Stream to the combined effects of heat and the motion of the earth on its axis. There is a constant tendency of the waters of the tropics towards the poles, and of those of the poles towards the tropics. In short, it would seem that the warm waters go to the poles to get cooled, and, in doing so, *force* those of the poles to come to the equator to get heated. Thus circulation is constantly kept up, but the currents so formed are endlessly modified by the obstructions they meet with in the islands and shallows of ocean and in the configuration of the land.

The value of a knowledge of this great "river in the ocean" is incalculable. In days of old, when daring mariners groped their way over the unknown waste of waters, many long and weary days and weeks were spent in battling against adverse currents and winds, or in lying helpless in the midst of dead calms,—evils which are now avoided by a knowledge of the flow of the ocean currents.

"Midway the Atlantic," says Maury, " in the triangular space between the Azores, Canaries, and the Cape de Verd Islands, is the *Sargasso* Sea. Covering an area equal in extent to the Mississippi valley, it is so thickly matted over with gulf weeds, that the speed of vessels passing through it is often much retarded. When the companions of Columbus saw it, they thought it marked the limits of navigation, and became alarmed. To the eye, at a little distance, it seemed substantial enough to walk upon. Patches of the weed are always to be seen floating along the outer edge of the Gulf Stream. Now, if bits of cork, or chaff, or any floating substance, be put into a basin, and a circular motion be given to the water, all the light substances will be found crowding together near the centre of the pool, where there is the least motion. Just such a basin is the Atlantic Ocean to the Gulf Stream, and the Sargasso Sea is the centre of the whirl. Columbus first found this weedy sea in his voyage of discovery. There it has remained to this day, moving up and down, and changing its position, like the calms of Cancer, according to the seasons, the storms, and the winds. Exact observations as to its limits and their range, extending back for fifty years, assure us that its mean position has not been altered since that time."

Mariners now know how to avoid this calm sea; moreover, they know how to avail themselves of *regular* winds and *regular* currents, and thus shorten voyages to a few weeks, which in former years required many months to accomplish.

The whirling winds that seem to blow in mad confusion round us, and the foaming billows of ocean that appear to leap and dash at their own wild will, are all under fixed, unvarying laws, by which our all-wise Creator has governed them from the beginning of time. There is much apparent disorder in this world of ours, but it is only *apparent.* Each successive discovery made by man serves to prove more clearly that He who in Scripture is described as riding upon the wind, and holding the ocean in the hollow of his hand, is not a God of confusion, but of order; and that all the varied elements, which seem to us so conflicting, are, to his omniscient eye, working in universal harmony.

"Modern ingenuity," continues the author just quoted, "has suggested a beautiful mode of warming houses in winter. It is done by hot water. The furnace and the caldron are sometimes placed at a distance from the apartments to be warmed. It is so with the Observatory. In this case, pipes are used to conduct the heated water from the caldron under the superintendent's dwelling over into one of the basement rooms of the Observatory—a distance of one hundred feet. These pipes are then flared out, so as to present a large cooling surface, after which they are united into one again, through which the water, being now cooled, returns of its own accord to the caldron. Thus cool water is returning all the time, and flowing in at the bottom of the caldron, while hot water is continually flowing out at the top.

"The ventilation of the Observatory is so arranged that the circulation of the atmosphere through it is led from this basement room, where the pipes are, to all other parts of the building; and in the process of this circulation, the warmth conveyed by the water to the basement is taken thence by the air, and distributed over all the rooms. Now, to compare small things with great, we have, in the warm waters which are confined in the Gulf of Mexico, just such a heating apparatus for Great Britain, the North Atlantic, and Western Europe. The furnace is the torrid zone, the Mexican Gulf and the Carribbean Sea are the caldrons, the Gulf Stream is the conducting pipe. From the Grand Banks of Newfoundland to the shores of Europe is the basement—the hot-air chamber—in which this pipe is flared out so as to present a large cooling surface. Here the circulation of the atmosphere is arranged by nature; and it is such that the warmth thus conveyed into this warm-air chamber of mid-ocean is taken up by the genial west winds, and dispersed in the most benign manner throughout Great Britain and the west of Europe.

"Every west wind that blows crosses the stream on its

way to Europe, and carries with it a portion of this heat to temper there the northern winds of winter. It is the influence of this stream upon climate that makes Erin the 'emerald isle of the sea,' and that clothes the shores of Albion in evergreen robes; while *in the same latitude* on this side, the coasts of Labrador are fast bound in fetters of ice."

*The winds* that blow upon the face of the great deep are not less subject to law than the waters of the sea. From the parallel of about 30° north and south nearly to the equator there are two distinct breezes, named the north-east and south-east *trade winds*, which blow, with but slight interruptions, perpetually round the world. The value of two such winds to navigators need scarcely be referred to. The cause of the trade winds is supposed to be the flow of cool atmosphere from the poles to the equator, and back thence to the poles. From some reason not yet ascertained, the cool air from the poles travels to the equator in the upper regions of the atmosphere. The currents from north and south meet about the parallel of 30°, and, pressing against each other, produce a calm, from beneath which calm two surface currents are ejected—one toward the equator as the north-east trades, the other towards the pole as the south-west passage winds. Having been heated at the equator, the winds again return toward the poles.

The little irregularities and variations in the winds, of which man is naturally observant, are the mere eddies and local deviations, which bear no proportion to the grand stream of atmospheric circulation which goes on perpetually round the globe. Thus the investigations of science throw light upon the passage of Scripture which tells us that " the wind goeth toward the south, and turneth about unto the north; it whirleth about continually, and the wind returneth again according to his circuits."

Among the many influences that the wind has upon the sea, one of the most curious is the creating of waterspouts.

A WATERSPOUT.

*Waterspouts* are immense columns of water which are caught up from the sea into the clouds. They are seen most frequently in warm latitudes, and are much and justly dreaded by sailors, as ships are often overwhelmed by them and sunk. They are usually seen to form under a dark cloud, when the sea becomes strangely agitated, the waves dart rapidly towards the centre of the agitated portion, whence they rise whirling round in a spiral direction towards the cloud, which sends down a long, dark tongue, or inverted cone, to meet them. When the two join, the waterspout is formed, and it continues often for a considerable time travelling over the surface of the sea.

Any ship coming within its influence would instantly be destroyed, for the mighty mass of whirling watery vapour is in many cases from fifty to eighty fathoms in diameter. It is said, however, that they can be broken and dispersed by a cannon ball, and that navigators often escape from their power by firing a gun through them.

The following account of a storm in which waterspouts were seen is extracted from Ellis's Polynesian Researches :—

### STORM AMONG THE SOUTH SEA ISLANDS.

About nine o'clock in the morning Mr. Ellis, Mr. Barff, five natives, and an English sailor, embarked in a small boat, intending to cross a channel of about twenty miles wide between two islands. The wind being fair they expected to reach the Riatean shore in three or four hours, and to arrive at the residence of the friends whom they wished to visit before the close of the day. They had not, however, been an hour at sea, when the heavens began to gather blackness, and lowering clouds intercepted the view of the receding shore as well as that of the opposite mountains. The wind became unsteady and boisterous; the sea rose, not in long heavy billows, but in short, cross, and broken waves—the most dangerous kind of sea for an open boat. Becoming uncertain of the direction in which they were driving, and fearing that they should be swamped, they took down their mast and sail, tied the masts, bowsprit, and oars together in a bundle with one end of a strong rope, and, fastening the other end to the bow of the boat, threw them into the sea. The bundle of masts, oars, &c., acted as a kind of breakwater or floating anchor, and not only broke the force of the billows that were rolling towards the boat, but kept it tolerably steady, while they were driven they knew not whither by the raging tempest.

The rain came down in blinding torrents, and most of the natives under the influence of fear sat down in the bottom of the boat, and shut their eyes or covered them with their hands, expecting each moment that the waves would close over them.

In a short time the rain abated and the northern horizon became somewhat clear, but scarcely had hope begun to spring up in their hearts when new cause for alarm presented itself. " *Ure ure tia moana!*" exclaimed one of the natives, and, looking in the direction in which he pointed, they saw a large cylindrical waterspout, extending, like a massive column, from the ocean to the dark and impending clouds. It was not very far distant, and seemed moving towards their apparently devoted boat, while the violence of the storm forbade their attempting to hoist a sail in order to get out of its way. The natives abandoned themselves to despair, and either threw themselves down in the bottom of the boat, or sat crouching on the keel with their faces buried in their hands. The sailor, however, kept at the helm, while Mr. Ellis and his companion sat silently in the stern, watching the alarming object before them. While thus employed they saw two other waterspouts, and subsequently a third, if not more, so that they seemed almost surrounded by them.

Some were well defined, extending in an unbroken line from the sea to the sky, like pillars resting on the ocean and supporting the clouds; others assuming the shape of a funnel or inverted cone attached to the clouds, and extending towards the waters beneath.   In some they imagined they

WATERSPOUTS.

could trace the spiral motion of the water, as it was drawn upwards to the clouds which every moment became more awfully black.   The spectacle would have been one of deep and curious interest in other circumstances, but their imminent danger rendered them more solicitous about their personal safety than the observation of these terrific and sublime wonders of the deep.

"The roaring of the tempest," writes Ellis, "and the hollow sounds that murmured on the ear, as the heavy billow rolled in foam, or broke in contact with opposing billows, seemed as if deep called unto deep; and the noise of waterspouts might almost be heard, while we were momentarily expecting that the mighty waves would sweep over us.

"I had once before, when seized with the cramp while bathing at a distance from my companions, been, as I supposed, on the verge of eternity.   The danger then came upon me suddenly, and my thoughts, while in peril, were but few. The danger now appeared more imminent, and a watery grave every moment more probable; yet there was leisure afforded for reflection, and the sensibilities and powers of the mind were roused to an unusual state of excitement by the conflicting elements on every side. A retrospect of life, now perhaps about to close, presented all the scenes through which I had passed in rapid succession and in varied colours, each exhibiting the lights and shades by which it had been distinguished. . . . . But the most impressive exercise of mind was that referring to the awful change approaching. . . . .

"The hours that followed were some of the most solemn I have ever passed in my life. Although much recurred to memory that demanded deep regret and most sincere repentance, yet I could look back upon that mercy that had first brought me to a knowledge of the Saviour with a gratitude never perhaps exceeded. Him, and him alone, I found to be a refuge, a rock in the storm of contending feelings, on which my soul could cast the anchor of its hope for pardon and acceptance before God. . . . . I could not but think how awful would my state have been, had I in that hour been ignorant of Christ, or had I neglected and despised the offers of his mercy."

During the whole of that day the storm continued, and at intervals they beheld, through the clouds and rain, one or other of the waterspouts, but they finally disappeared without doing them any damage. It is not easy for an individual who has never beheld them, to realize the sensations produced, when solitary voyagers on the Pacific, from their light canoes or deckless boats, descry these sublime objects towering from the water to the sky, while the powerful agitation of the former indicates the mighty process by which they are sustained.

Many are the narrow escapes which have been made from waterspouts, but we can only afford space to tell of one other. It occurred to a ship in the Pacific Ocean. It was sailing before a fresh breeze when a waterspout was descried coming towards it. The captain instantly summoned the crew on deck and prepared to take in sail. On it came nearer and nearer. The column was well defined, extending in an unbroken line from the sea to the clouds, which were neither dense nor lowering. Around the outside of the liquid cylinder was a kind of thick mist, and within, a substance resembling steam, ascending apparently with a spiral motion. The water at the base of the column was violently agitated, while the spray which was thrown off from the circle formed by the lower part of the column, rose several feet above the level of the sea. At first it bore down direct upon the ship, but when within a short distance it changed its course slightly and passed by, leaving the thankful crew to pursue their voyage.

Many gallant ships have sailed to southern climes and never more been heard of. May it not be possible that their loss was owing to the destructive power of waterspouts?

We are told that waterspouts sometimes break upon the land and do great damage. Upon one occasion one broke over the harbour of Honolulu in one of the South Sea Islands. "It was first observed," says Cheever, "moving along slowly, of about the thickness of a hogshead, accompanied by a violent ebullition of the water at its base. Upon touching the reef the column broke, causing a sudden rise of the sea of three feet on the beach. Great numbers of fish were said to have been destroyed by the force of the falling water. Other waterspouts have at different times broken on the land here, and have washed away houses and drowned inhabitants. They are experienced in the Atlantic, where I have myself observed them, as well as in the Pacific. Trees are torn up by them, valleys flooded, eminences ploughed away, deep pits excavated, and habitations, harvests, and cattle borne away."

MISCELLANEA of the sea. If being affected by the moon proves a creature mad, then, undoubtedly, the sea is a lunatic! The tide—in other words, the regular semi-diurnal advance and retreat of the sea upon the shore, are caused by the influence of the moon, which, owing to the law of gravitation, attracts toward it that portion of the sea over which at any time it happens to be passing, and thus raises a sort of protuberance or wave. At the *opposite* side of the earth a precisely similar wave or elevation of the sea takes place; the cause in this case being, that the attractive power of the moon tends to draw the earth away from the sea, while, in the former case, it tends to draw the sea away from the earth. Thus, by the same power—the attractive force of the moon—a similar result is obtained on two exactly opposite points of the earth, namely, the elevation of the sea; and thus *high* tides are produced. As the moon continues her progress round the world she draws, as it were, these two high tides along with her, and thus, necessarily, leaves the low tides behind her. The moon encircles the earth once every twenty-four hours; therefore, two full and two ebb tides occur every day.

But the moon is not alone in her influence on the tides. The sun also acts a part, but his distance being so great he affects them very little, until in the varied course of his evolutions he and the moon act in concert,—pull together, in fact, in the same direction,—and so vigorous is their united effort that they produce very high, or what we call *spring* tides. When these luminaries act in opposition the result is very low, or *neap* tides. Spring and neap tides occur twice a month. The tide takes six hours to rise and six to fall, but as the circling of the moon round the earth is not *precisely* within the twenty-four hours, so the tides are constantly changing a few minutes, not quite half an hour, every day. The earth at the tropics is nearer to the moon than elsewhere, so that the tides are highest there, while they diminish as we approach the poles.

There are numerous secondary influences at work in the world which modify the tides; thus, in the Mediterranean there is little or no tide, owing to the narrowness of the entrance at the Straits of Gibraltar, which prevents the tidal wave from having much effect; the conformations of land, too, in many places modify the tides; but the foregoing particulars are the broad outlines relative to the phenomenon of tides which it were well to bear in remembrance.

The salt in the sea is that which renders it so useful as a cleanser of the land. The ocean is, in fact, the scavenger of the world. Into it all that is filthy or noxious is ultimately conveyed and neutralized or dissipated. The saltness of the sea varies in different places, and in consequence of its saline properties the sea cannot freeze until it reaches a very low temperature, and the ice when formed is by no means perfect. The salt is expelled in the process of freezing; and when in the Polar regions the surface of sea-ice is melted by the summer sun and formed into pools, the water is found to be fresh and good.

The phosphorescence of the sea is one of the most curious and splendid of the phenomena in nature. Often the whole ocean is seen to sparkle with what appears to be a host of stars as bright as those in the sky, and the track left in the wake of a ship seems to be a sheet of liquid flame. When the sea is in this condition, spray thrown up by oars or dashed from the bow of a ship glitters like a mass of molten silver. For a long time the cause of this phosphoric light remained a deep mystery to scientific men, but they at last discovered that it is caused by the presence of myriads of animalculæ of the Medusa species, most of which are invisible to the naked eye, being not only minute, but excessively thin and transparent, and the degree of brilliancy with which these tiny creatures emit their beautiful light is supposed to depend on the condition of the atmosphere. The same species of phosphorescence is emitted by decaying vegetable matter, rotten wood, and dead fish. A traveller, in writing of his experiences in the Pacific Ocean, gives the following account of a remarkable phosphoric appearance of the sea :—

" We had often before observed luminous points, like sparks of fire, floating here and there in the furrow of our vessel, but now the whole ocean was literally bespangled with them. Notwithstanding the smoothness of the surface, there was a considerable swell of the sea, and, sparkling as it did on every part as with fire, the mighty heavings of its bosom were indescribably magnificent. It seemed as if the sky had fallen to a level with the ship, and all its stars, in tenfold numbers and brilliancy, were rolling about with the undulations of the billows.

" The horizon in every direction presented a line of uninterrupted light, while the wide space intervening was one extent of apparent fire. The sides of our vessel appeared kindling to a blaze, and as our bows occasionally dashed against a wave, the flash of the concussion gleamed half-way up the rigging, and illuminated every object along the whole length of the ship. By throwing any article over-board, a display of light and colours took place, surpassing in brilliancy and beauty the finest exhibition of fireworks. A lovely effect was produced by a line coiled to some length, and then cast into the water at a distance, and also by a bucket of water dashed from the side of the vessel. The rudder, too, by its motions, created splendid coruscations at the stern, and a flood of light by which our track was marked far behind us. The smaller fish were distinctly traceable by darting lines showing their rapid course, while now and then broad gleamings, extending many yards in every direction, made known the movements of some mon-ster of the deep."

Phosphorescence of the sea is frequently observed in the waters that wash our own shores, but never to such an extent as described above.

*The bottom* of the ocean, we need scarcely say, varies very considerably in depth beneath the surface, not only near land, but far away from any shore. There are mountain ranges and broad valleys in the sea's bed that correspond with those upon the dry land; and the mountain peaks of this ocean-world form the shallows and islands of the sea. There are forests too, bright, beautiful forests of sea-weeds and sponges, and gorgeously-coloured coral groves, that might well gladden the hearts of mer-men and maids, did such creatures exist to enjoy them; but they are not ten-antless,—the atmosphere around them—namely, water—swarms with fish of every name, shape, and size, which hover round and round the branches of these submarine groves, and poke their prying noses into the lovely coral caves. Strange sights they must witness there sometimes. Many a goodly cargo, many a bag of gold, lies hidden in these mysterious caverns, torn from the shipwrecked mariner, and tossed there to lie till that day when the secrets of the deep shall be revealed. This is no fanciful idea. The following poetic description, by Percival, is said by those who are most competent to judge to be true to nature:—

> "There, far below in the peaceful sea,
>     The purple mullet and gold-fish rove;
>  There the waters murmur tranquilly,
>     Through the bending twigs of the coral grove;
>  There, with its waving blade of green,
>     The sea-flag streams through the silent water,
>  And the crimson leaf of the dulse is seen
>     To blush like a banner bathed in slaughter.
>  There, with a light and easy motion,
>     The fair coral sweeps through the clear deep sea;
>  And the yellow and scarlet tufts of ocean
>     Are bending like corn on the upland lea.
>  And life, in rare and beautiful forms,
>     Is sporting amid those bowers of stone,
>  And is safe when the wrathful spirit of storms
>     Has made the top of the wave his own."

*The waves* of the sea, to which reference is above made, are by no means so large as we are led to suppose by writers who talk of "*mountain billows.*" Huge they are, undoubtedly, and to those who are tossed on their foaming crests they are invested with a dread sublimity, which, coupled with the smallness of the ship on which their safety depends, causes them to appear immensely larger; but they do not approximate to the height of mountains. To those who have witnessed an Atlantic storm it is scarcely possible to believe that the wildest waves do not rise much higher than twenty feet. Yet such is the fact; though of course the sheets of foam and blinding spray swept from their summits reach to a much greater height. Thus, in the dark confusion of elements during a furious storm, the summits of the waves may be continued upwards in solid-like banks of spray, which, mingling with the black over-hanging clouds or the thick descending rain, may cause the observer naturally to imagine that he beholds mountains of raging water.

The influence of the waves extends but a few fathoms below the surface of the sea. The wildest storm that ever lashed the angry billows into a seething foam leaves the unfathomable depth of ocean in the same perpetual tranquillity which it maintains during the most death-like calm.

It is a mistake to suppose that the *water* of waves rolls over the surface of the sea. The wave rolls on, but the water is left behind. A very simple way to obtain a correct idea of a wave's motion is, to grasp the end of a long piece of rope, and, raising the hand, give it one powerful shake or heave upwards and downwards; the *waves* that will be observed to run along it from end to end are precisely similar in action to those which *appear* to roll over the Atlantic. The waves of the rope roll forward, but the rope itself does not advance. It is not until waves approach the shore that the water really begins to move, for then it cannot sink downward, so is obliged to tumble forward in order to find its level. The speed of waves is proportioned to their size. The largest are said to travel at the rate of from thirty to forty miles an hour. If the water composing waves really rolled along, ships would necessarily be carried along with them at the same terrific speed ! Thus navigation would be impossible. But we know that waves pass under vessels, yet leave them far behind.

Let it be remembered that a wave is not a *thing*, but a

*motion*—an undulatory motion, imparted to water by the power of the winds.

*The depth* of the sea varies very much. Its extreme depth has never been ascertained, and, doubtless, never will be. Below eight or ten thousand feet ordinary sounding-leads become useless, because they cannot communicate an appreciable shock on striking the bottom at such a depth; and it is well known that ocean-currents can draw out the sounding-line long after the plummet has ceased to do so, thus deceiving the operator.

Many curious and ingenious, and not a few absurd, machines have been invented of late years in order to sound the depth of "blue water." Some have tried it with silk threads, others with spun yarn. Some thought that by exploding heavy charges of powder in the deep sea a *sound* would reach the surface which might determine the depth, from the rate at which sound travels through water. Others constructed leads with columns of air inclosed in them, which, they thought, might show the aqueous pressure to which they might be subjected; and one ingenious philosopher contrived a lead which should register the depth by means of clock-work; but all these contrivances failed to accomplish any satisfactory result.

At last the simple plan of fastening a cannon-ball to a piece of twine was suggested by an American, and put in practice; and this sounding instrument has been more successful than any other. Till within a few years back 5000 feet was the greatest depth that had been certainly ascertained; but the Americans have succeeded in sounding to a depth of 25,000 feet, or five miles. That there are greater depths still to be fathomed is highly probable.

Such are a few of the more interesting and curious features of the mighty ocean, whose history we are now tracing. We have touched briefly on that period in the history of man when the sea was an object of unfathomable mystery or superstitious fear, and when canoes and rafts were used, chiefly in rivers, and sometimes along the margin of the unknown deep. We shall now turn to the period when boats of larger size began to be built, and when men began to find out the truth of that word which was afterwards written in the sacred volume: "They that go down to the sea in ships, that do business in great waters; these see the works of the Lord, and his wonders in the deep."

But it was reserved to later generations to discover the order and harmony that reigns in the apparent confusion of the winds and waves; to observe more clearly how the Almighty directs and governs all the elements for the good of earth's innumerable inhabitants; to appreciate more fully the truth of that word: "The Lord is good to all, and his tender mercies are over all his works."

> "Break, break, break,
>   On thy cold grey stones, O sea!
> And I would that my tongue could utter
>   The thoughts that arise in me.
>
> Oh, well for the fisherman's boy,
>   That he shouts with his sister at play!
> Oh, well for the sailor lad,
>   That he sings in his boat on the bay!
>
> And the stately ships go on
>   To their haven under the hill;
> But oh for the touch of a vanish'd hand,
>   And the sound of a voice that is still!
>
> Break, break, break,
>   At the foot of thy crags, O sea!
> But the tender grace of a day that is dead
>   Will never come back to me."

ANCIENT GALLEY.

# CHAPTER V.

## ANCIENT SHIPS.

EVERYTHING must have a beginning, and, however right and proper things may appear to those who begin them, they generally wear a strange—sometimes absurd—aspect to those who behold them after a lapse of many centuries.

When we think of the trim built ships and yachts that now cover the ocean far and wide, we can scarce believe it possible that men really began the practice of navigation, and first put to sea, in such grotesque vessels as that represented above.   Yet such undoubtedly was the case.

In our third chapter reference has been made to the rise of commerce and maritime enterprise, to the fleets and feats of the Phœnicians, Egyptians, and Hebrews in the Mediterranean, where commerce and navigation first began to grow vigorous.   We shall now consider the peculiar structure of the ships and boats in which their maritime operations were carried on.

*Boats,* as we have said, must have succeeded rafts and canoes, and big boats soon followed in the wake of little ones ; and gradually, as men's wants increased, the magnitude of their boats also increased, until they came to deserve the title of little ships.  These enormous boats, or little ships, were propelled by means of oars of immense size ; and, in order to advance with anything like speed, the oars and rowers had to be multiplied, until they became very numerous.

In our own day we seldom see a boat requiring more than eight oars.  In ancient times boats and ships required sometimes as many as four hundred oars to propel them.

The forms of the ancient ships were curious and exceedingly picturesque, owing to the ornamentation with which their outlines were broken, and the high elevations of the bows and stern.  It may not be out of place, here, to present our readers with a picture of some of the curious—not to say grotesque—boats and ships used by the Chinese at the present day, and to remark that in their high antiquated sterns and elaborate ornamentation, they bear no small degree of resemblance to the ships of the ancients.  The cut gives a view of the entrance to the Hoan-ho River, and the curious looking craft, some of which are like resuscitated antediluvians, may be seen still by any one who chooses to go there to see them !

We have no authentic details of the minutiæ of the form or size of ancient ships, but antiquarians have collected a vast amount of desultory information, which when put together, enables us to form a pretty good idea of the manner of working them, while ancient coins and sculptures have given us a notion of their general aspect.  No doubt many of

these records are grotesque enough, nevertheless they must
be correct in the main particulars.

Homer, who lived 1000 B.C. gives, in his " Odyssey," an
account of ship-building in his time, to which antiquarians
attach much importance, as showing the ideas then pre-

valent in reference to geography and the point at which the art of ship-building had then arrived.  Of course due allowance must be made for Homer's tendency to indulge in hyperbole.

Ulysses, king of Ithaca, and deemed one of the wisest Greeks who went to Troy, having been wrecked upon an island, is furnished by the nymph Calypso with the means of building a ship, that hero being determined to seek again his native shore and return to his home and his faithful spouse Penelope,—

> "Forth issuing thus, she gave him first to wield
> A weighty axe, with truest temper steeled,
> And double-edged; the handle smooth and plain,
> Wrought of the clouded olive's easy grain;
> And next, a wedge to drive with sweepy sway;
> Then to the neighbouring forest led the way.
> On the lone island's utmost verge there stood
> Of poplars, pines, and firs, a lofty wood,
> Whose leafless summits to the skies aspire,
> Scorched by the sun, or seared by heavenly fire
> (Already dried).   These pointing out to view,
> The nymph just showed him, and with tears withdrew.
>     "Now toils the hero;  trees on trees o'erthrown
> Fall crackling round, and the forests groan;
> Sudden, full twenty on the plain are strewed
> And lopped and lightened of their branchy load,
> At equal angles these disposed to join,
> He smoothed and squared them by the rule and line.
> (The wimbles for the work Calypso found),
> With those he pierced them and with clinchers bound.
> Long and capacious as a shipwright forms
> Some bark's broad bottom to outride the storms,
> So large he built the raft; then ribbed it strong
> From space to space, and nailed the planks along.
> These formed the sides; the deck he fashioned last;
> Then o'er the vessel raised the taper mast,
> With crossing sail-yards dancing in the wind:
> And to the helm the guiding rudder joined
> (With yielding osiers fenced to break the force
> Of surging waves, and steer the steady course).
> Thy loom, Calypso, for the future sails
> Supplied the cloth, capacious of the gales.
> With stays and cordage last he rigged the ship,
> And, rolled on levers, launched her on the deep."

The ships of the ancient Greeks and Romans, of which

our engraving gives what may be considered a correct representation, were divided into various classes according to the number of " ranks," or " banks "—that is, *rows* of oars. *Moveres* contained one bank of oars ; *biremes*, two banks ; *triremes* three ; *quadriremes* four ; *quinqueremes* five ; and so on.   But the two latter were seldom used, being unwieldy, and  the oars in the upper rank almost unmanageable from their great length and weight.

Ptolemy Philopater, of Egypt, is said to have built a gigantic ship with no less than forty tiers of oars, one above the other !   She was managed by 4000 men, besides whom there were 2850 combatants ; she had four rudders and a double prow.   Her stern was decorated with splendid paintings of ferocious and fantastic animals ; her oars protruded through masses of foliage, and her hold was filled with grain !

That this account is exaggerated and fanciful is abundantly evident ; but it is highly probable that Ptolemy did construct a ship, if not several, of uncommon size.

The sails used in these ships were usually square, and when there was more than one mast, that nearest the stern was the largest.   The rigging was of the simplest description, consisting sometimes of only two ropes from the mast to the bow and stern.   There was usually a deck at the bow and stern, but never in the centre of the vessel. Steering was managed by means of a huge, broad oar— sometimes a couple at the stern.   A formidable " beak " was affixed to the fore-part of the ships of war with which the crew charged the enemy.   The vessels were painted black, with red ornaments on the bows, to which .latter Homer is supposed to refer when he writes of red-cheeked ships.

Ships built by the Greeks and Romans for war were sharper and more elegant than those used in commerce; the latter being round bottomed and broad in order to contain cargo.

The Corinthians were the first to introduce *triremes* into their navy (about 700 years B.C.), and they were also the first who had any navy of importance. The Athenians soon began to emulate them, and ere long constructed a large fleet of vessels both for war and commerce. That these ancient ships were light compared with ours is proved by the fact that when the Greeks landed to commence the siege of Troy they *drew up their ships on the shore.* We are also told that ancient mariners, when they came to a long narrow promontory of land, were sometimes wont to land, draw their ships bodily across the narrowest part of the isthmus and launch them on the other side. Moreover, they had a salutary dread of what sailors term "blue water,"—that is, the deep distant sea—and never ventured out of sight of land. They had no compass to direct them, and in their coasting voyages of discovery they were guided by the stars.

The sails were made of linen in Homer's time; subsequently sail-cloth was made of hemp, rushes, and leather. Sails were sometimes dyed of various colours and with curious patterns. Huge ropes were fastened round the ships to bind them more firmly together, and the bulwarks were elevated beyond the frame of the vessels, by wickerwork covered with skins.

Stones were used for anchors, and sometimes crates of small stones or sand; but these were not long of being superseded by iron anchors with teeth or flukes.

The Romans were not at first so strong in naval power

as their neighbours, but in order to keep pace with them they were ultimately compelled to devote more attention to their navies. About 260 B.C. they raised a large fleet to carry on the war with Carthage. A Carthaginian quinquereme which happened to be wrecked on their coast was taken possession of by the Romans, used as a model, and one hundred and thirty ships constructed from it. These ships were all built, it is said, in six days; but this appears almost incredible. We must not, however, judge the power of the ancients by the standard of present times. It is well known that labour then was cheap, and we have recorded in history the completion of great works in marvellously short time, by the mere force of myriads of workmen.

The Romans not only succeeded in raising a considerable navy, but they proved themselves ingenious in the contrivance of novelties in their war-galleys. They erected towers on the decks, from the top of which their warriors fought as from the walls of a fortress. They also placed small cages or baskets on the top of their masts, in which a few men were placed to throw javelins down on the decks of the enemy,—a practice which is still carried out in principle at the present day, men being placed in the tops of the masts of our men-of-war, whence they fire down on the enemy. It was a bullet from the top of one of the masts of the enemy that laid low our greatest naval hero Lord Nelson.

From this time the Romans maintained a powerful navy; they crippled the maritime power of their African foes, and built a number of ships with six, and even ten, ranks of oars. The Romans became exceedingly fond of representations of sea-fights, and Julius Caesar dug a lake in the Campus Martius specially for these exhibitions. These were not by any means *sham* fights. The unfortunates who manned the ships on these occasions were captives or criminals who fought as the gladiators did—to the death—until one side was exterminated or spared by imperial clemency. In one of these battles no fewer than a hundred ships and nineteen thousand combatants were engaged.

Such were the people who invaded Britain in the year 55 B.C. under Julius Caesar, and such the vessels from which they landed upon our shores to give battle to the then savage natives of our country.

A brief account of one of the greatest of the naval fights of ancient days, namely the battle of Salamis, cannot fail to prove interesting here. In ancient times war seems to have been not only a necessity but actually a pleasure to men, and some nations, such as Sparta in Greece, made it their sole occupation. The gospel of Jesus Christ—the message of *love*—had not been preached at that time, except to the Jews.

Xerxes, the son of Darius, king of Persia, was a man who seems to have taken special delight in conquest. Having returned (480 B.C.) from a successful expedition into Egypt, he resolved to invade Greece. A pretext for invasion did not seem to be necessary in those times. He simply remarked that he did not choose to buy the figs of Attica; he would possess himself of the country, and thus have figs of his own. Accordingly, Greece was invaded, and the Persians with their countless hosts were at first successful, being supported by the co-operation of an immense fleet of war-galleys and ships carrying provisions, which were ordered along the coast of Asia Minor towards the Hellespont. The Persian army amounted to above two millions of men. The fleet consisted of fourteen hundred and twenty-seven ships of war, besides a thousand smaller vessels, with crews amounting to six hundred thousand men.

Of all the states of Greece only two were found courageous enough to offer resistance to this overwhelming force. The Athenians and Spartans joined their forces together, and single-handed fought in defence of their native land. Their united forces did not amount to more than eleven thousand two hundred men. They were commanded by Themistocles. Their fleet consisted of only three hundred and eighty ships, but the knowledge of the Greeks in naval tactics, and of the seas in which they afterwards fought, was infinitely superior to that of the Persians. Their fleet was commanded by Eurybiades, but Themistocles directed all its operations.

### BATTLE OF SALAMIS.

After the famous battle of Thermopylae, where Leonidas and his three hundred Spartans sacrificed themselves for their country, the only hope left to the Greeks was their fleet which lay at Salamis. To cope successfully with such overwhelming forces seemed impossible, but to attack and destroy the Persian fleet, and so cut off supplies from the land forces, seemed not so hopeless ; for the overwhelming majority of the enemy's fleet was neutralized by the narrowness of the seas in which the battle was to be fought.

Considerable strategic genius and nautical knowledge were displayed by Themistocles in this famous engagement. In order to draw the enemy on to attack them in narrow waters, Themistocles caused it to be rumoured that the Greek fleet at Salamis was preparing for flight. The arti-

fice succeeded. Xerxes immediately gave orders that Salamis should be blockaded, and soon after the opposing fleets prepared for battle.

Themistocles, knowing that a periodical wind, which would be favourable, would soon set in, delayed the attack till it arose. Then he gave orders to advance, and the Greeks bore down upon the foe. The Persian fleet hastened to make a general attack, while their army lined the adjacent shores, and their monarch himself was seated on an eminence to view the approaching battle. The narrow strait prevented the numerous ships of the Persians from being regularly brought into action, while the zeal of the commanders to distinguish themselves in the presence of their king, tended to increase the confusion. Moreover, the wind blew directly in their teeth, and the height and heaviness of their vessels rendered them almost useless.

The Greeks on the other hand, having advanced in steady and exact order, used their ponderous beaks with terrible effect, running into the hostile ships, and sinking many of them. The confusion soon became general. The Greeks gave the enemy no time to recover. Attack followed attack, and soon many of the Persian ships were driven ashore. In the midst of this *melé* a heroine rose conspicuous. Artemisia, queen of Halicarnassus, who had come to the assistance of Xerxes with five ships, exerted herself with so much spirit, that the Persian monarch was heard to say that his soldiers behaved like women in the conflict, and the women like soldiers. But nothing could now retrieve the fortunes of the day. The Persians fled on all sides. Many ships were sunk—more were taken; above two hundred were burnt; the sea was so covered with corpses as to be scarcely visible (so says the poet

Æschylus) ; and the rest of the fleet was completely dispersed; while, on the other side, only forty Grecian galleys are said to have been sunk or destroyed ; but most of the crews saved themselves by swimming on board the other ships, or on the neighbouring shore of Salamis.

Three-deckers and great guns have done much in modern times to dye the sea with human blood ; but truly the ancients, in their grotesque galleys, effected enough of slaughter, one would think, to satisfy the thirst of the most sanguinary son of Mars !

# CHAPTER VI.

## EARLY VOYAGES.

THE idea of the ancients as to the shape of the earth was what we would now style peculiar, but we cannot deny that it was perfectly natural.

They thought that the world was flat, and who would blame them for thinking so? Homer was of this belief. He placed the fabled regions of Elysium and Tartarus beneath the earth, and supposed that the vaulted heavens rested on the summits of the highest mountains. He deemed the land of the Ethiopians the most distant part of the habitable globe, and the highest peak of the range of the Atlas mountains, in Africa, he deified, describing it as a giant supporting the canopy of the heavens on his shoulders. Colchos, on the Black Sea, was believed to be an ocean-city, in which was the Palace of the Sun! Here the fabled coursers of that luminary rested during the night. This was Homer's eastern confine of the globe.

Rhodope, or the Riphean Mountains, formed his northern limit; and the region beyond this was peopled by his fanciful and teeming brain by a race of creatures who lived in perfect felicity in the recesses of their sheltered valleys. They were represented as exempt from all ills, physical or moral; from sickness, the changes of the seasons, and even from death itself. In order to counterbalance this creation, he brought into being a race of Cimmerians, whom he placed near the mouth of the Sea of Azof, and doomed them to perpetual darkness.

Although a blind beggar, Homer was undoubtedly an original and mentally prolific fellow. He made quite a minute and interesting geographical sketch of the old world, which had only one fault, that of being somewhat incorrect. The Cyclops, a race of giants who had but one eye, were placed in Sicily; the Arimaspians (also one-eyed) inhabited the frontiers of India; and the Pigmies or Dwarfs were supposed by him to dwell in Africa, India, and the southern parts of the world.

Moreover, he peopled the earth and sea with monsters of frightful form and size, as well as with hideous giants, such as Polyphemus, who watched poor mariners in order to destroy them, and thereafter roast and devour their flesh. But we ought not to suppose that Homer invented all this. Doubtless the bold mariners who were driven to distant and unknown lands, and returned to tell of the wonders they had seen, furnished him with the ground-work of all that he so graphically related, and with a poet's license enlarged upon.

Homer's idea of the earth, as far as it can be gathered from his writings, was that it was a flat disc, surrounded by the river Ocean, and that it was about 600 miles in diameter. A century later, Hesiod states that he believed the space between the heavens and the earth was exactly the same as that between the earth and Tartarus, the abode of darkness, beneath it. He further tells us, that if a brazen anvil were tossed from heaven, it would take exactly nine days and nine nights to reach the earth, completing its journey on the tenth day. No doubt Hesiod thought he had ventured upon a daring flight of imagination when he said this, yet how wonderfully far short did he come of the truth.

Four hundred years after Homer another speculative philosopher started up and caused the sage folk of the world to open their eyes, by stating it as his belief that the earth's form was that of a short cylinder, like one of the men of a backgammon board, and that its surface was *concave*. Here we may see the working of fancy and observation. Anaximander, the philosopher in question, observed the convexity of the portion of the world in which he dwelt, and conceived the remainder of his idea. Thales, one of the seven sages, was the first to hit upon the truth. He declared his belief that the earth was spherical and that it rested on nothing! This was a bold idea, and few were disposed to receive it. Even Herodotus, the most celebrated traveller and historian of antiquity, who lived in the fifth century B.C., rejected the idea of the spherical form of the world as absurd. But Socrates, a century later, asserted his belief in this vexed question, the rotundity of the earth.

With such vague notions and limited knowledge of things in general, and of the earth's form in particular, we do not wonder that the ancients did not usually venture far from land or on long voyages. Some of the more daring among them did, however, perform voyages which are really marvellous, considering the nature of their vessels and their want of scientific knowledge and appliances.

Among the first recorded are the interesting

### VOYAGES OF HANNO, HIMILCON, AND PYTHEAS.

*Hanno* lived, it is believed, before the fifth century B.C. He was sent by the Carthaginians, then in the zenith of their maritime prosperity, on a voyage of discovery beyond the Pillars of Hercules, as the two rocky mountains on either side of the Straits of Gibraltar were then named. The great ocean beyond was unknown, yet the intrepid Hanno obeyed the order at once.

He was directed to establish colonies along the western shore of Africa, and so set sail with a fleet of sixty vessels —each vessel being propelled by fifty oars. No fewer than thirty thousand men and women embarked with him; Hanno set sail, passed the straits, proceeded down the African coast, and a week thereafter they founded a city and erected a temple to Neptune. Continuing their voyage they established five trading posts and entered into friendly intercourse with the natives, whom they termed Lixitæ.

Strange indeed were the sights which these bold navigators witnessed as they continued their adventurous voyage. All the natives were by no means so friendly as the Lixitæ. At one place where they attempted to land they were rudely driven off by savage fellows dressed in the skins of wild beasts, who sent showers of stones and other missiles at them. Then they came to a river in which monsters of the most hideous nature—gigantic and ferocious —were seen gambolling in the water or crawling on the muddy banks, namely crocodiles and hippopotami—familiar enough to men of the present age, but alarming and terrible to men who had not even heard of them before.

And well might these ancients be awed and amazed! We have a vivid recollection of our own wonder at the first view we had of the horrible tusks, the hideous red throat, and the cavernous jaws of a live hippopotamus! Had the monster been uncaged, other sensations, besides that of wonder, might perhaps have assailed us.

Voyaging on they came to a coast close along which arose high mountains covered with trees, from which the most delicious perfumes were wafted out to them upon the breeze. The wood of those trees was scented and beautifully tinted. Near to this place vast plains were observed on which many huge fires were blazing, and here the sounds of music and the shouts of thousands of natives were heard. But Hanno seems to have deemed it wise not to land, so he pushed on, and arrived at a fiery region where torrents of flame rushed down into the sea, and the earth was so hot that the foot could not rest upon it. In the midst of this region one mountain was seen, which rose above the rest and was named the chariot of the gods.

Here they met with a curious set of savages whom they described as being very rude indeed, and their skins uncommonly rough and hairy. It is conjectured that our adventurers had fallen in with a troop of the gigantic apes now known as gorillas, which they had mistaken for human beings! A conjecture which is strengthened by the fact that they were so wild that no intercourse could be held with them, and three females who were captured made such a violent and altogether unlady like struggle to escape, that they were obliged to kill them! A strange way of taming savages; but the men of old were not particular—they stripped off their skins and carried them back to Carthage.

This is all the information we have of this remarkable voyage. Antiquarians differ (by no means an unusual thing) in regard to its extent. Some give to Hanno's course an extent of three thousand miles, others say less than seven hundred. It is most probable that its utmost limit was a little to the south of Sierra Leone. Want of provisions compelled them to return home.

*Himilcon*, a contemporary of Hanno and also a Carthaginian, was sent on a voyage to the North of Europe, while his countryman was out upon the voyage just described. The only account we have of this voyage is contained in a Latin poem, from which we gather only the following meagre facts,—that Himilcon crossed the Bay of Biscay and discovered a race of bold athletic people, who recklessly ventured out to sea in boats made of skins sewed together. That some boats of this kind are safe and can stand a considerable sea, we now know from our intercourse with the Esquimaux who constantly use them.

Leaving these people they crossed, in the space of two days, a sea which brought them to an island which they named the Sacred Island, and which was undoubtedly Ireland. Near to this was another island, which they named Al-Bion. But we have no details of the voyage, neither do we know that Himilcon ascertained these to be islands by sailing round them. He most probably conjectured that they were such.

*Pytheas*, a learned astronomer and geographer, was the next who ventured out upon the great deep in search of unknown lands,—about 340 B.C. He was sent forth by the citizens of Marseilles, which was established by the Phocians and had originally been named Massilia.

Pytheas set sail for the north of Europe in a solitary ship and without mishap arrived, in the course of a few weeks in a wide gulf which turned out to be the British Channel, with Himilcon's island of Al-Bion on the left. Pytheas may be said to be the discoverer of Britain, for although Himilcon was the first to see it and to record the fact, the former was the first to sail round it and map its form correctly. He described it as having the form of an isosceles triangle, and mentions the inhabitants of the southern part of the island as being sociable, peaceful, industrious, and honest. They raised wheat and worked rich mines of tin. Here then we have the first faint shadows of the history of our native land, and it is worthy of remark that the characteristic features described by Pytheas as marking the natives of our country then, are those for which she has in all ages been celebrated. A cause this, not of self-glorification, but of thankfulness to God.

Pytheas continued his voyage northward until he reached an island, or continent; he knew not which. This he named Thule, and being unable to proceed further spoke of it as *Ultima Thule*, an expression which has now come to signify, in figurative language, the utmost limit of any point or region. No doubt this Ultima Thule was Shetland, but there are some who have deemed it to be Sweden or even Iceland. Pytheas made other important discoveries;—he entered the mouth of the Rhine, and discovered a river supposed to be either the Elbe or the Oder, and finally after a little less than a year's absence returned home.

Other voyages there were in those days, all more or less interesting; but we may not record them here, enough has been said to show their style and purpose. Oars were the chief if not the only propelling power in all of them. The land was hugged as much as possible and the stars at night were the seaman's guide. But little resulted from such voyages. They were not followed up; and it was not until the great discovery of the Mariner's Compass that the world began to estimate properly the value of the sea, and to devote all their energies to the advancement of navigation in all its branches. Sails came gradually to take the place of oars, though for a long period both were used in the same vessel, so that when one mode of propulsion failed the other became available. At length in a certain class of vessels sails superseded oars altogether—but it was long before the high fore-castle and quarter-deck were discarded. Strange looking clumsy craft these ancient ships must have been.

ANCIENT SHIP.

NORSE GALLEY.

# CHAPTER VII.

## THE PROGRESS OF NAVIGATION.

It is a curious fact that the crusades of the twelfth and thirteenth centuries were the chief cause of the advancement of navigation after the opening of the Christian era. During the first five hundred years after the birth of our Lord, nothing worthy of notice in the way of maritime enterprise or discovery occurred.

But about this time an event took place which caused the foundation of one of the most remarkable maritime cities in the world. In the year 476 Italy was invaded by the barbarians. One tribe, the Veneti, who dwelt-upon the north-eastern shores of the Adriatic, escaped the in-

'vaders by fleeing for shelter to the marshes and sandy islets at the head of the gulf, whither their enemies could not follow by land owing to the swampy nature of the ground, nor by sea, on account of the shallowness of the waters. The Veneti took to fishing; then to making salt, and finally to mercantile enterprises. They began to build, too, on those sandy isles, and soon their cities covered ninety islands, many of which were connected by bridges. And thus arose the far-famed city of the waters—"Beautiful Venice, the bride of the sea."

Soon the Venetians and their neighbours the Genoese monopolized the commerce of the Mediterranean.

The crusades now began, and for two centuries the Christian warred against the Turk in the name of Him who, they seem to have forgotten, if indeed the mass of them ever knew, is styled the Prince of Peace. One of the results of these crusades was that the Europeans engaged, acquired a taste for Eastern luxuries, and the fleets of Venice and Genoa, Pisa and Florence, ere long crowded the Mediterranean, laden with jewels, silks, perfumes, spices, and such costly merchandize. The Normans, the Danes, and the Dutch, also began to take active part in the naval enterprise thus fostered, and the navy of France was created under the auspices of Philip Augustus.

The result of all this was that there was a great moving, and to some extent, co-mingling of the nations. The knowledge of arts and manufactures was interchanged, and of necessity the knowledge of various languages spread. The West began constantly to demand the products of the East, and wealth began to increase, and the sum of human knowledge to extend.

Shortly after this era of opening commercial prosperity

in the Mediterranean, the hardy northmen performed deeds on the deep which outrival those of the great Columbus himself, and were undertaken many centuries before his day.

### DEEDS OF THE ANGLO-SAXONS AND NORTHMEN.

These races of men inhabited the borders of the Baltic, the shores of the German Ocean, and the coasts of Norway. Like the nations on the shores of the Mediterranean, they too became famous navigators, but unlike them, war and piracy were their chief objects of pursuit. Commerce was secondary.

In vessels resembling that at the head of this chapter, these nations went forth to plunder the dwellers in more favoured climes, and to establish colonies in other lands. In the seventh century they established the Anglo-Saxon dominion in England, and their celebrated King Alfred became the founder of the naval power of Britain, which was destined in future ages to rule the seas.

It was the Northmen who in huge open boats, pushed off, without chart or compass (for neither were yet invented), into the tempestuous northern seas, and, in the year 863, discovered the island of Iceland; in 983, the coast of Greenland, and, a few years later, those parts of the American coast now called Long Island, Rhode Island, Massachusetts, Nova Scotia, and Newfoundland. It is true they did not go forth with the scientific and commercial views of Columbus. Neither did they give to the civilized world the benefit of their knowledge of those lands; but although their purpose was simply selfish, we cannot withhold our admiration of the bold, daring spirit displayed by those early navigators, under circumstances of the greatest possible disadvantage—with undecked boats, meagre supplies, no scientific knowledge or appliances, and the stars their only guide over the trackless waste of waters.

## MARCO POLO.

In the course of time, one or two adventurous travellers pushed into Asia, and men began to ascertain that the world was not the insignificant disc, or cylinder, or ball, they had deemed it. Perhaps one of the chief among those said adventurous travellers was Marco Polo, a Venetian, who lived in the latter part of the thirteenth century. He made known the central and eastern portions of Asia, Japan, the islands of the Indian Archipelago, part of the continent of Africa, and the island of Madagascar, and is considered the founder of the modern geography of Asia. His brief account of the island of Japan—and which, be it observed, is the first account of that island given to the world,—is somewhat amusing,—

"Zipangu, or Cipango," he writes, "is an island in the Eastern Ocean, situated about fifteen hundred miles from the mainland. It is quite large. The inhabitants have fair complexions, are civilized in their manners, though their religion is idolatry. They have gold in the greatest abundance, but its exportation is forbidden. The entire roof of the sovereign's palace is stated to be covered with a plating of gold, as we cover churches and other buildings with lead. So famous is the wealth of this island, that Kublai Khan was fired with the desire of annexing it to his dominions. He sent out a numerous fleet, and a powerful army; but a violent storm dispersed and wrecked the ships, and thirty thousand men were thrown upon a desert island, a few miles from Cipango. They expected nothing but death or captivity, as they could obtain no means of subsistence. Being attacked from Cipango, they got in rear of the enemy, took possession of their fleet, and put off for the main island. They kept the colours flying from the masts, and entered the chief city unsuspected. All the inhabitants were gone except the women. They took possession, but were closely besieged for six months, until, despairing of relief, they surrendered, on condition of their lives being spared. This took place in the year 1284."

The adventures of this wonderful man, Marco Polo, were truly surprising, and although he undoubtedly exaggerated to some extent in his account of what he had seen, his narrations are for the most part truthful. He and his companions were absent on their voyages and travels twenty-one years. They saw the pearl-fisheries of Ceylon, and the diamonds of a kingdom named Murphili, where the people were in the habit of dropping pieces of meat into inaccessible valleys, in order that the diamonds there might stick thereto, and be brought up in the talons of vultures and eagles, a custom that calls at once to remembrance one of the incidents in the life of Sinbad the sailor. Marco alludes to the gigantic bird called the roc, which he declares could lift elephants into the air ! He became the favourite of Kublai Khan, emperor of China, and dwelt with him for some time at Pekin. He travelled far and wide over land and sea, and ultimately returned home, so changed that his best friends did not know him, but so rich in jewels and gold that they very willingly made his acquaintance over again.

This great traveller very quietly and coolly settled the question of the pigmies or dwarfs that were, as we have before mentioned, supposed to dwell in the southern parts of the world. In writing of Sumatra he says,—

"It should be known that what is reported respecting the mummies of pigmies sent to Europe from India, is only an idle tale; these pretended human dwarfs being manufactured in this island in the following manner :—The

PEARL DIVING.

country produces a large species of monkey, having a countenance resembling that of a man.  The Sumatrans catch them, shave off their hair, dry and preserve their bodies with camphor and other drugs, and prepare them generally so as to give them the appearance of little men. They then pack thém in wooden boxes and sell them to traders, by whom they are vended for pigmies in all parts of the world. But there are no such things as pigmies in India or anywhere else. It is mere monkey-trade."

*The Ceylon Pearl Fishery* above referred to, has long been a source of wealth to mankind. It was for a time in possession of the Dutch, and came into the possession of the British in 1796. A year or two after, the fishery yielded a revenue of nearly £200,000.

Pearls are found in oyster shells, and they are the result of a disease to which the fish is liable. Some have supposed that a grain of sand getting into the creature's body, proves so irritable, that it covers it over with several coats of a substance, or secretion, which forms the beautiful white pea-like globule, which we call a pearl.

The fishing season commences about the middle of February, and continues till the end of March. The boats, with their owners, the pearl divers, who are all Indians, come from the Coromandel coast and rendezvous in the bay of Condatchy, where they are numbered and contracted for. At ten o'clock each night, all the boats sail with the land-breeze for the banks, which they reach about sun-rise, and commence the fishing. The depth of water over the banks varies from three to fifteen fathoms ; but the best fishing is found in from six to eight fathoms. The crew of each boat consists of twenty men, ten of whom are divers ; the other ten remain in the boat to haul the divers up. Five divers descend at a time, while the others have leisure to recruit.

When about to descend, the diver seizes a rope with one hand, at the end of which is a stone which he grasps with his toes, and thereby hastens his descent; with the other hand he seizes a second rope, to the end of which is attached a basket. Thus prepared, he is lowered into the sea, and allowed to descend at the utmost speed the stone can take him. Arrived at the bottom, he fills his basket with osyters as quickly as possible, and when unable to remain longer under water, he makes a signal to his comrades above, who at once draw him to the surface. The stone is pulled up afterwards.

This process he continues as long as his strength will permit. Sometimes he makes from forty to fifty plunges a-day. The work is very fatiguing and hurtful. The time a diver continues under water seldom exceeds a minute; sometimes a little more, and occasionally, but very rarely, two minutes. It is even said that instances have been know of a diver remaining five minutes under water, but the assertion is not authenticated. The effects on the men, even although used to it from their infancy, are very severe, and sometimes the exertion is so violent, that on coming up, they discharge blood from the mouth, ears, and nostrils. A few of them rub their bodies over with oil, and stuff their ears with cotton, but the most are reckless, and use no precautions whatever.

Besides these evils, pearl-divers are subjected to the risk of being attacked by ground sharks while at the bottom, and of these monsters they are naturally very apprehensive.

After the boats return to shore, the oysters are piled in heaps, and allowed to remain until they have putrefied and become dry, when the pearl is easily extracted without being injured.

Such is the nature of the fishery, which has continued from the time of Marco Polo down to the present day.

Marco Polo died, but the knowledge of the East opened up by him—his adventures and his wealth, remained behind to stir up the energies of European nations—yet there is no saying how long the world would have groped on in this twilight of knowledge, and mariners would have continued to "hug the shore" as in days gone by, had not an event occurred which at once revolutionized the science of navigation, and formed a new era in the history of mankind. This was the invention of the mariner's compass.

MAN AT THE WHEEL.

# CHAPTER VIII.

### THE MARINER'S COMPASS.

"WHAT *is* the compass?" every philosophical youth of inquiring disposition will naturally ask. We do not say that all youths will make this inquiry. Many there are who will at once say, "Oh, I know! It's a needle with a card on the top of it—sometimes a needle with a card under it—which always points to the north, and shows sailors how to steer their ships."

Very well explained indeed, my self-sufficient friend; but you have not answered the question. You have told us what a compass is like, and one of the uses to which it is applied; but you have not yet told what it *is*. A man who had never heard of a compass might exclaim, "What! a needle! Is it a darning needle, or a knitting needle, or a drawing-through needle? And which end points to the north—the eye or the point? And if you lay it on the table the wrong end to the north, will it turn round of its own accord?

You laugh, perhaps, and explain; but it would have been better to have explained correctly at first. Thus :—

The mariner's compass is a small, flat bar of magnetized steel, which, when balanced on a pivot, turns one of its ends persistently towards the north pole—the other, of course, towards the south pole; and it does this in consequence of its being magnetized. Above—sometimes below this bar of steel, usually called "the needle," a card is fixed, whereon are marked the cardinal points—north, south, east, and west—with their subdivisions or intermediate points, by means of which the true direction of any point can be ascertained.

"Aha!" you exclaim, "Mr. Author, but you yourself have omitted part of the explanation. *Why* is it that the magnetizing of the needle causes it to turn to the north?"

I answer humbly, "I cannot tell;" but, further, I assert confidently, "Neither can anybody else!" The fact is known, and we see its result; but the reason why magnetized steel or iron should have this tendency—this polarity—is one of the mysteries which man has not yet been able to penetrate, and probably never will.

Having explained the nature of the compass, as far as explanation is possible, we present our reader with a picture of one.

COMPASS.

It will be seen that there are four large points—N.,

S., E., and W.—the cardinal points above referred to, and that these are subdivided by twelve smaller points, with one little black triangular point between each, and a multitude of smaller points round the outer circle.   To give these points their correct names is called "boxing the compass,"—a lesson which all seamen can trip off their tongues like A B C, and which most boys could learn in a few hours.

For the sake of those who are anxious to acquire the knowledge, we give the following explanation: Let us begin with north.   The large point midway between north and east (to the right), is *north-east.*   The corresponding point midway between N. and W. (to the left), is *north-west.*   A glance will show that the corresponding points towards the south are respectively *south-east* and *south-west* (usually written SE. and SW., as the two former points are written NE. and NW.)   Now, to read off the compass with this amount of knowledge is very simple. Thus,—*North, north-east, east, south-east, south, south-west, west, north-west, north.*   But be it observed that, in the language of the sea, the *th* is thrown overboard, except when the words north and south occur *alone.*   When conjoined with other points they are pronounced thus—nor'-east, sou'-east, and so on.

To come now to the smaller subdivisions, it will suffice to take a quarter of the circle.   The point midway between NE. and N. is "nor' nor'-east" (NNE.), and the corresponding one between NE. and E. is "east nor'-east" (ENE.)   These points are again subdivided by little black points, which are thus named:—The first, next the N., is "nor' by east" (N. by E.); the corresponding one next the E. is "east by north" (E. by N.)   The second *black* point from N. is "nor'-east by north" (NE. by N.), and the corresponding one—namely, the second black point from east —is "nor'-east by east" (NE. by E.)   Thus, in reading off the compass, we say—beginning at north and proceeding to east,—North, north by east, nor' nor'-east, nor'-east by north, nor'-east, nor'-east by east, east nor'-east, east by north, east; and so on with the other quarters of the circle.

So much for "boxing the compass."   The manner in which it is used on board ship, and the various instruments employed in connection with it in the working of a vessel at sea, will be explained shortly; but first let us glance at the history of the compass.

It is a matter of great uncertainty when, where, and by whom the mariner's compass was invented.

Flavio Gioia, a Neapolitan captain or pilot, who lived about the beginning of the fourteenth century, was generally recognised throughout Europe as the inventor of this useful instrument; but time and research have thrown new light on this subject.   Probably the Neapolitan pilot was the first who brought the compass into general notice in Europe; but long before 1303 (the year in which it was said to have been invented) the use of the magnetic needle was known to the Chinese.

*Loadstone*, that mineral which has the mysterious power of attracting iron, and also of imparting to iron its own attractive power, was known to the Chinese before the year 121, in which year a famous Chinese dictionary was completed, wherein the word *magnet* is defined as "the name of a stone which gives direction to a needle."   This proves not only that they knew the attractive properties of the loadstone, and its power of imparting these properties to metal, but also that they were aware of the polarity of a magnetized needle. Another Chinese dictionary, published between the third and fourth centuries, speaks of ships being guided in their course to the south by means of the magnet; and in a medical work published in China in 1112, mention is made of the *variation* of the needle,—showing that the Chinese had not only used the needle as a guide at sea, but had observed this one of its well-known peculiarities—namely, the tendency of the needle to point in a *very slight degree* away from the true north.

In the thirteenth century, too, we find mention made of the needle by a poet and by two other writers; so that whatever Flavio Gioia may have done (and it is probable he did much) in the way of pushing the compass into notice in Europe, he cannot be said to be the inventor of it. That honour doubtless belongs to the Chinese. Be that as it may, the compass *was* invented, and, in the fourteenth century, it began the revolution in maritime affairs to which we have before alluded.

The first compasses were curiously formed. The Chinese used a magnetized needle, which they placed in a bit of rush or pith, which was floated in a basin of water, and thus allowed to move freely and turn towards the poles. They also made them in the form of iron fish. An Arabian author of the thirteenth century thus writes:—" I heard it said that the captains in the Indian seas substitute for the needle and reed a hollow iron fish magnetized, so that, when placed in the water, it points to the north with its head and to the south with its tail. The reason that the fish swims, not sinks, is that metallic bodies, even the heaviest, float when hollow and when they displace a quantity of water greater than their own weight."

The use of the compass at sea is so simple that, after

what has been said, it scarcely requires explanation. When a ship sets sail for any port, she knows, first of all, the position of the port from which she sets sail, as well as that to which she is bound. A straight line drawn from the one to the other is her true *course*, supposing that there is deep, unobstructed water all the way; and if the compass be placed upon that line, the point of the compass through which it passes is the point by which she ought to steer. Suppose that her course ran through the east point of the compass; the ship's head would at once be turned in that direction, and she would continue her voyage with the needle of the compass pointing straight *across* the deck, and the east and west points straight *along* it.

But various causes arise in the actual practice of navigation to prevent a ship keeping her true course. Winds may be contrary, and currents may drive her either to the one side or the other of it; while land—promontories, islands, and shallows—compel her to deviate from the direct line. A vessel also makes what is called "lee-way," which means that, when the wind blows on her side, she not only advances forward, but also slides through the water sidewise. Thus, in the course of a day, she may get a considerable distance off her true course—in sea parlance, "make a good deal of lee-way."

To perform the voyage correctly and safely in the face of these obstacles and hindrances is the aim and end of navigation; and the manner of proceeding is as follows:—

The hour is carefully noted at starting, and from that moment, night and day to the end of the voyage, certain observations are made and noted in the ship's journal, called the Log. Every hour the rate at which the ship is going is ascertained and carefully noted. The point of the compass towards which the ship is to be steered is given by the captain or officer in command to the steersman, who stands at the wheel with a compass always before him in a box called the *"binnacle,"* as represented in the cut at the head of this chapter. The course is never changed except by distinct orders from those in command, and, when it is changed, the hour when the change takes place, and the new point to be steered are all carefully noted down. Thus at the end of the day, or at any other time if desired, the position of the ship can be ascertained by her course being drawn upon a chart of the ocean over which she is sailing, correct charts, or maps, being provided by the captain before starting.

The estimate thus made is, however, not absolutely correct. It is called the *"dead-reckoning,"* and is only an approximation to the truth, because allowance has to be made for lee-way, which can only be guessed at; allowance has also to be made for variations in the rate of sailing in each hour, for the winds do not always blow with exactly the same force during any hour of the day. On the contrary, they may vary several times within an hour both in force and in direction. Those variations have to be watched and allowed for, but such allowance may be erroneous in a greater or less degree. Currents, too, may have exerted an unseen influence on the ship, thus rendering the calculation still less correct. Nevertheless, dead-reckoning is often the only guide the sailor has to depend upon for days at a time, when storms and cloudy skies prevent him from ascertaining his true position by other means, of which we shall speak presently.

Of course, in the early days of navigation there were no charts of the ocean. The navigator knew not whither he was hurrying over the wild waste of waters; but by observing the relative position of some of the fixed stars to his course while sailing out to sea, he could form a rough idea of the proper course to steer in order to return to the port whence he had started.

The compass, then, shows the sailor the course he has been going, and the *log* (of which more presently) enables him to ascertain the rate at which he has proceeded; while his chronometers, or time-keepers, tell him the *time* during which the course and rate of sailing have been kept up. And many a long cruise on the unknown deep has been successfully accomplished in days of old by bold seamen, with this method of dead-reckoning, and many a mariner at the present day depends almost entirely on it, while *all* are, during thick stormy weather, dependent on it for days, and sometimes weeks together.

*The Log* to which we have referred, is the instrument by which the rate at which a ship is progressing is determined. It is a very simple contrivance; a triangular piece of wood about the size of a large saucer with a piece of stout cord fastened to each corner, the ends of the cords being tied together, so that when held up the "log," as it is called, resembles one of a pair of scales. One of the cords, however, is only temporarily attached to its corner by means of a peg, which when violently pulled comes out. One edge of the triangle is loaded with lead. The whole machine is fastened to the "log-line," another stout cord many fathoms long, which is wound on a large reel.

Heaving the log, as we have said, takes place every hour. One sailor stands by with a sand glass which runs exactly half a minute. Another holds the wooden reel, and a third heaves the log over-board, and "pays out" line as fast as he can make the reel spin.   The instant it is thrown the first sailor turns the sand-glass.   The log, being loaded on one side, floats perpendicularly in the water, remaining stationary of course, while the man who hove it watches sundry knots on the line as they pass over the stern of the ship, each knot representing a mile of rate of speed in the hour.   As the last grain of sand drops to the bottom of the glass the first sailor gives a sharp signal, and the second clutches and checks the line; examines the knot nearest his hand, and thus knows at once how many knots or miles the ship is sailing at that time.   The sudden stoppage of the line jerks the *peg*, before referred to, out of the log, thereby allowing the other two fixed cords to drag it flat and unresisting over the surface of the sea, when the line is reeled up and put by.   The flight of another hour calls for a repetition of the heaving of the log.

As scientific knowledge advanced, instruments of peculiar and more complicated form were devised to enable navigators to ascertain more correctly their position on the surface of the sea, but they did not, and never will, supersede the method by dead-reckoning, for this reason that the latter can be practised at all times, while the former are useless unless the sun, moon, or stars be visible, which in some latitudes they are not for many days and weeks during which clouds and fogs shroud the bright sky from view.

*The Quadrant* is the chief of those instruments, of which a representation is given below.   To give a succinct account of this would take up more space than we can spare.   It may suffice the general reader to say that by observing the exact position of the sun at noon, or of the moon or a star, in relation to the horizon, the precise *latitude* of a ship— that is, her distance north or south of the equator—is ascertained. The method of "taking an observation" is complicated, and difficult to explain and understand. We

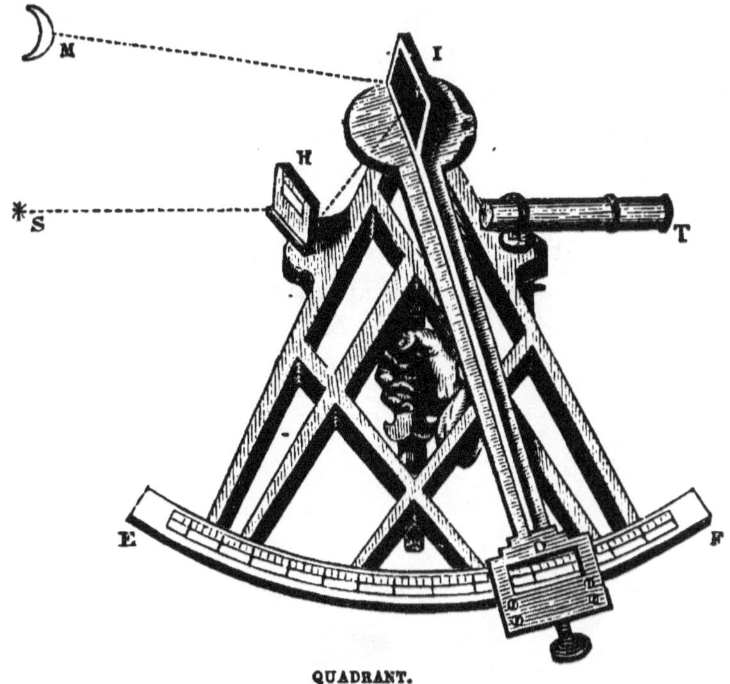



QUADRANT.

refer those who are curious on the point to treatises on navigation.

*Chronometers* are exceedingly delicate and perfect time keepers, or watches, which are very carefully set at the commencement of the voyage. Thus the *time* at the *meridian*, whence the vessel started is kept up during the voyage. By means of an observation of the sun with the quadrant, or sextant (a somewhat similar instrument), the true time at any particular point in the voyage may be ascertained. A *difference* is found to exist between the time, at the spot where the observation is taken, and the time of the chronometer. A calculation founded on this difference gives the ship's *longitude*, that is, her distance east or west of the meridian that passes through Greenwich. That meridian is an imaginary line drawn round the world longitudinally, and passing through the north and south poles, as the equator is a line passing round it latitudinally.

Thus, then, a ship's latitude and longitude having been ascertained, and a line being drawn through the first, parallel to the equator, and through the second, parallel to the first meridian, the point where these two lines intersect is the exact position of the ship upon the sea.

# CHAPTER IX.

### EARLY PORTUGUESE DISCOVERIES.

As we have seen in foregoing chapters the size and form of ships had gradually been much improved. The compass and other scientific appliances had been discovered, cannon also, and gunpowder, had been invented, and seamen had become more courageous and venturesome.

Still, however, men continued to "hug the land," and dreaded to face the unknown dangers of the open sea. But at last the Portuguese nation began that career of maritime enterprise which won for it the admiration of the world.

### EARLY PORTUGUESE DISCOVERIES.

About the beginning of the fourteenth century (1330), the Canary Islands, lying on the west coast of Africa, were re-discovered by the accident of a French ship being blown off the coast in a storm, and finding shelter amongst them. This group had been known to the ancients under the name of the Fortunate Islands, but had been forgotten for more than a thousand years. During the course of the century the Spaniards plucked up courage to make discoveries and settlements upon them, although by so doing they were compelled to undergo that much dreaded ordeal, sailing *out of sight* of their fondly "hugged" land!

In the beginning of the next century arose a prince, Don Henry, son of John I. of Portugal, whose anxiety to promote discovery, and to find a passage by sea round the coast of Africa to India, induced him to send out many expeditions, all of which accomplished something, and many of which added very extensively to the geographical knowledge of the world at that time. Navigators sent out by him from time to time discovered the Madeira Islands; sailed along the western coast of Africa a considerable distance; ascertained the presence of gold dust among the savages on the gulf of Guinea; discovered the Azores, besides numerous other islands and lands; crossed the equator, and approached to within about eighteen hundred miles of the southmost cape of Africa.

The discovery of gold dust stirred up the energies of the Portuguese in a remarkable degree, and induced them cheerfully to undertake ventures which without that inducement they would probably never have undertaken at all. Moreover, they had now learned to quail less at the idea of losing sight of land, and towards the end of the fifteenth century (1486), *Bartholomew Diaz*, an officer of the household of John II., achieved the grand object which had long been ardently desired by the Portuguese, he doubled the great southern Cape of Africa, which King John named the " Cape of Good Hope," although Diaz had named it the " Cape of Tempests."

The circumstance is thus alluded to by a poet of that period,—

> "At Lisboa's court they told their dread escape,
> And from her raging tempests named the Cape.
> 'Thou southmost point,' the joyful King exclaimed,
> '*Cape of Good Hope* be thou for ever named!'"

But a man of greater renown than Bartholomew Diaz was now about to step upon the stage, and outshine all previous actors in the scene. He was a Genoese by birth, and his name was,—

### CHRISTOPHER COLUMBUS.

"The world is flat," said philosophers even in the days of Columbus. But centuries before bold-thinkers had asserted that it was round, and in all ages there were some who held that, so called, absurd doctrine. Among these " absurd thinkers," was Christopher Columbus; and one of the expressions of contempt used against him by the *wise* men of Portugal, to whom he long and fruitlessly appealed for assistance to carry out his daring schemes, was this,—"he is a *foreigner* who asserts that the world is round like an orange, and that there are places where people walk on their heads!"

Aye, he did assert that the world was round like an orange, and of his revilers he might have said that as far as wisdom went it mattered little whether *they* walked upon their heads or on their feet.

Columbus was born in Genoa in the year 1435. He, with his brother Bartholomew, followed his father's trade, that of a wool-comber, till he was ten years of age, when he was sent to the University of Pavia; but he soon returned to wool-combing, at which he continued till he was fourteen. Then he took to the sea. In course of time he made a voyage of discovery to Iceland; afterwards joined the Genoese fleet under command of his great-uncle, and became a naval warrior, fighting the Venetians and Neapolitans, and chasing the pirates of the Mediterranean for about sixteen years, when he was wrecked on the coast of Portugal.

In Lisbon his brother Bartholomew had settled and become a drawer of plans and charts. Columbus joined him, and married an Italian lady. He was in the prime of life at this time; an enthusiastic and a religious man. The idea that he should be the means of diffusing the knowledge of the gospel of Jesus Christ, seems to have fired his soul with an unquenchable flame. And truly had it not been unquenchable the long, long years of disappointment he experienced would have effectually extinguished it.

He brooded over the idea, and sought to carry it out for years. At the age of forty he proposed to the senate of Genoa to sail through the Pillars of Hercules, proceed straight *west* till he reached the East Indies, and circumnavigate the globe!

The globe! "there is no globe," doubtless thought the Genoese, so they declined his offer, on the plea of poverty. But Columbus was not to be put down. He made a similar offer to King John II. of Portugal, who with his councillors treated the proposal as absurd, and also declined it. Again he tried the Government of Genoa, and was a second time refused. Nothing daunted, he carried his proposal to Ferdinand and Isabella of Spain. The former threw cold water on him; the latter, to her honour be it recorded, received, encouraged, and finally, having sold part of her jewels for the purpose, equipped him for his long-desired and long-procrastinated voyage across the unknown seas. But many years had been wasted in these fruitless appeals to governments, and Columbus had reached the age of fifty-five before his first voyage of discovery began.

And now the hopes of this great man were about to be realized. On the 30th of April 1492 he received letters-patent from the joint sovereigns of Spain, granting him the following privileges and titles, in the event of his accomplishing the object of his voyage,—

"He should receive the title of Grand Admiral of the Ocean."

" He should be Viceroy and Governor-General of all islands and mainlands he might discover."

" He should levy a tax upon all productions, spices, fruits, gold, silver, diamonds, pearls, &c., discovered in or exported from the lands under his authority."

" His titles should descend to his posterity for ever."

Kings and Queens were lavish in magnificent promises in those days, but not careful to fulfil them. Columbus performed his share of this bargain; that his royal patrons did not is evident from the fact that he died at last in neglect and extreme poverty, when broken health and old age had brought his celebrated and useful labours to a close.

It is a wise and merciful arrangement of God that the future is concealed from mortal view. Columbus thought not of the future. The present was his, and he set about vigorous and immediate preparations. But difficulties met him at the very outset. No sailors could be got to volunteer on what seemed to all a wild, or, at least, a desperate venture. Criminals, condemned or awaiting trial, were offered pardon if they chose to embark with Columbus!

The harbour of Palos was selected as the port of departure. But the mariners of Palos disappeared! they hid themselves; the ship carpenters of Palos grew sick, and it seemed as if the whole world conspired to prevent the undertaking.

At length three brothers named Pinzon, all sailors, agreed to join Columbus; others took courage on witnessing their bold conduct; three vessels were provided, and were finally got ready for sea.

Now the ships of Columbus, though small, were by no means so small as many historians would have us believe. They were three in number, and named respectively the

*Santa Maria,* the *Pinta* and the *Nina.* Columbus commanded the first with a crew of sixty-six men; Alonzo Pinzon the second with a crew of thirty men, and Vincent Pinzon commanded the third, with a crew of twenty-three men. But the smallest of the three, the *Nina,* afterwards when at sea, took on board fifty-six men in addition to her own crew, a number of cannon, and part of the rigging of the *Santa Maria* without making any perceptible difference in her draught of water. *Santa Maria* measured ninety feet at the keel; had four masts, two being square-rigged, and two with the lateen-sails peculiar to Mediterranean craft. Her main deck extended from stem to stern, and her double deck on the poop was twenty-six feet long. Her sides were pierced for cannon, she had a complicated arrangement of ropes, blocks and pulleys, and carried eight anchors. The other two vessels, however, were decked only forward and aft; the centre being entirely open. The little fleet was only provisioned for one year.

Everything connected with the sailing of the squadron was marked by deep solemnity, and, as should ever be the case, by earnest prayer to Him who prospers or thwarts the efforts of man according to His own will.

When the vessels were about ready for sea, Columbus retired for a time to a monastery, and spent his days and nights in prayer and meditation.

Early on the morning of the third of August 1492 the fleet set sail. The crews, having previously marched in procession to the monastery, where they confessed their sins, and offered up prayer for success in their enterprise, went on board. The inhabitants of Palos crowded to the shore to witness the departure of those whom they scarcely expected ever to see again; the royal standard, representing the crucifixion, was hoisted at the main of the Admiral's ship; Columbus, standing on the quarter-deck, gave orders to hoist the sails "in the name of Jesus Christ;" a fair wind wafted them speedily out to sea, and the memorable voyage began.

One does not wonder much that the sailors—these first navigators of the Atlantic—grew terrified as they sailed onward into the unknown ocean, and reeled upon the foam of its stormy billows for weeks and weeks together.   But one is compelled to wonder at the cool calm self-possession of the extroardinary man who pushed westward, ever westward, undismayed by the dangers and uncertainties that surrounded him, or the cowardice and mutinous threatenings of his crews.

Columbus began a journal the day he sailed, and from that time gave himself little rest night or day.   He watched the flight of birds; sounded the depth of the ocean; noted the appearance of the weeds that floated upon it; and in short allowed nothing to escape the notice of his eminently practical mind.

Soon the fears of the men began to be aroused by the unwonted appearances by which they were surrounded.  The course being south-west the familiar stars began to sink on the horizon, and entirely new constellations appeared to view, One day the compass was observed to deviate a little from the pole-star !  Here was a subject to startle the stoutest-hearted of the men.   Their hitherto unfailing guide showed symptoms of wavering from its course.   Having done so in a small degree, might it not do so in a greater, and, perhaps, become useless in course of time?  Columbus viewed this *variation of the needle* with amazement, but he concealed his feelings, and quietly and gravely told the alarmed crews, "that the needle did not point directly to the pole, but that in particular circumstances it described a compass round it." This silenced the men for the time; but soon other causes of fear arose.

The trade winds before which they were sailing, blew so long and steadily from east to west that the men were suddenly struck with the idea that it would never change, and so all hope of being able to sail back to Spain was gone! Here was a dreadful state of things ! The thought drove them to open mutiny, and possibly they might have been tempted to some murderous act against their Admiral, had not a contrary wind sprung up at that very time, as if to rebuke their hasty conduct.

' Relieved from anxiety on this score, they were soon filled with new terrors on coming to a region where the sea-weed covered the ocean so thickly that the ship could scarcely move, and it seemed as if they were to be for ever set fast in the semi-solid mass. This was the *Sargasso Sea* referred to in a previous chapter. To add to their alarm they were for a long time surrounded by a calm so deep that it resembled the very death of Nature. No phantom that the imagination could conjure up, was too absurd to obtain belief. They expected the weedy mass to open, and frightful monsters of the deep to appear and gulp them unceremoniously down. They fancied they had at last reached the end of the world and must necessarily perish. Little wonder then that mutinous murmurs again broke out. We can sympathize with those men, for it must be borne in mind that they had not the scientific knowledge, the enthusiasm, or the genius of Columbus to buoy them up.

At length they escaped this, as they did other dangers,

and continued their westward way. Columbus kept two "logs," one, correctly, for his own private use, the other, with the length of each day's advance *shortened* in order to deceive his men. Columbus departed from his usual integrity of character in this matter. He seems to have forgot that the Bible, which he reverenced, has pronounced a curse against those who say, "Let us do evil that good may come." On the 1st of October, one of the officers declared that they were 1700 miles distant from the Canaries. The admiral's log, however, gave 2100 miles as the true distance.

At last the crews could no longer be restrained. They insisted on the ships' prows being turned homeward. Even the brothers Pinzon, and the other officers of the squadron joined in the mutiny, and some of the more daring hinted that it would be well to throw the admiral into the sea. Finding that neither expostulation, exhortation, nor threatening was of any avail, Columbus at last yielded to their importunity so far as to propose that they should continue the voyage for three days more, saying that, if at the end of that time no land were discovered he should instantly return. This proposal did not seem to the men extravagant or unfair, and Columbus felt that he did not hazard much in making it, for indubitable signs of their approach to land had appeared for several days past. The water had gradually become shallow; flocks of strange birds, and among them pigeons, were seen; a staff curiously wrought and ornamented had been picked up, and weeds of a different kind from any they had yet observed had been passed. A cane which seemed to have been lately cut, and a thorn with red fruit upon it were also found.

At length an island appeared on the horizon. It was

first seen by the crew of the *Pinta,* who fired a cannon and instantly began to chant the *Te Deum,* in which they were speedily joined by the crews of other ships. As they drew near, extensive flat and verdant fields were seen, other parts of the island were clothed with wood and diversified with rivulets.

Overjoyed at the sight the crews repented of their disobedience to Columbus, and, passing from one extreme to the other, they looked up to the man whom, a short time before, they had threatened and insulted, as one whom God had endowed with penetration and perseverance above the common lot of mortals,—in which opinion they were undoubtedly not far from the truth.

Arrayed in gorgeous robes, Columbus landed, set up the royal standard, and took possession of the new land for the crown of Castile and Leon, all his followers kneeling on the shore, kissing the ground and weeping in the extravagance of their joy, while crowds of natives watched their proceedings in speechless amazement. They regarded the strangers as a superior order of beings, who had thunder and lightning at command, and believed them to be children of the sun, who had descended to stay for a little among the children of men.

Thus were the *West* India Islands discovered, on Friday, the 12th October, 1492. The island on which they landed was one of the Bahama group, and was named by its discoverer *San Salvador* in memory of our Saviour.

Columbus imagined that he had come upon the *East* Indies, but he had made a far more important discovery. He had touched the confines of the New World, that mighty continent which was named America after a Florentine merchant and seaman, Amerigo Vespucci, who did indeed visit the New World two years *after* Columbus, but who had not a shadow of title to the honour, which was conferred upon him, long after the discovery was made, by either an ignorant or a false Frenchman, who republished a narrative of Amerigo's voyage, and claimed for him the right to have the continent named after him.

During that year and on several successive voyages, Columbus discovered and named many of the neighbouring islands. He also discovered the continent of South America in 1498. But we must not omit to mention that the continent of North America had been discovered previous to that time—in 1497 by John Cabot, a Venetian pilot resident at Bristol, and his son Sebastian, who was born in England.

We would fain linger a while with Columbus; it is not our purpose, however, to write his memoir. Other matters claim our attention. The discoveries of the Spaniards under Columbus close the records of the fifteenth century. Those of the sixteenth open with the exploits of the Portuguese under *Vasco da Gama*, and the Spaniards under Ferdinand *Magellan*. The former, doubling the Cape of Good Hope, sailed to Calicut, and was thus the first to achieve the long-desired object of proceeding from Europe to India by sea. The latter in 1519 discovered and passed those straits on the extreme south of America that bear his name, but his career was cut short by his being murdered by the natives of one of the Philippine islands.

## CHAPTER X.-

### SHIPS OF THE FIFTEENTH, SIXTEENTH, AND SEVENTEENTH CENTURIES.

DURING the 15th, 16th, and 17th centuries, the navy of England made long and rapid strides in improvement, especially under the fostering care of Henry VII.  Indeed, the Royal Navy may be said to have begun to assume real importance in that monarch's reign, although it had nominally existed for more than a hundred years.  The "*Great Harry*," built in 1488, was probably the first three-masted man of war that ever belonged to the nation, and she was the first vessel in which port-holes for cannon on the lower deck were cut.  Previously, the guns were discharged over the bulwarks.  The largest of Henry's ships, named "*Le Grace de Dieu*," may be appropriately styled the father of the British navy.  She was 1000 tons burden, had four masts and carried 80 guns; she was built in 1515.

But the first really gigantic ship of those days was built in the reign of Charles I. at Woolwich dockyard about the year 1637, and was named—

### "THE ROYAL SOVEREIGN."

The annexed engraving gives a good idea of her appearance.  This vessel is sometimes spoken of as "*the Sovereign of the Seas*."  The following account of her was published at the time of her destruction by fire in 1696, and is quoted from "Charnock's History of Marine Architecture :—

"The *Royal Sovereign* was the first great ship that was ever built in England; she was then designed only for splendour and magnificence, and was in some measure the occasion of those loud complaints against ship-money in the reign of Charles I., but being taken down a deck lower, she became one of the best men of war in the world, and so formidable to her enemies, that none of the most daring among them would willingly lie by her side. She had been in almost all the great engagements that had been fought between France and Holland; and in the last fight between the English and French, encountering the 'Wonder of the World,' she so warmly plied the French admiral, that she forced him out of his three-decked wooden castle, and chasing the *Royal Sun* before her, forced her to fly for shelter among the rocks, where she became a prey to lesser vessels, that reduced her to ashes. At length, leaky and defective herself with age, she was laid up at Chatham, in order to be rebuilt; but, being set on fire by negligence, she was, upon the 27th of this month (January), devoured by that element which so long, and so often before, she had imperiously made use of as the instrument of destruction to others."

A very elaborate and quaint description of this vessel was sent to Charles I., from which we give the following extract verbatim. The author, Thomas Heywood, after describing minutely her decorations, goes on to say,—

"There is one thing above all these for the world to take especiall notice of, that shee is besides tunnage just so many tuns in burden as their have beene yeares since our blessed Saviours incarnation, namely, 1637, and not one under or over.   A most happy omen, which though it was not first projected or intended, is now by the true computation found so to happen.   It would bee too tedious to insist upon every ornament belonging to this incomperable vessel, yet thus much concerning her outward appearance. She hath got two galleries of a side, and all parts of the ship are carved also with trophies of artillery, and types of honour, as well belonging to land as sea, with symboles, emblemes, and impresses appertaining to the art of navigation; as also, their two sacred majesties badges of honour, armes, eschutcheons, &c. . . . .

"Her length by the keele is 128 foote, or thereabout, within some inches.   Her mayne breadth or widnesse from side to side 48 foote.   Her utmost length from the fore-end of the sterne, *a prora ad puppim*, 232 foote.   She is in height, from the bottome of her keele to the top of her lanthorne, 76 foote, she beareth five lanthornes, the biggest of which will hold ten persons to stand upright, and without shouldring or pressing one the other.

"She hath three flush deckes, and a forecastle, an halfe decke, a quarter decke, and a round house.   Her lower tyre hath thirty ports, which are to be furnished with demi-cannon and whole cannon throughout, being able to beare them.   Her middle tyre hath also thirty ports for demi-culverin, and whole culverin.   Her third tyre hath twentie-sixe ports for other ordnance.   Her forecastle hath twelve ports, and her half decke hath fourteene ports.   She hath thirteene or fourteene ports more within board for murdering-pieces, besides a great many loopholes out of the cabin for musket-shot.   She carrieth, moreover, ten pieces of chase ordnance in her right forward, and ten right aff, that is, according to land service; in the front and the reare. She carrieth eleaven anchors, one of them weighing foure thousand foure hundred, &c., and according to these are her cables, mastes, sayles, cordage, which, considered together, seeing Majesty is at this infinite charge, both for the honour of this nation, and the security of his kingdome, it should bee a great spur and encouragement to all his faithful and loving subjects to bee liberall and willing contributaries towards the ship money."

But long before this great ship was built, England had begun to prove her superiority on the ocean. Among many other naval triumphs achieved during the centuries of which we now write, was her

### DEFEAT OF THE SPANISH ARMADA.

This remarkable event took place in the year 1588, and while it exhibits the maritime enterprise of the Spaniards, and the extent of their naval force, it at the same time shows their lamentable want of pluck.

Encouraged by the immense superiority of its fleet over that of the British, and anxious to crush the Protestant religion, being encouraged thereto by the Pope, Spain resolved to invade Britain with an Armada consisting of 130 large ships, having 20,000 land forces on board. Besides these, 34,000 land troops were prepared to join from the Netherlands.

In very natural consternation, Queen Elizabeth of England hastily marshalled her troops by land and sea to meet the invaders. She had only 30 small vessels wherewith to oppose the enemy's. But among the commanders of that fleet there were men of renown,—Drake, Frobisher, Hawkins, and others. With characteristic daring the British attacked the Armada in the Channel, and gave them such a warm reception, that the Spanish vessels were fain to seek refuge on the coast of Zealand.  Instead of invading our country, the Spaniards now only thought of getting home as fast as possible; but the wind being contrary they resolved to sail round by the Orkneys.  They were followed and harassed by the British fleet as far as Flamborough Head, off which they encountered a terrible storm which completed their defeat.  Thus God mercifully came to our aid, and saved the country not only from the horrors of invasion, but from the withering blight of popery.

Seventeen ships, having on board 5000 men, were wrecked on Ireland and the western isles, and of the whole Armada only 53 ships returned to Spain to tell the tale of their ignominious discomfiture.

Dr. Motley, in his new work, " The History of the United Netherlands," gives the following spirited

### ANECDOTE OF THE SPANISH ARMADA.

In crossing the Bay of Biscay the ships were tossed about by a very severe storm.  Many of the galley slaves were English prisoners, to whom this storm proved a great blessing.

"David Gwynn, a Welsh mariner, had sat in the Spanish hulks a wretched galley-slave—as prisoner of war—for more than eleven years, hoping year after year for a chance of escape from bondage.  He sat now among the rowers of the great galley, the *Vasana*, one of the humblest instruments by which the subjugation of his native land to Spain and Rome was to be effected.  Very naturally, among the ships which suffered most in the gale, were the four huge unwieldy galleys—a squadron of four under Don Diego de Medrado, with their enormous turrets at stem and stern, and their low and open waists.  The chapels, pulpits, and gilded Madonnas proved of little avail in a hurricane. The *Diana*, largest of the four, went down with all hands; the *Princess* was labouring severely in the trough of the sea, and the *Vasana* was likewise in imminent danger. So the master of this galley asked the Welsh slave, who had far more experience and seamanship than he possessed himself, if it were possible to save the vessel. Gwynn saw an opportunity for which he had been waiting eleven years. He was ready to improve it. He pointed out to the captain the hoplessness of attempting to overtake the Armada. They should go down, he said, as the *Diana* had already done, and as the *Princess* was likely at any moment to do, unless they took in every rag of sail, and did their best with their oars to gain the nearest port. But in order that the rowers might exert themselves to the utmost, it was necessary that the soldiers, who were a useless incumbrance on deck, should go below. Thus only could the ship be properly handled. The captain, anxious to save his ship and his life, consented. Most of the soldiers were sent beneath the hatches; a few were ordered to sit on the benches among the slaves.

"Now there had been a secret understanding for many days among these unfortunate men, nor were they wholly without weapons. They had been accustomed to make toothpicks and other trifling articles for sale out of broken sword-blades and other refuse bits of steel. There was not a man among them who had not thus provided himself with a secret stiletto. At first, Gwynn occupied himself with arrangements for weathering the gale. So soon, however, as the ship had been made comparatively easy, he looked around him, suddenly threw down his cap, and raised his hand to the rigging. It was a preconcerted signal.

The next instant he stabbed the captain to the heart, while each one of the galley-slaves killed the soldier nearest him; then, rushing below, they surprised and overpowered the rest of the troops, and put them all to death. Coming again upon deck, David Gwynn descried the fourth galley of the squadron, called the *Royal*, commanded by Commodore Medrado in person, bearing down upon them, before the wind. It was obvious that the *Vasana* was already an object of suspicion. 'Comrades,' said Gwynn, 'God has given us liberty, and by our courage we must prove ourselves worthy of the boon.' As he spoke there came a broadside from the galley *Royal* which killed nine of his crew. David, nothing daunted, laid his ship close alongside of the *Royal*, with such a shock that the timbers quivered again. Then at the head of his liberated slaves, now thoroughly armed, he dashed on board the galley, and, after a furious conflict, in which he was assisted by the slaves of the *Royal*, succeeded in mastering the vessel, and putting all the Spanish soldiers to death. This done, the combined rowers, welcoming Gwynn as their deliverer from an abject slavery which seemed their lot for life, willingly accepted his orders. The gale had meantime abated, and the two galleys, well conducted by the experienced and intrepid Welshman, made their way to the coast of France, and landed at Bayonne on the 31st, dividing among them the property found on board the two galleys. Thence, by land, the fugitives, 466 in number— Frenchmen, Spaniards, Englishmen, Turks, and Moors, made their way to Rochelle. Gwynn had an interview with Henry of Navarre, and received from that chivalrous king a handsome present. Afterwards he found his way to England, and was well commended by the queen."

We must pause now in the record of the progress of discovery; a history of which is not the object we have in view in this work. To recount, even briefly, the adventurous voyages of the Dutch and of the English at this period—to tell of Drake, Hawkins, Frobisher, Cabot, Jacques Cartier, Balboa, Magellan, Cavendish, Raleigh, Barentz, Hudson, and a host of others, whose achievements are chronicled in almost every language, and whose very names, "familiar as household words," call up vivid pictures of ships, and storms, and battles upon the deep, encounters with wild beasts and savage men, torrid zones and frozen seas; to tell of these, we say, even briefly, would overload the pages of many a weighty tome. We shall therefore quit the historical account of the progress of man upon the ocean, and turn to the *Second Part* of our work.

THE DOCKS.

# PART II.

## MODERN NAVIGATION—DISCOVERY AND ADVENTURE.

---

## CHAPTER I.

### DOCKS.

HAVING now brought the subject of navigation down to the commencement of modern discovery, and thus cleared the way to the introduction of what may be called modern navigation, our remaining space shall be devoted more thoroughly to a miscellaneous collection of the countless anecdotes of adventures, the discoveries and shipwrecks, that crowd the pages of maritime history; and, in fulfilling this task, special regard shall be had to the distinctive peculiarities of ships of different kinds and countries.

Preliminary to this, however, we will conduct our young readers (of course with their permission) to the dock-yards, where ships are modelled and moulded, and launched, and loaded with the rich and varied freights which they are destined to carry far and wide across the stormy seas.

### THE DOCK-YARD.

If we were a maker of riddles, we would ask our reader, "Why is a ship like a human being?" and having added, "d'ye give it up?" would reply, "Because it commences life in a cradle," but, *not* being a frabricator of riddles, we *don't* ask our reader that question. We merely draw his attention to the fact that ships, like men, have not only an infancy but also have cradles,—of which more here-after.

Let us enter one of those naval nurseries, the dock-yard. What a scene it is! What sawing, and thumping, and filing, and grinding, and clinching, and hammering without intermission, from morn till noon, and from noon till dewy eve! What a Babel of sounds and chaos of indescribable material!

That little boy whom you observe standing under the shadow of yonder hull, his hands in his pockets (of course,) his mouth open (probably), and his eyes gazing up fixedly at the workmen, who cluster like bees on the ribs and timbers of yonder infant ship—has stood there for more than an hour, and he will stand there, or thereabouts, for many hours to come, for it happens to be a holiday with him, and he dotes on harbours and dock-yards.   His whole being is wrapped up in them.

And this is natural enough.   Most boys delight to gaze on incomprehensible and stupendous works.   Let us, you and I, reader, follow this urchin's example, keeping our mouths shut, however, save when we mean to speak, and our eyes open.

There are ships here of every shape and size, from the little coasting vessel to the great East-Indiaman, which, in its unfinished condition, looks like the skeleton of some dire megatherium of the antediluvian world.   Some of these infant ships have an enormous shed over them to protect them from the weather ; others, however, are destitute of such protection, for ships like men, it would seem, are liable to vicissitudes of fortune, while the " great ones " of the dock-yard world are comfortably housed, the small ones are not unfrequently exposed to the fitful buffetting of the rude elements even from their birth.

There are ships here, too, in every state of progression. Here, just beside you, is a " little one " that was born yesterday.   The keel has just been laid on the blocks, and it will take many a long day of clinching, and sawing, and hammering, ere that infant assumes the bristling appearance of an antediluvian skeleton.   Yonder is the hull of a ship almost completed.   It is a gigantic infant, and wears an aspect of a very thriving child; it evidently has a robust constitution and a sturdy frame.   Perhaps we may re-visit the dock-yard to-morrow and see this vessel launched.

Besides these two, there are ships with their ribs partially up, and ships with their planking partially on, and in a more distant part of the yard there are one or two old ships hauled up high and dry to have their bottoms repaired and their seams re-pitched, after many a rough and bravely fought battle with the ocean waves.

Now that we have gazed our fill at the general aspect of the dock-yard, let us descend a little more to particulars. We shall first tell of the,—

*Nature and use of docks.* There are two kinds of docks, dry and wet. A dry dock is usually constructed with gates to admit or shut out the tide. When a ship arrives from a long voyage, and needs repair to the lower part of her hull, she must be got out of the water somehow or other. This object is frequently attained in regard to small vessels, by simply running them gently on the flat sand or mud beach of a bay or harbour, so that, when the tide retires, they shall be left dry. But it would be dangerous as well as inconvenient to do this with large ships, therefore dry docks have been constructed for this purpose. They are so built that when the tide is full the dry docks are also full. When thus full of water, the gates of a dry dock are opened, and the large ship is dragged slowly in, after which the gates are shut. The tide then retires, but before this takes place, the ship has been propped up on all sides with timbers, in such a way that she stands upright, "upon an even keel," and thus, the pressure on her hull being equally distributed, she is not damaged. Then the water is let out by means of sluices in the gates, or it is pumped out, and the ship left dry. When the tide returns, the gates and sluices are all shut, and its entrance into the dock prevented, until such time as the ship is repaired, when water is let slowly in. As the vessel floats, the props and supports fall away, the gates of her hospital are opened, and off she goes again, in all the vigour of recruited health to wing her way over the billows of the great deep.

A wet dock is somewhat similar to a dry dock, the chief difference being that ships, while in it, are kept floating in water.

Docks are not only used, however, for repairing and building ships, they are also used for loading and unloading them, and as ships are arriving and departing from them almost constantly, the busy, bustling, active scene they present is always agreeable and interesting.

The principal docks of the United Kingdom are as follows :—

| | |
|---|---|
| Docks on the Thames, namely,— East and West India Docks ; London Docks ; St. Katherine's Docks ; Commercial Docks ; Victoria Docks. Southampton Docks. | Liverpool and Birkenhead Docks. Bristol Docks. Hull Docks. Glasgow Docks. Dundee Docks. Leith Docks. |

So much for docks in passing. Let us now turn our attention to the process of,—

## BUILDING A SHIP.

As we think it highly improbable that any of our readers intend to become either ship carpenters or ship architects, we will not worry them with technical explanations. To give an easily understood and general idea of the manner of building a ship, is all we shall attempt. The names of those parts only that are frequently or occasionally referred to in general literature shall be given.

The term *ship* is employed in two significations. In familiar lauguage it denotes any large or small vessel that navigates the ocean with sails. In nautical language it refers solely to a vessel having three masts, each consisting of a lower-mast, a top-mast, and a top-gallant-mast. At present we use the term ship in the familiar sense.

Elaborate and complicated drawings having been prepared, the builder begins.

The *keel* is the first part of a ship that is laid. It is the beam which runs along the bottom of a boat or ship from one end to the other. In large ships the keel consists of several pieces joined together. Its uses are, to cause the ship to preserve a direct course in its passage through the water, to check the lee-way which every vessel has a tendency to make, and to moderate the rolling motion. The keel is also the groundwork, or foundation, on which the whole superstructure is reared, and is therefore immensely strong and solid. The best wood for keels is teak, as it is not liable to split.

Having laid the keel firmly on a bed of wooden block in such a position that the ship when finished may slide into the water, stern foremost, the shipbuilder proceeds next to erect the stem and stern posts.

*The stem-post* rises from the *front* end of the keel, not quite perpendicularly from it, but sloping a little outwards. It is formed of one or more pieces of wood, according to the size of the ship, but, no matter how many pieces may be used, it is always a uniform single beam. To this the ends of the planks of the ship are afterwards fastened. Its outer edge is called the *cut-water*, and the part of the ship around it is named the *bow*.

The *stern-post* rises from the opposite end of the keel, and also slopes a little outwards. To it are fastened the ends of the planking and the framework of the *stern* part of the ship. To it also is attached that little but most important part of a vessel, *the rudder.* The rudder (also called the helm) is a small piece of timber extending along the back of the stern-post, and hung moveably upon it by means of what may be called large iron hooks and eyes. By means of the rudder, the mariner guides the ship in whatever direction he pleases. The contrast between the insignificant size of the rudder and its immense importance is very striking, and its power over the ship is thus referred to in Scripture, " Behold also the ships, which, though they be so great, and are driven of fierce winds, yet are they turned about with a very small helm, whithersoever the governor listeth." The rudder is moved from side to side by a huge handle or lever on deck, called the tiller, but as in large ships the rudder is difficult to move by so simple a contrivance, an arrangement of ropes or chains and pulleys are attached to it and connected with the drum of a *wheel* at which the steersman stands. In the largest ships two, and in rough weather, four men are often stationed at the wheel.

*The ribs* of the ship next rise to view. These are curved wooden beams which rise on each side of the keel and are bolted firmly to it. They serve the same purpose to a ship that bones do to the human frame. They support and give strength to it as well as form.

*The planks* follow the ribs. They are broad, and vary in thickness from two to four inches. These form the outer skin of the ship, and are fastened to the ribs, keel, stem-post and stern-post by means of innumerable pins of wood or iron called tree-nails. The spaces between the planks are caulked, that is *stuffed* with oakum, which substance is simply the untwisted tow of old and tarry ropes. A figure-head of some ornamental kind having been placed on the top and front of the stem-post, just above the cut-water and a flat ornamental stern with windows in it, sometimes, to light the cabin, the hull of our ship is complete. But the interior arrangements have yet to be described, although of course they have been progressing at the same time with the rest.

*The beams* of a ship are massive wooden timbers which extend across from side to side in a series of tiers. They serve the purpose of binding the sides together, of preventing them from collapsing, and of supporting the decks, as well as of giving compactness and great strength to the whole structure.

*The decks* are simply plank floors nailed to the beams, and serve very much the same purposes as the floors of a house. They also help to strengthen the ship longitudinally. All ships have at least one complete deck, most have two, with a half-deck at the stern called the *quarter-deck*, and another at the bow called the *fore-castle*. But the decks of large ships are still more numerous. Those of a first-rate man-of-war are as follows,—we begin with the lowest, which is considerably under the surface of the sea,—

The Orlop-deck; the Gun-deck; the Middle-deck; the Upper-deck; the Quarter-deck; and the Poop—the latter deck being the highest deck of all, a very small one, at the stern.

Thus a man-of-war is a floating house with six stories, the Poop being the garret, and the Orlop-deck the cellars. The upper decks are lighted by sky-lights, those further down by port-holes (or gun-holes), and windows, the lowest of all by candles or lamps, day-light being for ever banished from those gloomy sub-marine regions !

*The bulwarks* rise above the upper deck, all round the

ship, and serve the purposes of protecting the upper deck
from the waves, and supporting the *belaying-pins* to which
the ropes are fastened.  In ships of war the top of the
bulwarks form a sort of trough all round the ship, in
which the hammocks, (the swinging-beds) of the men are
stowed away every morning.  This trough is termed the
*hammock-nettings*, and the hammocks are placed there to be
well aired, while, in action, they serve to protect the crew
from musketry.

*The wheel*, which has been already referred to, stands
usually at the stern of the ship, on the quarter-deck; but
it is sometimes placed on an elevated platform amid-ships,
so that the steersman may see more clearly where he is
going.

*The binnacle* stands directly in front of the wheel.  It
is a species of box, firmly fixed to the deck, in which is
placed the compass.  It is completely covered in, having a
glass window through which the man at the wheel can
observe the course he is steering.

*The capstan* stands on the main-deck, sometimes near
the centre of the vessel, at other times near the bow or the
stern.  It is a massive block of timber moving on a pivot
which is turned round by wooden levers called capstan
bars or *hand-spikes*, and is used for any purpose that
requires great *tractive* power.  The drawing in of the cable
for instance, or warping the ship, which means that a
rope is fixed on shore, or by an anchor to the bottom of
the sea, and the other end of it is coiled round the capstan,
so that when the capstan is forced round by the hand-
spikes the rope coils on to it, and the ship is slowly dragged
forward.

*The windlass* is simply a horizontal, instead of a perpendicular capstan.  Its sole purpose is for heaving up the anchor, and it is placed close to the bow of the ship.

*The galley*, or cooking house, is usually near to the windlass, in the front part of the vessel.  Here the cook reigns supreme; but this nautical kitchen is wonderfully small.  It is just big enough to hold the fire-place and " coppers," with a small shelf on which the cook (always a man and often a negro) performs the duties of his office.

The various decks below are partitioned off, by means of plank walls which are called *bulk-heads*, into a variety of berths and apartments; and the greater part of the centre of the vessel (in merchantmen) is called the " *hold* " and is reserved for cargo.

*The hull* of the ship, being thus far advanced, now gets a coat of tar all over it, which preserves the wood from the action of the weather, and helps to render the seams watertight.  Some vessels are sheathed from the keel to a short way above their water-line with thin sheets of copper, to preserve them more effectually from tear and wear, and especially to defend them against those barnacles and marine insects that would otherwise fasten to them.

Being now ready to be launched from her cradle into the sea—her future home—we will proceed in our next chapter to describe the process of launching.

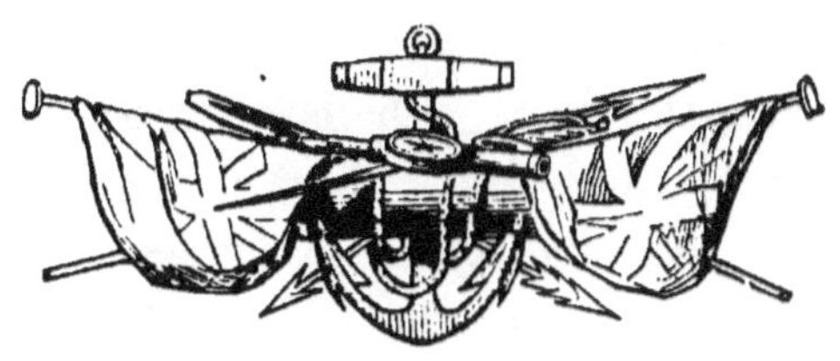

THE LAUNCH.

## CHAPTER II.

### THE LAUNCH.

SHIPS begin life with a retrograde movement.   They imitate
the crabs, in other words they are launched stern foremost.
Whether great or small, long or short, whether clothed
in patrician copper, or smeared with plebeian tar, they all
start on their first voyage with their stern-posts acting the
part of cut-water, and, also, without masts or sails.   These
necessary adjuncts and a host of others are added after
they have been clasped to the bosom of their native sea.
One notable exception there is to this rule, the launch of

the far-famed *Great Eastern*, which monster of the deep was forced into her element *sidewise*, of which a full account will be found in another part of this volume.

*The cradles* on which ships are launched are wooden frameworks, so constructed as to slide down an inclined plane, called the *ways*, bearing their burdens along with them into the water. When the ship is ready for launching, the *shores*, or supports that have kept her so long in position are knocked away one by one, until the entire weight of the ship rests on the cradle. The *ways* are then well greased, and it only remains to knock away one or two remaining checks to allow the vessel to seek her future home by means of her own weight.

But before this last act is done, a day must be fixed for the launch ; friends of the owners must be invited to go on board during this her first voyage ; a fair maiden must be invited to go through the ceremony of giving the ship her name ; paragraphs must go the round of the newspapers ; as the hour draws near, crowds of human beings, young and old, male and female, must hurry to the spot to witness the great event, and hundreds of little boys must beg leave from school (if they can) ; in short, a great stir must be made, and a great day must dawn before the last shores are knocked away, and the noble structure be permitted to rush down that inclined plane, and for the first time cleave the waves.

Many are the launches that have taken place since ship-building began, and were we to search among the records of such events for the most striking and interesting, we should have to leave this work, perhaps, unwritten. Unquestionably the *most* interesting and peculiar of all launches was that of the *Great Eastern*, but as an account of that will be found in its proper place we will at this time content ourself with giving one of the most recent, as well as interesting, that has come under our notice, namely, the

### LAUNCH OF THE BLACK PRINCE.

This is a vessel of war, of a species which has been invented very recently.  It is sheathed with armour of iron, so as to be impenetrable by cannon shot.  A full account of her will be found on page 247.  At present it will suffice to say that she was built by the Messrs. Napier of Glasgow, and is upwards of 6000 tons burden.

On the day of the launch the weather was most unpropitious.  Rain fell in torrents, but the launch of a great ship—of a more than usually heavy and peculiar ship—was too great an event to miss on account of the bad weather. Rain might moisten the clothes, but it could not damp the enthusiasm of the good citizens of Glasgow.  Umbrellas in thousands darkened the very earth, and long before the appointed hour, a patient and expectant crowd of certainly no less than 50,000 persons thronged the neighbourhood of the building-yard, and lined the banks of the Clyde.

Every kind of vehicle was engaged to convey sight-seers to the scene, and special steamers were hired, and crammed to suffocation, with people who could not find other means of transit.  As the hour approached, (half-past two), great excitement prevailed ; while a magnificent display of gay flags, and the enlivening strains of musical bands, united their influences to wage a spirited war with the depressing showers of rain.

" The arrangements for the launch, both to ensure safety and expedition were very complete.  The Messrs Napier had previously taken the precautionary measure of getting the river deepened opposite their building-yard, thereby securing a depth of water at high tide of more than thirty feet. The chain, cable, and hawsers used in checking the vessel were of a massive and heavy description. The bars composing the links of the chain cables were [illegible] inches in thickness, and the hawsers, which were made of hemp, were 24 inches in circumference. Two chain cables, and one large hawser, were attached at one end to the bow of the vessel; the cables were fastened at the other end to large anchors, weighing five tons each, which had been imbedded in the north side of the river ; and the hawser was attached to an anchor of similar dimensions, which was imbedded not far from the bow of the vessel. Checking hemp hawsers and a chain cable of equal strength were also attached to the vessel's quarter, and two anchors also of five tons in weight. The anchors were so solidly fixed in the ground that it would have been difficult to conceive how they could have been dragged from their position, even though the combined weight and velocity of the vessel had been brought to bear upon them. At the bow of the ship was an 18-inch hydraulic machine, capable of exerting a pressure of nearly 900 tons upon the vessel, if she did not slide away by her own weight on the removal of the dogshores. The ram was placed so as to act right upon the breast of the vessel, at the point where the bow rounds itself into the keel. For hours previous to the time fixed for the launching, spectators were moving in all directions through Messrs. Napiers' yard, to gratify a curiosity very natural on an occasion which had drawn together many thousands of all classes. As two o'clock approached, the anxiety of the spectators increased, and two spacious stands, erected to accommodate ladies, with covered seats, were speedily filled with fair occupants, while the gentlemen, with heroic patience, were submitting to a thorough drenching from the unceasing rain outside. At two o'clock the carpenters began to knock away the bilge blocks, and were occupied in this operation nearly three-quarters of an hour. The vessel was then held firm for a minute or two, by means of two 'dogshores,' till the interesting ceremony of naming the ship was performed. For this purpose a covered stand had been erected at the bow of the vessel which was named the *Black Prince* by Miss Elizabeth Malcolm Napier, grand-daughter of Mr. Robert Napier, and daughter of Mr. John Napier, of the firm of Messrs. Napier.

"The expectation and excitement had reached its height when the signal was given to remove the dogshores. This was done, but the vessel did not move. The hydraulic machine was immediately worked, and slowly the heavy ram was seen to advance, easing up the bow by its tremendous pressure of 900 tons._ For several minutes the distance travelled by the vessel was almost infinitesimal, but gradually the speed quickened ; she rushed along the ways with tremendous and ever-increasing velocity, and darting stern foremost through the water, was floating like a cork in a few seconds more than five or six hundred yards down the river.

"All fears of any hitch in the launch were now over, and the spectators on the south side of the river relieved their feelings by loud and renewed cheers, which were re-echoed from the spectators on the opposite bank.

"The graceful and easy movement of the vessel down the ways into the water was the theme of general remark. There was no lurch or unsteadiness in her whole progress into the river. Several of the checking chains and cables were never put to the strain, and the noble looking vessel was rounded and brought to a right position in the river without jerk or accident of any kind."

Thus was launched one of the first " mailed " warriors of the sea.

And now, having shown how the launching of our ship is accomplished, let us turn to consider the next step towards completion, for there is yet much to be done ere she is able to brave the tempest.

### RIGGING A SHIP.

Although fitting-in the lower masts of a ship cannot well be deemed a part of the rigging, we will nevertheless describe the operation here.

As the lower masts of a large ship are from five to six feet in circumference it is manifest that some powerful mechanical contrivance is required to raise them over the bulwarks and put them in an upright position, into their appointed places. Such contrivances, in the form of enormous cranes, are fixed in some of the larger docks, but the most usual method is to have the masts put in by means of

*The Shear Hulk.* This is a strongly built hull of a ship, moored in a part of the river or harbour that will afford depth of water to float any sized vessel alongside. It has one stout mast with two immense beams attached to it near the deck, and sloping outwards over the bulwarks in such a way that their ends overhang the deck of the vessel into which masts are to be placed. These sloping beams are prevented from falling overboard altogether, and their slope is regulated, by blocks and tackles from the mast of the hulk. By means of this contrivance, which is just a gigantic crane, the ponderous lowermasts of large ships are raised and lowered into their places.

When these are fixed the rigging of the ship commences. The method of putting it up cannot prove interesting to general readers, not even to boys, for when they take to rigging model ships they do not require the mechanical contrivances that are necessary in rigging large vessels. But all readers of sea-stories and nautical history will find it of the utmost advantage to their clear understanding of what they read, to have a general idea of the names and uses of the principal parts of a ship's rigging. We will, therefore, devote a small space to the explanation of this subject. And, first, let us examine the

*Masts.* These vary in size, form, and number, in different ships, but in all they serve the same purpose—to support the sails. Lower masts of large vessels are never formed out of one tree. They are found to be stronger when built up of several pieces which are fastened together by strong iron hoops. Masts sometimes consist of three distinct parts. The *lower*-mast, *top*-mast, and *top-gallant* mast. In most large ships there are three masts, each having three parts. The centre mast, being the largest, is the *main-mast*, the front one, which is next in size, is the *fore-mast*, and the one next the stern, the smallest, is called the *mizzen*.

Although we have spoken of *lower-masts*, for the sake of clearness, the name is never used. The name of the mast itself designates the lower part of it. To name the masts in order, we have the

| Fore-mast. | Main-mast. | Mizzen-mast. |
|---|---|---|
| Fore-top-mast. | Main-top-mast. | Mizzen-top-mast. |
| Fore-top-gallant-mast. | Main-top-gallant-mast. | Mizzen-top-gallant-mast. |

THE MAIN-TOP.

The parts of the different masts are connected and secured by means of *cross-trees* and *caps*, which are named after the mast and part of the mast to which they belong. Thus, we have the *fore-top*, the *fore-top-mast cross-trees*, the *main-top* and *main-top-mast cross-trees*, &c. Observe, particularly, that the *fore-top*, *main-top*, and *mizzen-top* are the platforms or cross-trees at the tops of the *lower* masts and not—as might well be supposed by landsmen—the extreme tops of these masts. The button-like objects on the summits of the masts are called the *trucks*; which, besides forming a sort of finish to them, are fitted with small *pulleys* through which *signal-halyards*, or cords for hoisting the flags, are rove.

In our woodcut you have a representation of the *main-top* of a large ship. In first rate men-of-war the "*tops*" are so large that a number of men can be stationed on them. Besides their other purposes they are very frequently used as a place of punishment for the midshipmen, or "middies," (the boy-officers), who are often sent there to air themselves, and profit, if they can, by calm reflection in exalted solitude.

*Shrouds* and *stays* are the thick ropes that keep the masts firmly in position. They form part of what is termed the "standing gear" of a ship, in other words, the ropes that are fixtures, to distinguish them from the "running-gear," those moveable ropes, by means of which the sails and boats and flags, &c., are hoisted. Nearly all the ropes of a ship are named after the mast, or yard, or sail, with which they are connected—thus we have the *main-shrouds*, the *main-top-mast shrouds*, and the *main-top-gallant shrouds*. The *main back-stay*, the *main-top-gallant back-stay*, and so on— those of the other masts being similarly named, with the exception of the first word, which, of course, indicates the particular mast referred to. Shrouds rise from the "*chains*" which are a series of blocks called " dead eyes " fixed to the sides of the ship, the shrouds are fixed to these and also to the masts near the tops—they serve the purpose of preventing the masts from breaking *sideways.* Back stays prevent them from breaking *forward,* and *fore stays* prevent them from breaking *backward* or "aft." Besides this, shrouds have little cross ropes called *ratlines* attached to them, by means of which rope-ladders the sailors ascend and descend the rigging to *furl,* that is, tie up,—or *unfurl,* that is, to untie or shake out the sails.

Our cut represents a sailor boy ascending the mizzen - top-mast-shrouds.

*Yards* are the heavy wooden cross-poles or beams to which the sails are attached.

*Reef points* are the little ropes which may be observed hanging in successive rows on all sails, by means of which *parts* of the sails are gathered in, and tied round the yards, thus reducing their size in stormy weather. Hence

ASCENDING THE RIGGING.

such nautical expressions as "taking in a reef" or a "double reef," and " close reefing," which last implies that a sail is to be reduced to its smallest possible dimensions. The only further reduction possible, would be folding it up altogether, close to the yard, which would be called "furling" it, and which would render it altogether ineffective. In order to furl or reef sails, the men have to ascend the masts and "*lay-out*" upon the yards. It is very dangerous work in stormy weather. Many a poor fellow, while reefing sails in a dark tempestuous night, has been blown from the yard into the sea, and never heard of more. All the yards of a ship, except the three largest, can be hoisted and lowered by means of *halyards.* The top-gallant masts can also be lowered, but the lower masts, of course, are fixtures.

The *bowsprit* of a ship is a mast, which projects out horizontally, or at an angle, from the bow. It is sometimes in two or three pieces, sometimes only in one. To it are attached the *jib-sail* and the *flying-jib*, besides a variety of ropes and stays which are connected with, and support the foremast.

The *cat-heads* are two short beams which project from the bows on either side and support the ship's anchors when not in use.

*Miscellaneous.* The openings in the decks are called *hatches* ; the staircases which descend to the cabins are called *companions.* The pulleys by which sails, &c., are hoisted, are named *blocks. Braces* are the ropes by which sails are fixed tightly in any position. Hauling a rope *taut* means hauling it tight. The *weather* side of a ship means the side which happens to be presented to the wind ; the *lee* side that which is away from the wind, and, therefore, sheltered. The *starboard* side means the right side, the *larboard* signifies the left ; but as the two words resemble each other, to prevent mistakes the word *port* is always used for larboard in shouting orders. *Heaving the lead*, is the act of throwing a heavy leaden plummet with a line attached into the sea, to ascertain its depth. It is thrown from the *chains* as far as possible ahead of the ship, so that it may reach the bottom and be perpendicularly beneath the man who heaves it when the ship comes up to the spot where it entered the water. A peculiar and musical cry is given forth by the heaver of the lead each time he throws it. The fore-castle is the habitat of the ordinary sailors, and is usually in nautical parlance, termed the *foeg-s'l.*

Most of what we have just described applies more or less to every ship; but this will be seen in future chapters; meanwhile we would seriously recommend all those who have found this chapter a dry one, to turn back to the head entitled " Rigging the ship," and from that point read it all over again with earnest attention.

OUTWARD BOUND.

# CHAPTER III.

### OUTWARD BOUND—DANGERS OF THE COAST—WRECKS IN THE GREAT GALE OF FEBRUARY 1861.

A LONG cruise now lies before us.  Our ship is launched and rigged and victualled, and nothing now remains but to hoist our sails, up with our anchor, and singing a jovial song the while, sweep out before the wind across the rolling seas.

> "I love, Oh! how I love to ride
> On the fierce foaming bursting tide!"

If you can echo the sentiments of that song, reader, then come with us and we will give you enough—perchance more than enough—of it.

There is danger on the *deep*—every one knows that—but every one does not know that there is greater danger on the shallow sea.   As we have explained before, ancient mariners feared the deep sea, and "hugged the land."   They little thought that they hugged their greatest foe.

Plenty of sea-room and blue water is the delight of the sailor in modern days, because, blow high, blow low, his ship, if a good one, can usually ride out the fiercest storm. But when he approaches land,—then begins his real danger. Then comes the risk of quicksands and sunken rocks, or of gales springing up and casting his bark, a battered wreck, upon that dread of seamen—a *lee-shore*.   This being the case, ships engaged in the coasting-trade are constantly exposed to greater risks than those that plough the distant sea, and when a gale springs up, all vessels that chance to have neared their desired haven are in peculiar danger at that time.   Let us then begin with *coasting vessels.*

The records of disaster on our shores too clearly prove the danger of nearing the land.

Our illustration presents several vessels, which although they all at times venture out into blue water, are more frequently found passing from point to point along our shores. The best way perhaps of showing the dangers to which we have above referred will be to describe some of the terrible scenes that occured during a recent and terrific gale.

WRECKS IN THE GREAT GALE OF FEBRUARY 1861.

No accounts can be more graphic than those of the newspapers of the day from which we quote.

"Off the Wicklow coast the storm was terriffic.  About eleven o'clock on Saturday morning, at full tide, a fine brig was seen beating in towards the mouth of Bray River.  A few moments and she was seen to strike broadside to, the waves breaking over her in clouds of spray to the height of her topmasts.  Her name, the *Endeavour*, Drogheda, could be plainly read.  She was then within some thirty yards of the shore, and five men could be seen leaning helplessly over the side of the gunwale, with hands clasped beseechingly to those who crowded quickly to the spot.  For nearly an hour the five men clung to the vessel, watching with death-stricken faces the anxious crowd, who, for the most part, could only return the stony gaze.  At length, after repeated failures, one gallant boatman took advantage of a retiring wave, rushed almost under the black hull of the brig, and cast a rope right into the grasp of one of the men.  With just strength enough left, he fastened this to a stout hawser, which was quickly drawn ashore.  Meanwhile the vessel was madly oscillating from side to side, her masts trembling like whips, and the sails flying away in ribbons.  Three of the men speedily got ashore by the rope, but two still remained behind, and seemed to be engaged in a struggle as to which was to go next.  At length the youngest sprang over the side and succeeded in escaping, the last man, who was evidently fast losing strength, and who could be seen to shake as with an ague, gazing hopelessly and helplessly on the people.  It becoming quite evident that he could make no effort to save himself, a gallant young fellow, James Lacy, the son of Mr. Lacy of Bray Head, at once volunteered to dare the fearful alternative of trying to reach the ship.  Three times he essayed to get footing on the dark slippery sides of the rolling vessel, which, amid the cheers of those on shore, he at last succeeded in doing.    Lashing the man round the waist with a rope, with a great effort he raised him to the top of the gunwale; but the man, stiff and powerless as if dead, fell back on the deck again.    With another effort young Lacy succeeded in fairly pushing the almost dead man over the side, when he at once fell into the raging surf with the rope from his body still secured, fortunately, across the connecting hawser.    A gallant rush was at once made into the waves by some gentlemen and boatmen, who secured the drowning man, a terrible wave at the very moment boiling round the little group in a mass of foam."

Another paper gives a short summary of the amount of loss as follows :—

"Some faint idea may be formed of the devastation occasioned by the late storm when we mention that on Monday no fewer than 135 losses were reported at Lloyd's, a number which has never been equalled.    This, however, by no means represents the actual loss, for, as many vessels engaged in the coasting trade had sailed from various ports on the east coast but a few hours before the sudden storm burst upon them, there is only too much reason to fear that a large portion of these small craft have foundered, with all on board.

"A calamity similar to that at Whitby occurred in the vicinity of Wells, on the Norfolk coast, near Cromer.  While the gale was at its height, on Saturday morning, about nine o'clock, a barque called the *Favourite*, Captain Summers, bound to Torre del Mar from Hartlepool, was driven on shore on the Blakewell West Sands.    The moment the ship was seen, a party of eight fishermen nobly ventured out to the rescue of the crew of the stranded barque.    The sea was running very high, and, on nearing the sand, the boat was capsized, and, melancholy to relate, the whole of the poor fellows were drowned. They were all married, and have left large families. The crew of the stranded ship were afterwards rescued by another party of fishermen who put off from Blakeney. The barque will become a total wreck. Another vessel was lost near the same place—the schooner *Kingston* from Hartlepool for Plymouth.

"In the Tees bay, a fleet of colliers exceeding sixty in number are announced to have been wrecked.

"A sad sacrifice of life took place on the coast at the mouth of the bay, near Redcar. The brig, *Lady de Crespignie*, Captain Price, belonging to Colchester, and the schooner *Apollos*, of Schiedam, laden with coals, were carried on to the Redcar rocks, where they became total wrecks, and every soul on board them met with a watery grave. A very heavy sea broke in over the beach, and the following vessels were driven ashore:—The *Roman Empress*, Captain Driver, bound to the Mediterranean from Shields, on the Marsk Sand; the brig *Mary*, from Sunderland for the Thames; the *Eustace*, Captain Thompson, master, bound to London from Sunderland; the brig *Odessa*, bound to London; the *Koh-i-Noor*, Wildridge, master, from Shields for London; and the *Marie Clotilde*, bound to Hartlepool. Most of these ships were going to pieces when the last accounts left."

The wreck of a vessel called the *Merchant* shows the extreme danger encountered by those brave men who form the crews of our life-boats. It occurred on the coast, in the Whitby district. Seven ships were driven ashore there, and the crew of the life-boats had already been

making prodigious efforts to save life.  An eye-witness
thus describes the thrilling scene:—

"The *Merchant* was driven to the beach just to the
north of the pier.  The life-boat was again immediately
launched and manned by the same noble fellows who had
saved the lives from all the wrecked ships.  The sea was
now dreadful and the danger imminent.  The men in the
life boat were warned not to go; but, undaunted, they
proceeded and had got to sea, when it was observed from
the shore that the schooner *Roe*, lying between the *Merchant* and the coast, greatly obstructed the management of
the life-boat, and, in consequence, it was carried to the
stern of the *Merchant*.  While attempting to get the boat
to lee-ward of the vessel, she was upset by a tremendous
cross sea, between the stern of the *Merchant* and the shore,
and the unfortunate boatmen were immediately immersed
in the raging sea.  The scene will never be forgotten.  The
brave fellows had on cork belts, which kept them up for a
short time, and they struggled hard for their lives, and
that within forty yards of the shore and the pier.  A
rocket was fired over them, but the line was not reached
by any of them.  Thousands, regardless of the sea washing
over them, lined the pier and the shore, and among them
were the wives, children, and relatives of the poor drowning men.  Some were only restrained by force from jump-
ing into the sea, with the vain hope of saving their dear
relations.  The shrieks of the women and children as the
poor fellows disappeared one by one were most heart-
rending.  No assistance, however, could be rendered.  One
of the crew succeeded in getting on the bottom of the life
boat, which never righted, and, after clinging to it for some
time, and receiving fearful seas, was dashed off and perished.

Only one out of the crew of thirteen succeeded in reaching the shore, and this is attributed to a cork waistcoat which he wore in addition to the ordinary belt."

Of those thirteen men only one was unmarried. The rest left eleven widows and forty children totally unprovided for by this awful calamity.

It must be remembered that all this and a great deal more that we cannot even touch upon, much less give in detail, occurred during the short but terrible course of *one* storm; and it is a fact of the most deeply solemn and saddening character, that every gale we landsmen hear sweeping past our windows is *certain* to dash many a ship to pieces on our shores, and send many a soul with awful suddenness into the presence of its Creator.

Happy, thrice happy, those who, at such an hour, have not to turn with despairing cries, *for the first time*, to our blessed Saviour. And well does it become those on shore who call themselves Christians, to betake themselves to their knees when the fierce tempests blow, and, in the name of Jesus, pray that human beings on the sea may be saved from the angry waves.

In a recent number of a periodical we find the following curious and sad paragraph :—

" *The Wreck Chart.*—We have lying before us a remarkable map, the wreck chart of the British Isles for 1858. It is to be found in a return to Parliament, carefully prepared by the Board of Trade. The chart is of the same appearance as an ordinary map of these islands, except that the whole line of coast, from the Orkneys to the Land's End, is dotted with a series of black marks. Each mark indicates either a shipwreck or some casualty to a vessel nearly approaching that disaster. A most melancholy effect has

BRIGANTINE.
CUTTER
SLOOP.

this chart when this key to its object is given. The whole coast, particularly the approaches to our great commercial cities, bristles with dottings, which indicate clearly the site where some noble ship has gone to destruction with her human freight. All round our coast, with the aid of this map, we can trace clearly the frightful work of destruction during the past year. In 1858 the number of vessels wrecked on the coast and in the seas of the United Kingdom was 1170; of these 354 were total wrecks, and 50 were sunk by collision, making the number totally lost 404. By these disasters the lives of 1895 persons were imperiled, of which number 340 persons were actually lost. This is the dark side of the doleful map. It has, however, a bright side, and on that we find that, by the life boats of the National Life Boat Institution, those of local bodies, and various other craft, 1555 of our fellow creatures were, during the past year, rescued from a watery grave."

The coasting trade, then, is replete with danger, yet it is carried on with the utmost vigour, and there are always plenty of "hands," as seamen are called when spoken of in connection with ships, to man the vessels. The traffic in which they are engaged is the transporting of the goods peculiar to one part of our island to another part where they are in demand.

We shall describe the vessels represented in our plate, and begin with the smallest.

## SLOOPS.

Like all other vessels, sloops vary in size, but none of them attain to great magnitude. As a class they are the smallest decked vessels we have. From 40 to 100 tons burden is a very common size. A sloop of 40 tons burden is what we call a *little* ship, and one of 100 tons is by no means a big one. The hull of such a vessel being intended exclusively to carry cargo, very little space is allowed for the crew. The cabins of the smaller sized sloops are seldom high enough to permit of an ordinary man standing erect. They are usually capable of affording accommodation to two in the cabin and three or four in the forecastle, and such accommodation is by no means ample. The *class* to which vessels belong is determined, chiefly, by the number of their masts and the arrangement and form of their sails.

The distinctive peculiarity of the sloop is, that it has but one mast; and its rig is, nautically speaking, *fore-and-aft*—that is to say, the sails are spread with their surfaces parallel to the sides of the vessel, *not* stretched upon yards *across* the vessel. The term "fore-and-aft" is derived from the *forward* part and the *after* part of the ship. *Fore-and-aft* sails, then, are such as are spread upon yards which point fore and aft, not across the ship. We conceive this elaborate explanation to be necessary for some readers; and, therefore, don't apologize for making it. A ship whose sails are spread *across* the hull is said to be *square-rigged*. Sometimes a sloop carries a square top-sail.

The mast, yards, and sails of a sloop are as follows:—As has been already said, one of the distinctive peculiarities of a sloop is, that it has only *one* mast. This mast is sometimes formed of one *stick*, sometimes of two; the second, or *top-mast*, being fastened to the top of the lower mast by *cross-trees* and *cap*, in such a way that it may be hoisted or lowered at pleasure. A sloop has usually four sails,—a main-sail, fore-sail, gaff, and jib. The *main-sail* is behind the lower mast; it reaches from within a few feet of the deck to the top of the lower mast, and spreads out upon two yards towards the stern or after part of the ship, over which it projects a few feet. The lower yard of the main-sail is called the boom, and the upper the main-sail-yard. This is by far the largest sail in the sloop. Above it is spread the *gaff*, which is comparatively a very small sail, and is used when the wind is not very strong. The *fore-sail* is a triangular sheet, which traverses on the *fore-stay*; that is, the strong rope which runs from the lower mast-head to the bow, or front part of the sloop. On the bowsprit is stretched the *jib*, another triangular sail, which reaches nearly to the top of the lower mast. The only sail that rises above the lower mast is the gaff. In stormy weather this sail is always taken down. If the wind increases to a gale the jib is lowered, and lashed to the bowsprit. Should the gale increase, a reef is taken in the main-sail. One, two, three, and sometimes four reefs are taken in, according to the violence of the storm; when the last reef is taken in, the sloop is under *close-reefed* main-sail. Increased violence in the storm necessitates the taking in of the main-sail and *lying-to* under the fore-sail, or a part of it. Lying-to is putting the sloop's head to the wind, and placing the helm in such a position that it tends to turn the vessel in one direction, while the gale acting on the fore-sail tends to force it in another, and thus it remains stationary between the two opposing forces. Many vessels thus *lie-to*, and ride out the severest storm. Sometimes, however, a dreadful hurricane arises, and compels vessels to take in all sails and "*scud under bare poles*"—that is, *drive before* the wind without any sails at all, and it is at such seasons that man is forced to feel his utter helplessness and his absolute dependence on the Almighty. Of course, there are slight variations in the rig of sloops—some have a *square-sail*, and some have a *flying-jib;* but these are not distinctive sails, and they are seldom used in small craft.

Our Illustration represents a sloop under full sail, main-sail, gaff, fore-sail, and jib, sailing with a side wind.

Now it may strike some of our observant readers, that in our engraving the cutter and the sloop, although acted upon by the same wind, are sailing in precisely opposite directions. Perchance our sceptical friends may think they have "caught us napping," putting upon paper what was never seen in nature. Nevertheless, this apparent paradox may be explained thus:—

Suppose a vessel with the bow and stern sharp and precisely alike, so that it might sail backwards or forwards with equal facility. Suppose, also, that it has two masts exactly the same in all respects—both of them amidships, one near the bow, the other near the stern. Suppose, further, a square sail stretched between the two masts quite flat, and remember that this would be a fore-and-aft sail, namely, one extending along the length, not across the breadth of the vessel.

Well, now, were a breeze to blow straight against the side of such a vessel, it would either blow it over, flat on its side, or urge it slowly *sideways* over the water, after the fashion of a crab. Now remove one of these masts—say the stern-most one—and erect it close to the lee-side of the vessel (that is, away from the wind-ward side), still keeping the sail extended. The immediate effect would be that the sail would no longer present itself *flatly* against the wind, but diagonally. The wind, therefore, after dashing against it would slide or whisk violently off in the direction of the mast that had been removed, that is, towards the stern. In doing so it would of course give the vessel a shove in the opposite direction, on the very same principle that a boy, when he jumps violently off a chair, not only sends his body in one direction, but sends the chair in the opposite direction. So, when the wind jumps off the sail towards the stern it sends the ship in the opposite direction, namely, forward. Reverse this; bring back the mast you had removed to its old place in the centre of the deck, and shift the *front* mast near to the lee-bulwarks. The wind will now slide off the sail towards the *bow*, and force our vessel in the opposite direction, namely, backward.

By means of the rudder, and placing the sails in various positions so as to cause them to press against the masts in a particular manner, vessels can be made to sail not only with a side wind but with a breeze blowing a good deal *against* them—in nautical phrasology, they can be made to sail "close to the wind." In short, they can sail in every direction except directly in the "teeth" of the wind. Some ships sail closer to the wind than others; their powers in this respect depending very much on the cut of their sails, and the form of their hulls.

*The Lighter* is a small rough clumsy species of coasting vessel usually of the sloop rig. It is used for discharging cargoes of large vessels in harbours, and off coasts where the depth of water is not great. Lighters are usually picturesque-looking craft with dingy sails, and they seldom carry top-sails of any kind. Being seldom decked they are more properly huge boats than little ships. But lighters are not classed according to their rig,—they may be of any rig, though that of the sloop is most commonly adopted. In the annexed wood-cut you have a specimen of one very much in use. The sail of this boat is kept extended by means of a *sprit* or wooden pole which is fastened low

THE LIGHTER.

down on the mast just above the heads of the crew; its other end being fastened to the upper outside corner of the sail, which, in consequence of this arrangement, is called a *sprit* sail. The sprit in the cut is on the other side of the sail, but its presence is indicated by a diagonal line on the canvas.

## THE CUTTER.

This species of vessel is similar, in all respects, to the sloop, the only difference being that it is better and more elegantly built. Gentlemen's pleasure yachts are most frequently cutters, but yachts may be of any form or rig— that is, they may belong to any *class* of vessels without changing their name of *yacht*. Cutter yachts are much more elegantly moulded and rigged than the sloops that we have just described. They are *clipper-built*—that is, the hull is smoothly and sharply shaped; the cutwater, in particular, is like a knife, and the bow wedge-like. In short, although similar in general outline, a cutter-yacht bears the same relation to a trading sloop that a racer does to a cart horse. Their sails, also, are larger in proportion, and they are fast-sailing vessels; but, on this very account, they are not such good *sea-boats* as their clumsy brethren, whose bluff or rounded bows rise on the waves, while the sharp vessels cut through them, and often deluge the decks with spray.

In our Engraving we have a sloop-rigged yacht sailing with a light *side* wind, with main-sail, gaff, fore-sail, and jib set, and the *Union Jack*, our well-known national flag, flying at the *peak*.

The yard observed stretching across the vessel is that on which a square-sail is sometimes spread when the cutter is running before a fair wind.

*The Schooner* is the most elegant, and, for small craft, the most manageable vessel that floats. Its proportions are more agreeable to the eye than those of any other species of craft, and its rig is in favour with owners of yachts, especially with those whose yachts are large. The schooner's distinctive peculiarities are, that it carries two masts, which usually "*rake aft*," or lean back a good deal; and its rig is chiefly fore-and-aft, like the sloop. Of the two masts the *after* one is the *main-mast*. The other is termed the *fore-mast*. The sails of a schooner are—the *main-sail* and the *gaff* on the main-mast; the *fore-sail*, *fore-top-sail*, and *fore-top-gallant-sail* (the two last being square sails), on the fore-mast. In front of the fore-mast are the *stay-sail*, the *jib*, and the *flying-jib*; these last are triangular sails. If a schooner were cut in two in the middle, crosswise, the front portion would be in all respects a sloop with a square top-sail; the stern part would also be a sloop, minus the bowsprit and the triangular sails *before* the mast. Schooners sometimes carry a large square-sail, which is spread when the wind is "dead aft." They are much used in the coasting trade, and one of their great advantages is that they can be worked with fewer "hands" than sloops of the same size.

## THE BRIGANTINE.

A specimen of this vessel is given in our engraving. Its rig is a mixture of that of the sloop and brig, which latter vessel shall be described hereafter. The Brigantine is *square* rigged on the fore-mast, and sloop-rigged on its after or mizzen mast. Of its two masts the front mast is the larger, and, therefore, is the main-mast. In short a brigantine is a mixed vessel, being a brig forward, and a sloop aft.

SCHOONER

Such are our coasting vessels; but it must be borne in mind that ships of their *class* are not confined to the coast. When built very large they are intended for the deep ocean trade, and many schooners approach in size to full-rigged "ships."

Reference having been made to life boats, we shall, before leaving this department of our subject devote a chapter to them, and to an account of the heroism of a young woman who dwelt in a lighthouse on our stormy coasts not many years ago.

THE LIFE BOAT.

# CHAPTER IV.

### GRACE DARLING.

THERE are not many women who, like Joan of Arc, put forth their hands to the work peculiarly belonging to the male sex, and achieve for themselves undying fame. And among these there are very few indeed, who, in thus quitting their natural sphere and assuming masculine duties, retain their feminine modesty and gentleness.

Such an one was Grace Darling. She did not, indeed, like those to whom we have just referred, altogether quit her station and follow a course peculiar to the male sex; but she did once seize the oar and launch fearlessly upon the raging sea and perform a deed which strong and daring men might have been proud of; which drew forth the wondering admiration of her country, and has rendered her name indissolubly connected with the annals of heroic daring in the saving of human life from vessels wrecked upon our rock-bound shores.

Grace Darling was born in November 1815, at Bamborough on the Nothumberland coast. Her father was keeper of the lighthouse on the Longstone, one of the Farn Islands lying off that coast; and here, on a mere bit of rock surrounded by the ocean, and often by the howling tempests and the foaming breakers of that dangerous spot, our heroine spent the greater part of her life, cut off almost totally from the joys and pursuits of the busy world. She and her mother managed the domestic economy of the lighthouse on the little islet, while her father trimmed the lantern that sent a blaze of friendly light to warn mariners off that dangerous coast.

In personal appearance Grace Darling is described as having been fair and comely, with a gentle modest expression of countenance, about the middle size, and with nothing in the least degree masculine about her. She had reached her twenty-second year when the wreck took place in connection with which her name has become famous.

The Farn Islands are peculiarly dangerous. The sea rushes with tremendous force between the smaller islands, and, despite the warning light, wrecks occasionally take place among them. In days of old, when men had neither heart nor head to erect lighthouses for the protection of their fellows, many a noble ship must have been dashed to pieces there, and many an awful shriek must have mingled with the hoarse roar of the surf round these rent and weather-worn rocks.

A gentleman who visited the Longstone rock in 1838, describes it thus :—

" It was, like the rest of these desolate isles, all of dark whinstone, cracked in every direction, and worn with the action of winds, waves, and tempests, since the world began. Over the greater part of it was not a blade of grass, nor a grain of earth; it was bare and iron-like stone, crusted, round all the coast as far as high-water mark, with limpet and still smaller shells.  We ascended wrinkled hills of black stone, and descended into worn and dismal dells of the same ; into some of which, where the tide got entrance, it came pouring and roaring in raging whiteness, and churning the loose fragments of whinstone into round pebbles, and piling them up in deep crevices with sea-weeds, like great round ropes and heaps of fucus.  Over our heads screamed hundreds of hovering birds, the gull mingling its hideous laughter most wildly."

One wild and stormy night in September 1838, such a night as induces those on land to draw closer round the fire, and offer up, perchance, a silent prayer for those who are at sea, a steamer was battling, at disadvantage with the billows, off St. Abb's Head.  She was the *Forfarshire*, a steamer of three hundred tons, under command of Mr. John Humble, and had started from Hull for Dundee with a valuable cargo, a crew of twenty-one men and forty-one passengers.

· It was a fearful night; the storm raged furiously and would have tried the qualities of even a stout vessel; but this one was in very bad repair, and her boilers were in such a state that the engines soon became entirely useless, and at last they ceased to work. We cannot conceive the danger of a steamer left thus comparatively helpless in a furious storm and dark night off a dangerous coast.

In a short time the vessel became quite unmanageable, and drifted with the direction of the tide, no one knew whither. Soon the terrible cry arose, " breakers to lee-ward," and immediately after the Farn lights became visible. A desparing attempt was now made by the captain to run the ship between the islands and the mainland, but in this he failed, and about three o'clock she struck heavily on a rock bow foremost.

The scene of consternation that followed is indescribable. Immediately one of the boats was lowered, and with a freight of terror-stricken people pushed off, but not before one or two persons had fallen into the sea and perished in their vain attempts to get into it. This party in the boat, nine in number, survived the storm of that awful night, and were picked up the following morning by a Montrose sloop. Of those left in the ill-fated ship some remained in the after part, a few stationed themselves near the bow thinking it the safest spot. The captain stood helpless, his wife clinging to him, while several other females gave vent to their agony of despair in fearful cries.

Meanwhile the waves dashed the vessel again and again on the rock, and at last a larger billow than the rest lifted her up and let her fall down upon its sharp edge. The effect was tremendous and instantaneous ; the vessel was literally broken into two pieces, and the after part, with the greater number of the passengers in the cabin, was swept away through the Pifa Gut, a tremendous current which is considered dangerous even in good weather. Among those who thus perished were the captain and his wife. The fore part of the steamer, with the few who had happily taken refuge upon it, remained fast on the rock. Here eight or nine of the passengers and crew clung to the windlass, and a woman named Sarah Dawson with her two little children lay huddled together in a corner of the fore cabin exposed to the fury of winds and waves all the remainder of that dreadful night. For hours each returning wave carried a thrill of terror to their hearts, for the shattered wreck reeled before every shock, and it seemed as if it would certainly be swept away into the churning foam before daybreak.

But daylight came at last, and the survivors on the wreck began to sweep the dim horizon with straining eye-balls as a faint hope at last began to arise in their bosoms. Nor were these trembling hopes doomed to disappointment. At the eleventh hour God in his mercy sent deliverance. Through the glimmering dawn and driving spray, the lighthouse-keeper's daughter from the lonely watch-tower descried the wreck, which was about a mile distant from the Longstone. From the mainland, too, they were observed; and crowds of people lined the shore and gazed upon the distant speck, to which, by the aid of telescopes, the survivors were seen clinging with the tenacity of despair.

But no boat could live in that raging sea, which still lashed madly against the riven rocks, although the violence of the storm had begun to abate. An offer of £5 by the steward of Bamborough Castle failed to tempt a crew of men to launch their boat. One daring heart and willing hand was there, however. Grace Darling, fired with an intense desire to save the perishing ones, urged her father to launch their little boat. At first he held back. There was no one at the lighthouse except himself, his wife and

BRIG.

Page 70.

daughter. What could such a crew do in a little open boat in so wild a sea? He knew the extreme peril they should encounter better than his daughter, and very naturally hesitated to run so great a risk. For besides the danger of swamping and the comparatively weak arm of an inexperienced woman at the oar, the passage from the Longstone to the wreck could only be accomplished with the ebb tide, so that unless the exhausted survivors should prove to be able to lend their aid they could not pull back again to the Lighthouse.

But the earnest importunities of the heroic girl were not to be resisted. Her father at last consented, and the little boat pushed off with the man and the young woman for its crew. It may be imagined with what a thrill of joy and hope the people on the wreck beheld the boat dancing on the crested waves towards them; and how great must have been the surprise that mingled with their other feelings on observing that one of the rowers was a woman!

They gained the rock in safety; but here their danger was increased ten-fold, and it was only by the exertion of great muscular power, coupled with resolute courage, that they prevented the boat being dashed to pieces against the rock.

One by one the sufferers were got into the boat. Sarah Dawson was found lying in the fore cabin with a spark of life still trembling in her bosom, and she still clasped her two little ones in her arms, but the spirits of both had fled to Him who gave them. With great difficulty the boat was rowed back to the Longstone, and the rescued crew landed in safety. Here, owing to the violence of the sea, they were detained for nearly three days, along with a boat's crew which had put off to their relief from North Sunderland; and it required some ingenuity to accommodate so large a party within the narrow limits of a lighthouse. Grace gave up her bed to poor Mrs. Dawson; most of the others rested as they best could upon the floor.

The romantic circumstances of this rescue, the isolated position of the girl, her youth and modesty, and the self-devoting heroism displayed upon this occasion, thrilled through the length and breadth of the country like an electric shock, and the name of Grace Darling became for the time as well known as that of the greatest in the land; while the lonely lighthouse on the Longstone become a point of attraction to thousands of warm admirers, among whom were many of the rich and noble. Letters and gifts flowed in upon Grace Darling continually. The public seemed unable to do enough to testify their regard. The Duke of Northumberland invited her over to Alnwick Castle, and presented her with a gold watch. A public subscription, to the amount of £700, was raised for her. The Humane Society presented her with a handsome silver tea-pot and a vote of thanks for her courage and humanity. Portraits of her were sold in the print shops all over the land, and the enthusiasm which at first was the natural impulse of admiration for one who had performed a noble and heroic deed, at last rose to a species of mania, in the heat of which not a few absurdities were perpetrated.

Among others, several of the proprietors of the metropolitan theatres offered her a large sum nightly on condition that she would appear on the stage, merely to sit in a boat during the performance of a piece illustrative of the incident of which she was the heroine! As might have been expected of one whose spirit was truly noble, she promptly declined all such offers. God seems to have put his arm tenderly round Grace Darling, and afforded her special strength to resist the severe temptations to which she was exposed.

All proposals to better her condition were rejected, and she returned to her home on the island rock, where she remained with her father and mother till within a few months of her death. The fell destroyer, alas! claimed her while yet in the bloom of womanhood. She died of consumption on the 20th of October 1842, leaving an example of self-devoting courage in the hour of danger, and self-denying heroism in the hour of temptation, that may well be admired and imitated by those whose duty it is to man the life-boat, and launch to the rescue on the stormy waves, in all time to come.

## LIFE-BOATS.

A life-boat is a large boat formed in such a way that it cannot sink and cannot easily be overturned by rough seas. Its object is to rescue the passengers and crews of vessels wrecked upon the coast; and from what has been said in a former chapter as to its great usefulness in saving human life, the reader will readily believe that scientific and phil-anthropic men have given much earnest thought to the best methods of constructing it.

By means of floats, air-tight compartments, &c., the life-boat is made so buoyant that it will "live," as sailors express it, in a sea upon which no other boat could venture without being instantly swamped. The men are provided with cork and air jackets or belts, in order to prevent their sinking should they chance to be washed overboard; and the more effectually to prevent such a catastrophe, they usually lash themselves to the seats or "thwarts." Of course such a boat is constantly washed over by the waves, but even when full of water it cannot sink. The chief danger the life-boat runs is that of being upset altogether, or being thrown upon a rock and having her planks stove in, or being dashed against the side of the vessel whose crew it has been brought to succour.

In former years wrecked crews had only to look for deliverance to the poor fishermen who dwelt upon the coast where they chanced to have been wrecked. Now, however, philanthropists have formed a society, named the "*Royal National Life-boat Institution*," whose principal objects are to construct and fit out as many life-boats as their funds will admit of, and to reward with medals and sums of money such persons as shall distinguish themselves in the saving of life from wrecks.

That this institution is actively engaged and doing its work well, may be gathered from the following paragraph, which we extract verbatim from a newspaper published in March of last year (1861):—

"ROYAL NATIONAL LIFE-BOAT INSTITUTION.—A meeting of this institution was held yesterday—Mr. Thomas Chapman, F.R.S., in the chair. Rewards amounting to £156 were voted to the crews of life-boats of the society, for saving the crews of various wrecked vessels during the late heavy gales. Applications for life-boats were made from Tynemouth, in Northumberland; Peterhead, in Scotland; and Aberystwith in Wales. It was reported at the meeting that her Majesty the Queen, in appreciation of the important and philanthropic character of the work of the society, had signified her intention to become an annual subscriber of £50 to its funds. Within the last two months, the institution had expended nearly £3000 on its life-boat stations."

Another extract from the "Illustrated London News" of Nov. 1859, shows how the agents of this society work, and the feeling that exists in the public mind regarding it.

"On the first instant, (Nov. 1859) when it was blowing

a heavy gale from the S.S.W. the screw steamer *Shamrock* of Dublin, was seen to ground on the south end of the Holm Sands. The Lowestoft beachmen, seeing the sea breaking heavily over her, and from their experience know- ing that no time was to be lost, collected their people and immediately launched the life-boat, which is in connection with the Royal National Life-boat Institution, for their rescue. When the life-boat reached the steamer the sea was breaking over the mast-heads, but she was providen- tially enabled to anchor in a most advantageous position ahead of her; and although the sea broke over her and re- peatedly filled her, this excellent life-boat, as often in her buoyancy clearing herself of the seas, was at length, with difficulty, enabled to approach the steamer. A communica- tion was then established with the wreck by means of ropes, and the whole of the crew (fourteen men) were hauled by lines through the sea to the life-boat and brought safely to the shore. This act has been pronounced as daring a rescue from shipwreck as was ever witnessed.

"Early on the morning of the 26th ult., this life-boat again put off, during a heavy gale from the southward, to the rescue of the crew of five men of the schooner *Lord Douglas*, of Dundee. On the life-boat's return to the shore the gale split her foresail, which compelled her to run on Corton Reach. Having procured another sail and changed some of her men, she went off again to the assistance of the crew—four in number—of another vessel, the Silva, of Glasgow, which was on Corton Sands. The men on the wreck were drawn into the life-boat by lines. The foresail was again split by the violence of the gale, and she was compelled for safety to take the beach at Yarmouth. The neighbouring life-boat stationed at Pakefield, has also during the recent gales rendered noble services in saving life from wrecks.

"The National Life-boat Institution has voted the crews of these life-boats nearly £100 for their valuable exertions during the recent storms. Last summer the society built a new house for the Lowestoft life-boat, at a cost of £158.

"We append some particulars of the operations of the life-boats of the Royal National Life-boat Institution during the present year. It appears that these boats have been called into active operation on fifty-six different occasions, on various points of our coast. The result has been that one hundred and thirty-four lives have been saved off twenty-three wrecks, besides the assisting of five vessels safely into port. On twenty-three occasions it happened that when the life-boats had put off, in reply to signals of distress, the vessels either got out of danger or their crews were rescued by other means. Again, crews assembled several times to give assistance, but were not required to put off to sea. For these several exertions the crews were paid nearly £600.

"Nearly all these services took place in stormy weather and heavy seas, and often in the dark hours of night, and yet, it is gratifying to add, not a single accident happened either to the boats or to the gallant fellows who had manned them. On these occasions, and at the quarterly periods of exercise, the life-boats of the society were manned probably by no less than four thousand persons. Such practical proofs as these of the immense value of the National Life-boat Institution in a maritime country like ours, cannot possibly be overrated, and surely it has the highest claims on our support. The more we hear of its operations at various parts of the coast, the more we feel urged to press its claims on public notice."

The society has stations all round our coasts, although not nearly so many as could be desired, and the good done is incalculable.

One of the great objects to be attained in cases of wrecks · is, to pass a line between the wreck and the shore by means of which a stout rope may be drawn to or from the vessel and connected with it, by which many, sometimes all of those on board, may be saved. The great difficulty is to get the line thrown on board, and in order to overcome this several machines have been invented by which a line may be thrown. One of those machines is a small cannon from which the end of the line is shot over the wreck. Another machine used for saving life is a large buoy or float, provided with ropes by means of which a drowning man may grasp and support himself until assistance arrives. This buoy is supplied with a blue light which can be fired by pulling a cord, so that, when it is dark, a bright glare guides those who are in search to the objects they desire to succour. A representation of this buoy is given in the annexed wood-cut.

It is one of the prominent features of the present age that men strive by every means to turn scientific knowledge to useful account. It is not enough that we should wonder at the discoveries of science, and expatiate on the wisdom and power of Him who made the universe. In these days we endeavour to press science into the service of art, and, while we admire the wisdom displayed in all that increasing knowledge unfolds to us, we adore the *love* that prompted our heavenly Father to put so much power and so many wonderful materials into the hand of man, for the express purpose of conducing to his temporal prosperity and happiness.

THE LIFE-BUOY.

By careful study of the varied phenomena connected with the currents in the ocean and in the atmosphere, scientific men are now enabled with considerable certainty to foretell the coming of a storm, and even to point out its probable course. By ingenious appliance of the well-known agent electricity, we can instantly communicate our thoughts and our knowledge from one end of the kingdom to the other. By the union of these two powers, it is now proposed to telegraph to the lighthouses along our coast at what time a storm may be expected, and in what direction it will probably blow, so that, by means of preconcerted signal-lights ships nearing our ports may be warned of the coming danger and put in possession of information sufficient to enable them to avoid it. A central office is proposed, to which meteorological information should be telegraphed from all quarters, and from which the digested information could be transmitted to lighthouses and sea-ports.

Maury, the eminent and pious American philosoper, from whose admirable work, the "*Physical Geography of the Sea*," we have already quoted, gives his opinion on this subject, as follows:—

He holds that, though storms cannot be predicted in all cases, they may in many; and this by the establishment of a central office to which meteorological observations should be transmitted by telegraph from a wide circle of surrounding stations, and compared together. He points out that, taking a general view of the world, the coasts of Britain are peculiarly dangerous, for they seldom fail to present a lee-shore to the sailor in any and every wind that blows. On the other hand, the geographical position of these islands is such as would enable them to give early and valuable warnings to countries eastward, of western storms. Predictions of weather founded on observations at any one point would exhibit uncertainty and confusion, but when derived from observations at many and distant points, instantaneously communicated and combined, order and sequence appear, and the progressive march of special storms can be traced. Hence a central meteorological office is in a vastly more favourable position for judging of the weather than any single ship, though steered by a scientific commander, amply provided with barometers and thermometers. To every ship, therefore, when it comes into the neighbourhood of our iron-bound shores, after its solitary voyage through the watery waste, it would be one of the greatest boons conceivable if each lighthouse should hang out a signal, intimating what Captain Maury well calls "the invisible dangers of the atmosphere," thereby indicating to the mariner from what quarter he may presently expect a storm to break forth, which coast will be dangerous, and which safe for him, to be found in the neighbourhood of. Had any such system been in operation when that magnificent Australian liner, the Royal Charter, with its hundreds of passengers, came in sight of our shores, after the long voyage, with its precious freight from the other side of the world, the dire calamity which ensued could never have occurred. That sad wreck (an account of which will be found in another part of this volume) shocked the public mind for a moment grievously, yet it is but a drop in the great aggregate of the nation's losses in the same manner, and from the same causes, as the public notifications of more than a thousand wrecks in the year testify.

## CHAPTER V.

### THE BRIG.

ADVANCING step by step in our investigation of the peculiar rig and build of ships, we come to the *brig*. This species of craft is usually, but not necessarily, larger than those that have yet been described; it is generally built on a larger scale than the schooner, and often approaches in magnitude to the full sized, three-masted ship.

The distinctive features of the brig are, that it has *two* masts, both of which are *square-rigged*. It is a particularly serviceable species of craft, and is much used in foreign trade.

### THE RIGGING OF THE BRIG.

The advantage of the square-rig over the fore-and-aft rig is, that the sails, being smaller and more numerous, are more easily managed, and require fewer men, or "hands," to work them. Thus, as we increase the size of our vessel, the more necessity is there that it should be square-rigged. The huge main-sail of the sloop and schooner could not be applied to large vessels; so that, when men came to construct ships of several hundred tons burden, they were compelled to increase the *number* of masts and sails, and diminish the *size* of them; hence, probably, brigs were devised *after* schooners. The main-mast of a brig is the aft one.

The sails are named after the masts to which they are fastened,—namely, the *main-sail*—above that the *main-top-sail*—above that the *main-top-gallant-sail*—and sometimes a very small sail, named the *royal*, is spread above all. Behind the main-sail there is a small fore-and-aft sail, similar to the main-sail of a schooner, which is called the *boom-main-sail*. On the fore-mast is a similar sail, which is called the *try-sail*. Attached to the respective yards of square-rigged ships there are smaller poles or arms which can be pushed out at pleasure, and the yard lengthened, in order to receive an additional little sail, or wing, on each side. These wings are called *studding-sails*, or *stun-sails*, and are used only when the wind is fair and light. They are named after the sails to which they are fastened; thus, there are the main-stun-sails, the *main-top stun-sails*, and the *main-top-gallant stun-sails*, &c. The foremast of a brig is smaller than the main-mast. It carries a *fore-sail, fore-top-sail, fore-top-gallant-sail*, and *fore-royal*. Between it and the bowsprit are the *fore-stay-sail, jib*, and *flying-jib*. The three last sails are nearly similar in *all* vessels. All the yards, &c., are hoisted, and shifted, and held in their position by a complicated arrangement of cordage, which in the mass is called the running-rigging, in contradistinction to the standing-rigging, which, as we have said, is *fixed*, and keeps the masts, &c., immovably in position. Yet every rope, in what seems to a landsman's eye a bewildering mass of confusion, has its distinctive name and specific purpose.

Our coloured engraving represents a brig in the most dangerous of all positions, namely, off a lee-shore in a gale, endeavouring to "weather" a point, that is, trying to sail round without being dashed against it. She is sailing as close to the wind as possible. She would get on much better if she were to ease off a point or two to the left, and so let the wind blow more flatly against her sails; but were she to do this she would run the risk of being blown on the point of land before she weathered it. She sails, it will be observed, under her fore-sail, fore-top-sail, and main-top-sail,—the main-sail and boom-main-sail being clewed up, and her top-gallant-masts being lowered till only their tops are seen above the top-mast cross-trees. The top-gallant yards have been lowered on deck and stowed away till the gale moderates. No doubt the jib too is hoisted, but it is hid from view by the fore-sail and the spray.

The brig at the head of the chapter is sailing with "a wind on her quarter," that is almost, but not quite, "astern." And be it carefully noted here, that "a wind on the quarter" is the best that can blow for most vessels, because it acts on vessels in such a way that *all* the sails "draw," or are filled. She has not the wind, however, *quite* on her quarter. It is nearly fair, or " dead aft,"—the main-sail being clewed up to let the wind get at the fore-sail, shows this. On this brig are set the main-top, main-top-gallant, fore, fore-top, and fore-top-gallant sails, also the jib and flying jib.

Brigs and schooners, being light and handy craft, are generally used by pirates and smugglers in the prosecution of their lawless pursuits, and many a deed of bloodshed and horror has been done on board such craft by those miscreants.   The following is one of the blackest we have ever fallen in with:—

### STORY OF ALEXANDER TARDY.

Alexander Tardy was a native of the island of St. Domingo, and one of the most dreadful characters by nature that ever lived.   Having shown a bad unsettled disposition in boyhood, we are not surprised to find that in youth he gave up mercantile pursuits and went to sea as steward of a ship.   This was shortly after the commencement of the present century.   This situation he left under suspicion of having poisoned the captain.

From this time forward he led the life of an unsettled wanderer—sometimes in one employment, sometimes in another, but chiefly spending his life as a thief.   Being at one time on board a vessel bound for Charleston, he poisoned several of the passengers and charged the crime on the negro cook, who was tried, condemned, and executed, although, as may be supposed, he protested his innocence to the last.

This miscreant seems to have been unable to resist the desire to poison his fellow-creatures, even when he could have no possible reason for the perpetration of the diabolical act.   On another occasion he attempted to poison the passengers in a ship bound for Philadelphia; but on this occasion was seized and condemned to seven years hard labour.

Being liberated at the end of his term, Tardy now gave himself up to the commission of every species of crime that man is capable of committing. At last, while staying at Havanna, in Cuba, he formed the bold and dreadful plan of going on board a vessel, poisoning the captain and all the crew, and thus possess himself of a ship and cargo at once.

To accomplish this, he took into his confidence three Spaniards, desperadoes quite equal to himself in villany. Their names were Felix, Pepe, and Courro. Having consulted together, they resolved to take passage on board the *Crawford*, an American brig, commanded by Captain Brightman, which was about to sail for New York with a cargo consisting of sugar, coffee, molasses, &c. Captain Brightman happened to be unwell at the time of starting, and Tardy sought to ingratiate himself in the character of a doctor. Courro shipped as Tardy's servant, while Felix and Pepe gave themselves out to be merchants, and, in order to support this assumed position, took on board with them a box full of lead and iron, which they gave in charge to the captain, saying that it contained 17,000 dollars in gold. The crew of the *Crawford* consisted of Mr. Dobson the mate, and five seamen. Besides these there were four other passengers, one of whom was a Spaniard named Ginoulhiac, another was a Mr. Robinson, part owner of the cargo. Altogether, there were fifteen souls on board the ill-fated brig.

On the 28th of May, 1827, the *Crawford* put to sea;—ere that voyage was done, only Dobson the mate, Gibbs the cook, and Ginoulhiac the Spanish passenger, survived to tell of the dark deed of blood that had been perpetrated upon the sea.

Dobson, the mate, describes the events of the tragedy thus :—

" The brig proceeded on the voyage with variable

winds, but with every prospect of making a fair passage. One morning, after the vessel had been at sea for a few days, the wind being light and the weather fair, I sat down to breakfast on deck with Tardy and the other cabin passengers. Captain Brightman was still indisposed and confined to his berth.

"During breakfast Tardy acted as master of the ceremonies, and helped me to bacon, fried eggs, and a bowl of chocolate, all which politeness, of course, excited no suspicion. Soon after breakfast I descended to the cabin for the purpose of taking some repose, having been engaged all night on duty, but I had hardly lain down for a minute, when I was attacked with a violent headache, throbbing about the temples, and sickness of the stomach. Unable to make out the cause of this sudden illness, I sent for Tardy, who, having felt my pulse and inquired into the symptoms of the disease, declared that there was bile on the stomach, and recommended an emetic. Mr. Robinson, having overheard the prescription, dissuaded me from taking any medicine whatever, and recommended repose. I therefore had my mattress removed to the open air on deck, where I lay until eight o'clock in the evening, by which time the vomiting had ceased, and I felt a good deal relieved.

"During the day I had a conversation with Mr. Robinson, who communicated his fear that an attempt had been made by the Spaniards to poison them, as the whole crew seemed to be sick, and who proposed that, to guard against anything of this kind in future, their own cook should prepare food for the crew and other passengers, while Courro, who acted as the servant of Felix and Tardy, might act as cook for the Spaniards. Nothing, however, was settled upon definitely, and, as the vessel was going safely in her course, I lay down for the night, but with orders to be awaked if the breeze should spring up.

" I had slept, I think, about an hour and a half, when I was waked by dreadful shrieks proceeding from all parts of the vessel. Starting up with the apprehension that we were boarded by pirates, I ran forward to the forecastle, and there a horrid scene of slaughter met my sight. I learned that Courro was the first to wake, and perceiving that the time was come for action, he called up Tardy and the Spaniards. Tardy then cut the throat of Dolliver (one of the seamen) and gave the signal, when the Spaniards set up dreadful cries which roused everybody; and, as any one came up, either from the cabin or forecastle, he was immediately stabbed.

" The American carpenter was the first to make his way from the cabin, and was stabbed by Pepe; but the blow not proving mortal a struggle ensued, which lasted for a short time, when he fell and was dispatched by an axe. During the continuance of this struggle, Captain Brightman rushed on deck, and received a blow from Felix which laid him prostrate. The Irish passenger met the same fate, and Robinson was supposed to have thrown himself from the cabin windows into the ocean, upon seeing the death of the Irishman.

" Courro was equally successful at the forecastle, and stabbed, successively, Potter, Gibbs, and Bicknell. Deane, who slept on deck, was not discovered in the darkness, and threw himself overboard without being wounded. When in the water, he entreated that a barrel, plank, or oar, or something might be thrown out to support him as he was ready to sink, and these entreaties were seconded by Mr.

Robinson (who was also in the water), but all in vain; and they both doubtless soon sank to rise no more.

"In the meantime, being wounded, I had made the best of my way to the rigging, which had not escaped the notice of Tardy, who called out in a loud voice for me to descend, which I refused to do; but upon repeated assurances that if I came down my life would be spared, I at length ventured down upon the deck, and was immediately surrounded by Tardy and his companions.  Tardy now began to question me about the box which Felix had brought on board, and what had become of it.  I replied that I had seen the box, and put it in the captain's state-room, but could not tell what had become of it, if it were no longer there.  Tardy then explained that the Spaniards had applied to the captain for the box, and upon his refusal to give it up, they had resolved, instead of going to the United States to seek a precarious redress from the laws, to take the law into their own hands, and had accordingly killed the captain and taken possession of the vessel; that as the deed was now done, it would be useless to go to the United States, and they had determined to sail for Europe; and that, if I would assist them, they would not only save my life, but I should be well paid for my services when the cargo was disposed of.

"Of course this plausible story was a mere fabrication, in order to excuse the murders and the seizure of the vessel; but as I was not in a condition to dispute the accuracy of the statement, I offered no objection to it, and consented to do that which was requested of me, whereupon I obtained permission to lie down on my mattress and take some repose.  In the course of the morning, after the work of destruction had been completed, the Spaniards set up loud cries of exultation, and, intoxicated with their success, walked about the deck, which, as well as the sails and rigging, was everywhere dyed with blood, and they occasionally resorted to a bottle of liquor placed on the hencoop.

"They were not, however, so far gone as to neglect the clearing away of all traces of the murders. They washed the deck and rigging, and painted the sails to conceal the blood with which they were stained. During the day all the papers belonging to the brig were torn up and thrown overboard, and all the chests and trunks which had belonged to the passengers and crew were ransacked for plunder. The American flag was also destroyed, and materials were produced for making a Spanish flag, which Mr. Ginoulhiac (who seems to have been spared, probably because he was a Spaniard) was required to put together."

Thus far we have quoted the account given by the mate. After this these miscreants sailed about for some time, uncertain what to do. At last Tardy resolved to run for Norfolk to procure hands and provisions. But Tardy's cup of iniquity was now full. He to whom vengeance belongeth led the murderers blindly to their fate. Having reached their port, and cast anchor about a hundred yards from the shore, Tardy ordered Dobson, the mate, to get the boat ready to land him. Dobson obeyed with alacrity, got possession of an oar, and, while the Spaniards were aloft furling the sails, he suddenly pushed off and sculled towards the land, intending instantly to give information of the vessel's character to the authorities.

Tardy saw, when too late, the mistake he had committed in allowing the mate to enter the boat alone, and he knew that his doom was fixed. Without a moment's hesitation he went into the cabin, sat down upon a box of dollars—

his ill-gotten gains—and terminated his existence by cutting his throat.   Meanwhile Dobson gave information, the ship was taken possession of and the Spaniards secured, all of whom, excepting Ginoulhiac, were tried, condemned, and executed a month afterwards.

# CHAPTER VI.

## CAPTAIN COOK.

As we have now come to treat of the larger species of craft that plough the ocean, we shall proceed to visit those lands, of which, without the aid of ships, we should never have known the existence. We will, in fact, circumnavigate the world, and, in doing so, we shall put ourselves under one of the greatest circumnavigators the world ever knew, namely—

## CAPTAIN COOK.

This celebrated man was born at Marton, in Yorkshire, in 1728. His parents were poor; his scholastic education scanty; but his was one of those vigorous spirits that seem to thrive best in adverse circumstances. James Cook educated himself, rose to be a captain in the royal navy, and distinguished himself signally in the service. But all his early doings sink into insignificance when compared with his labours as a discoverer and circumnavigator of the world. He commenced his career of discovery as a lieutenant.

It is not our intention to write a biography of Cook. Our object, in this chapter, will be to select a few interesting anecdotes from his adventures. "Cook's Voyages" are as familiar to us and as celebrated as the "Adventures of Robinson Crusoe," and we would deem it gross injustice to write a book on man's deeds upon the ocean without giving a prominent place to this prince of navigators, who fell, alas! while yet in the strength and vigour of his days, and while engaged in prosecuting his useful and interesting discoveries among the islands of the South Seas. He was murdered by savages in the year 1779.

### OBJECT OF COOK'S FIRST VOYAGE.

In the introduction to the beautiful illustrated edition of Cook's Voyages, published by Tallis and Co., from which work our quotations are made—the object for which Cook was first sent forth to the unknown regions of the South Seas, is thus stated:—

"In the latter part of the year 1767, while Wallis and Carteret [two eminent navigators] were still at sea, it was resolved by the Royal Society, that it would be proper to send persons into some part of the South Sea, to observe the transit of the planet Venus over the sun's disc, which, according to astronomical calculation, would happen in the year 1769; and that the islands called Marquesas de Mendoza, or those of Rotterdam or Amsterdam, were the fittest places then known for making such observations.   (It was fixed, however, that the island of Otaheite or Tahiti, which had just been discovered by Wallis, should be the point of observation.)

"This resolution having been communicated to his Majesty [George III.], he directed that a vessel should be fitted out for the purpose.   The command was intrusted to Lieutenant Cook, who had recently been employed in surveys in Newfoundland, and had been pointed out as an officer specially qualified for the service; and he was appointed by the Royal Society.   With him were associated, Mr. Charles Green, assistant at the Royal Observatory of Greenwich, Mr. (afterwards Sir Joseph) Banks, long so well known as president of the Royal Society, and Dr. Solander, a Swede, and pupil of the celebrated Linnæus.

"The vessel employed on this occasion was the *Endeavour*, a barque of 370 tons, built for the coal trade.   A vessel of this class was preferred by Cook to any other.   The colliers are particularly distinguished as excellent sea-boats, and their build allows more room, and permits them to take the ground or be laid on shore with more safety than any other vessels of equal size. They also require fewer men for their navigation."

A representation of this species of vessel, the *barque*, will be found in our next engraving, accompanied with a detailed account of its peculiar rig.

The officers and crew, including the scientific gentlemen, consisted of eighty-four men, besides the commander. "The barque was victualled for eighteen months, and took on board ten carriage, and twelve swivel guns, with good store of ammunition and other necessaries. The instructions given to the commander were, after making the necessary astronomical observations at Otaheite, to prosecute the design of making discoveries in the South Seas, returning home by way of Good Hope."

We can fancy with what exulting enthusiasm a man like Captain Cook would receive such an untrammelled commission to sail at will through the unknown regions of ocean and plough a track, if he could, entirely round the world. He was daring, enthusiastic, scientific, genial, and self-reliant, and the results of this and of his succeeding voyages were of the utmost importance to the interests of science and humanity; while the details are full of stirring incident and romantic adventure, as well as of minute and interesting accounts of new and curious species of birds, beasts, and fish.

As Captain Cook wrote his own account of those voyages, we will let him speak for himself.

### CURIOUS CREATURES OF THE SEA.

On the passage out, strange creatures were discovered in the sea, in regard to which Cook says :—

"Mr. Banks and Dr. Solander had an opportunity of observing many marine animals, of which no naturalist has hitherto taken notice, particularly a new species of the *Oniscus;* and an animal of an angular figure, about three inches long and one thick, with a hollow passing quite through it, and a brown spot on one end, which they conjectured might be its stomach. Four of these adhered together by their sides when they were taken, so that at first they were thought to be one animal, but upon being put into a glass of water they soon separated, and swam about very briskly. These animals are of a new genus, to which Mr. Banks and Dr. Solander gave the name of *Dagysa*, from the likeness of one species of them to a gem.

" Several specimens of them were taken, adhering together sometimes to the length of a yard or more, and shining in the water with very beautiful colours.

"Another animal of a new genus they also discovered, which shone in the water with colours still more beautiful and vivid, and which indeed exceeded in variety and brightness anything that we had ever seen. The colouring and splendour of these animals were equal to those of an opal. One of them lived several hours in a glass of salt water, swimming about with great agility, and, at every motion, displaying a change of colours almost infinitely various.

"We caught also among the rigging of the ship, when we were at the distance of about ten leagues from Cape Finisterre, several birds which have not been described by Linnæus ; they were supposed to have come from Spain, and our gentlemen called the species *Motacilla velificans*, as they said none but sailors would venture themselves on board a ship that was going round the world. One of them was so exhausted, that it died in Mr. Banks's hand almost as soon as it was brought to him."

Again, just after crossing the " line," as the equator is called by seamen, Cook refers to other discoveries thus : —" In the evening of the 29th (October) we observed that luminous appearance of the sea which has been so often mentioned by navigators, and to which such various causes have been assigned ; some supposing it to be occasioned by fish, which agitated the water by darting at their prey, some by the putrefaction of fish and other marine animals, some by electricity, and others referring it to a great variety of different causes. It appeared to emit flashes of light exactly resembling those of lightning, only not so considerable; but they were so frequent, that sometimes eight or ten were visible at the same moment.

"We were of opinion that they proceeded from some luminous animal, and upon throwing out the casting net our opinion was confirmed ; it brought up a species of *Medusa*, which, when it came on board, had the appearance of metal violently heated, and emitted a white light. With these animals were taken some very small crabs, of three different species, each of which gave as much light as a glow-worm, though the creature was not so large by nine-tenths."

### FIRST MEETING WITH SAVAGES.

Captain Cook proceeded southward on his voyage till he passed out of the warm latitudes and reached the celebrated Straits of Magellan at the southern point of South America. Here he fell in with natives of Terra del Fuego.

" Having taken the boat on board," he writes, " I made sail into the strait, and at three in the morning anchored in twelve fathom and a half, upon coral rocks, before a small cove, which we took for Port Maurice, at the distance of half a mile from the shore. Two of the natives came down to the beach expecting us to land ; but this spot afforded so little shelter that I at length determined not to examine it. I therefore got under sail again about two o'clock and the savages retired into the woods.

" At two o'clock we anchored in the bay of Good Success, and after dinner I went on shore, accompanied by Mr. Banks and Dr. Solander, to look for a watering place and to speak to the Indians, several of whom had come in sight. We landed on the starboard side of the bay near some rocks, which made smooth water and good landing. Thirty or

forty of the Indians soon made their appearance, at the end
of a sandy beach on the other side of the bay, but seeing
our number, which was ten or twelve, they retreated.

"Mr. Banks and Dr. Solander then advanced about one
hundred yards before us, upon which two of the Indians
returned, and, having advanced some paces towards them,
sat down. As soon as they came up the Indians rose, and
each of them having a small stick in their hand threw it
away, in a direction both from themselves and the strangers,
which was considered as the renunciation of weapons in
token of peace. They then walked briskly towards their companions, who had halted about fifty yards behind them, and
beckoned the gentlemen to follow, which they did.

"They were received with many uncouth signs of friendship; and in return they distributed among them some beads
and ribbons, which had been brought on shore for that purpose, and with which they were greatly delighted. A mutual
confidence and good-will being thus produced our parties
joined ; the conversation such as it was became general, and
three of them accompanied us back to the ship.

"When they came on board, one of them, whom we took
to be a priest, performed much the same ceremonies which
M. Bougainville describes and supposes to be an exorcism.
When he was introduced into a new part of the ship, or
when anything that he had not seen before caught his attention, he shouted with all his force for some minutes,
without directing his voice either to us or his companions.

"They ate bread and some beef, but not apparently with
much pleasure, though such part of what was given as they
did not eat they took away with them ; but they would
not swallow a drop of wine or of spirits ; [like sensible
fellows, Cook might have added !] they put the glass to their

lips, but, having tasted the liquor, they returned it with strong expressions of disgust.    Curiosity seems to be one of the few passions which distinguish men from brutes, and of this our guests appeared to have very little.    They went from one part of the ship to another, and looked at the vast variety of new objects that every moment presented themselves, without any expression either of wonder or pleasure; for the vociferations of our exorcist seemed to be neither."

After having been on board for a couple of hours these unprepossessing savages expressed a desire to go ashore, so the boat was ordered immediately and they were landed. The account thus given of these poor creatures does not give us a high opinion of them, and the engraving which accompanies the description gives the features of a very repulsive visage.    They seem to stand low in the scale of humanity.

### A QUARREL WITH THE OTAHEITEANS.

Very different indeed were the natives just described to those of Otaheite, at which island Captain Cook arrived some time after.    They were savages, it is true, but conducted themselves with a degree of natural politeness and urbanity that made them great favourites with the sailors. The wisest arrangements, however, and best intentions of a commander may be frustrated by the folly of his subordinates.    An incident that occurred soon after their arrival proves this.    Having appointed thirteen marines and a petty officer to guard the tent they had pitched near the shore, Cook and some of his officers went to explore the interior of the island in search of hogs for food.    They were accompanied by an old chief named Owhaw :—

" As we were crossing a little river that lay in our way, we saw some ducks, and Mr. Banks, as soon as he had got

over, fired at them and happened to kill three at one shot.
This struck them with the utmost terror, so that most of
them fell suddenly to the ground, as if they had been shot
at the same discharge.    It was not long, however, before

OTAHEITE.

they recovered from their fright, and we continued our route,
but we had not gone far before we were alarmed by the report of two pieces, which were fired by the guard at the tent.
We had then straggled a little distance from each other, but
Owhaw immediately called us together, and, by waving his
hand sent away every Indian who followed us except three,

each of whom, as a pledge of peace on their part, and an entreaty that there might be peace on ours, hastily broke a branch from the trees and came to us with it in their hands.

" As we had too much reason to fear that some mischief had happened we hasted back to the tent, which was not distant above half a mile, and when we came up we found it entirely deserted, except by our own people.  It appeared that one of the Indians, who remained about the tent after we left it, had watched his opportunity, and, taking the sentry unawares, had snatched away his musket.  Upon this the petty officer, a midshipman who commanded the party, perhaps from a sudden fear of further violence, perhaps from the natural petulance of power newly acquired, and perhaps from a brutality in his nature, ordered the marines to fire.  The men, with as little consideration or humanity as the officer, immediately discharged their pieces among the thickest of the flying crowd, consisting of more than a hundred, and observing that the thief did not fall, pursued him and shot him dead.

" We afterwards learned that none of the others were either killed or wounded."

Happily no evil came of this affair, and soon after the natives and sailors were as friendly as ever.

The traffic carried on at this time was chiefly with beads in exchange for articles of food.  A single bead as big as a pea was sufficient to purchase five or six cocoa-nuts, and as many bread-fruit.  This latter article of food is so peculiar that we shall describe it.

### BREAD FRUIT,

Bread fruit grows on a tree peculiar to the South Sea Islands, about the size of a middling oak.  It has obtained its name in consequence of the strong resemblance of the edible part of it to the crumb of loaf bread. "The leaves of the tree are frequently a foot and a half long, of an oblong shape, deeply sinuated like those of the fig-tree, which they resemble in consistence and colour, and in the exuding of a white milky juice upon being broken. The fruit is about the size and shape of a child's head, and the surface is reticulated, not much unlike a truffle. It is covered with a thin skin, and has a core about as big as the handle of a small knife. The eatable part lies between the skin and the core, and is as white as snow. It must be roasted before it is eaten, being first divided into three or four parts. Its taste is insipid with a slight sweetness, somewhat resembling that of the crumb of wheaten bread mixed with a Jerusalem artichoke."

We have given this particular account of the bread fruit, because it is a curious and much used article of food in those islands, and also because its history is connected with a series of perhaps the most romantic incidents in real life that have ever burst upon the astonished world, to verify the saying that "truth is strange, stranger than fiction." We refer to the Mutiny of the Bounty, and the subsequent settlement of Pitcairn Island, details of which will be found in the next chapter.

### A SKIRMISH WITH THE SAVAGES.

One day the *Endeavour* was anchored off one of the islands, and two boats were sent in shore to take soundings. "In the meantime," says Cook, "the natives to the number of near four hundred, crowded upon us in their canoes, and some of them were admitted on board.

"To one who seemed to be a chief, I gave a piece of broad cloth, and distributed some trifling presents among the rest.

"I perceived that some of these people had been about the ship when she was off at sea, and that they knew the

SOUTH SEA CANOES.

power of our fire-arms, for the very sight of a gun threw them into manifest confusion.

"Under this impression they traded fairly; but the people in one of the canoes took the opportunity of our being at dinner to tow away our buoy. A musket was fired over them without effect; we then endeavoured to reach them, with some small shot, but they were too far off. By this time they had got the buoy into their canoe, and we were obliged to fire a musket at them with ball. This hit one of them, and they immediately threw the buoy overboard. A round shot was then fired over them, which struck the water and went ashore. Two or three of the canoes immediately landed their people, who ran about the beach, as we imagined, in search of the ball.

"After the ship was removed into deeper water and properly secured, I went with the pinnace and yawl, manned and armed, accompanied by Mr. Banks and Dr. Solander, and landed upon the island, which was about three quarters of a mile distant. We observed that the canoes which were about the ship did not follow us upon our leaving her, which we thought a good sign ; but we had no sooner landed than they crowded to different parts of the island and came on shore.

"We were in a little cove, and in a few minutes were surrounded by two or three hundred people, some rushing from behind the heads of the cove, and others appearing on the tops of the hills. They were all armed, but they came on in so confused and straggling a manner that we scarcely suspected they meant us any harm, and we were determined that hostilities should not begin on our part. We marched towards them, and then drew a line upon the sand between them and us, which we gave them to understand they were not to pass.

"At first they continued quiet, but their weapons were held ready to strike, and they seemed to be rather irresolute than peaceable. While we remained in this state of suspense, another party of Indians came up, and now growing more bold as their nnmber increased, they began the dance and song which are their preludes to a battle. Still, however, they delayed the attack, but a party ran to each of our boats and attempted to draw them on shore. This seemed to be the signal, for the people about us at the same time began to press in upon our line.

"Our situation was now become too critical for us to remain longer inactive. I therefore discharged my musket, which was loaded with small shot, at one of the forwardest, and Mr. Banks and two of the men fired immediately afterwards. This made them fall back in some confusion ; but one of the chiefs, who was at the distance of about twenty yards, rallied them, and running forward, waving his *patoo-patoo* (war-club), and calling loudly to his companions, led them to the charge. Dr. Solander, whose piece was not yet discharged, fired at this champion, who stopped short on feeling the shot, and then ran away with the rest. They did not, however, disperse, but got together upon a rising ground, and seemed only to want some leader of resolution to renew their attack.

"As they were now beyond the reach of small shot, we fired with ball ; but as none of them took effect they still continued in a body, and in this situation we remained about a quarter of an hour. In the meantime the ship, from whence a much greater number of Indians were seen than could be discovered in our situation, brought her broadside to bear, and entirely dispersed them by firing a few shot over their heads. In this skirmish only two of the Indians were hurt with the small shot, and not a single life was lost, which would not have been the case if I had not restrained the men, who, either from fear or the love of mischief, showed as much impatience to destroy them as a sportsman to kill his game.

"When we were in quiet possession of our cove, we laid down our arms and began to gather celery, which grew here in great plenty. After a little time we recollected to have seen some of the people hide themselves in a cave of one of the rocks; we therefore went towards the place, when an old Indian, who proved to be the chief that I had presented with a piece of broad-cloth in the morning, came out with his wife and his brother, and in a supplicating posture put themselves under our protection. We spoke kindly to them, and the old man then told us that he had another brother, who was one of those that had been wounded by the small shot, and inquired with much solicitude and concern if he would die. We assured him that he would not, and at the same time put into his hand both a musket ball and some small shot, telling him that those only who were wounded with the ball would die, and that the others would recover; at the same time assuring him that if we were attacked again, we should certainly defend ourselves with the ball, which would wound them mortally. Having now taken courage, they came and sat down by us; and as tokens of our perfect amity, we made them presents of such trifles as we happened to have about us."

### NEW ZEALAND WAR-CANOE.

We have already made reference to the canoes of the South Sea Islanders, in the beginning of this work. Cook refers to those of New Zealand thus:—

" The ingenuity of these people appears in nothing more than in their canoes. They are long and narrow, and in shape very much resemble a New England whale boat. The larger sort seem to be built chiefly for war, and will carry from forty to eighty or a hundred armed men. We measured one which lay ashore at Tolaga; she was $68\frac{1}{2}$ feet long, 5 feet broad, and $3\frac{1}{2}$ feet deep. The bottom was sharp, with straight sides like a wedge, and consisted of three lengths, hollowed out to about 2 inches, or $1\frac{1}{2}$ inch thick, and well fastened together with strong plaiting. Each side consisted of one entire plank, 63 feet long, 10 or 12 inches broad, and about 1¼ inch thick; and these were fitted and lashed to the bottom part with great dexterity and strength.

" A considerable number of thwarts were laid from gunwale to gunwale, to which they were securely lashed on each side, as a strengthening to the boat. The ornament at the head projected 5 or 6 feet beyond the body, and was about 4½ feet high. The ornament at the stern was fixed upon that end as the stern-post of a ship is upon her keel, and was about 14 feet high, 2 feet broad, and 1½ inch thick. They both consisted of boards of carved work, of which the design was much better than the execution. All their canoes, except a few at Opoorage or Mercury Bay which were of one piece and hollowed by fire, are built after this plan, and few are less than 20 feet long. Some of the smaller sort have out-riggers, and sometimes two are joined together, but this is not common.

"The carving upon the stern and head ornaments of the inferior boats, which seemed to be intended wholly for fishing, consists of the figure of a man, with a face as ugly as can be conceived, and a monstrous tongue thrust out of the mouth, with the white shells of sea-ears stuck in for eyes. But the canoes of the superior kind, which seem to be their men-of-war, are magnificently adorned with open-work, and covered with loose fringes of black feathers, which had a most elegant appearance. The gunwale boards were also frequently carved in a grotesque taste, and adorned with tufts of white feathers placed upon black ground. The paddles are small and neatly made. The blade is of an oval shape, or rather of a shape resembling a large leaf, pointed at the bottom, broadest in the middle and gradually losing itself in the shaft, the whole length being about six feet. By the help of these oars they push on their boats with amazing velocity."

### A NARROW ESCAPE.

Mr. Ellis, to whose book reference has already been

made, and who visited the South Sea Islands nearly half a century later than Cook, tells us that the *single* canoes used by some of the islanders are far safer than the *double canoes* for long voyages, as the latter are apt to be torn asunder during a storm, and then they cannot be prevented from constantly upsetting.

Single canoes are not so easily separated from their outrigger. Nevertheless, they are sometimes upset in rough seas; but the natives don't much mind this. When a canoe is upset and fills, the natives, who learn to swim like ducks almost as soon as they can walk, seize hold of one end of the canoe, which they press down so as to elevate the other end above the sea, by which means a great part of the water runs out; they then suddenly loose their hold, and the canoe falls back on the water, emptied in some degree of its contents. Swimming along by the side of it, they bale out the rest, and climbing into it pursue their voyage.

Europeans, however, are not so indifferent to being overturned as are the savages. On one occasion, Mr. Ellis, accompanied by three ladies, Mrs. Orsmond, Mrs. Barff, and his wife, with her two children and one or two natives were crossing a harbour in the island of Huahine. A female servant was sitting in the fore-part of the canoe with Mr. Ellis's little girl in her arms. His infant boy was at its mother's breast, and a native with a long light pole, was paddling or pushing the canoe along, when a small buhoe, with a native youth sitting in it, darted out from behind a bush that hung over the water, and before they could turn or the youth could stop his canoe, it ran across the outrigger. This in an instant went down, the canoe was turned bottom upwards, and the whole party precipitated into the sea.

The sun had set soon after they started from the opposite side, and, the twilight being very - short, the shades of evening had already thickened round them, which prevented the natives on shore from seeing their situation. The native woman, being quite at home in the water, held the little girl up with one hand, and swam with the other towards the shore, aiding, at the same time, Mrs. Orsmond, who had caught hold of her long hair, which floated on the water behind her. Mrs. Barff, on rising to the surface, caught hold of the outrigger of the canoe that had occasioned the disaster, and, calling out loudly for help, informed the people on shore of their danger, and speedily brought them to their assistance. Mrs. Orsmond's husband, happening to be at hand at the time, rushed down to the beach and plunged at once into the water. His wife, on seeing him, quitted her hold of the native woman, and grasping her husband, would certainly have drowned both him and herself, had not the natives sprung in and rescued them.

Mahinevahine, the queen of the island, leaped into the sea and rescued Mrs. Barff; Mr. Ellis caught hold of the canoe and supported his wife and their infant until assistance came. Thus they were all saved.

The only fear the natives have on such occasions is an attack by sharks. These voracious monsters are deified by some of the natives, and nothing would at one time induce them to hurt them, but Mr. Ellis mentions one instance in which a native showed very little respect to this fish.

### CATCHING A SHARK.

"I was once," says he, "in a boat on a voyage to Bora-bora, when a ravenous shark, approaching us, seized the blade of one of the oars, and, on being shaken from it, darted at the keel of the boat which he attempted to bite. While he was thus employed, the native whose oar he had seized, leaning over the side of the boat, grasped him by the tail, succeeded in lifting him out of the water, and with the help of his companions, dragged him alive into the boat, where he began to flounder and strike his tail with rage and violence. Mr. Tyeman and myself, for we were sailing together, were climbing up on the seats out of his way, but the natives, giving him two or three blows on the nose with a small wooden mallet, quieted him, and then cut off his head. We landed the same evening, when, I believe, they baked and ate him."

There are many varieties of canoes among these Islanders. The accompanying wood-cut exhibits a very curious one, described by Cook as being peculiar to the Friendly Islands. The most remarkable feature about it was the sail, which, being suspended by a spar from a forked mast, could be so turned that the prow' of the boat became the stern and *vice versa*. It sailed with equal rapidity in either direction.

### BEAUTIFUL ISLES.

The innumerable islands of the South Seas, present a most diversified appearance. Some hilly, some mountainous, and others low and flat, but all exceedingly beautiful. Those lying to the southward of the Marquesas are thus described :—

"They are low, narrow islands, of coralline formation; and though among them some few, as Gambier's Islands, are hilly, the greater number do not rise more than three feet above the level of high water. The names of Crescent, Harp, Chain, Bow, &c., which some of them have received from their appearance, have been supposed to indicate their shape. Those already known seem to be increasing in size, while others are constantly approaching the surface of the water. Sometimes they rise like a perpendicular wall from

CANOE OF THE FRIENDLY ISLANDS.

the depths of the ocean to the level of its surface. At other times, reefs or groves of coral, of varied and beautiful form and colour, extend, in the form of successive terraces below water, to a considerable distance around.

"Here islands may be seen in every stage of their progress; some presenting little more than a point or summit of a branching coralline pyramid, at a depth scarcely discernible through the transparent waters; others spreading, like submarine gardens or shrubberies, beneath the surface; or presenting here and there a little bank of broken coral and sand, over which the rolling wave occasionally breaks; while a number rise like long curved or circular banks of sand, broken coral, and shells, two or three feet above the water, clothed with grass, or adorned with cocoa-nut or palm trees."

These remarkable islands are often found in the form of a ring or circle, enclosing a sheet of water or lagoon of considerable extent.  To these lagoons there is always, at least, one narrow entrance or opening by which ships may pass from the heaving breast of the Pacific, into a quiet pond. Many of the coral islands, in fact, wall off, as it were, a portion of the Pacific, thus forming the most splendid natural harbours in the world.  "In the island of Hao, the Bow Island of Captain Cook, it is said, ships may sail many miles after entering the lagoon.  The narrow strip of coral and sand enclosing the basin is sixty or seventy miles in length, although exceedingly narrow.  The stillness of the surface of the bright blue water, within the lagoon, the border of white coral and sand by which it is surrounded, the dark foliage of the lofty trees by which it is sheltered, often reflected from the surface of the water, impart to the interior of these low islands an aspect of singular beauty and solitude, such as is but seldom presented by the more bold and romantic scenery of the higher lands."

Most of these lovely islands are inhabited, but, alas, many of them, even at the present day, are scenes of bloodshed, cruelty, and human depravity, that men in civilized lands can scarcely conceive of.

### THE SAVAGES.

The habits of many of the natives, especially those of the Feejee group, are horrible in the extreme.  Those savages are exceedingly ferocious and fond of war, and are addicted to cannibalism.  They feast on the flesh of their enemies, and a captive child has been known to have been fed on the flesh of her own parent. But they do not restrict themselves to the flesh of their enemies. Human flesh is actually regarded as a dainty; and when a chief desires a feast he sends and kills a slave, whose body is roasted in an oven, in order to gratify his monstrous appetite.

The dress of these poor wretches is exceedingly scanty; sometimes a mere shred of native cloth wrapped round the loins. They also tatoo their bodies to a very great extent, so much so that they look at last as if they were clothed with skin-tight garments, covered with quaint and complex devices.

Tatooing is the puncturing the skin in various places with sharp needles of bone, and rubbing dark-colouring substance into the punctures. The operation is exceedingly painful, and sometimes the natives die under it.

Their whole countenances are much disfigured by this practice. Each chief has imprinted on his face the marks and involutions peculiar to his family or tribe; while the figures tatooed on the faces of his dependants and retainers, though fewer in number, are the same in form as those by which the chief is distinguished. This tatooing of the face of a New Zealander thus answers the purpose of the particular stripe or colour of a Scotch Highlander's plaid—marks the clan to which he belongs. It is considered highly ornamental, and, in addition to the distinguishing lines or curves, the intricacy and variety of the pattern thus permanently fixed on the face, constitutes one principal distinction between the chiefs and the common people. It may, therefore, be regarded as the crest, or coat of arms, of the New Zealand aristocracy. The same observation also applies to the inhabitants of the South Sea Islands generally.

Like all savages, these Islanders are given to boast of their physical powers and prowess. Ellis says:—"The warriors of New Zealand delight in swaggering and bravado, for while my companion was talking with some of Korokoro's party, one of them came up to me, and several times brandished his patupatu over my head, as if intending to strike, accompanying the action with the fiercest expression of countenance, and the utterance of words exceedingly harsh, though to me unintelligible. After a few minutes he desisted, but when we walked away he ran after us; and, assuming the same attitude and gestures, accompanied us till we reached another circle, where he continued for a short time these exhibitions of his skill in terrifying.

"When he ceased, he inquired rather significantly, if I was not afraid. I told him I was unconscious of having offended him, and that, notwithstanding his actions, I did not think he intended to injure me. The New Zealanders are fond of endeavouring to alarm strangers, and appear to derive much satisfaction in witnessing the indications of fear they are able to excite."

Some of the customs of these people are thus described by Cook. "Before beginning the onset (at a battle) they join in a war-song, to which they all keep the exactest time, and soon raise their passion to a degree of frantic fury, attended with the most horrid distortion of their eyes, mouths, and tongues, to strike terror into their enemies; which, to those who have not been accustomed to such a practice, makes them appear more like demons than men, and would almost chill the boldest with fear. To this succeeds a circumstance, almost foretold in their fierce demeanour—horrid, cruel, and disgraceful to human nature—

which is, cutting in pieces, even before being perfectly dead, the bodies of their enemies, and, after dressing them on a fire, devouring the flesh, not only without reluctance, but with peculiar satisfaction.

"One might be apt to suppose that people capable of such excess of cruelty, must be destitute of every human feeling, even amongst their own party. And yet we find them lamenting the loss of their friends, with a violence of expression which argues the most tender remembrance of them. For both men and women, upon the death of those connected with them, whether in battle or otherwise, bewail them with the most doleful cries; at the same time cutting their foreheads and cheeks with shells or pieces of flint, in large gashes, until the blood flows plentifully and mixes with their tears.

"The children are initiated, at a very early age, into all the practices, good or bad, of their fathers; so that you find a boy or girl, nine or ten years old, able to perform all the motions and imitate the frightful gestures which the more aged use to inspire their enemies with terror, keeping the strictest time in their song."

## AMUSEMENTS—DIVING AND SWIMMING EXTRAORDINARY.

It is a curious fact that some of the games played by the little naked savage children of the South Sea Islands are very similar to our own. A traveller who had sauntered to a part of the sea-beach of one of the islands to watch the children at play, tells us that one band was busily employed in playing blind-man's-buff. Another group were walking on stilts that raised them three feet or so from the ground; while others were engaged in flying kites. These kites were of all shapes and sizes—made of thin cloth of native manufacture, and were raised to a great height by means of twine, made of the fibrous husk of the cocoa-nut.

But the amusement which these people take the greatest delight in—old as well as young—is swimming and diving in the sea; and the expertness exhibited by them is most extraordinary. They have two principal games in the water; one of which consists in diving off a sort of stage, erected close to deep water, and chasing each other in the sea. Some of them go down to extraordinary depths; others skim along on the surface or roll over like porpoises, or diving under each other, come up unexpectedly and pull each other down by a leg or an arm. They never seem to tire of this sport, and from the great heat of the water in the South Seas, they can remain in it for hours at a time without feeling chilled.

Even infants just able to walk waddle down to the beach, throw themselves into the water, and strike boldly out to sea like ducklings. Mothers, too, jump in with their little infants at their breasts, and gambol with them in the water, as mothers in this civilized land sport with their little ones on grassy lawns.

One would think that swimming miles out to sea, and diving fathoms down into the deep, to disport among the lovely coral groves at the bottom, with, now and then, the chance of being bitten in two by a shark, would be excitement enough for these savages. By no means! They must add to these amusements that riotous, boisterous, and somewhat dangerous one called 'winning in the surf,' which is practised as follows:—

On the shores of those islands of the Pacific that are not guarded by a breakwater of coral, there falls, with slow regular majestic thunder, a mighty billow which never goes down, even in the calmest weather.  It is not the result of wind, it is the termination of that long rolling swell that moves across the wide sea in a calm; the ocean's breathing, as it were, while asleep.  In storms, of course, this billow mounts in size, and rages along intermixed with a thousand superficial waves, and when it reaches the shore it bursts into foam upon the rocks with a savage fury that bids fair to demolish the solid earth itself.  But even in the deadest calm the billow rises with its great broad glossy back glittering with the sunbeams, until it approaches to within a mile of the shore.  Then it becomes like an emerald wall, its crest overlaps, ripples, breaks, and, with a deep solemn roar it rushes on, a world of snowy water to engulf the beach.  It is on this crested wave that the natives ride.

They assemble in hundreds on the beach, each with a short flat board in his hand.  Just after a billow has broken they rush into the surf with loud yells, and are carried off by the seething foam of the receding wave.  For some time the swimmers continue to strike out to sea, breasting over the swell like hundreds of black seals. There they all turn, and, watching an approaching billow, mount on its white crest; each laying his breast on the short flat board above mentioned, they come rolling towards the shore, careering on the summit of the mighty wave, with a speed that seems to threaten their total destruction, while the onlookers shout and yell in an ecstasy of excitement and delight.  Just as the monster wave is about to fling its bulky length upon the shore, most of the swimmers slide back into the trough behind it.  Others, slipping off their boards, seize them in their hands, and plunging through the watery waste, swim out to repeat the amusement, while a few come reckless on, amid the churning foam and spray, to the shore.

### MURDER OF CAPTAIN COOK.

Cook was murdered, during his third voyage, by the natives of the Owhyhee, one of the Sandwich Islands, in Febrary 1779.

Toward the evening of the 13th of that month, a theft committed by a party of the islanders on board the *Discovery*, gave rise to a serious disturbance. Pareea, a chief of some importance, was accused of the theft, and a struggle ensued in which he was knocked down. This passed over without anything more serious, but the incident raised a feeling of anger in the breasts of the natives that led to a still more serious and fatal quarrel.

On the following morning the cutter of the *Discovery* was stolen. Cook felt that he could not allow so great an offence to pass unpunished, and being determined to recover his boat he went on shore with a party of marines, intending to invite Tereoboo, the king of the island, on board his ship, and hold him as a hostage until the boat should be returned.

The old king, not suspecting the object of his visitors, readily consented, and agreed also to take his two sons along with him. Captain King, who accompanied Cook on this voyage, thus relates the details of this melancholy affair :—

"Things were in this prosperous train, the two boys being already in the pinnace, and the rest of the party having advanced near the water-side, when an elderly woman called Kaneekabareea, the mother of the boys, and one of the king's favourite wives, came after him, and with many tears and entreaties, besought him not to go on board. At the same time two chiefs who came along with her laid hold of him, and insisting that he should go no further, forced him to sit down. The natives, who were collecting in prodigious numbers along the shore, and had probably been alarmed by the firing of the great guns, and the appearances of hostility in the bay, began to throng round Captain Cook and their king.

"In this situation the lieutenant of marines, observing that his men were huddled close together in the crowd, and thus incapable of using their arms, if any occasion should require it, proposed to the captain to draw them up along the rocks, close to the water's edge; and the crowd readily making way for them to pass, they were drawn up in a line, at the distance of about thirty yards from the place where the king was sitting. All this time the old king remained on the ground, with the strongest marks of terror and dejection in his countenance. Captain Cook, not willing to abandon the object for which he had come on shore, continued to urge him in the most pressing manner to proceed; whilst, on the other hand, whenever the king appeared inclined to follow him, the chiefs who stood round him interposed, at first with prayers and entreaties, but afterwards, having recourse to force and violence, insisted on his staying where he was. Captain Cook, therefore, finding that the alarm had spread too generally, and that it was in vain to think any longer of getting him off without bloodshed, at last gave up the point; observing to Mr. Phillips, that it would be impossible to compel him to go on board, without the risk of killing a great number of the inhabitants.

" Though the enterprise that had taken Cook ashore had now failed and was abandoned, yet his person did not appear to have been in the least danger, till an accident happened which gave a fatal turn to the affair.  The boats which had been stationed across the bay, having fired at some canoes that were attempting to get out, unfortunately killed a chief of the first rank.  The news of his death arrived at the village where Cook was, just as he had left the king, and was walking slowly toward the shore.  The ferment it occasioned was very conspicuous.  The women and children were immediately sent off, and the men put on their war-mats and armed themselves with spears and stones.  One of the natives, having in his hand a stone and a long iron spike (which they call a pahooa), came up to the captain, flourishing his weapon, by way of defiance, and threatening to throw the stone.  The captain desired him to desist : but the man persisting in his insolence, he was at length provoked to fire a load of small shot.  The man having his mat on, which the shot was not able to penetrate, this had no other effect than to irritate and en-courage the natives.  Several stones were thrown at the marines; and one of them attempted to stab Mr. Phillips with his *pahooa*, but failed in the attempt, and received from him a blow with the butt end of his musket.  Cook now fired his second barrel, loaded with ball, and killed one of the foremost of the natives.

" A general attack with stones immediately followed, which was answered by a discharge of musketry from the marines and the people in the boats.  The islanders, contrary to the expectations of every one, stood the fire with great firmness, and before the marines had time to re-load, they broke in upon them with dreadful shouts and yells.

What followed was a scene of the utmost horror and confusion.

"Four of the marines were cut off amongst the rocks in
their retreat, and fell a sacrifice to the fury of the enemy.
Three more were dangerously wounded; and the lieutenant,
who had received a stab between the shoulders with a
pahooa, having fortunately reserved his fire, shot the man
who had wounded him just as he was going to repeat his
blow.   Our unfortunate commander, the last time he was
seen distinctly, was standing at the water's edge, and calling out to the boats to cease firing and to pull in.   If it be
true, as some of those who were present have imagined,
that the marines and boatmen had fired without his orders,
and that he was desirous of preventing any further bloodshed, it is not improbable that his humanity on this occasion proved fatal to him.   For it was remarked that whilst
he faced the natives, none of them had offered him any
violence, but that, having turned about to give his orders
to the boats, he was stabbed in the back and fell with his
face into the water.

"On seeing him fall, the islanders set up a great shout,
and his body was immediately dragged on shore, and surrounded by the enemy, who, snatching the daggers out of
each other's hands, showed a savage eagerness to have a
share in his destruction."

Thus fell one of the greatest navigators and discoverers
of modern times, in his fifty-second year.   His name will
live in the memory of man as long as the annals of maritime discovery are loved and read.   The good which has
accrued to the human family by his labours is incalculable,
and the bulky volumes in which those labours are recorded
by his own pen are more stirring and much more interest-

ing than the pages of romance; for those distant isles of the sea have been visited by the messengers of the gospel of our Lord and Saviour Jesus Christ, and many of the savage isles which, in Cook's day, were the scenes of horrible cruelty and disgusting practices, are now the peaceful abodes of industrious Christian men and women. Of this, more in the next chapter.

Meanwhile let us say a word in reference to the class of vessel in which Captain Cook performed his first voyage.

### THE BARQUE.

The vessel next in size larger than the brig, is the *barque.* It does not follow, however, that its being larger constitutes it a barque.   Some brigs are larger than barques, but *generally* the barque is the larger vessel.   The difference between a barque and a brig is that the former has *three* masts, the two front ones being square-rigged, and the mizzen being fore-and-aft rigged.   The centre mast is the main one.   The rigging of a barque's two front masts is almost exactly similar to the rigging of a brig, that of the mizzen is similar to a cutter.   If you were to put a fore-and-aft rigged *mizzen-mast* into the after part of a brig, that would convert it into a barque.

The term *clipper* simply denotes that peculiar sharpness of build and trimness of rig which ensures the greatest amount of speed, and does not specify any particular class. There are clipper sloops, clipper yachts, clipper ships, &c. A clipper barque, therefore, is merely a fast sailing barque.

The peculiar characteristics of the clipper build are, knife-like sharpness of the cutwater and bow, and exceeding correctness of cut in the sails, so that these may be drawn as tight and *flat* as possible.   Too much bulge in a sail is a

CLIPPER BARQUE

disadvantage in the way of sailing. Indeed, flatness is so important a desideratum, that experimentalists have more than once applied sails made of *thin planks of wood* to their clippers; but we do not know that this has turned out to be much of an improvement. The masts of all clippers, except those of the sloop or cutter rig, generally rake aft a good deal—that is, they lean backwards; a position which is supposed to tend to increase speed. Merchant vessels are seldom clipper-built, because the sharpness of this peculiar formation diminishes the available space for cargo very much. Another disadvantage in clippers is, that they are usually bad sea-boats, that is, being extremely sharp in the bow, they *cut through* the waves instead of *rising over* them in stormy weather, and thus deluge their decks with water. They are best adapted for still waters. And of course, in moderate weather they make rapid voyages on the ocean.

# CHAPTER VII.

### THE "MESSENGER OF PEACE."

THERE are few records in the annals of ship-building, so interesting as the account of the building of Williams's missionary ship, the " Messenger of Peace."

In order to spread the gospel amongst the natives of Polynesia Mr. Williams was at times in the habit of taking passage in a ship, land on one and another of the islands in passing, and sometimes allow the ship to leave him there, trusting to the arrival of another to take him off. Some of the islands, however, being out of the usual course of ships he had to wait sometimes an inconveniently long time. In order to remedy this evil and render himself more independent in his movements he resolved to build a little ship !

The boldness of the mind that could entertain such an idea, and the force of the will that could carry it out to completion, can only be adequately understood by those who knew intimately the difficulties the missionary had to overcome ere his little ark was launched upon the deep.

First of all he knew nothing at all about ship-building; then he had few tools except two or three of the lighter and more ordinary kind used by carpenters; his materials, too, were not well adapted for the purpose they had to serve, and the natives who assisted him were as ignorant as little children. Yet in the face of all these and many more difficulties he accomplished his object of

### BUILDING A MISSIONARY SHIP.

Mr. Williams was naturally a good mechanic, and he possessed an invincible will,—two circumstances which account for the almost miraculous achievement of converting himself into a ship-builder in a single day, and launching a good serviceable ship, of nearly eighty tons burden in the short space of three months. The account reads like one of the marvellous deeds of our old friend Robinson Crusoe.

"My first step," says Williams, "was to make a pair of smith's bellows; for it is well known that little can be done towards the building of a ship without a forge. We had but four goats on the island, and one of these was giving a little milk, which was too valuable to be dispensed with, so that three only were killed, and, with their skins, as a substitute for leather, I succeeded, after three or four days' labour, in making a pair of smith's bellows. These, however, did not answer very well; indeed I found bellows-making to be a more difficult task than I had imagined, for I could not get the upper box to fill properly; in addition to which my bellows drew in the fire.

"To complete my perplexities the rats, which at Raratonga were like one of the plagues of Egypt, as if by general consent congregated during the night in immense numbers and devoured every particle of the goat-skin, and, on entering the workshop in the morning, I was mortified by the discovery that nothing remained of my unfortunate bellows but the bare boards. This was really vexatious, for I had no material to supply the loss. Still bent upon the accomplishment of my object, and while anxiously considering the best means 'to raise the wind,' for that was essential to my success, it struck me that, as a pump threw water, a machine constructed on the same principle must of necessity throw wind."

Acting upon the thought the ingenious missionary very soon did "raise the wind" to good purpose. He made a box about eighteen or twenty inches square and four feet high; put a valve at the bottom, and fitted in a damper, similar to the piston in the cylinder of a steam engine. This was loaded with stones, to force it down with considerable velocity, and affixed to it was a long lever by which it was again raised.

Before placing this curious machine to the fire it was tried, and, to the immense delight of the pastor and his savage and wondering flock, it blew a strong and furious blast. But, alas! it was not yet perfect. On bringing it into contact with the devouring element its deficiencies soon became apparent. In the first place it was found that there was too great an interval between the blasts, and secondly that it sucked in the fire so fast that in a few minutes it was in a blaze! However, the evil was remedied by the construction of a valve at the back of the pipe which communicated with the fire, and opened to let out the wind and shut when the machine was filling.

A little thought soon enabled Williams to overcome the other inconvenience, namely, the long interval between the blasts while the machine was being filled with air. He concluded that if one box gave one blast, two boxes would double it, and that, by working the boxes alternately a continuous blast might be kept up. The novel pair of bellows worked admirably. It is true they were somewhat uncouth and heavy; eight men being required to work them, but labour was cheap and the natives were delighted with the employment.

An anvil was the next implement required. For this a stone was used. A pair of carpenters' pincers answered for tongs, and charcoal made of the cocoa-nut tree served for coals. With these simple implements all the iron-work of the ship was afterwards made.

The open-mouthed and wide-eyed amazement of the natives at all the proceedings of their missionary was very amusing. "The first iron the natives saw worked," he writes, " excited their astonishment exceedingly, especially the welding of two pieces together. Old and young, men and woman, chieftain and peasant, hastened to behold the wonder, and when they saw the ease with which heated iron · could be wrought they exclaimed, 'Why did not we think of heating this hard stuff also, instead of beating it with stones? What a reign of dark hearts Satan's is!'"

Nothing, however, excited more interest than the pumps that were fitted to the ship after it was built. Even the king was so much delighted that he frequently had his favourite stool carried on board, and entertained himself for hours pumping out the bilge water!

But we are digressing. As Williams and his wondering assistants had no saws they split the trees in half with wedges, and then they adzed them down to the thickness of planks with small hatchets of which they happened to possess a few, and which they converted into adzes, after a sort, by tying them to crooked pieces of wood as handles. But some of the planks of the future ship behoved to be bent, and they had no apparatus for steaming them. This difficulty was overcome by a piece of bamboo being bent to the shape of the planks required, and given as a pattern to the willing natives who went into the woods and sought till they found several trees crooked by nature into the requisite form. By splitting these, planks suited to their purpose were obtained.

Having very little iron they fastened the planks to the frame of the vessel by boring large augur-holes through the timbers and also the outer and inner planks, into which they drove wooden pins, or trenails. As a substitute for oakum they used cocoa-nut husk, but as this was not plentiful enough on the island the deficiency was supplied by dried banana stumps, native cloth, and other substances.

At every step those energetic ship-builders encountered difficulties, but they were never arrested long in their work. Not only had they to fashion their materials, but they had frequently to make the implements by which those materials were fashioned.

Thus they made excellent cordage from the bark of the *hibiscus*, but before accomplishing this a rope machine had to be constructed. Again capital sheaves were made for the blocks out of aito, or iron-wood ; but in order to produce those sheaves a turning lathe had to be made.

For sails they used mats, on which the natives were wont to sleep, sewed together and quilted to resist the wind. The hanging of the rudder proved an extremely difficult matter, for having no iron sufficiently large for pintles (or rudder-hinges), they were obliged to make use of a piece of a pick-axe, a cooper's adze, and a large hoe. These were found afterwards to serve their purpose very well, but being doubtful of their strength Williams wisely prepared a substitute for a rudder in case of emergency.

This vessel was two-masted ; sloop rigged, and carried a main-sail, fore-sail, and jib. Her length was about sixty feet, and her breadth eighteen. She was completed and launched in fifteen weeks, and her name was *The Messenger of Peace.*

Perhaps a more singular vessel was never before built, either as to the peculiarity of the circumstances or her object, for she carried the richest cargo that ever floated on the sea. She was insured, too, without money. No raging billows, or howling winds, or breaking surf upon a lee shore could touch her lading, for she was freighted with the gospel of life.

It is to be regretted that Mr. Willliams did not leave a still more minute account of the details of this remarkable vessel. Even what we have got was written at the urgent request of his friends, for his own modesty would have induced him to pass over the building of the *Messenger of Peace* with a few words.

FIRST VOYAGE OF WILLIAMS'S SHIP.

As the first voyage of so curious a ship, as that which we have just described, must prove interesting to every one, we shall insert it here, partly in the missionary's own words. He says :—

" Thinking it prudent to try our vessel before we ventured to Tahiti, which was seven or eight hundred miles from us (!) I determined on a visit to our interesting station at Aitutaki, which was only about one hundred and seventy miles distant. The king, Makea, never having seen any other island, determined to accompany me.

" Raising our wooden and stone anchors, and hoisting our

mat sails, I took my compass and quadrant and put to sea, accompanied only by natives. We had not proceeded above six miles from the shore, when, in shifting the sails, the natives, not observing what was said to them, and not being acquainted with maritime usages, let the foresail go, and as the wind was very strong, it broke our fore-mast. Providentially, however, about twelve or fifteen feet above the deck was left standing ; and having cleared the wreck, and hoisted a part of our sail on the broken mast, we turned back and were thankful to find that we should reach the land, although several miles to leeward of the harbour.

" We filled a cask with stones, which in addition to our wooden anchor, we hoped might hold the vessel outside the reef ; and if not, I resolved upon the desperate alternative of running upon it, by which the vessel, in all probability, would have been dashed to pieces ; but this was preferable to being driven from the island, with a scanty supply of provisions and the ship in a crippled state, in a track where there was not an island within a thousand miles. Having, however, a number of natives on board, and making them all work, we succeeded by sunset, contrary to expectation, in reaching the harbour in safety.

" We got a new mast, repaired our damages, and, in a few days, sailed again. Having a strong and favourable wind we reached Aitutaki on Sabbath morning, in time to conduct the services of the day."

Here they remained eight or ten days and then prepared for their return voyage. But this was by no means so prosperous as the voyage out, and the alarm of the poor king became quite touching. The weather was boisterous, and a strong sea running, which, during the night, gave the vessel several severe blows. Having never been at sea before, his majesty expressed some alarm, and asked Mr. Williams seriously if the ship would be knocked to pieces. On being assured that there was no danger he was for a time satisfied, but not so fully as to allow the missionary for one moment out of his sight. On every occasion that Mr. Williams went on deck the king followed him, and when he went below again, down went the king also; in short he appeared to believe that there was no safety except close to the missionary's side !

The wind being unfavourable they were three days and three nights in returning to Raratonga. On the second evening the king began to get restless and anxious, fearing that they had missed the island and were sailing into " wide gaping space." On the third evening as the sun descended beneath the horizon, and no land appeared, his distress amounted almost to despair, and he expressed a belief that he should never see his beloved island again, refusing all consolation, even although Mr. Williams assured him that he should behold his kingdom that very night.

At the time indicated Raratonga did come into view, and the joy expressed by poor Makea on beholding it was unbounded. Nothing, however, appeared to excite his astonishment so much as the accuracy with which the missionary could tell the time when land would be seen.

On entering the harbour they were struck with the improved appearance of the mission house, which had been left surrounded by and almost buried in the *debris* of the ship-building. It was beautifully neat and clean. The garden was well cultivated and fenced in, while the fruit of the dark red mountain plantain, and golden banana, fully ripe, were smiling a welcome through the splendid leaves which surrounded the trunks that bore them.

' On landing Mr. Williams found that this improved state of things was the result of a remark made by his wife some time before to her female scholars, to the effect that she would like to have the pathway and garden put in order before the return of her husband. Delighted to have an opportunity of showing their gratitude and love to the missionaries, they at once replied, "We will not leave a chip against which, on his return, he shall strike his feet."

The cargo brought back by the *Messenger of Peace* on this her first voyage was somewhat peculiar. It consisted principally of pigs, cocoa-nuts, and cats ! The king embarked about seventy of the first and a large number of the last for the improvement of his own beloved dominions which were nearly destitute of pigs, but overflowing with rats for whose special edification the cats were imported.

The rats were so numerous that nothing edible was safe from them, and it is worthy of remark that the rats of Raratonga ranked boots and shoes, and leather trunks in their list of edible substances. Williams says, " The rats were astonishingly numerous, so much so, indeed, that we never sat down to a meal without two or more persons to keep them off the table. When kneeling down at family prayer they would run over us in all directions, and we found much difficulty in keeping them out of our beds."

Rendered desperate by the encroachments of these wretches, " war to the knife " was declared against them by the natives upon one occasion. All the able-bodied, male and female, old and young, turned out, and so great was the slaughter that no less than thirty baskets made of cocoa-nut leaves were filled with the bodies of the slain. Yet in spite of this the numbers of the enemy did not appear to be in the least diminished. Hence the cargo of cats, as a last resource.

But, strange to say, the cats, although good fighters and true to their new king, did not turn out to be nearly so destructive to the rats as the pigs were !　These last were savagely voracious, and did good service in ridding the island of the intolerable nuisance.

## DEATH OF WILLIAMS.

Like his predecessor in discovery, Captain Cook, this noble-hearted missionary poured out his blood upon the shores of one of the islands of the South Seas.　He fell while endeavouring to conciliate the natives of the island of Erromanga, and so win them to Christ.　Captain Morgan, who commanded the ship in which he sailed to the New Hebrides group, thus details his melancholy fate :—

" The event happened the day after we left the island of Tanna.　There the natives received us most kindly, and Mr. Williams remarked he had never been received more kindly by any natives.

" We proceeded to Erromanga, and hove to on the south side all night.　On reaching Dillon's Bay we lowered the whale boat, and took in Mr. Williams, Mr Harris, Mr Cunningham and myself, with four hands.　The natives were wild in their appearance and extremely shy.　They spoke a different language from that of the windward Islands, so that Mr. Williams could not understand a word they said.　He made them some presents and tried to persuade them to come into our boat, but did not succeed, so we left them and pulled up the bay, while some of the natives on shore ran along the rocks after the boat.

" On reaching the head of the bay, we saw several natives standing at a distance.　We made signs to them to come towards us, but they made signs for us to go away.　We threw them some beads on shore, which they eagerly picked up, and came a little closer, and received from us some fish-hooks and beads, and a small looking-glass. On coming to a beautiful valley between the mountains, having a small run of water, we wished to ascertain if it was fresh, and we gave the chief a boat-bucket to fetch us some. In about half an hour, he returned running with the water, which I think, gave Mr. Williams and myself more confidence in the natives. They ran and brought us some cocoa-nuts, but were extremely shy. Mr. Williams drank of the water the native brought, and I held his hat to screen him from the sun.

" He seemed pleased with the natives and attributed their shyness to the ill-treatment they must have received from foreigners visiting the island on some former occasion. Mr. Cunningham asked him if he thought of going on shore. I think he said he should not have the slightest fear, and then remarked to me, ' Captain, you know we like to take posses-sion of the land, and if we can only leave good impressions on the minds of the natives, we can come again and leave teachers ; we must be content to do a little ; you know Babel was not built in a day.'

" He did not intend to leave a teacher this time. Mr. Harris asked him if he might go on shore, or if he had any objections ; he said, ' No, not any.' Mr. Harris then waded on shore ; and as soon as he landed the natives ran from him, but Mr. Williams told him to sit down. He did so, and the natives came close to him and brought him some cocoa-nuts and opened them for him to drink."

Mr. Williams then landed and endeavoured to calm the fears of the natives by offering them presents of cloth and trinkets which they accepted, but still were very shy and evidently regarded the strangers with suspicion. A few children were seen playing in the woods, which was regarded as a good sign by the visitors, but the total absence of women was a circumstance which made the peaceable disposition of the natives doubtful, because when mischief was intended these savages always took the precaution to send their women away.

At last three of the party advanced towards the wood. Captain Morgan's letter continues :—"All three walked up the beach, Mr. Harris first ; Mr. Williams and Mr. Cunningham followed. After they had walked about a hundred yards, they turned to the right alongside of the bush, and I lost sight of them. Mr. Harris was the furthest off. I then went on shore, supposing we had found favour in the eyes of the people. I stopped to see the boat anchored safely, and then walked up the beach towards the spot where the others had proceeded ; but before I had gone a hundred yards the boat's crew called out to me to run to the boat."

The captain immediately ran, followed by Mr. Cunningham, the only one of the three who escaped, and whose narrative gives the details of what occurred after the trio had entered the bushes. He says :—

"The looks and manners of the savages I much distrusted, and remarked to Mr. Williams that probably we had to dread the revenge of the natives in consequence of their former quarrel with strangers, wherein perhaps some of their friends had been killed. Mr. Williams, I think, did not return me an answer, being engaged at the instant repeating the Samoan numerals to a crowd of boys, one of whom was repeating them after him. Finding a few shells on the bank, I picked them up. On noticing they were of a species unknown to me, I was in the act of putting them into my pocket when I heard a yell, and instantly Mr. Harris rushed out of the bushes about twenty yards before me.    I instantly percieved it was run or die.    I shouted to Mr. Williams to run (he being as far behind me as Mr Harris was in advance) and I sprung forward through the natives that were on the banks of the brook, who all gave way.

"I looked round and saw Mr. Harris fall in the brook, and the water dash over him, a number of savages beating him with clubs.    Mr. Williams did not run at the instant I called to him, till we heard a shell blow ; it was an instant, but too much to lose.    I again called to Mr. Williams to run, and sprang forward for the boat, which was out of sight ; it was round a point of bush.

"Mr. Williams, instead of making for the boat, ran directly down to the beach into the water, and a savage after him. It seemed to me that Mr. Williams's intention was to swim off till the boat picked him up.    At the instant I sighted the boat I heard a yell behind me, and looking round, found a savage close after me with a club.    I stooped, and, picking up a stone, struck him so as to stop his further pursuit.

"The men in the boat had, on seeing Mr. Williams and me running, given the alarm to Captain Morgan, who was on the beach at the time.    He and I jumped into the boat at the same instant ; several stones were thrown at the boat.

" Mr. Williams ran into deep water, and the savage close after him.    On entering the water he fell forward, but did not attempt to swim, when he received several blows from the club of the native on the arms and over the head.    He twice dashed his head under water to avoid the club, with which the savage stood over him ready to strike the instant he arose.    I threw two stones from the boat which for a moment arrested the progress of the other native, who was a few paces behind ; but it was only for an instant. The two rushed on our friend and beat his head, and soon several others joined them. I saw a whole handful of arrows stuck into his body.

" Though every exertion was used to get up the boat to his assistance, and though only about eighty yards distant, before we got half the distance our friend was dead, and about a dozen savages were dragging the body on the beach, beating it in the most furious manner. A crowd of boys surrounded the body as it lay, in the ripple of the beach, and beat it with stones, till the waves dashed red on the shore with the blood of their victim. Alas ! that moment of sorrow and agony—I almost shrieked in distress.

" Several arrows were shot at us, and one passing under the arm of one of the men, passed through the lining and entered the timber. This alarmed the men who remonstrated, as, having no fire-arms to frighten the savages away, it would be madness to approach them as Mr. Williams was now dead."

The boat was, therefore, rowed back to the ship and an attempt was made to recover the body, which proved unsuccessful, as the savages had dragged it into the woods.

Thus perished one of the greatest missionaries that ever left our shores. An effort was afterwards made to recover his remains, but his savage murderers confessed that they had devoured his body, and also that of Mr. Harris. Only a few bones were recovered and conveyed to Samoa where they were interred.

The dreadful news fell upon the islanders throughout Polynesia with the stunning violence of a thunder-bolt. So bitter and heart-rending was the lamentations of the native

Christians everywhere, that their heathen countrymen joined in the wail from sheer sympathy.

The intelligence travelled from one island to another like a black cloud of woe. When the ship reached Tanna in the New Hebrides the first question asked by the eager natives was, " Where is Williamu ?" (so they pronounced his name), and when the sad truth was told they hung upon the hand of Mr. Cunningham and wept like children.

On arriving at Samoa, the first canoe that reached them was guided by a middle-aged man, who, as soon as they were within hail, called out to the native teachers to inquire for " Missi William." The agonizing effect produced upon this man when the death of his beloved missionary was announced is described as. heart-breaking. He seemed at once unhinged ; he dropped his paddle, and stooped his head and wept. He paddled his canoe alongside for some time making occasional inquiries, ever and anon bursting out into fresh cries and tears.

It was at the dark hour of midnight that poor Mrs. Williams was awakened to learn the awful news. Her agony was indescribable, and who can wonder ? · She was at first, and for a considerable time, utterly paralyzed. Her anguish was too deep for tears. But the bereaved widow did not sorrow alone. The missionary's biographer writes, " Had the death scene in Egypt been that night repeated in Samoa, lamentations more bittter, and cries more piercing, could scarcely have attended it, than those which this intelligence awakened. In a short time every sleeping native had been aroused, and through the morning twilight they were seen grouped together in solemn and sorrowful communication, while everywhere might be heard the sounds of distress."

The natives crowded round the house anxious to see Mrs.

Williams and comfort her as much as they could by mingling their tears with hers; but she could not bear it for many hours. At last one named Malietoa was admitted. "As soon as he entered the room, he burst forth into the most passionate expressions of distress, weeping, beating his breast, and crying, "Alas! Williamu, Williamu, our father, our father! He has turned his face from us! We shall never see him more! He that brought us the good word of salvation is gone! O cruel heathen; they know not what they did! How great a man they have destroyed!"

After giving utterance to this outburst of inexpressible feeling he turned to Mrs. Williams, who was lying on a sofa. Kneeling by her side, he gently took her hand, and, while the tears flowed fast down his dusky cheeks, he said, in the softest and most soothing tones, "O my mother! do not grieve so much; do not kill yourself with grieving. You too will die with sorrow, and be taken away from us, and then, oh, what shall we do? Think of John, and of your very little boy who is with you, and think of that other little one in a far distant land, and do not kill yourself. Do love, and pity, and compassionate us."

Who will doubt the divine power of the blessed gospel, when it can bring savage, cannibal lips to utter such words of tender sympathy and consolation as these?

We will not, after what has been written, presume to pass an eulogium on the character of Mr. Williams. To live beloved by thousands whom he has benefitted, and to die passionately lamented by whole tribes of reformed savages, is enough to stamp a man "great" in the highest possible sense of the term. His history is briefly recorded in the inscription on the tomb at Samoa which marks the spot where his bones lie. It runs thus:—

"Sacred to the memory of the Rev. John Williams, father of the Samoan and other missions, aged 43 years and 5 months, who was killed by the cruel natives of Erromanga, on Nov. 20th, 1839, while endeavouring to plant the Gospel of Peace on their shores."

FULL-RIGGED SHIP.

# CHAPTER VIII.

### FIRST-RATE MAN-OF-WAR.

WE now come to consider the largest class of vessel that
floats upon the sea, namely, the *full-rigged ship*, the distinctive pecularity of which is that its three masts are *all*
square-rigged together, with the addition of one or two fore-
and-aft sails.   As the fore and main masts of a "ship" are
exactly similar to those of a barque, which have been already
described, we shall content ourself here with remarking that
the *mizzen-mast* is smilar in nearly all respects to the other
two, except that it is smaller.   The sails upon it are,  the
*spanker* (a fore and aft sail projecting over the quarter-
deck), the *mizzen-top sail* and *mizzen-top-gallant sail*, both

of which are square sails.   Above all these a ship sometimes puts up small square-sails called the *royals.*

The best specimen of a "ship" which can be presented
to our view is a

## FIRST-RATE LINE-OF-BATTLE SHIP.

Within the last few years a gigantic steamer has been
built (of which we shall treat in another chapter), but, with
the exception of this, the line-of-battle ship is the most
magnificent and formidable vessel that floats.   Few of the
works of man are more interesting than a first-rate man-of-
war, and all who have the opportunity ought to complete
their knowledge of our ocean homes by paying a visit to
this the king of ships.

It spreads an immense cloud of canvas, and its towering
sides are pierced with *port-holes* in two, and, as in *first-rates,*
in three formidable tiers.   Our plate represents a full-rigged
line-of-battle ship.   All the sails are hoisted with the
exception of the *stay-sail* and the *stun-sails,* which latter,
as we have said, are never spread except in *light-fair* winds.

We may here remark that ships sometimes carry small
"*sky-scrapers*" above the royals.   The complement of a
first-rate line-of-battle ship is upwards of a thousand men.
The vessel is, in fact, a floating town, in which nearly all
the ordinary professions and trades are carried on as
vigorously and as regularly as on shore.   Besides the
captain, lieutenants, masters, chaplain, surgeons, assistant-
surgeons, midshipmen, clerks, schoolmasters, &c., gunners,
boatswains, seamen, and marines (or naval soldiers), there
are carpenters, cooks, sailmakers, ropemakers, armourers,
coopers, and barbers, who work steadily at their respective
trades.   Everything is conducted by rule, and with the

utmost regularity. Were this not the case, we can easily conceive the inextricable state of confusion into which every-thing would be thrown. In so magnificent a vessel there are various peculiarities of detail which merit notice. The tops of the lower masts, instead of being mere cross-trees, as in vessels of smaller size, are large platforms, planked over and railed in, on which bodies of men may be stationed. They are called the *main-top*, *fore-top*, and *mizzen-top* respectively, and the main-top of a first-rate man-of-war can accommodate forty or fifty men. The guns of which there are from one hundred to one hundred and thirty, vary in size, and carry shots of from fourteen to sixty-eight pounds weight. They are managed by ropes and blocks, and each gun requires a number of men to work it.

As the rigging of all three-masted ships is much the same, we will not enumerate the masts, sails, and rigging of a line-of-battle ship. Should the reader wish to know them, let him turn to Chapter II., Part II., where he will find pretty full details on such matters, many of which are applicable to this as to other vessels. We shall now turn to the

## INTERIOR ARRANGEMENTS.

A first-rate line-of-battle ship is called a "*ship of the line*," because in naval warfare it usually forms one of a line of large vessels which advance in preconcerted arrange-ment to the attack. Smaller vessels of war do not form part of the line, but move about more independently, somewhat after the manner of skirmishing troops in the army.

A first-rate is also called a "*three-decker*," because it has three distinct decks, or floors, or storeys, extending the entire length of the ship, on which heavy guns are planted. There are also smaller half-decks of which we shall speak presently.

The three decks are named the *upper gun-deck* or *spar-deck*; the *middle or main gun-deck*, and the *lower gun-deck.* Below this is the *orlop-deck*, on which are no guns, it being beneath the surface of the water. Below this is the hold. Returning to the upper gun-deck we find the *quarter-deck*, occupying the after part of the vessel, behind (or, as sailors have it "abaft") the main-mast, and sometimes above the sternmost part of this deck there is a *poop*. In the front part of the ship rises a small deck, called the *fore-castle.* The uses and arrangements of these decks are as follows,—

The *upper deck* comprises the following several portions: —the *poop* which covers the commodore's cabin, on the highest part of the stern. The *quarter-deck* is a sacred spot on board a man of war. It is appropriated exclusively to the use of the officers, no one else being allowed to set foot on it except in the discharge of duty. Even the midshipmen, or "middies," although they belong to the class of officers, are only allowed to perambulate the larboard side of the quarter-deck. Here the power that represents royalty is supposed to sit enshrined, hence no one ever goes upon it, not even the captain, without touching his cap, not to the individuals who may chance to be upon it, but to the locality itself. The centre part of the upper deck, called the waist, between the main and fore masts is occupied partly by the larger boats, and by the spare spars which are always carried, to replace any of the booms, top-masts, or yards that may be accidentally broken or carried away. On each side of the boats are unencumbered spaces called the gangways, which are free to the sailors. The fore-castle also belongs to the men. It extends from the fore-mast to the bow of the ship. Hence, when it is said, so and so went to sea *before the mast*, it is meant that he went as an ordinary sailor—was a denizen, in fact, of the fore-castle.

All round the edges of the ship runs a box or trough called the *hammock nettings* in which the men stow their hammocks, or beds, tightly rolled up during the day, and so perfect are the arrangements on board a man-of-war, that a thousand men can lash up and stow away their hammocks in the nettings in a few minutes and without the slightest confusion. The guns on this upper are the lightest in the ship.

The *main-deck* comes next. Here we find, commencing aft, the captain's cabin, over the door of which hangs the timepiece of the ship, and in front of which always paces a sentry. Marines, who in fact and in appearance are *naval soldiers*, do all the sentry duty on board ship, carrying a musket just as soldiers do on shore. They are a distinct and separate class from the sailors or jack-tars, and are trained and drilled very much in the duties of soldiers.

The duty of the sentry before the captain's cabin, besides guarding the entrance, is to note the time and call out the half hours to the officer of the watch on deck, who orders a boy to strike the bell. Thus the time is announced, but not in our shore-going style. Time at sea is divided into watches and reckoned by bells. Seven watches constitute the twenty-four hours. Five of these are four hours long, the other two are short watches of two hours each, and are termed the *dog-watches*. At the end of the first half hour of a watch the bell is struck *one;* the next half hour *two;* and so on up to *eight*, which terminates the four hours of the watch, and then they commence with *one bell* again at the end of the first half hour of the succeeding watch. Consequently one never hears, "What o'clock is it?" but "How many bells is it?"

The space extending from the captain's cabin to the main-mast is the *half-deck*, which is always kept a clear space. Near the fore-mast is the *galley*, or cooking range for the captain. The guns on this main-deck are of the largest size. They are always kept in splendid order, ready for action, with their shot piled or laid securely to prevent rolling, beside them. To the beams overhead hooks are attached to which the hammocks are slung at bed-time. The space allowed for each hammock is very scrimp; but in order to prevent the evil effects of crowding, it is so arranged that the man to whom each alternate hammock belongs shall form part of the "watch on deck," while the others (facetiously termed the "*watch* below!") are sound asleep. Thus the empty hammocks are squeezed up by the sleepers on either side. When the watch is relieved, the full hammocks are emptied at the same moment that the empty hammocks are filled. The port-holes of the main-deck are always kept open, except in very bad weather, so that it is well aired.

The *lower-deck* lies immediately under the main-deck. On the furthest aft portion of it, reaching forward to the mizzen-mast, is the *ward-room*. Here dwell the lieutenants, surgeons, purser, master, and chaplain. Close by the fore-mast is the ship's galley, the exclusive domain of the cook, whose office is by no means a sinecure, seeing that he has periodically to fill the mouths of the entire ship's company, lieutenants and middies included, with the exception of the commodore and captain, and the favoured few who may be privileged to mess with them. All the available space on this deck between the guns is occupied by mess chests, and mess lockers, in which latter the pots, pans, spoons, and victuals used by the sailors are kept.

All that portion of this deck which extends from the foremast to the bow is devoted to the sick. It is the ship's hospital, and is called the *sick-bay.* Here the doctor reigns supreme. This being the lowest gun-deck the ports are always closed when the sea becomes rough; hence it is not so well ventilated as could be wished, and the sick are doomed to a miserable existence.

Mr. Charles Nordhoff, in his "man-of-war life," gives the following graphic account of his own experience of the

### MISERIES OF THE SICK-BAY.

Nordhoff went to sea as a little boy, and, falling sick soon after going on board his ship, was carried to the sick-bay and laid in a hammock.

"Here," he says, "I lay sick for many days. My sickness, or else the paregoric which was given me for medicine, stupefied me. My existence seemed to me as a dream; objects and events passing about me I was merely conscious of, without receiving from them any impression. The doctor ordered a mustard plaster to be applied to my breast. Two days after I was cupped and then blistered. I stood it all, not with fortitude, but with apathy. There seemed scarcely sufficient life left in my body to suffer. I said nothing, ate nothing, and drank nothing but water for nine days.

"In the meantime the sick-bay was filled with sick men, many of them having upon them the loathsome diseases contracted in their debaucheries on shore. Several men died. While I was yet lying very low, the occupant of the

hammock adjoining mine (our beds touched) died.   He
was an Englishman, a strong man, in the prime of life, and
he parted from existence very reluctantly.   The chaplain
was with him in his last moments; and as he and the sick-
bay steward closed the dead-man's eyes, I heard the latter
whisper, pointing to me :—

"'That little boy will be next, sir.'"

But that little boy was *not* next.   He recovered and lived
to pen the lines we have just quoted.

"To be sick on board ship," he continues, "seems to be
the very height of earthly misery.   The sickroom on shore,
surrounded as it is by every comfort, by all the appliances,
invented by art or suggested by love, which can make the
sufferer's lot more bearable, waited on by sympathizing
friends, watched with anxious and loving care, is yet far
from desirable.   But to be bed-ridden on board ship is a
horrible fate.   Cooped up with dozens of others in a narrow
space on one of the lower decks, badly ventilated, and reek-
ing with all the odours peculiar to sick-rooms and to ship
holds, annoyed constantly by the fretful complaint, the dull
moan of pain, or the hollow cough, half stifled perhaps by
the feverish gasping of a neighbour, whose close proximity
makes it impossible for one to get a breath of fresh air, the
invalid lies in his cot, hour after hour, and day after day,
thinking and thinking, until his brain is bewildered and his
soul grows weary and faint.   At stated intervals, a steward
or loblolly boy makes the round of all the hammocks and
cots, and supplies the wants of the sick.   Twice a day, once
at nine A.M., and again at four P.M., the dull monotony
is invaded by the doctor's visit.   At dark, or in bad weather,
the port-holes are closed, thus shutting out the last remnant
of fresh air, and a dingy lantern, hung to the beams, sheds

a faint light around its immediate proximity, by which the utter darkness of the outskirts is only made more clearly tangible. And there the sick man lies, his cot swinging with the motion of the vessel, the bilge water rushing across the deck, the timbers creaking and groaning in concert with the moan of pain, until, after an almost interminable night, the bustle and noise overhead announce the advent of another day of misery."

Turning from this digression let us continue our examination of the ship's interior. We have described three decks. Let us descend to the fourth, which is called,—

The *Orlop-deck*. There are no guns here, for the good reason that the orlop-deck is below the ship's water-line. For the same reason there is no light, except that produced by lanterns. At the after-part of this deck is a deep cavernous apartment termed the *bread-room*. Its name sufficiently explains its use. Next to this are the private rooms of the ward-room officers. The central part of this deck is termed the *cock-pit*. This, in time of war, is a room of horrors, for here the wounded men are carried and the often overtasked surgeons ply their amputating knives, while the shrieks of the sufferers mingle with the groans of those who wait their turn, and with the dull thunder of artillery overhead. Next to this are the *steerages*, where the middies, and the purser's and ship's clerks mess; the boatswains', gunners', sail-makers', and carpenters' rooms; and, further forward, just under the sick-bay, are the rooms appropriated to the reception of boatswains', carpenters', and sail-makers' stores.

To the *hold* is the next, and our lowest descent. It lies below the orlop-deck and contains the powder magazines, shot, wet provision, such as beef and pork, flour and other dry provisions, chain cables, water-tanks, and an endless variety of articles too numerous to mention.

The *boats* of a man-of-war are usually six in number and are of various sizes. The smaller boats are hung at the sides of the vessel; the larger ones are hoisted on deck. They are as follows; the long-boat, or, as it is sometimes called, the launch, is the largest, having a mast and sails and frequently a deck. -It is useful in conveying stores to the ship, and in time of war is armed and equipped for going on services that the ship could not attempt. Up rivers, for instance, and in other shallow waters, or for " cutting out," that is, stealthily attacking vessels at night, or when becalmed. But all of the larger boats are used more or less for the same purpose. The barge is the next, then the pinnace, the cutter, the jolly-boat, and the gig,— the last being a small, long, narrow, and exceedingly neat boat, appropriated exclusively to the use of the captain when he wishes to go ashore or to visit another vessel.

Such are the interior arrangements and armament of a line-of-battle ship. Before proceeding to tell of what such vessels can do and have done, we shall briefly run over a few curious and interesting

### MISCELLANEOUS FACTS.

The total weight of a first-rate line-of-battle ship when fully equipped for a cruise, has been estimated to be upwards of 3000 tons. If we consider that an ordinary cart of coals is about one ton in weight we may form some idea of what those figures represent. There are several anchors of which the *best bower* is the largest; it weighs about five tons and costs about £350. The cable is usually made of iron-chain. Cables vary in size. Not long ago they were made of hemp and were sometimes so much as 25 inches in circumference. A cable of such dimensions and about 100 fathoms or 600 feet long, cost upwards of £400. Chain cables have entirely superseded these, however, being stronger, less cumbrous, and more easily managed.

The strength of the cable and the power of the windlass by which it is raised are enormous. A striking illustration of this occurred on board a merchant vessel once. The anchor had got foul of the rocks in such a way that when they attempted to pull it up it would not move. The whole crew was summoned, and every man that could lay hold of a part of a handspike lent his weight to turn the windlass, round which the chain cable was wound, but all to no purpose. So great was the strain that the bow of the ship was pulled deep into the water and the stern raised up considerably. Still the anchor held on. The captain, being very loth to lose a good cable which he would have been compelled to slip had the anchor remained fast, ordered the men to remove a large portion of the cargo to the stern of the vessel, which was done, and the weight brought the ship almost quite straight again. Then the crew heaved once more on the windlass, and at last the anchor came away with a jerk so tremendous that the whole ship trembled with the shock. On bringing the anchor to the surface it was found that the fluke which had been fouled was bent completely back so as to form a right angle with the shank—showing at once the excellence of both anchor and cable, and the tremendous strain to which they had been subjected.

The length of a first-rate is usually upwards of 200 feet; the breadth about 60 feet. The height of the mainmast is about 200 feet. The total cost of such a vessel—hull, rigging, sails, stores, and guns, is estimated at about

£100,000. About fifty acres of land are required to grow the oaks that are used in the building of a single first-rate man-of-war—supposing each acre to contain forty of the finest oaks. In other words, two thousand oaks are required to build a man-of-war! every one of which must be a hundred years old. Such an amount of timber would be sufficient to build the wood-work of about seven hundred cottages.

A man-of-war is usually, when about to proceed to sea, provisioned and watered for six months, and is supplied with powder, and shot, sails, and rigging, and spare clothing, sufficient to last during a cruise of three years.

## THE CREW.

We have already said that the crew of a first-rate man-of-war numbers about one thousand souls. Every one will easily understand that in a ship, where the men are constantly called into sudden action and sent swarming about the decks and rigging, nothing but the strictest discipline can prevent utter confusion.

The discipline on board men-of-war is so rigidly enforced, that the most perfect order and thorough harmony prevails in every part of the busy hive. A glance at the human machinery of such a vessel, is quite as interesting as an inspection of an intricate and beautiful piece of mechanism.

At the head of all stands the Commodore, and the ship of the fleet in which he hoists his pendant is called the flag-ship. He, however, interferes very little with the management of the ship. His duties are to guide and direct the movements of the fleet. Setting him aside, therefore, the chief officer of the ship is the *Captain*, who orders, directs, and is responsible for everything, including the ship itself. His power is despotic. The *First Lieutenant* is perhaps the most important officer in the ship. He sees to having the captain's orders obeyed, and upon his judgment and discretion very much depends. His duties are very laborious. He does not, like the others, keep watch every alternate four hours, but is on duty all day. He thoroughly inspects the vessel alow and aloft at least once every day, to see that all is in good order and kept clean, and makes a report thereon to the captain. The captain speaks to the crew through the first lieutenant, and all who have occasion to make reports to the captain must do it through the same individual, who is, therefore, possessed of great power and influence. In short he superintends everything and commands everybody. At quarters, that is, when the ship is prepared for action, the first lieutenant has charge of the quarter-deck. The other lieutenants have charge of the deck alternately every four hours. When at sea the officer of the watch, or of the deck, sails the ship—sees that she is kept on her course—keeps a reckoning of her speed, and deviations from the course, and takes note of the weather and of everything that may occur—whether at night or during the day, within the ship or without it—during his watch. All of which he enters on the log-slate when the watch is relieved.

The *sailing master* is one who cannot be said to rank either after or along with the rest of the officers, inasmuch as his peculiar office is permanent, and does not admit of promotion either into it from a lower, or out of it into a higher rank. His duty is to keep the ship's reckoning, to note the bearings and distance of the nearest land or the port to which the ship is bound, and report the same to the captain. He also manages the storing of the hold, and has supervision over nearly all the stores of the ship.  In fact, he exercises as nearly as may be the functions of a captain in the merchant service.

The *purser* is, curiously enough, called an "idler," although he is usually one of the busiest men in the ship. The surgeon and his assistants, and the chaplain are also thus styled—the reason being that none of the three are expected to keep watch, their professional duties being incompatible with such a routine arrangement.  These officers share the same cognomen with the cook and his satellites, and the officer's servants, all of whom, being on constant duty during the day, are relieved from taking part in the regular watches.  The purser's office is a highly responsible one.  He has special charge of all the cash, provisions, and clothing in the ship, and keeps all the accounts. In fact, he is a nautical accountant and man of business.

The *midshipmen* are boy-officers of the ship, the sky-larking, mischievous, dare-anything rascals who order about the men as if they, the mids, were giants, and the others pigmies; whose duty it is to learn their profession, and whose aspiration it is to become first lieutenants, or captains if possible, and admirals if they can.  They muster the watch at night; at quarters they muster the guns' crews; and at sea, one of them has charge of the fore-castle.  They take the sun's altitude at noon, and work out the ship's reckoning by it; they keep journals of the cruise, which are periodically inspected; and in port, one takes charge of every boat that leaves the ship.  Their self-imposed duties are innumerable and eccentric in the extreme, ranging—not literally, but metaphorically—from "pitch and toss to manslaughter."  There are usually about two dozen of them on board a first-rate.

Next come the warrant officers—the *boatswain, gunner, sail-maker,* and *carpenter.* The first of these, the "bo's'n," has charge of the rigging, and is responsible for its efficient condition. He has, moreover, a silver whistle and a stentorian voice, with both of which he calls the men to duty when required to do so. Of the crew, we can only afford space to say that there are quarter-masters, captains of forecastle, captains of tops, &c. Rope-makers, caulkers, armourers, coxswains, coopers, stewards, able-bodied and ordinary seamen and boys.

The *marines* are a sort of ship-police force in time of peace, and sharp-shooters in action. The sailors are apt to regard them with contempt; but their services on board in the way of keeping order in time of peace, and fighting in time of war, are the reverse of contemptible. When posted on the "tops" and among the rigging, they can keep up a galling fire on the decks of an enemy, in close action. It was a ball from the "mizzen-top" of the *Redoubtable* that killed Nelson.

Such is a man-of-war, and such the general arrangements and details of that class of vessels which, for centuries past, have been the bulwark of our country, and earned for themselves the title of the "Wooden Walls of Old England."

## THE BLACK PRINCE.

"There were giants in those days," is said of the men of old. Truly, in reference to naval affairs, it may now be said, "There are giants in *these* days." In times not long gone by men clad themselves in steel from top to toe ere they went forth to battle. Now-a-days our ships of war are beginning literally to don coats of mail, and soon our brave tars will have to change their tune and sing, not of the wooden, but of the *iron*, walls of Old England.

Magnitude and strength seem to be the ruling passions of the day. The *Great Eastern* is the climax of the first— the *Black Prince* of the second. That great instigator to all that is war-like; that ingenious inventor of curious and deadly cannon; that fomentor of discord, disturber of the world's peace, and favourite son of Mars, Napoleon III., some years ago, took it into his head to build a ship of war which should be strong enough to run right into and sink an enemy's vessel, and from whose steel-plated sides cannon balls should rebound harmlessly into the sea, and against which shell should be shattered to atoms. He not only planned, but he built and launched this monster vessel, and most appropriately (so appropriately that we might almost fancy it was sarcastically) called it the *"Gloire!"*

England was surprised, became alarmed, and followed suit with the *Warrior*, and now the two countries are vieing with each other in constructing vessels which will sink by means of their artillery, or overwhelm with their gigantic battering-ram charge anything that floats upon the sea. What is to be the result when these steel-clad warriors of the ocean enter the lists against each other, no one can tell—the Yankees would probably "guess" there will be a "universal smash,"—we trust that we shall be for ever left in ignorance, and that no necessity will arise to test their tremendous powers.

As the general principles on which these steel-plated ships are built are very similar, an account of the *Black Prince*, the launch of which we described in a previous chapter, will suffice to give an idea of what they are.

The dimensions of the *Black Prince* are as follows:—

| | |
|---|---|
| Extreme length, about ... ... ... | 420 feet. |
| Length between perpendiculars ... ... | 380 ,, |
| Extreme breadth ... ... ... ... | 58 ,, |
| Depth from spar deck ... ... ... | 41½ ,, |
| Builders' measurement ... . . ... | 6173 tons. |

This vessel is to be armed with Armstrong guns; and the engines, though nominally 1250 horse power, may, it is said, be wrought up to about 4000 or 5000.

But the great peculiarity of this ship is, the enormous strength of its build and the thickness of the steel plates with which it is sheathed.

About 213 feet of each side of the vessel is rendered impervious to shot or shell, by armour plates of wrought iron, from 15 to 16 feet long, 3 to 4 broad, and 4½ inches thick, each plate averaging *upwards of four tons.* Their edges are planed, and they are fitted together with tenon and groove joints.

In order to deaden the effect of shot, 18 inches of Indian teak wood are interposed between the armour and the "skin," or really water-tight iron shell of the vessel. The teak is of two thicknesses,—10 and 8 inches—the former being laid with the length-way of the plank, running fore and aft, and the other layer of 8 inches being placed vertically. This sheathing of iron and wood extends from a little above the gunwale to about 5½ feet below the water line.

The armour-sheathed space is pierced on the main or gun-deck with thirteen port-holes on each side for 26 guns. These ports are contracted to about two feet, in consequence of the carriage being so constructed that the gun pivots round a point near the outer edge of the port.

The central armour-clad space and the bottom of the ship are divided into water-tight compartments in order to keep the vessel afloat if seriously damaged, and by this means any damage to the exterior plating, and the flooding arising from it, will be merely local.

The moulded depth of the vessel is 41 feet. The armour plates cover 22 feet in depth of the top sides, 16 of which will be exposed above the water line, the armour thus descending about 6 feet below the surface of the water. The intention of government originally was that the vessel should be a steam ram, for the purpose of running down an enemy's vessel, and it was accordingly constructed with a stem of dimensions and strength commensurate with the work it was designed to accomplish. But the stem might be shattered by the collision, or it might be completely blown away, and so might the stern, which is not protected with armour. Yet, even should the stem and stern be thus blown to atoms, a new stem and stern are lying ready-made underneath! The keel of the vessel is placed internally where it forms one of an extensive set of girders which run fore and aft, and between these deep floor-plates are introduced, to the lower edge of which and to the girders the plating of the bottom is attached. The frames, which consist of 10-inch plates and angle irons, are rivetted to the inside cage of the floors, and a great part of the bottom is then plated over on the inside of these, and made perfectly water-tight, thus forming a double security in case of injury to the bottom from grounding or any other cause. The vessel is built in compartments, so that, in the event of any part receiving damage, the damage is confined to the particular locality. For this purpose there are strong iron - bulkheads running longitudinally from within a few yards of the stern, - on each side of the vessel.

The figure-head, which represents Edward the Black Prince in a complete suit of armour of the period, has been carved with much artistic skill from a built block of wood 16 feet in length, by Messrs Kay and Reid, ship-carvers, Glasgow.

# CHAPTER IX.

## THE MUTINY OF THE BOUNTY.

LIGHTS and shadows vary the aspects of nature, moral as well as physical. This work being a sort of picture of nautical affairs—a somewhat sketchy and miscellaneous one, no doubt—we think it advisable to change the tone of our colouring here, and turn from the *deeds* to the *misdeeds* of man-of-war's-men. And the best illustration we could bring forward perhaps is

## THE MUTINY OF THE BOUNTY.

This subject will again convey us to the romantic and sunny regions of the South Seas.

Seventeen years after Cook's return from his first voyage, a number of merchants resident in London, and connected with the West India trade, being desirous of introducing the bread-fruit tree into the West India Islands as an article of food, preferred a request to government that a vessel should be fitted out and sent to the South Seas for the purpose of procuring specimens and transporting them to the West Indies.*

Government agreed. A small vessel of 215 tons was purchased and carefully fitted out with all the necessary appliances for her peculiar duty, under the able superintendence of Sir Joseph Banks. Lieutenant Bligh, who had

---

* For description of bread-fruit, see page 192.

previously sailed with Captain Cook in the *Resolution*, was appointed to command the ship, which was named the

"THE BOUNTY" AT OTAHEITE.

*Bounty*, and which was stored and victualled for a cruise of eighteen months.

The *Bounty* sailed from Spithead on the 23d of December 1787, having on board a crew consisting of the commander (Bligh), one master, three warrant officers, one surgeon, two master's mates, two midshipmen, and thirty-four petty officers and seamen; besides two botanists—David Nelson and his assistant William Brown—who were to take charge of the transport of the bread-fruit trees, and any other plants that might be gathered by the expedition,—forty-six souls in all.

The voyage out was rough and tempestuous. They tried in vain to double Cape Horn, and were compelled to go by the Cape of Good Hope instead, but at last arrived safely at Otaheite, and anchored in Matavai Bay, on the 26th October 1788.

At this time Otaheite had been visited only once or twice by discovery ships, and no missionaries had yet been sent to it. The natives were, therefore, absolute savages; but they seem to have always been much the reverse of savage in their dispositions. At least the crew of the *Bounty* found them extremely kind and hospitable; so much so, that, during the six pleasant months they spent at the island collecting plants, the natives and the sailors became much attached to each other.

Besides collecting plants, the crew spent much of their time in wandering among the groves of that lovely island, or in rowing about its coral shores, shooting birds or procuring fresh water.

Upwards of one thousand plants of the bread-fruit tree, having been secured and planted in tubs specially prepared for their reception, the *Bounty* put to sea once more, and the crew unwillingly bade adieu to the hospitable shores of Otaheite.

But the kindness of the natives, the romantic beauty of

the island, and the genial sunny climate had so captivated the men, that three of them resolved to desert and remain behind. They accordingly watched their opportunity, seized one of the boats and escaped, carrying with them a chest of fire-arms and ammunition. They were, however, speedily captured, and, on writing a humble letter of repentance, were pardoned.

But dark schemes were hatching among the men; and on the 28th of April 1789 they broke out into open mutiny. Fletcher Christian, the master's mate, was the ringleader. He was a young and able man of a quick daring spirit. It is said that Lieutenant Bligh had given offence to this man, and also that the mutiny was partly caused or at least precipitated by Bligh's hasty and stern character. There may be some truth in this, but he seems to have had the comfort of his men at heart if we may judge by the following remark made by him in reference to keeping watch :—

"I have always considered this (the division of the ship's company into three watches) a desirable regulation, when circumstances will admit of it, on many accounts, and am persuaded that unbroken rest not only contributes much to the health of the ship's company, but enables them more readily to exert themselves in cases of sudden emergency."

At dawn of day on the 28th, Christian, with a number of the men whom he had gained over, got possession of fire-arms, under pretence of shooting a shark, and rushed into the cabin where their commander was sleeping. Bligh started up in amazement, on seeing himself surrounded by men armed with cutlasses and pistols, and instantly called loudly for assistance. But no assistance came, for nearly all the crew either favoured the mutineers, or were overawed by them.

Having bound Bligh's hands behind him they forced him rudely on the deck without even allowing him to dress, and kept guard over him while the boatswain and others were compelled to lower the launch into which Bligh and eighteen men who refused to join the mutineers were thrust. Having flung them a few pieces of pork, a few pounds of bread, some gallons of water and a few stores, the boat was cut adrift and left floating on the wide ocean.

Fletcher Christian then took the command of the *Bounty*, issued a dram to his fellow mutineers, and sailed for Otaheite, shouting for joy at having thus rid themselves of their commander.   Little did those wretched men know the misery that awaited them !

Lieutenant Bligh escaped after encountering with his companions unparalleled perils and sufferings, details of which we reserve for the next chapter.   No sooner was government informed of what had occurred than they sent out the *Pandora* frigate, under Captain Edwards, to hunt down the mutineers and bring them to justice.   Eighteen months after the *Bounty's* last departure from Otaheite, the *Pandora* anchored in Matavia Bay.   Three of the mutineers immediately came on board and surrendered themselves. They were put in irons, and soon after eleven others were captured.

It was found that two of their number named Churchill and Thompson were dead.   One of these, Churchill, had been made a king soon after quitting the *Bounty*; a neighbouring king had taken a fancy to him, invited him to his court, made him his chief friend, and, dying soon after, left him his kingdom !   Thompson who accompanied Churchhill became envious of his companion's honours, and shot him. The natives, enraged at the murder of their king, instantly retaliated and stoned Thompson to death.

From journals found in possession of the prisoners it was learned that after casting the boat adrift with Captain Bligh and his companions the mutineers sailed to the island of Toobouai where they anchored on the 25th of May 1789, having previously thrown all the bread fruit plants overboard. Here they proposed to settle, but being short of supplies of various kinds they resolved to go to Otaheite for them.

Reaching that island on the 6th June they palmed upon the simple natives a story to the effect, that having fallen in with Captain Cook at a newly discovered island where he meant to settle, Lieutenant Bligh and part of their crew had remained to assist Cook, and that Christian had been placed in command of the *Bounty* and sent for an additional supply of hogs, goats, fowls, and bread fruit.

The natives at once believed this story, supplied their visitors with whatever they required, and the *Bounty* again sailed from Otaheite ; eight native men, nine women and seven boys accompanied them on this trip. On the 26th of June they anchored a second time at Toobouai and imdiately landed and set about building a fort.

But here they found no rest. Quarrels and disputes constantly arose among themselves, and they had frequent skirmishes with the natives, many of whom were shot. At last the place became so disagreeable that they resolved to abandon it and return to Otaheite, where, it was agreed, those who chose might settle, and those who preferred it might remain in the ship and go where they pleased. Accordingly Toobouai was abandoned, and on the 20th September, they once more anchored in Matavia Bay. Here sixteen of the men went ashore. The remaining nine with Christian at their head sailed from Otaheite on the night of the 21st September. They took with them nineteen natives—seven men and twelve women. What became of them shall be told in the sequel.

Captain Edwards had now secured the fourteen mutineers who were still alive, but no account whatever could be obtained of the *Bounty* or of the nine remaining men. He therefore gave up the search and commenced his homeward voyage. However much these mutineers deserved punishment we cannot but feel that they were treated with unnecessary barbarity on board the *Pandora*. They were confined in irons in a place called the " Pandora's Box," which was built on the after part of the quarter-deck, was only eleven feet in length, and could only be entered by a scuttle in the roof. From this some of the unhappy prisoners were ere long released by the total wreck of the ship, which struck on a coral reef off the coast of New Holland and went down.

### WRECK OF THE PANDORA.

Some of the mutineers taken on board the *Pandora* protested that they were innocent, having taken no active part in the mutiny, but remained silent and unwilling spectators of it, and there is no doubt that this was the case. Among them was young Heywood, and Stewart, the midshipmen, and Morrison the boatswain's mate. But they were all treated alike and confined in the " Pandora's Box."

On the 29th of August the *Pandora* arrived at the coast of New Holland, close to a reef of coral called the " Barrier Reef." A boat was sent to sound for the opening in the reef, but in the course of the night the ship drifted past it. In his narrative of the wreck, laid before the court-martial, Captain Edwards says, " On getting soundings the topsails were filled; but before the tacks were hauled on board, and other sail made and trimmed, the ship struck upon a reef. We had a quarter less two fathoms on the larboard side, and three fathoms on the starboard side. The sails were braced about different ways, to endeavour to get her off, but to no purpose. They were then clewed up and afterwards furled, the top-gallant yards got down and the top-gallant masts struck.

" Boats were hoisted out with a view to carry out an anchor, but, before that could be effected, the ship struck so violently on the reef, that the carpenter reported she made eighteen inches of water in five minutes, and in five minutes after this that there were four feet of water in the hold. Soon after, eight and a half feet water was reported.

" About ten we perceived that the ship had beaten over the reef, and was in ten fathoms water; we therefore let go the small bower anchor, cleared away the cable, and let go the best bower, in fifteen and a half fathoms, some of the guns were thrown overboard, and the water gained on us only in a small degree, so we flattered ourselves that with the assistance of a thrummed top-sail, which we were preparing to haul under the ship's bottom, we might be able to lessen the leak, and to free her of water."

In this expectation, however, Captain Edwards was disappointed. During the night the water gained upon them despite their utmost efforts at the pumps. Three of the crew of the *Bounty* were let out of their " box " to assist in working the pumps. The others offered their assistance and begged earnestly to be allowed a chance of saving their lives; but no answer was vouchsafed to them by their heartless commander, and two additional sentinels were placed over them,—a most unnecessary piece of precaution, seeing that they were all ironed and handcuffed, besides being confined in their cage.

Seeing no prospect of escape these wretched men betook themselves to prayer. Meanwhile the ship showed evident signs of being about to sink; and the crew hastily betook themselves to the boats. As Captain Edwards passed over their prison-house on his way to the boats young Heywood earnestly implored him to have mercy on them. But the captain passed on without reply.

The ship was at that time lying on her broadside, with the larboard bow completely under water. Fortunately the master-at-arms possessed a heart not quite so hard as that of his commander. In slipping from the roof of the " Pandora's Box " into the sea, he let the keys of the prisoners' irons fall through the scuttle which he had opened just a few minutes before, and thus enabled them to commence their liberation. It is said that the master-at-arms let fall the keys by *accident*—we cannot believe it; undoubtedly it was done by design. But there was a kinder heart than even his there. William Moulter, a boatswain's mate, remained with the prisoners to assist in releasing them from their shackles, saying, as he did so, that he would set them free or go to the bottom along with them.

While they were thus engaged the ship went down, and the master-at-arms and all the sentinels sank to rise no more. The cries of the drowning men were fearful, and more than half an hour elapsed ere all the survivors were picked up by the boats.

Poor Stewart, the midshipman, and three of the other

prisoners went down with their hands manacled. The rest escaped. Young Heywood sprang overboard, seized a plank and was making for the shore when a boat picked him up. Morrison, one of the men, swam about with his handcuffs on until a boat came to his assistance.

Those who had escaped took refuge on a small sandy islet and hauled up the boats to repair those that were damaged. Then the people were mustered, and it was found that eighty-nine of the ship's company and ten of the mutineers were saved—thirty-one of the former and four of the latter had perished. After suffering great hardships the remnant of the *Pandora's* crew reached the island of Timor, and getting on board a ship there, returned to England.

Here the mutineers were tried for mutiny and piracy, and part of them condemned to death. Several of their number, however, who had not taken active part in the mutiny of the *Bounty* were acquitted, and some were pardoned; among the latter were young Heywood and Morrison.

Such was the end of this portion of the crew of the *Bounty*. Turn we now to Lieutenant Bligh and his companions.

OPEN BOAT IN A GALE.

# CHAPTER X.

### BLIGH'S EXTRAORDINARY BOAT VOYAGE.

FEW situations in which men can be placed are more dangerous or dreary than that of being out upon the wide ocean in an open boat.

That the risk is very great may be gathered, in some degree, by a glance at the annexed woodcut where a party of youths are seen caught in a squall and obliged to lower their sail in order to close-reef it. The water here is seen lipping up to the very edge of the gunwale near the stern, while it dashes past the bow in white foam. Obviously the great danger lies in the simple fact of the boat being *open*. Size is, comparatively, an unimportant matter. If the boat were decked over, it might venture out even upon the Atlantic with some degree of security ; but, however large a boat may be, if it is not decked, the risk of being swamped in stormy weather is very great, because the waves break into it faster than they can be baled out, and no one who is not either mad, or at least influenced by a very strong and overpowering motive, will risk his life by going to sea in an open boat. Of course by "going to sea" is meant undertaking a long voyage.

Nevertheless, although this be true, there are many instances on record of wonderful voyages having been accomplished in open boats. In some cases, men have been driven off shore in a gale and compelled to undertake such voyages.

In others their ships have gone down in the distant ocean, leaving them floating in their open boats like mere specks upon the sea ; and sometimes, as in the instance we are about to consider, mutinous crews have put the comrades who would not join them into an open boat and cut them adrift.

It will be remembered that in our last chapter we related how the mutineers of the *Bounty* had put Lieutenant Bligh and some of the men into an open boat and cast them loose. We shall now relate a few of the details of Bligh's

## EXTRAORDINARY BOAT VOYAGE.

When Fletcher Christian and his merciless companions set their commander adrift in the boat, they flung them a small quantity of provisions and a few stores which, together with the crew, sank the boat so deep in the water that one would have expected that the first breeze of wind would have filled and swamped it.

The boat in which these nineteen men found themselves floating in the midst of the Pacific Ocean, was the launch. Its length was 23 feet; its breadth 6 feet 9 inches.  In this, without awning or covering of any kind and with a small allowance of food—scarce enough to sustain life, they encountered heavy storms and endured the severest privations and sufferings from cold and exposure during a voyage of several thousands of miles.

The names of the men thus cast away are as follows :— Lieutenant Bligh ; John Fryer, master; William Elphinstone, master's-mate ; John Hallet, midshipman ; Thomas Hayward, midshipman ; William Peckover, gunner ; William Cole, boatswain ; William Purcell, carpenter ; Thomas Ledward, surgeon's-mate ; John Samuel, clerk and steward ;

David Nelson, botanist; Lawrence Labogue, sailmaker; Peter Linkletter, quarter-master; John Norton, quarter-master; George Simpson, quarter-master's-mate; Thomas Hall, ship's cook; John Smith, commander's cook; Robert Lamb, butcher; and Robert Tinkler, a boy.

None but a man of decided firmness and energy of character could have carried himself and his companions through the dangers and trials of that voyage in safety. Lieutenant Bligh proved himself fully equal to the emergency.

His first care after the *Bounty* left them was to examine the condition of his boat and the amount of his provisions. These last were very meagre. They consisted of one hundred and fifty pounds of biscuit, thirty pounds of pork, six quarts of rum, six bottles of wine, and twenty-eight gallons of water. Of stores they had a few pieces of canvas, some twine and cordage, four cutlasses, a quadrant, and a compass.

The condition of the launch and her crew is beautifully and forcibly expressed in the following lines :—

"The boat is lowered with all the haste of hate,
  With its slight plank between thee and thy fate;
  Her only cargo such a scant supply
  As promises the death their hands deny;
  And just enough of water and of bread
  To keep, some days, the dying ofrm the dead.
  Some cordage, canvas, sails, and lines, and twine,
  But treasures all to hermits of the brine,
  Were added after, to the earnest prayer
  Of those who saw no hope save sea and air;
  And last, that trembling vassal of the Pole,
  The feeling compass, navigators' soul.

     *      *      *      *

  The launch is crowded with the faithful few
  That wait their chief—a melancholy crew,
  But some remained reluctant on the deck
  Of that proud vessel, now a moral wreck—
  And viewed their captain's fate with piteous eyes;
  While others scoffed his augured miseries,
  Sneered at the prospect of his pigmy sail,
  And the slight bark, so laden and so frail."

Being within about thirty miles of the island of Tofoa, Bligh resolved in the first instance to proceed thither in order to procure, if possible, bread fruit and water. But the natives who lined the beach turned out to be of exceedingly treacherous and fierce disposition. One of the chiefs earnestly entreated Bligh to spend the night there, and upon his refusing to do so, he exclaimed angrily, " Then we will kill you." Thereupon he gave a signal, and immediately about two hundred savages rushed upon the sailors and attacked them with stones, which flew about their heads like a shower of shot. Fortunately none were seriously hit, and they all succeeded in getting safely into the boat with the exception of John Norton, the quarter-master, who boldly ran up the beach to cast off the stern fast. Upon this brave but unfortunate man the natives rushed, and in a few minutes stoned him to death.

The crew of the launch pushed hastily off to sea, but were followed by several canoes, laden with stones, from which the attack was continued. Having no fire-arms, the only defence they could make was to throw back the stones which happened to lodge in the boat, but in this mode of warfare the savages were much more expert, and it is probable the Europeans would have been murdered had they not hit upon the ruse of throwing part of their clothing into the sea. As they expected, the natives stopped to pick up the garments, and the crew of the boat pulled lustily till beyond the reach of stones. Soon after, night coming on, the pursuit was abandoned.

Before this occurred, however, one or two bread-fruits and a few small cocoa-nuts had been gathered, and added to their slender stock of provisions.

The eyes of the wretched men in the launch were now

turned anxiously towards their commander, in whose energy and knowledge they felt their hope of deliverance depended. It is to be hoped that, among men in such desperate circumstances, there were some who earnestly looked to a higher Power for deliverance. The commander now informed his men that he meant to steer straight for a Dutch settlement on the island of Timor, distant above three thousand six hundred miles, and added that the only chance they had of accomplishing such a voyage successfully was to place themselves voluntarily on a fixed allowance of food, which, on careful calculation, he said, would afford each man one ounce of bread and quarter of a pint of water per day !

To this the men readily agreed, and that night, it may be said, the perilous voyage began. They gave up all idea of steering for any of the islands of the Pacific, knowing full well that the natives, seeing their helpless condition, would slay and devour them.

"We bore away," says Bligh, "across a sea where the navigation is but little known, in a small boat, twenty-three feet long from stem to stern, deeply laden with eighteen men. I was happy, however, to see that every one seemed better satisfied with our situation than myself. It was about eight o'clock at night on the 2d of May 1789, when we bore away under a reefed lug-foresail, and having divided the people into watches, and got the boat into a little order, we returned thanks to God for our miraculous preservation, and, in full confidence of his gracious support, I found my mind more at ease than it had been for some days past."

But this happy frame of mind was not to last long. At dawn of the following day the sun arose red and fiery—a sure indication of coming storms—and ere the day had far advanced the gale burst upon them in all its fury; so fierce was it that, we are told, the sail of the boat was actually *becalmed* when between the heavy billows, while, when on the top of the seas, it proved almost more than they could carry, yet they did not dare to take it in. The sea curled constantly over the gunwale, and incessant baling was necessary to keep them afloat.

In order to lighten the boat, all their superfluous clothing, with some spare sails and cordage were thrown overboard, and the biscuit was stowed in the carpenter's chest to preserve it from the spray that lashed over them.

Bligh had apportioned the provisions so as to last eight weeks, that being the time that would be probably required under ordinary circumstances to complete the voyage; and being a man of firm character he resolved to enforce the rules as to food at the risk of his life if need be. As the men were exhausted with baling, and thoroughly wet, a tea-spoonful of rum and quarter of a bread-fruit were served out to each, but, in spite of this, their limbs were so benumbed with cold when day-light came, that they could scarcely continue the work of baling, upon which, under God, the lives of all depended; another tea-spoonful of rum was therefore served out, by which they felt much revived.

That day the boat was kept running before the wind. Five small cocoa-nuts were served out for dinner, and in the evening a few pieces of bread-fruit were distributed for supper, after which they commended themselves to God in prayer.

The gale continued till the morning of the 5th, when it began to abate, and now Bligh prepared a small log-line with which he afterwards marked more correctly than heretofore their progress over the unknown ocean. The sufferings of the poor fellows from fatigue and cold were extreme, for, in addition to their laborious work and exposure, they had not sufficient room in the bottom of the boat to stretch their limbs when they lay down to rest, and usually awoke with severe cramps. To add to their misfortunes, the biscuit, it was found, had been much damaged during the gale, part of it was quite decayed and unfit for food. Nevertheless it was carefully preserved.

On the 6th they came in sight of islands, but, remembering the reception at Tofoa, the sight of land aroused fear instead of joy in their breasts. On the same day they hooked a fish. Circumstanced as they were, such an event created a burst of anxious delight, which, alas, was almost instantly changed into a groan of disappointment, in consequence of the fish escaping while they were endeavouring to get it over the side of the boat. That night each man supped on an ounce of damaged biscuit, and quarter of a pint of water.

Next day they were pursued by two canoes, which, however, failed to overtake them, although they did not give up the chase till the afternoon. Well was it for them that these natives did fail, and that the people in the boat had resolution enough to refrain from attempting to land, for the islands they were passing turned out to be part of the Feejee group, the inhabitants of which are now known to be the fiercest and most addicted to cannibalism, as well as the most cruel and inhospitable, of all the islanders of the South Seas.

Soon after this heavy rain came on, and every effort was made to collect the shower. By this means their stock of fresh water was increased to thirty-four gallons, and their thirst, for the first time since they were turned adrift, was thoroughly quenched. But the consequences of the rain were hurtful in other respects, for everything in the boat and on their persons was soaked, and being compelled to sleep all night in this condition, unable, from want of room, to make any exertion to warm themselves by means of muscular effort, they were seized with severe shiverings.

On the 8th, therefore, Bligh deemed it advisable to issue a slightly more substantial breakfast, and served to each man an ounce and a half of pork, half a pint of cocoa-nut milk, an ounce of biscuit, and a tea-spoonful of rum, which last, though so small in quantity, is said to have been of the greatest service.

During all this time, and, indeed, during the whole voyage, Bligh kept a short journal in a small book which had been used in the *Bounty* for the insertion of signals. He says, in regard to it, " It is with the utmost difficulty that I can open a book to write, and I feel truly sensible I can do no more than point out where these lands are to be found, and give some idea of their extent."

Yet the persevering commander on that forlorn voyage, continued to keep the journal to the end, and it, with several other weather-stained relics, are now in possession of his daughters.

Bligh now adopted a more certain method of doling out the scanty allowance. " Hitherto," he says, " I had issued the allowance by guess, but now I made a pair of scales, with two cocoa-nut shells, and having accidentally some pistol balls in the boat, twenty-five of which weighed one pound, or sixteen ounces, I adopted one of these balls as the proportion of weight that each person should receive of bread at the times I served it out. I also amused all hands with describing the situation of New Guinea and New

Holland, and gave them every information in my power, that, in case any accident should happen to me, those who survived might have some idea of what they were about, and be able to find their way to Timor, which at present they knew nothing of more than the name, and some not even that. At night I served a quarter of a pint of water and half an ounce of bread for supper."

Bligh entertained his men thus during a brief respite of a few hours' fine weather and sunshine, which they availed themselves of to dry their clothes and sails. But this was scarcely accomplished when another gale, accompanied by thunder, lightning, and rain, burst upon them, and again drenched them all to the skin.

On the 10th it was very severe. The sea broke over them so constantly that they were compelled to run before the wind, and to keep two men constantly baling. The allowance, too, was still further reduced, one twenty-fifth part of a pound of biscuit, and quarter of a pint of water, being the allowance for breakfast, and the same at dinner and supper. Occasionally, when the weather was very bad, half an ounce or so of pork, and a tea-spoonful of rum was added.

" In the evening of the 12th," says Bligh, " it still rained hard, and we again experienced a dreadful night. At length the day came, and showed a miserable set of beings, full of wants, without anything to relieve them. Some complained of great pain in the bowels, and every one of having almost lost the use of his limbs. The little sleep we got was in no way refreshing, as we were constantly covered with the sea and rain. The weather continuing bad, and no sun affording the least prospect of getting our clothes dried, I recommended to every one to strip and wring them through the sea-water, by which means they received a warmth that, while wet with rain water, they could not have."

The gale continued unabated during several days, and as the nights were intensely dark, not a star being visible, they were often very uncertain as to their steering. Yet, although islands were seen more than once, they held on their miserable course, preferring the chance of being starved to death in an open boat, to the risk of being killed and eaten by the savages.

The night of the 16th was horribly dark and tempestuous, and they expected each moment that the boat would be overwhelmed. That day was also marked by the issue of an ounce of pork in addition to the ordinary allowance. The bad weather continued, and several days later Mr. Bligh speaks of some of his people seeming half dead, while their appearance was "horrible."

"During the whole of the afternoon of the 21st," he says, "we were so covered with rain and salt water that we could scarcely see. We suffered extreme cold, and every one dreaded the approach of night. Sleep, though we longed for it, afforded no comfort; for my own part I almost lived without it. On the 22d our situation was extremely calamitous. We were obliged to take the course of the sea, running right before it, and watching with the utmost care, as the least error in the helm would in a moment have been our destruction. It continued through the day to blow hard, and the foam of the sea kept running over our stern and quarters.

"The misery we suffered this night exceeded the preceding. The sea flew over us with great force, and kept us baling with horror and anxiety. At dawn of day I found every one in a most distressed condition, and I began to fear that another such night would put an end to the lives of several who seemed no longer able to support their sufferings. I served an allowance of two tea-spoonfuls of rum; after drinking which, and having wrung our clothes, and taken our breakfast of bread and water, we became a little refreshed."

Next day the wind moderated, the sun came out to cheer their drooping spirits, and Bligh speaks, for the first time, of seeing "cheerful faces" about him. Wretched as was their condition they experienced some degree of comfort and warmth,—the first they had felt during the previous fifteen days. This moment of breathing time was employed by the commander in examining into the state of the provisions, which he found so reduced that a further reduction in the allowance became absolutely essential. He expected that a mutinous spirit would be roused in the poor fellows when this was announced, but to his surprise they at once agreed to it on the necessity being explained.

It was important that the rate of consumption should be so proportioned that the stock might last six weeks longer. Accordingly it was arranged that the allowance in future should be one twenty-fifth part of a pound of bread for breakfast, and the same quantity for dinner, as usual, but that the proportion for supper should be discontinued!

It seemed as if God, in his mercy, smiled upon this instance of self-denial on the part of those weary and worn-out men, for the very next day, about noon, some noddies—a small species of sea-fowl, about the size of a pigeon—came so near the boat that one of them was caught by the hand.

This little bird was divided, with its entrails, into

eighteen portions.  Then one of the sailors was made to turn his back upon the feast, while another sailor pointed separately to each portion, saying " *Who shall have this ?* " Thus every one felt that he had an equal chance with the rest of getting the best portion, and all grumbling at supposed unfairness was avoided.  Curiously enough the poor commander fared worst upon this occasion, for, much to the amusement of the men, the beak and claws were included in the share that fell to him !

On the same evening several boobies approached, and one of them was caught and divided in the same manner. It was about the size of a duck.  The blood was given to three of the men who had been most distressed for want of food.  Of course it was eaten raw.  Even had they possessed the means of cooking it, these half famished men would not have delayed their meal for such a trifle.  On the 26th another booby was caught.

The heat of the sun now became even more distressing than cold and rain had been before, and some of the people were seized with a languor and faintness that rendered them indifferent to life.

At last, on the 28th, about one in the morning, the sound of breakers was heard by the man at the helm, and soon after they approached the "barrier reef," which runs along the eastern coast of New Holland.  The sea broke furiously over this reef, but within the water was as smooth as a pond.  Along it they steered until an opening was found, and passing in with a strong stream, they at last found themselves in smooth water, and returned thanks to God who had brought them thus far in safety.  But their terrible voyage was not yet done.  Here they could only rest and recruit their strength for a few days.

Oysters were found on the rocks in great abundance. Fresh water was also found; but above all, rest—sound, sweet, refreshing repose to their wearied limbs and minds —was obtained.

With returning health, as is too often the case in such circumstances, came a mutinous spirit. Bligh ordered some of the crew to go along the shore to gather supplies. They grumbled at what they considered too severe duty, and one of them told his commander that he was as good a man as himself.

Bligh says, "It was not possible for one to judge where this might have an end if not stopped in time. To prevent, therefore, such disputes in future, I determined either to preserve my command or die in the attempt; and, seizing a cutlass, I ordered him to lay hold of another and defend himself; on which he called out that I was going to kill him, and immediately made concessions. I did not allow this to interfere further with the harmony of the boat's crew, and everything soon became quiet."

About this time—June 1st—Nelson, the botanist, became very ill; two of the men also began to show symptoms of sinking under the effects of the exposure and suffering they had endured, notwithstanding their recent rest. But the voyage to the nearest habitable part of the globe could not be delayed on this account; so, on the 3d, the little boat once more launched out into the open sea.

Soon they were again reduced to the old allowance—the twenty-fifth of an ounce of biscuit, carefully weighed in the cocoa-nut scales, with the pistol bullet; and ere long they were reduced to worse straits than before. The surgeon and one of the stoutest sailors broke down.

"On the morning of the 10th, after a comfortless night," says Bligh, "there was a visible alteration for the worse in many of the people, which gave me great apprehensions. An extreme weakness, swelled legs, hollow and ghastly countenances, a more than common inclination to sleep, with an apparent debility of understanding, seemed to me the melancholy presage of an approaching dissolution. The surgeon and Lobogue, in particular, were most miserable objects. I occasionally gave them a few tea-spoonfuls of wine out of the little that remained, which greatly assisted them. The hopes of being able to accomplish the voyage was our principal support. The boatswain very innocently told me that he really thought I looked worse than any in the boat. The simplicity with which he uttered such an opinion amused me, and I returned him a better compliment."

But the sufferings of this much enduring crew were soon to terminate; with some in restoration to health and to their native land; with others in the last quiet resting-place of man. On the 11th, Mr. Bligh told his companions that they were approaching Timor; and, accordingly, the next day they arrived at that island, where the people received them with the utmost hospitality and kindness; vieing with each other in acts of kindness, while they gazed in horror and pity at the living skeletons who, with tears streaming from their eyes, and words of thankfulness to God upon their lips, landed on their shores.

Two months they remained here to recruit; then they set forth on their return to England. But all of them did not reach it. Of the nineteen who were forced from the *Bounty* by the mutineers, thirteen survived to tell the tale of their wonderful voyage and almost miraculous escape.

Besides John Norton, who was stoned by the savages of Tofoa, Nelson, the botanist, perished at Timor. Two others died at Batavia, and another on the passage home. The surgeon, Mr. Ledward, was left behind, and never again heard of.

"Thus happily ended," says Bligh, in conclusion, "through the assistance of Divine Providence, without accident, a voyage of the most extraordinary nature that ever happened in the world."

# CHAPTER XI.

### PITCAIRN ISLAND.

Much has been said, in preceding chapters, of the mutiny of the *Bounty* and its consequences; but we have not yet done with it. The most remarkable result of that mutiny has yet to be told.

The inspired psalmist says, "Surely the wrath of man shall praise thee, the remainder of wrath shalt thou restrain;" and never, probably, was the truth of this prophecy more strikingly or evidently set forth than in the colonization and finally the conversion of

### PITCAIRN ISLAND.

When Fletcher Christian left Otaheite in the *Bounty*, he took with him, as has been said, several native men and women. The following were the comrades who accompanied him:—Edward Young, midshipman; John Mills, gunner's mate; Matthew Quintal, seamen; William M'Coy, seaman; Alexander Smith *alias* John Adams, seaman; John Williams, seaman; Isaac Martin, seaman; and William Brown, gardener.

These, with Christian and the Otaheitans, numbered altogether twenty-eight souls. They sailed from Matavai Bay, in 1790; and a long but fruitless search was made for them; in the course of years they were forgotten, and the story of the mutiny of the *Bounty*, and all connected with, became at last a tale of other days.

Nearly twenty years passed away. At the end of that period an American trading vessel, having gone far out of her course in the southern Pacific, where few ships have ever occasion to go, approached one of those solitary islands against whose steep and iron-bound shores the never-silent surf of the ocean bursts with tremendous violence, so as to render landing in boats, except in a few places and at certain times, extremely difficult.

- This was Pitcairn Island,—a spot so remote and out of the usual course of vessels that only once or twice at the most had it been seen, and perhaps never visited, since its discovery.

Here, to his amazement, the American captain found a colony of *natives* who *spoke English !* and on inquiry he found them to be the descendants of the mutineers of the *Bounty* who had landed there twenty years before ! Only one of the men who had sailed with Bligh, namely, Smith, *alias* John Adams, was alive. The others had been murdered. About four years after their arrival the Otaheitans secretly conspired against the Englishmen and killed them all with the exception of Adams, whom, however, they wounded severely in the neck with a pistol-ball. On the same night the exasperated women, who had all become the wives of the deceased Englishmen, arose and murdered the Otaheitans. Thus John Adams was the only man left alive on the island. Recovering from his wound this man set to work with the nine women and a few small children to till the ground of their island home, which produced abundance of yams, cocoa-nuts, bananas, and plantains. They had besides plenty of hogs and poultry.

From Adams's narrative we learn that Fletcher Christian and his comrades, after quitting Otaheite, sailed away in search of an uninhabited island.   He fell in with Pitcairn, and ran the *Bounty* aground in order the more conveniently to get the live-stock, &c., landed.   Then he set the ship on fire, and thus rendered any future effort to escape from the island hopeless.

Everything went on smoothly for a time, but soon they began to quarrel and finally to murder each other, until, as has been described, the whole of the full grown males, except Adams, were destroyed.   When Pitcairn was, we may say, rediscovered by the American captain in 1808, the population of the island amounted to about thirty-five, all of whom spoke English and were described as having been educated by John Adams "*in a religious and moral way.*" The grace of God had indeed touched the heart of this man, as we shall see presently.

Six years passed, and no further notice was taken of Pitcairn Island.   But in the year 1815 a letter was received at the Admiralty from Sir Thomas Staines, commander of the *Briton*, to the following effect :—

"I have the honour to inform you that on my passage from the Marquesas Islands to this port on the morning of the 17th Setember, I fell in with an island where none is laid down in the Admiralty charts.   I therefore hove to until daylight and then closed to ascertain whether it was inhabited, which I soon discovered it to be, and to my great astonishment found that every individual on the island (forty in number) spoke very good English.   They proved to be the descendants of the deluded crew of the *Bounty*.

" A venerable old man, John Adams, is the only surviving Englishman who last quitted Otaheite in her, and whose exemplary conduct, and fatherly care of the whole of the little colony, could not but command admiration.   The pious manner in which all those born on the island have been reared, the correct sense of religion that has been instilled into their young minds by this old man, has given him the pre-eminence over the whole of them, to whom they look up as the father of one and the whole family.

" A son of Christian was the first-born on the island ; he is now about twenty-five years of age, and is named Thursday October Christian.

This young man, with such remarkable names, is described as being a fine tall youth full six feet high, with dark hair and an open pleasing countenance. He wore no clothes except a piece of cloth round his loins, and a straw hat ornamented with black cock's feathers, so that his fine figure and muscular limbs were shown to great advantage. Captain Pipon who wrote an account of this visit, says, " Added to a great share of good humour, we were glad to trace in his benevolent countenance all the features of an honest English face."

Thursday October Christian was accompanied on board the *Briton* by another fine handsome youth named George Young, a son of Young, the midshipman. Sir Thomas Staines took these young men into the cabin and set before them something to eat, when, to his inexpressible astonishment, the semi-savages rose up, clasped their hands together, and one of them said in solemn tones the familiar words, " For what we are going to receive, the Lord make us truly thankful."

Surprised beyond measure by all he heard and saw, Sir Thomas landed, with considerable difficulty, owing to the surf, and was met by old John Adams on the beach. He was accompanied by his wife, a very old woman, and nearly blind, and by a number of the inhabitants, all of whom were described as being graceful in form, healthy and robust, and particularly good-natured in their expressions and manners.

The women were clothed in cloth of their own manufacture, and the form of their dress was extremely simple. One piece of cloth reaching from the waist to the knees, and another piece thrown loosely over their shoulders in the form of a mantle, was all their costume. But what surprised and delighted their visitors most was the simple modesty of these descendants of the mutineers and their deep sense of religion. They had been impressed by old Adams with the propriety and necessity of returning thanks to the Almighty for the many blessings they enjoyed, and they never thought of touching food without first asking a blessing of Him who gave it. Besides this they were in the habit of repeating the Lord's Prayer and the Creed morning and evening.

The means by which this remarkable state of things was brought about was, the conversion of John Adams many years after he had landed on the island, and long after all his companions of the *Bounty* had perished. The only books saved from this vessel were a copy of the Bible and a Book of Common Prayer.

In the year 1810 he first became seriously impressed, and from that time forward to the day of his death, he led a consistent religious life, and spent his time and energies in training the young people around him. The Holy Spirit blessed his efforts, and the name of Jesus ere long became precious to many of those who dwelt in that remote island of the sea. A man of the name of Buffett, a sailor, was left there by a whale ship in later years and became of the greatest assistance to Adams in the capacity of a schoolmaster.

Captain Beechy, of the *Blossom*, gives the following account of the people of Pitcairn in 1825 when Adams was in his sixty-fifth year :—

" During the whole time I was with them I never heard them indulge in a joke or other levity ; and the practice is apt to give offence. They are so accustomed to take what is said in the literal meaning, that irony was always considered falsehood in spite of explanation. They could not see the propriety of uttering what was not strictly true for any purpose whatever. The Sabbath-day is devoted entirely to prayer, reading, and serious meditation. No boat is allowed to quit the shore, nor any work whatever to be done, cooking excepted, for which preparation is made the previous evening.

" I attended their church on this day, and found the service well conducted. The prayers were read by Adams, and the lessons by Buffett ; the service being preceded by hymns. The greatest devotion was apparent in every individual, and in the children there was a seriousness unknown in the younger part of our communities at home. In the course of the litany they prayed for their sovereign and all the royal family with much apparent loyalty and sincerity. Some family prayers which were thought appropriate to their particular case were added to the usual service, and Adams, fearful of leaving out any essential part, read in addition those prayers which are intended only as substitutes for others.

" A sermon followed, which was very well delivered by Buffet ; and lest any part of it should be forgotten, or escape attention, it was read three times. The whole concluded with hymns which were first sung by grown-up people and afterwards by the children. . . . .

" All that remains to be said of these excellent people is, that they appear to live together in perfect harmony and contentment ; to be virtuous, religious, cheerful, and hospitable beyond the limits of prudence, to be patterns of conjugal and parental affection, and to have very few vices."

The village was described as forming a pretty square ; the upper corner, near a large banyan tree being the site of the cottage that John Adams built with his own hands. Opposite to this was the cottage of Thursday October Christian. In the centre was an open plot of grass, fenced in to keep the hogs and goats out. In the houses they had tables, chairs, chests, and bed-steads, and indeed every comfort that could be desired.

The first severe blow this interesting colony received was the death of its " father," good old John Adams, which took place in 1829. He had indeed acted the part of father and pastor to them since the period of his conversion. Although an illiterate man he could read well, and taught himself to write late in life. He celebrated all marriages and baptisms according to the rites of the Church of England, but never ventured on confirmation or the sacrament of the Lord's supper.

John Adams passed away, but his place was ere long ably filled by George Nobbs, a gentleman whose history is almost as romantic as that of Adams himself.

Mr. Nobbs served as a midshipman and afterwards as a lieutenant in the British navy for many years, during which he saw much service and distinguished himself on many occasions. He was taken prisoner by the Spaniards off the coast of Chili in 1822. He was exchanged with other prisoners soon after, and took passage for England in 1822 in a ship which had shortly before touched at Pitcairn's

Island.   Mr. Nobbs was so captivated by the account of the happiness of the people of that island, that be resolved to visit it.   He had led an adventurous and stirring life, had sailed round the world four times, had encountered many dangers, and was now anxious to find a peaceful home where he could be of use to his fellow-creatures.   But it was no easy matter to get to Pitcairn, as ships never went directly thither, and for nearly two years he wandered about seeking in vain for a passage.   At last he formed the bold resolution of going there in a boat alone, if he could find no one willing to accompany him!   At Callao, in Peru, he met the owner of a launch who agreed to accompany him if he would fit out the boat.   This Mr. Nobbs did, and, in a mere boat these two men set out by themselves on a voyage of three thousand five hundred miles, which they accomplished in forty-two days.   The owner of the launch died soon after their arrival in 1828, and Mr. Nobbs at once began his labour of love amongst the islanders, and became the successor of John Adams when he died, in the following year.

We cannot follow the fortunes of this interesting colony further.   It still flourishes under its beloved pastor, who, only a few years ago, was ordained, and introduced to Queen Victoria just previous to his setting out, with the intention, we believe, of spending the remainder of his days among the Christian descendants of the mutineers of the *Bounty*.

# CHAPTER XII.

STEAM FRIGATE—BLOWING UP OF THE AMPHION—BURNING OF THE KENT—FOUNDERING OF THE MAGPIE AND ROYAL GEORGE.

IN our account of the Battle of the Nile mention has been made of *frigates*. These are vessels of war and in the accompanying illustration is shown the general appearance of a

## STEAM FRIGATE.

The word "frigate" is used to denote a particular class of war-vessel, the distinguishing feature of which is that it has only a *single tier* of guns all round. The frigate is a full-rigged ship in all respects, and may or may not have the addition of steam without its distinctive character being in any degree affected thereby. The frigate in the engraving is a screw steamer ; but, as we purpose to enter at large, in another place, into the subject of steam vessels, we will merely remark here, that the screw propeller by which this vessel is worked, projects from the stem under the water ; it will be observed that the jib and flying-jib of this frigate are taken down, and the main and fore-sails are clewed up, in order to check speed as she approaches harbour. This is further accomplished by the screw being reversed, so as to act as a drag upon the hull, while for the same end the sails of the fore-mast are *backed*. Sails can only be backed when the wind is somewhat ahead. When the wind is fair they cannot be backed until the ship is turned towards the wind in some degree.

STEAM FRIGATE.

Screw propellers are found to be of the utmost importance in naval warfare, especially in frigates, which serve the purpose of *light troops*, so to speak, to ships of the line, rendering them independent of wind as long as the coals last, and enabling them to proceed up deep rivers which could not be entered without the aid of steam. Frigates usually carry from forty to fifty guns in a single tier.

### BLOWING UP OF THE AMPHION.

On the 22d of September 1796 there occurred a most appalling catastrophe, which threw a deep gloom at the time over Plymouth, and desolated many a home.

On that day the *Amphion* frigate lay alongside the sheer-hulk taking in her bowsprit close to the dockyard pier. Being on the eve of sailing she was crowded not only with her crew but with more than a hundred men, women, and children, who had come to take farewell of relations or to attend to the duties of getting the ship ready for sea. Little did that bustling crowd think that so many of them were about to enter so soon upon eternity.

The captain, Israel Pellew, was seated at dinner, in company with Captain Swaffield of the *Overyssel*, a Dutch sixty-four, and the first lieutenant of the *Amphion*, at the time of the explosion—about four o'clock in the afternoon. Suddenly a shock like an earthquake was felt all over Plymouth, while the sky toward the dock appeared red as if on fire. The inhabitants, with consternation depicted on their countenances, rushed into the streets. All knew that some appalling catastrophe had taken place ; soon the truth was ascertained—the *Amphion* frigate had blown up.

Then the horrified people hastened to the dock where a scene of the most awful and heart-rending nature presented itself. The riven and blackened wrecks of masts, spars, and rigging, were strewn in all directions, and the deck of the sheer-hulk alongside of which the frigate had lain, was covered with human blood. But the sights of that dreadful scene were scarcely more terrible than the cries of woe that filled the air as fathers, sisters, mothers, wives, brothers, rushed about among the mangled corpses, searching for beloved relatives, while the mutilated forms were being collected and conveyed to the hospital.

So complete and terrible was the destruction of human life that very few of the unfortunates on board the frigate survived to tell either what occurred or how it happened.

It was conjectured that the explosion was caused by the gunner, who was not a very sober man, and who was suspected of stealing the powder. If so, the wretched man paid the penalty of his misdeeds with his life. He was among those who perished.

Just one instant before the explosion took place, the sentinel at the cabin door happened to look at his watch. Next instant he was insensible, and when he recovered he found himself on shore comparatively unhurt. At the same moment the party in the cabin were thrown with extreme violence against the upper deck. Captain Pellew, although stunned, retained sufficient presence of mind to rush to the cabin window, through which, he was blown, by a second explosion, into the water. He was picked up almost uninjured.

Not so Captain Swaffield, who was in all probability killed by the first shock, as his body was afterwards found with the skull crushed together. The lieutenant sustained little injury, and escaped through the cabin windows much in the same manner as did his captain.

Several other singular escapes were made. One poor little child was found alive and very little hurt clasped tightly to its mother's breast, but that bosom was icy cold, and the mother's warm heart had ceased to beat, for the whole of the poor creature's body below the waist had been literally blown away. Yet that fearful wrench had failed to unlock the tremendous grasp that love had circled round the child.

Another escape was very remarkable, showing, as indeed nearly all such catastrophes do, how obviously the Almighty protects, from apparently unavoidable death, those whose time to die has not yet come. The boatswain was standing on the bow of the frigate, giving directions to some of the men who were out on the bowsprit rigging out the jib-boom, when he was sent like a rocket into the air, and fell insensible into the sea in the midst of a mass of wreck and rigging. On recovering consciousness he succeeded in extricating himself, and was finally picked up and carried ashore, having sustained no greater injury than a broken arm.

It is supposed that there could not have been fewer than three hundred persons on board the *Amphion* when she blew up. Of that number only eleven were saved—the captain, two lieutenants, a boatswain, a marine, four sailors, one woman, and a child.

### BURNING OF THE KENT.

Of all the dangers to which men are exposed, that of fire at sea is, perhaps, the most imminent and appalling. In the howling storm hope clings to the mariner to the very last; but when, to the fury of elemental strife without is added the raging of fire within, then, indeed, the

firmest nerves are shaken, and the stoutest hearts begin to
quail, and the most reckless and hardened of the crew begin
to call upon God for mercy.

SHIP ON FIRE.

On the 28th of February 1825, a large East Indiaman
was driving gallantly before a gale across that proverbially
stormy sea the Bay of Biscay. She was the *Kent*, a
splendid newly built vessel which had sailed from the
Downs only nine days before, on her voyage to Bengal and
China. She carried out troops with many of their wives
and children, and the total number of souls on board,

including her crew, was six hundred and forty. Upwards of forty of these were women, and more than sixty were children.

On the night referred to, the gale increased every moment in violence, and the towering billows of that far-famed sea tossed the huge vessel as if she were a cork. But her timbers were new and strong; her crew was good; and her commander, Captain Cobb, was brave and self-reliant. No doubt, the sea-sick landsmen, and the poor women and children trembled as they heard the fury of the elements, and felt their rude shock, especially when some of the cabin furniture broke loose and was dashed about; but the old tars at the wheel, and men who were accustomed to the sea, thought little, probably, of so stiff a gale.

As the violent tossing increased, the captain deemed it necessary to send below to see that all was fast in the hold. An officer and two seamen were, therefore, sent below with a lantern. They found that a cask of spirits had broken loose. The officer sent the men for some pieces of wood to secure it, and while they were absent on this errand he held the cask steady with one hand, and grasped the lantern in the other. At that moment the ship gave a heavy lurch, causing the officer to drop the lamp. In his haste to catch it he let go his hold of the cask, which was stove by another lurch of the ship; the spirits gushed out, and in an instant the hold was in a blaze.

The lambent blue flame that burst up the hatchways was quickly followed by a dense black smoke that told its own tale. The ship was on fire, and so thoroughly was the wood-work below ignited, that all hope of extinguishing the flames very soon vanished. Still every possible effort was made to subdue them. Captain Cobb proved himself equal to the terrible emergency, and gave his orders as coolly and collectedly as if there were no danger.

The terror that spread throughout the doomed ship may be described but cannot be conceived; and it was increased to its utmost pitch when the captain, as a last resource, ordered the lower deck to be scuttled, and the lower ports opened to admit the sea. As the black water rushed freely into the ship, hissing into the raging fire, and mingling clouds of hot steam with the rolling smoke, it seemed to the panic-stricken passengers that they were only privileged to choose between a death by drowning or by fire.

Nearly all the six hundred and forty people in the ship rushed upon the upper deck in frantic terror and confusion, many of them almost in a state of nudity. Some of the women and children were rushing about in search of husbands or fathers with an undefined feeling of hope that safety might be found beside the strong arms and loving hearts that were wont to protect them; but, alas! the pride of man was brought low on that dreadful occasion, and his arm, in most cases, was paralyzed. Some fell on their knees and prayed aloud for mercy; others stood silent and stupified; while many cried aloud in despair and agony. In the poet's words,—

> "Then shrieked the timid, and stood still the brave."

Many a secret trait of character is brought to light at such times that would fill a calm observer with surprise. Some who are noted for stern severity of disposition exhibit blanched cheeks and the tremours of unmanly fears, while others—and most frequently the females—seem to rise above the present danger, and in looking up to Him who alone can deliver them, find a comfort and exhibit a composure that might well convince us of the truth of that word, " God is a very present help in trouble." Not only did many of the ladies and soldiers' wives find comfort at that hour on board the *Kent* in reading the Bible and in prayer, but they were enabled even to console, in some degree, the raving *men* around them.

When the terror and confusion was at its height, a man who had been sent to the mast-head uttered a shout, and waving his cap, cried, " A sail on the lee-bow!" The change from despair to hope was instantaneous. A sail was soon observed, and the sailors greeted her with three enthusiastic cheers, while flags of distress were hoisted and guns fired to attract attention. The stranger proved to be the *Cambria*, a small brig of 200 tons, on her way to Vera Cruz, in Mexico. The boats of the *Kent* were immediately lowered, and the females and children placed in them and rowed to the brig. Afterwards the men left, and Captain Cobb was among the last to quit the burning wreck. But this work of transferring six hundred human beings from one ship to another in such a sea was not accomplished without difficulty and terrible loss of life.

The only way of getting into the boats after they had been launched was by sliding down a rope suspended from the spanker-boom over the stern. This the men did one at a time; but the hearts of many failed when they came to attempt to creep out on the small spar which at one moment almost dipt into the sea, and the next was lifted nigh forty feet above it; while those who overcame this difficulty and slid down the rope, sometimes hung a minute in mid-air, or were plunged several times into the water before they managed to drop into the boat.

Fortunately the soldiers maintained the most thorough

discipline throughout the whole of this trying scene, but in spite of every precaution many fell into the sea and were drowned. Some of the sick and a few of the poor children were suffocated in their cabins. One man fell into the blazing hold; and a few of the men refused to quit the ship. For what reason no one can tell. Probably the excitement and terror of their situation had destroyed their reason.

Before the wreck of the *Kent* was finally abandoned, about eighty human beings perished, twenty of whom were children.

But although thus mercifully saved from immediate danger, the situation of those on board the *Cambria* was such as to cause extreme anxiety. Upwards of six hundred persons were huddled into a small vessel of only 200 tons, without food to last for more than a few days, and obliged to risk suffocation in the cabins and hold, for the state of the weather compelled the crew to keep the hatches closed. God, in his goodness, however, sent them a favourable gale, and on the 3d of March they arrived in safety at Falmouth Harbour.

## FOUNDERING.

When a ship fills with water and sinks, she is said to founder. Many a gallant ship has sailed from port, with spreading sails and flying colours; with friends waving adieu on the pier-head, and hopeful sailors on the deck and rigging replying with a cheer—disappeared on the horizon, and—never more been heard of.

Long years have passed. Loving, anxious hearts have beat in hope, and tearful eyes have gazed out to sea in sad expectancy. Long, long years have passed—still the anxious cye, and the *constant* examination of "*Shipping intelligence*" have proved that there is such a thing as hoping against hope; but the heart has been again and again "made sick,"—the absent ship returns not—the world, long years ago, has forgotten her, and ceased to look for her arrival, "for," they say, "she must have *foundered at sea*." And thus, year by year, hundreds of our fellow-creatures perish;

SCUDDING BEFORE THE GALE.

hundreds of our bereaved fellow-creatures wail for the dear ones lost to them for ever; yet we pay but little heed to such terrible facts until, perchance, in the providence of God, the blow delivered on so many around is at last suffered to descend on *us*.

Ships founder in many ways, and the destruction is usually so instantaneous and complete that very few human beings, of all the thousands who have been on board such vessels when they went down, have lived to tell the cause, or relate the details. Sometimes a ship is upset in a squall, fills, and goes done at once. Sometimes it springs a leak and gradually sinks. At other times, while scudding before the gale, under bare poles, and with masts partially gone (as represented in our woodcut), a mighty wave lifts its white crest higher than the surrounding billows, falls with a thunder-clap on the devoted vessel, crushes in her deck, and sweeps her from the face of the raging sea in a single moment, leaving not even a shattered remnant of the wreck to show that she once had been there.

But of all the instances of foundering we ever heard of, the following is the most singular and terrible. Our information is derived from Gilly's admirable work, "Ship-wrecks of the Royal Navy."

### FOUNDERING OF THE MAGPIE.

The *Magpie* was a small schooner which sailed under Lieutenant Smith, in 1826, to the western shores of the Island of Cuba. The object of the cruise was to capture a pirate vessel which had become the scourge of that neighbour-hood.

On the 27th of August she was cruising off the Colorados Roads, on the west coast of Cuba. "The day had been extremely sultry, and towards evening the schooner lay becalmed, awaiting the springing up of the land breeze, a blessing which only those can appreciate who have enjoyed its refreshing coolness after passing many hours beneath the burning rays of a tropical sun.

„ " About eight o'clock a slight breeze sprung up from the westward. Towards nine it shifted to the southward, and a small dark cloud was observed hovering over the land. This ominous appearance, as is well known, is often the precursor of a coming squall, and seems as if sent as a warning by Providence.

" The lurid vapour did not escape the practised eye of the mate, who immediately reported the circumstance to Mr. Smith. All hands were turned up, and in a few minutes the schooner was placed in readiness to encounter the threatened danger.

" In the meantime, the cloud had gradually increased in size and density. The slight breeze had died away, and a boding stillness reigned around. Suddenly a rushing, roaring sound was heard; the surface of the water, which a moment before was almost without a ripple, was now covered with one white sheet of foam. The schooner was taken aback; in vain her commander gave the order to cut away the mast—it was too late, and in less than three minutes from the first burst of the squall, the devoted vessel sank to rise no more.

" At this fearful juncture, a vivid flash of lightning darted from the heavens, displaying for a moment the pale faces of the crew struggling in the water; the wind ceased as suddenly as it had begun, and the ocean, as if un-conscious of the fearful tragedy that had so lately been enacted upon its surface, subsided into its former repose."

. Such is a brief, startling account of the foundering of the *Magpie*. But the story does not end here. One of her crew, a gunner's mate, named Meldrum, succeeded in laying hold of a pair of oars that were floating near to the spot where he rose. Clinging to these, he supported himself for some time in silence and almost in a state of stupor. At length his horrible situation forced itself upon him with fearful intensity. He thought of his late comrades, and peered into the surrounding gloom, but nothing was to be seen, the darkness was too intense. He listened, but not a sound met his ear save the ripple of the waves, and the beating of his own heart. So agonizing were his thoughts, that he at last began to envy those who were gone, when a voice came faintly towards him. Pushing in the direction whence it came, he found one of the schooner's boats floating, keel uppermost, with seven persons clinging to it. One of these was Lieutenant Smith.

In a few minutes the lieutenant spoke to the men, some of whom were lying across the keel, and urged them to make an effort to right the boat and bale out the water, as, on their succeeding in this depended, in all probability, their deliverance from death. Encouraged by his words, the men who were on the keel slipped into the water, and after some time they managed to turn the boat over, and two of the men got in and began to bale her out with their caps.

Hope now began to re-animate the men as they watched the gradual diminishing of the water, but it was suddenly and rudely changed into terror by the cry from one of them of " a shark! a shark!"

The horror of the poor fellows at this, the most dreaded of all dangers, cannot be conceived. Their self-possession forsook them, they attempted to climb into the boat and at once upset her. Mr. Smith alone maintained his coolness. He encouraged them to resume their efforts to right and bale out the boat, and, as no sharks appeared, they followed his advice.

The night passed away, and the morning dawn broke, and they were succeeding in their efforts to empty the boat, when, a second time, the dreaded cry was raised. This time it was not a false alarm, the monsters were actually seen, and, in the panic that followed, the boat was again upset. For a few minutes the men remained uninjured, though the sharks actually rubbed against them as they darted to and fro, as if stirring themselves up to commence the work of destruction. But it was not long before a fearful shriek told that the first victim had perished. He had been seized by a leg, and the water round the spot where he was dragged down was dyed with his blood.

In the midst of this awful scene, Lieutenant Smith never lost his self command, but encouraged the men to recommence their efforts to turn the boat. Once more they were successful, and some of them had clambered in, when poor Smith was seized by a leg. It was torn from his body, but, with unparalleled heroism, he suppressed the cry of agony that rose to his lips, lest he should alarm his companions. In a minute more, a shark seized the other leg and tore it off. The hero's endurance was now indeed tried to the utmost. With a deep groan he relaxed his hold of the boat, and would have sunk altogether, had not those who were baling seized him and dragged him in. Smith gave his last instructions to one of the men. He exhorted him, in the event of his escaping, to tell the admiral that the men had done their duty, and that no blame could be attached to them, " And tell-him," he said, in conclusion, "I have but one favour to ask, and that is that he will promote Meldrum to be a gunner."

Towards evening this gallant and unselfish man appeared to sink rapidly, but ere he breathed his last, the sharks, which during the day had left their victims, re-appeared. In the panic that ensued, the boat gave a lurch and upset, and the well-nigh lifeless body of the unfortunate lieutenant sank to rise no more.

And now, deprived of the cheering voice of their brave commander, the remaining men once more attempted the weary task of turning the boat and baling it out, but soon two of them, giving way to despair, let go their hold and sank. Four men were now left, and these succceded in getting into the boat, but, before they had emptied it of water, two of the four sprang over the side in a fit of delirium, and disappeared.

Meldrum and Maclean alone remained. They persevered in the work of baling till the boat was almost dry, but their relief seemed to be only temporary. Again and again their anxious eyes scanned the horizon—still no sail appeared, and they thought with horror of the fate that awaited them —death by starvation—and were tempted to end their sufferings as some of their companions had already done. Hour after hour passed. The sun rose and sank and rose again, and the two solitary men sat, gazing in mute despair on the sea.

Suddenly, about eight in the morning, a white speck appeared on the horizon. They sprung up in hopeful expectation. It looked like a sail—it *was* a sail! It stood towards them, and as the sails and hull gradually rose to view, the spirits of the castaways revived. Just as deliverance seemed to be certain, the brig, when about half a mile distant, slightly altered her course. Those on board had not seen the boat. The two men shouted with the vehemence of despair, but their voices failed to travel so great a distance. Possibly they had been weakened by prolonged want and suffering. In this extremity, Meldrum, who happened to be a good swimmer, sprang overboard, and struck out in a direction that might, perhaps, enable him to intercept the brig. It was a desperate hazard. Success or death hung on the result—death not only to himself but to his comrade.

Maclean watched the bold swimmer as he breasted the waves, becoming less and less distinguishable, until he was altogether lost in the distance. Then he gazed at the brig, and watched her every movement with the intensity of one who felt that, under God, his life depended on her.

Meanwhile Meldrum accomplished two-thirds of the distance, when his strength began to give way. A few minutes more and he knew that the vessel would have passed. Throwing all his remaining strength into the effort, he shouted loud and long. The cry was heard. The brig was hove-to, the boat was lowered, in a few minutes the gallant sailor was saved, and it was not long before his comrade also was received on board in safety.

## FOUNDERING OF THE ROYAL GEORGE.

In the year 1782, the *Royal George*—a first-rate line-of-battle ship of 100 guns—foundered at her moorings in Portsmouth harbour, under the most singular circumstances, and attended by a fearful loss of life.

This magnificent vessel was fitting out, at the time of the accident, for the purpose of joining the fleet that was destined to sail to the relief of Gibraltar, at that time undergoing its prolonged and celebrated siege. It is said of the *Royal George*, by one who wrote at the time of her loss, that " she was the oldest first-rate in the service, her keel having been laid down in 1751.  She was rather short and high than agreeing with the rules of proportion at present laid down, yet so good a sailer that she has had more flags on board than any vessel in the service.  [This refers to her having been the *flag-ship* of the admirals commanding the fleet].  Lord Anson, Admiral Boscawen, Lord Rodney, and several other principal officers, had repeatedly commanded in her.  Lord Hawke commanded the squadron in her, which fought the French under Conflans, when the *Superbe* of seventy guns was sunk by her cannon, and the *Soleil Royal* of eighty-four was driven on shore and burnt."

Some of the planks of the *Royal George* had to be removed before the vessel was deemed in a fit state to go to sea.  In ordinary circumstances the work of renewing them would have been done in a dry dock, but haste was requisite, the ship was already almost equipped, and, as the planks referred to were not far below its water-mark, it was thought that by *careening*, that is, pulling the ship a little over to one side so as to raise the other slightly out of the water, the end in view might be accomplished.

Accordingly early in the morning of the 29th of August the work of careening began, yet so little was thought of it that the duties of taking in stores and provisions, &c., were not interrupted.  The admiral himself—Kempenfelt—was engaged in writing in the cabin, and an immense number of people were on board, either attending to their several duties or taking leave of their friends.  A victualling vessel lay alongside, and, in short, everything was going on as usual.  Besides the officers and crew, amounting to about nine hundred men, there were upwards of three hundred women and children, relatives of the men, on board at the time.

The danger of thus careening a ship in calm water is not very great, but, unfortunately, it was found that repairs had to be effected lower down on the hull than had been anticipated, and it lay a little more over on its side than had been intended. The scuppers of the lower deck had been left open, so that the water began to enter slowly. At this juncture an unexpected squall struck the ship, and she began to heel over to an alarming extent. The order was instantly given to beat to quarters to right the ship ; but alas ! it was too late. The ports were all open, the sea rushed in, and, in a moment, the *Royal George* filled and went down. So sudden was the catastrophe that men had barely time to shout " The vessel is sinking !" when it disappeared with all on board.

All who were between decks sank to rise no more, and these were the greater number of the people on board. Many of those who were on the upper deck, including the guard, were saved by the boats of the fleet, which instantly pulled to the rescue of the drowning men. The saved amounted to about three hundred in all ; the lost to from nine hundred to one thousand, and among the latter was Admiral Kempenfelt and a number of his officers. The victualling ship alongside was dragged down in the whirlpool, and several vessels not far distant narrowly escaped.

It is impossible to conceive the effect of such a terrible scene, and it is awful to think of the suddenness with which so many human beings were at that hour called into eternity to meet their God.

In the course of after years, some of the guns and other

materials, and a few portions of the hull, were recovered, by means of the diving-bell; but, with these trifling exceptions, the loss of the *Royal George* in Portsmouth harbour was as complete as if it had occurred in the midst of a tempest far out at sea.

RIVER STEAMER ON THE HUDSON.

## CHAPTER XIII.

### RIVER STEAMERS.

One night, in the year 1807, a terrible sight was witnessed by the inhabitants of the banks of the river Hudson, in America.

Men love what is marvellous, and they will go a long distance out of their way to see that which is terrific and horrible; but, on the night in question, there was no need to go far. The farmers had only to look out of their windows, and the sailors of the shipping had only to lift their heads above the bulwarks, to behold a sight that appalled the stoutest hearted, and caused the very hair on the craniums of the timid to stand on end.

The object that caused so much consternation was—a "monster of the deep!" In some parts of the river, men could not tell what it was like, for the night was dark when it passed, but a dark shadowy idea they obtained by the light of the fire which the creature vomited from its jaws;

and they formed a tremendous conception of its size and power from the speed at which it travelled, the splashing which it made, and the hideous groans with which it burthened the night air.

This "fiery monster of the deep" was the *first* river steamer, the *Clermont !*

Before going further into the details of this the first of a class of ships which have, within the last fifty years, almost completely changed the whole system of navigation, let us take a cursory glance at the first attempts made to propel ships by means of steam.

The subject has occupied mankind much longer than many people suppose. So long ago as the year 1543, a naval captain of Spain applied an engine to a ship of about two hundred tons, and succeeded in moving it at the rate of about two miles an hour. The nature of his engine the captain kept secret, but it was noted that part of it consisted of a caldron of boiling water!

This we are told by Thomas Gouzales, the director of the royal archives of Simancas; but his veracity is now called in question,—at any rate nothing further was afterwards heard of the discovery.

The first authentic record we have of steam navigation occurs in a work written by the Marquis of Worcester in 1665, in which allusion is made to the application of engines to boats and ships, which would " draw them up rivers against the stream, and, if need be, pass London Bridge against the current at low water."

Many attempts, more or less successful, were made by ingenious men from time to time.—Papin of France in 1690; Jonathan Hulls in 1736; and M. Genevois in 1759, were each successful to a certain extent in constructing working models, but nothing definite resulted from their labours. Yet we would not be understood to undervalue the achievements of such men. On the contrary, it is by the successive discoveries of such inquiring and philosophical men that grand results are at last attained. The magnificent structures that crowd the ocean were not the creations of one era, or the product of one stupendous mind. They are the result of the labours of thousands of men whose names have never been known to fame.

The men who, working upon the materials supplied by preceding generations, brought the propulsion of boats by steam nearest to perfection, *just before* the commencement of navigation, were Mr. Miller of Dumfries, Mr. Taylor his friend, and tutor in his family, and Mr. Symington,—all of whom were, in a very important degree, instrumental in ushering in the great event. Symington, in 1788, fitted an engine to a large boat, in which he attained the speed of seven miles an hour.

The man to whom the credit belongs of introducing *steam navigation* is undoubtedly Mr. Fulton of America. This gentleman, who was contemporary with those just mentioned, visited France and England, in the former of which he endeavoured unsuccessfully to carry out his projects, while in the latter he met with Symington and obtained much valuable information from him.

We have no sympathy whatever with those who seem to rake in to the credit of their own country every discovery and invention they possibly or plausibly can. We did much *towards* the commencement of steam navigation, but we did not begin it. We pushed considerably in advance of other nations in the invention of apparatus by which boats might be propelled by steam; we constructed models, tried it on a small scale, and found the thing to answer admirably; but we rested there. Meanwhile an enterprising American came and saw our achievements, ordered an engine in England, carried it across the Atlantic, and *commenced* the era of steam navigation, on the river Hudson, by building and launching

### THE FIRST STEAMER.

Robert Fulton, in conjunction with Chancellor Livingston of America, planned, built, and launched a boat in the spring of 1807, which they named the *Clermont*. It was propelled by steam, and averaged the rate of five miles an hour on its first voyage from New York to Albany, a distance of nearly one hundred and fifty miles.

All discoveries and novelties, great and small, are treated with ridicule at first by the mass of mankind, so it is not to be wondered that the crowds which flocked to the wharf to see the *Clermont* start on her first trip were somewhat satirical and jocose in their remarks. But when the steam was turned on, and they heard the first of that series of *snorts* that was destined, ere long, to shake the trembling air of land and sea, and saw the great uncouth paddle-wheels—all guiltless of paddle-*boxes*—revolve powerfully in the water and churn it into foam, a shout, tinged, doubtless, with prophetic fervour, greeted the triumphant engineer as his little steamboat darted from the shore.

Colden, in his Life of Fulton, speaks thus of the *Clermont's* first voyage:—

"She excited the astonishment of the inhabitants of the shores of the Hudson, many of whom had not heard even of an engine, much less of a steamboat. There were many descriptions of the effects of her first appearance upon the people of the banks of the river. Some of these were ridiculous, but some of them were of such a character as nothing but an object of real grandeur could have excited. She was described by some who had indistinctly seen her passing in the night, as a monster moving on the waters, defying the winds and tide, and breathing flames and smoke ! She had the most terrific appearance from other vessels which were navigating the river when she was making her passage. The first steamboat (as others yet do) used dry pine wood for fuel, which sends forth a column of ignited vapour many feet above the flue, and whenever the fire is stirred, a galaxy of sparks fly off, which, in the night, have a very brilliant and beautiful appearance.

"This uncommon light first attracted the attention of the crews of other vessels. Notwithstanding the wind and tide, which were adverse to its approach, they saw with astonishment that it was rapidly coming towards them ; and when it came so near that the noise of the machinery and paddles was heard, the crews—if what was said in the newspapers of the time be true—in some instances shrunk beneath their decks from the terrific sight, and left their vessels to go on shore, whilst others prostrated themselves, and besought Providence to protect them from the approaches of the horrible monster which was marching on the tide and lighting its path by the fires that it vomited !"

The *Clermont* became a regular passenger boat on the Hudson, and the progress of steam navigation continued to advance, until nearly all the navigable rivers of the world, and the great ocean itself, were covered with these clanking ships of commerce, which have added more to the comfort, the wealth, and the power of man—the power of doing good as well as evil—than the feeble human mind can conceive.

### THE COMET.

It was not until five years after the Americans set us the example, that we launched our first passenger steamboat, the *Comet*, a vessel of about twenty-five tons, with engines of three horse power. This little vessel was started by Henry Bell, of Helensburgh, on the Clyde. It began its career in 1812, and plied regularly for two years.

Like her predecessor the *Clermont*, she was regarded with no small degree of scepticism, and with a large amount of surprise by the thousands who saw her set forth. Nevertheless she soon proved her value, became a success-ful speculation to her owners, and was, ere long, followed by many other vessels of a similar kind.

### THE ARGYLE, AFTERWARDS NAMED THE THAMES.

In 1813 the *Argyle* was launched. This vessel was the first European steamer that pushed out into the more dangerous navigation of the open sea-coast. She was pur-chased by a company in London. On her passage she was as nearly as possible wrecked on a lee-shore, but, by her steam-power, was enabled to go straight against the wind at the rate of three and a half knots an hour, and so escaped.

One of the passengers has left us an interesting account of this interesting voyage, from which we cull one or two paragraphs :—

" The weather had now become so stormy and bad that our captain determined to put in to the port of Wexford, his great object being to navigate the vessel safely to London, rather than, by using great dispatch, to expose her to unnecessary risk. We put to sea again at two o'clock P.M., on May 30th, and steered for St. David's Head, the most westerly point of Wales. During our passage across St. George's Channel, one of the blades of the starboard -paddle-wheel became out of order: the engine was stopped and the blade cut away. Some hours afterwards a similar accident happened to the other wheel, which was remedied in the same manner.

"About two o'clock in the afternoon, twelve hours after leaving Wexford, we reached the pass of Ramsay: we remained there for three hours to oil the engine, and to give the stoker, who had not quitted his post an instant since leaving Wexford, a little rest. In a short time several boats were seen coming to our assistance, the idea prevailing here, as at Wexford, that our vessel was on fire. We landed on the island of Ramsay, a most desolate spot, containing only one habitation; we, however, procured some bread, butter, milk, cheese, and ale, with which we returned to the vessel, and commenced steaming through the straits and across St. Bride's Bay.

"The weather had now become unfavourable, and the sea ran alarmingly high in the bay. On the south side of St. Bride's Bay, between Skomar Island and the mainland, is a nasty passage called Jack Sound. Our pilot warned us of the danger of attempting this passage excepting at high water and with a favourable wind, as there were several formidable whirlpools which would seize the vessel and carry her on the rocks. Captain Dodd, however, who knew the power of his engine, insisted on going through the sound, in order to save five hours and another night at sea. The pilot repeated his remonstrances, at the same time trembling for fear; but we passed through all the whirlpools with the greatest ease. Nothing, however, can be conceived more frightful than the aspect of some of the rocks, and especially of those called the Bishop and his Clerks. Had we been in a sailing vessel our position would have been most perilous; but our steam was all-powerful and brought us safely to Milford Haven.

"We put to sea again late on the evening of the 31st, and on Friday morning we were in the middle of the Bristol Channel, with no land visible; but, towards evening, we discovered the high coast that terminates England in the west. As the weather, however, again assumed a gloomy aspect, our new pilot judged that it would be imprudent that night to double Land's End, so we shaped our course towards St. Ives.

"On approaching the shore we perceived a crowd of small vessels making towards us with all possible rapidity, by means of oars and sails. Here, as elsewhere, the alarm was taken, on seeing a vessel, judged to be on fire, steering towards the town, and all the disposable craft immediately put to sea. All the rocks commanding St. Ives were covered with spectators; and, when we entered the harbour, the aspect of our vessel appeared to occasion as much surprise amongst the inhabitants, as the ships of Captain Cook produced on his first appearance amongst the islanders of the South Seas.

"Another night passed, a night of storm and danger, but the little *Thames* (the vessel had been re-named by the new company who purchased her) behaved nobly, and next day reached Plymouth. Here," continues the narrative, " the harbour-master, who had never seen a steam-vessel before, was as much struck with astonishment when he boarded the *Thames*, as a child is on getting possession of a new plaything. He steered the vessel, and we passed round several ships of war in the sound. The sailors ran in crowds to the sides of their vessels as we passed them, and mounting the rigging, gave vent to their observations in a most amusing manner.

"We left Plymouth at noon on the following day, and steamed without interruption to Portsmouth, where we arrived on Friday, June 9th, having accomplished one hundred and fifty miles in twenty-three hours. At Portsmouth astonishment and admiration were, if possible, more strongly evinced than elsewhere. Tens of thousands of spectators were assembled to gaze on the *Thames;* and the number of vessels that crowded around us was so great that it became necessary to request the admiral to give us a guard to preserve some degree of order.

"We entered the harbour in the most brilliant style, steaming in, with the assistance of wind and tide, at the rate of from twelve to fourteen miles an hour. A court-martial was at the time sitting on board the *Gladiator* frigate, but the novelty of our steamboat presented an irresistible attraction, and the whole court came off to us, excepting the president, who was obliged by etiquette to retain his seat until the court was regularly adjourned. On Saturday, June 10th, the port-admiral sent his band and a guard of marines at an early hour on board; and soon afterwards he followed, accompanied by three admirals, eighteen post-captains, and a large number of ladies. The morning was spent in steaming amongst the fleet, and running over to the Isle of Wight. From Portsmouth we proceeded to Margate, which we reached on Sunday morning. Here we remained until the following day, when we embarked for our final trip, at half-past eight in the morning, and about six in the evening arrived at Lime-house, where we moored."

We have entered thus at considerable length into this voyage, because, besides being the first steam sea-voyage, it serves to exhibit very distinctly how great and how rapid has been the progress of steam navigation within the last fifty years. In reading such an account as this, in these days of "ocean-mail steamers " and "Great Easterns," we can scarcely believe that in it reference is made, not to the middle ages, but to the year 1813.

In the accompanying engraving are represented a merchant screw-steamer and a river-steamer or tug-boat; both of which may be seen in hundreds every day on the Thames and the Clyde. Of the first of these we shall speak again. The steamboat that heads this chapter is an

## AMERICAN RIVER-STEAMER.

Owing to the immense distance, sometimes more than a thousand miles, that the American inland steam craft proceed up rivers, they are constantly liable to come into extremely shallow waters; they are therefore built very differently from those of this country, which are chiefly used in the comparatively deep waters at the mouths of our largest rivers. They are long, broad, and very flat in the bottom; but they tower upwards, deck upon deck, to such an extent that they sometimes almost cease to resemble boats, and become more like to floating castles. Everything, in short, is above deck, engines and all; and as they are gaily painted, they look very imposing as they dart round a richly wooded point, or through a rippling narrow in the lovely lakes and rivers of the West.

The decorations of American river boats are in many instances of the most gorgeous and regal kind. Pier-glasses, painted panels, stained glass, gilded cornices, polished chairs and tables of the most costly woods, and sofas cushioned with the richest velvets, constitute the furniture of the cabins. These boats are remarkably fast sailers, and have powerful engines, partly for the purpose of attaining very high speed, and partly to enable them to stem the strong currents of the rapids against which in many places they have to contend. They are a little apt to upset, owing to the slight hold they have of the water; and in many of them men are stationed with trucks loaded with heavy weights, ready to be dragged quickly to either side of the steamer when the passengers rush to one side for the purpose of gazing at a passing view in the landscape.

In some of the wilder parts of that remarkable land the river-steamers have a decided tendency to blow up; owing, first, to the fact that most of the engines are high-pressure; and second, to the seemingly irresistible desire the captains have to *sit* on the safety valve!—a practice which undoubtedly secures their *superior* elevation in case of a blow up; but this does not afford much consolation, probably, to those who are killed.

## OCEAN-STEAMERS.

After that momentous era when steam was first successfully applied to useful purposes, human progress and improvement in all departments of science and art seemed to have been hooked on to it, and to have thenceforth rushed roaring at its tail, with truly "railroad speed," towards perfection !

Scarce had the first model steamboat splashed with its ungainly " blades " the waters of a pond, than river traffic by means of steamboats began. And no sooner had this been proved to be a decided success than daring schemes were laid to rush over old ocean itself on wheels.   Men were not long about it, after the first start was made.   Their intellectual steam was up, and the whirl of inventive effort racked the brains of engineers as the wheels of their steamboats tortured the waters of the deep.

And here again the name of Fulton comes into notice. Early in 1814 he conceived the idea of constructing a steam vessel of war, which should carry a strong battery with furnaces for red-hot shot.   Congress authorized the building of such a ship, and before the end of the same year it was launched.   Fulton died the following year, but the fame of that enterprising engineer will never die.

The new vessel received the rather quaint title of the *Fulton the First*.   She consisted of *two* boats joined together. Those who were appointed by Congress to examine her and report, give the following account of this curious man-of-war :—

"She is a structure resting on two boats and keels, separated from end to end by a channel 15 feet wide and 66 feet long.   One boat contains the caldrons of copper to prepare her steam ; the cylinder of iron, its piston, lever, and wheels, occupy part of the other.   The water wheel revolves in the space between them.   The main or gun-deck supports the armament, and is protected by a parapet, 4 feet 10 inches thick, of solid timber, pierced by embrasures. Through thirty port-holes as many thirty-two pounders are intended to fire red-hot shot, which can be heated with great safety and convenience.   Her upper or spar-deck, upon which several thousand men might parade, is encompassed by a bulwark, which affords safe quarters.   She is rigged with two stout masts, each of which supports a large lateen yard and sails.   She has two bowsprits and jibs, and four rudders, one at each extremity of each boat, so that she can be steered with either end foremost.   Her machinery is calculated for the addition of an engine which will discharge an immense column of water, which it is intended to throw upon the decks and through the port-holes of the enemy, and thereby deluge her armament and ammunition.

"If in addition to all this we suppose her to be furnished, according to Mr. Fulton's intention, with hundred-pound columbiads, two suspended from each bow, so as to discharge a ball of that size into an enemy's ship ten or twelve feet below her water-line, it must be allowed that she has the appearance, at least, of being the most formidable engine for warfare that human ingenuity has contrived."

Certainly she was; and even at the present time the *Fulton the First* would cut no insignificant figure if placed alongside our gunboats and floating batteries.

It is not easy to get intelligent men to believe in things that savour of the marvellous; yet there seems to be a point past which, if once a man be got, he will go on to believe almost anything, no matter how absurd.   In those days few people in Europe would credit the truth of this ship's proportions; but when, in the course of time and from indubitable testimony, they were compelled to believe, they flew to the opposite extreme of incredulity and believed anything, as the following curiously comical paragraph will show.   It is said to have appeared in a Scotch treatise on steamships, and is intended for a "full, true, and particular account" of this monstrous American man-of-war steamer.   After giving her dimensions three times larger than they were in reality, the author continues :—"The thickness of her sides is thirteen feet of alternate oak plank and cork wood.   She carries forty-four guns, four of which are hundred pounders; quarter-deck and forecastle guns, forty-four pounders : and further to annoy an enemy attempting to board, can discharge one hundred gallons of boiling water in a minute; and, by mechanism, brandishes three hundred cutlasses with the utmost regularity over her gunwales ; works also an equal number of heavy iron spikes of great length, darting them from the sides with prodigious force and withdrawing them every quarter of a minute ! "

This vessel, although probably intended for an ocean-steamer, was never used as such, as the war between England and America ceased soon after it was launched.  But not long after, a vessel propelled by steam ventured to cross the Atlantic, and thus became the parent of commercial steam navigation.   This vessel was

## THE SAVANNAH STEAMER.

Unfortunately, little information as to this the first ocean steamer has been chronicled.

She was launched at New York on the 22d of August 1818, and in the following year made her first voyage to Savannah, from which she sailed for Liverpool soon after, and crossed the Atlantic in twenty-five days.—during eighteen of which she used her engines.

The *Savannah* was about 350 tons burden, and was on this occasion commanded by Captain Moses Rodgers.  She was fitted with machinery for taking in her wheels in stormy weather, which was found to work admirably ; and she is mentioned as having been seen on the ocean going at the rate of nine or ten knots.

From Liverpool this steamer went to St. Petersburg and afterwards returned to Savannah in safety.

This was the insertion of the wedge.  Our own country

did not follow the lead until 1838, when the good people of New York were thrown into a state of excitement by the arrival of two steamers, the *Sirius* and the *Great Western* from England. So long a time had elapsed since the voyage of the *Savannah* that men had well-nigh forgotten it, and were disposed to regard these vessels as the *first* ocean-steamers. Indeed some narrow-minded and ungenerous writers have asserted that they *were* the first—totally ignoring the prior claim of the *Savannah*.

From that period ocean-steamers began to run frequently across the Atlantic. They now do so regularly, as well as to many other parts of the world.

# CHAPTER XIV.

## STEAMBOAT EXPLOSIONS—OCEAN MAIL-STEAMERS—WRECK OF THE ROYAL CHARTER.

Since steam navigation began many a noble steamboat has been wrecked, and many thousands of human lives have been lost. River and ocean steamers alike have been destroyed, by tempest, by accident, by fire, and by the explosion of boilers. Volumes might be filled with the sad details of such melancholy events, but we cannot do more than select one or two, at random, as illustrations of the calamities of this kind which are permitted to fall upon man.

About thirty years ago, there occurred on one of the American rivers the following

### STEAMBOAT EXPLOSION.

The details of this dreadful event are thus narrated by an eye-witness :—

"On the morning of the 24th February 1830, the *Helen M'Gregor* steamboat stopped at Memphis, on the Mississippi river, to deliver freight and land a number of passengers, who resided in that section of Tennessee. The time occupied in so doing could not have exceeded three quarters of an hour. When the boat landed, I went ashore to see a gentleman with whom I had some business. I found him on the beach, and after a short conversation I returned to the boat I recollect looking at my watch as I passed the gangway ; it was half-past eight o'clock. A great number of persons were standing on what is called the boiler deck, being that part of the upper deck situated immediately over the boilers. It was crowded to excess, and presented one dense mass of human bodies. In a few minutes we sat down to breakfast in the cabin. The table, although extending the whole length of the cabin, was completely filled, there being upwards of sixty cabin passengers, among whom were several ladies and children.

"The number of passengers on board, deck and cabin included, was between four and five hundred. I had almost finished my breakfast, when the pilot rung his bell for the engineer to put the machinery in motion. The boat having just shoved off, I was in the act of raising my cup to my lips, the tingling of the pilot bell yet on my ear, when I heard an explosion resembling the discharge of a small piece of artillery. The report was perhaps louder than usual in such cases, for an exclamation was half uttered by me that the gun was well loaded, when the rushing sound of steam and the rattling of glass in some of the cabin windows, checked my speech and told me too well what had occurred.

"I almost involuntarily bent my head and body down to the floor. A vague idea seemed to shoot across my mind that more than one boiler might burst, and that, by assuming this posture, the destroying matter would pass over without touching me.

"The general cry of, 'A boiler has burst!' resounded from one end of the table to the other; and, as if by a simultaneous movement, all started on their feet. Then commenced a general race to the ladies' cabin, which lay more towards the stern of the boat. All regard to order or deference to the sex seemed to be lost in the struggle for which should be first and furthest removed from the dreaded boilers. The danger had already passed away.　I remained standing by the chair on which I had been previously sitting.　Only one or two persons stayed in the cabin with me.　As yet, no more than half a minute had elapsed since the explosion; but in that brief space how had the scene changed!

" In that ' drop of time ' what confusion, distress, and dismay!  An instant before, and all were in the quiet repose of security—another, and they were overwhelmed with alarm or consternation.　It is but justice to say, that in this scene of terror the ladies exhibited a degree of firmness worthy of all praise.　No screaming, no fainting: their fears, when uttered, were not for themselves, but for their husbands and children.

" I advanced from my position to one of the cabin doors, for the purpose of inquiring who were injured, when, just as I reached it, a man entered by the opposite one, both his hands covering his face, and exclaiming, ' O God! O God! I am ruined!'　He immediately began to tear off his clothes. When stripped, he presented a most shocking spectacle. His face was entirely black; his body without a particle of skin.　He had been flayed alive.　He gave me his name and place of abode, then sank in a state of exhaustion and agony on the floor.

" I assisted in placing him on a mattress taken from one of the berths, and covered him with blankets.　He complained of heat and cold as at once oppressing him.　He bore his torments with manly fortitude, yet a convulsive shriek would occasionally burst from him.　His wife, his children were his constant theme;—it was hard to die without seeing them—' it was hard to go without bidding them one farewell.'　Oil and cotton were applied to his wounds, but he soon became insensible to earthly misery.

" Before I had done attending to him, the whole floor

of the cabin was covered with unfortunate sufferers. Some bore up under the horrors of their situation with a degree of resolution amounting to heroism. Others were wholly overcome by the sense of pain, the suddenness of the disaster, and the near approach of death. Some implored us, as an act of humanity, to complete the work of destruction and free them from present suffering.

"To add to the confusion, persons were every moment running about to learn the fate of their friends and relatives—fathers, sons, brothers; for in this scene of unmixed calamity it was impossible to say who were saved, or who had perished. The countenances of many were so disfigured as to be past recognition.

"My attention after some time was particularly drawn towards a poor fellow, who lay unnoticed on the floor, without uttering a single word of complaint. He was at a little distance removed from the rest. He was not much scalded; but one of his thighs was broken, and a principal artery had been severed, from which the blood was gushing rapidly. He betrayed no displeasure at the apparent neglect with which he was treated. He was perfectly calm. I spoke to him. He said he was very weak, but felt himself going—it would soon be over. A gentleman ran for one of the physicians. He came, and declared that if expedition were used he might be preserved by amputating the limb; but that to effect this it would be necessary to remove him from the boat. Unfortunately the boat was not sufficiently near to run a plank ashore. We were obliged to wait until it could be close hauled. I stood by him calling for help. We placed him on a mattress and bore him to the guards. There we were detained some time, from the cause we have mentioned. Never did anything appear to me so slow as the movements of those engaged in hauling the boat.

"I knew, and he knew, that delay was death—that life was fast ebbing. I could not take my gaze from his face; there all was coolness and resignation. No word or gesture indicative of impatience escaped him. He perceived, by my loud and perhaps angry tone of voice, how much I was excited by what I thought the barbarous slowness of those around. He begged me not to take so much trouble—'they were doing their best.' At length we got him on shore. It was too late—he was too much exhausted, and died immediately after the amputation.

"As soon as I was relieved from attending on those in the cabin, I went to examine that part of the boat where the boiler had burst. It was a complete wreck—a picture of destruction. It bore ample testimony to the tremendous force of that power which the ingenuity of man had brought to his aid. The steam had given everything a whitish hue; the boilers were displaced; the deck had fallen down; the machinery was broken and disordered. Bricks, dirt, and rubbish, were scattered about. Close by the bowsprit was a large rent, through which, I was told, the boiler, after exploding, had passed out, carrying one or two men in its mouth.

"Several dead bodies were lying around. Their fate had been an enviable one compared with that of others; they could scarcely have been conscious of a pang ere they ceased to be. On the starboard wheel house lay a human body, in which life was not yet extinct, though apparently there was no sensibility remaining. The body must have been thrown from the boiler-deck, a distance of thirty feet. The whole of the forehead had been blown away. The brains were still beating.

OCEAN MAIL STEAMER.

"The number of lives lost will in all probability never be distinctly known.  Many were seen flung into the river, most of whom sank to rise no more.  I am inclined to believe that between fifty and sixty must have perished. The cabin passengers escaped owing to the peculiar construction of the boat.  Just behind the boilers were several huge iron posts, supporting, I think, the boiler-deck; across each post was a large circular plate of iron, of between one and two inches in thickness.  One of these posts was placed exactly opposite the head of the boiler which burst. Against this plate the head struck, and penetrated to the depth of an inch; then broke and flew off at an angle, entering a cotton bale to the depth of a foot.  The boiler head was in point-blank range with the breakfast table in the cabin, and had it not been obstructed by the iron post, it must have made a clear sweep of those who were seated at the table."

Instances innumerable might be given of similar explosions, attended often with more or less loss of life, that have occurred on the lakes and rivers of America within the last half century.  In countries where low-pressure, or condensing engines are used, accidents of this kind are much less frequent.

## OCEAN MAIL-STEAMERS.

To such a pitch of perfection has steam navigation now arrived, that the mails are carried, with as steady regularity as if on land, across those stormy oceans over which not half a century ago ships ploughed their course with uncertain speed, and on which went forth, three hundred and seventy years ago, Columbus and his compeers, in utter ignorance of the world that lay beyond the seas.

Our engraving gives an illustration of one of those magnificent vessels which now ply regularly between America and on what is termed the " Overland Route to India." She is a paddle-steamer, with two funnels, and engines of nine hundred horse power. The rig is in most points very similar to that of a barque, namely, square-rigged fore and main-masts, and sloop-rigged mizzen.

These ocean-steamers are of immense size, and their interior fittings resemble those of a gorgeous palace. The *Persia* is the largest of them, with the exception of the *Great Eastern*, which being a unique colossus of the deep we do not class with other vessels. She shall be fully treated of in another chapter. The *Persia* is 376 feet long by 75 feet broad, about three thousand tons burden, and has engines of nine hundred and thirty horse power. She carries nearly three hundred first-class passengers, and is fitted up in a style of the utmost luxury and magnificence.

Nearly all the large steamers are now built of iron, that substance being found in many respects superior to wood; but as the *Great Eastern* is an iron vessel, and is described elsewhere, we shall, in order to avoid repetition, omit further reference to the peculiarity of their construction here.

Iron ships, however, have peculiar faults of their own, as the awful wrecks that sometimes take place too clearly prove.

One of the saddest and most fatal of those that have occurred of late years, was the

## WRECK OF THE ROYAL CHARTER.

Many and many a time has the raging sea opened its ravening maw to swallow the ships, and property, and lives of men ; but seldom has it swept so many human beings into eternity so suddenly, and under such deeply melancholy circumstances, as when it dashed the *Royal Charter* on the rocks of Anglesea—just an hour or two from port, and at the termination of a long successful voyage.

Ah! little do men know *what a day or an hour* may bring forth. On board that doomed steam vessel there was a clergyman. He must have been a good man, for he had gained the affection of all the passengers, who, on the day before that on which they expected once more to tread their native land, subscribed of the gold they were bringing home from the Australian mines, and presented a costly gift to him. Before that next day came, the clergyman and those with whom he sailed were on their knees crying to God for deliverance from the fearful storm ; and before the morning dawn had brightened into day, he with more than four hundred of the passengers and crew were numbered with the dead.

It is past now. Men have ceased to talk, as they once did in solemn tones, of the "Wreck of the *Royal Charter;*" but there are those living now in our land whose riven hearts will carry the memory of that awful wreck to the grave.

The *Royal Charter* sailed from Melbourne for Liverpool, on the 26th of August 1859, having on board three hundred and eighty-eight passengers, and a crew of one hundred and twelve men and officers. She was an iron-built screw-steamer of about two thousand seven hundred and nineteen tons, and two hundred horse power, and was considered a first-rate vessel. Her cargo was small, consisting chiefly of wool and skins; but she carried a rich freight of gold. Many of the passengers were returning home from the mines with the golden produce of long years of hard, hard toil. Yet we can well believe they thought little of their gold as they neared the cliffs of England, unless, perhaps, they thought of how much joy it might be the means of giving to dearly loved ones " at home."

It is estimated that the value of the gold dust and specie on board could not have been far short of £500,000.

On Tuesday evening, the 26th of October, she was off the coast of Anglesea, near Point Lynas, at which time there was a violent gale blowing from the E.N.E. Captain Taylor, who commanded her, continued to throw up signal rockets for several hours, in the hope of attracting a pilot; but none came. The gale increased in violence, and, not having a powerful engine, the vessel continued to drift toward the beach. It was pitch dark—no help was near—a rock-bound coast was on the lee. The captain, therefore, let go both anchors. But the gale had now become a perfect hurricane, and lashed the sea up to madness, and in spite of the engines, which were worked at their full power, the *Royal Charter* continued to drift toward the shore. One of the passengers who were saved gives the following narrative of the wreck :—

"On Tuesday night when the gale became so strong, opposite the Skerries, the ladies and many of the passengers became exceedingly nervous. For my part, however, I had such confidence in the captain, officers, and ship, that I went to bed at ten o'clock. I could only doze, and was aroused in an hour or two by the fearful storm. I heard a voice in the cabin crying out, ' Come directly, we are all lost! I will take your child; come along directly.'

"The voice was that of Captain Withers, a passenger, who had lost his own vessel in the South Pacific. I jumped out of bed and opened the cabin door, but all were gone from there. Hastily putting on a few articles I ran on deck. The ship bumped heavily two or three times against the ground. On going into the general saloon I found it crowded with ladies and gentlemen in the utmost state of tremour. Families were all clinging to each other; the young children were crying out piteously, whilst parents were endeavouring to soothe them with cheering hopes.

"The Rev. Mr. Hodge, a Church of England clergyman, belonging to East Retford, instituted a prayer-meeting, and a great number of passengers fervently participated in the service. The ship struck, however, so fearfully, and the huge waves came down upon her with such tremendous force, rushing into the cabin through the skylights, broken by the falling rigging and hatches, that all became absorbed in the idea of personal danger.

"All tried to soothe the ladies and children. Captain Withers came into the cabin, remarking, 'Now, ladies, you need not be at all afraid; we are on a sandy beach, and imbedded in the sand; we are not ten paces from the shore, and the tide will leave us dry, and in ten minutes you will all be safe.' Dr. Hutch, a government medical officer, also cheered the passengers. Captain Taylor came down afterwards to give encouragement, and he made a similar representation, which had the effect of greatly allaying the excitment. Great order was consequently kept on board.

"At half-past five o'clock the bumping went on worse than ever, until at last the water came rushing in. When day-light began to peep I was knocked by the force of the waves with great violence against the side of the saloon, and the screams were now dreadful. It was impossible to know what to do. I went on deck, but with the greatest difficulty maintained my equilibrium. At this time a great sea came against the broadside and divided the ship into two, just at the engine-house, as one would smash a pipe stump, and the sea washed quite through her. The two parts 'slewed' round, and became total wrecks. Parties were carried down with the debris, and as many must have been killed as drowned.

"Having made up my mind that I had best jump overboard on the lee side, I attempted to descend by a rope, but fell deep into the water, which was so thickly strewn with portions of the wreck that I had to open up a passage with my head. I was repeatedly thrown ashore, and as often washed back, until some people on shore managed to rescue me. By this time I was almost worn out and insensible."

Such is the sad statement of one who went through the perils of that awful night, and was among the few who were mercifully preserved. But there are some incidents which occurred that are not alluded to in the above narrative.

Most of those who were saved owed their lives, under God, to a Maltese seaman named Joseph Rodgers, who boldly leaped into the sea, and succeeded in conveying a rope to the shore. Had the vessel held together for two or three hours longer, there is little doubt that most, if not all, of the passengers and crew of the *Royal Charter* would have landed in safety; but the rope had been fastened only a short time, and a few only of those nearest to it had gained the rocky ledge, when the vessel broke up and sank. In the course of his evidence given before the commission appointed to inquire into this wreck, Rodgers said :—

"About half-past ten o'clock the watch was called to put the ship about. I went aft to haul in the spanker sheet on the port side. After the main-top-sail was set, they clewed it up again. They went up aloft to furl the sails, and the wind was so strong, that the roving poles were broken. I was nearly pitched off the yard. I came down and said I could not furl the sail ; and Mr. Stephens told me to go back again and make it fast to the yard-arm. Shortly after this the port anchor was let go, and after that the starboard anchor was let go. When both the chains parted, we cut away the masts, and she went ashore. Captain Taylor gave me an order to clear away the port life-boat. The mizzen-stay, being cut away, came down by the run, and fell upon the life-boat. When the ship struck upon the rocks I was on the forecastle, and I asked the boatswain's mate what he was going to do ; and he said, 'Go you ashore, and I will go too.' I went inside the forecastle, and found a chap with a line, and he said, 'Are you going ashore?' I said 'Yes.' I went on the top-gallant forecastle, and made the rope fast round my waist. Mr. Stephens asked me what I was going to do, and wanted to give me a life-buoy, but I said 'No,' and I lowered myself down by a flying jib-boom. I was washed back three times to the ship, but at last succeeded in getting ashore, where I saw some people, and they said, 'Give us the line,' and they took me away. I wanted to stop to pull the hawser ashore, but they would not let me."

For this brave deed the noble fellow afterwards received, from the National Life-boat Institution, a gold medal, a sum of £5, and a vote of thanks engrossed on vellum.

But neither strength nor courage were of any avail on that fatal morning. Captain Withers was right when he said, in endeavouring to calm the fears of the ladies, 'that they were only ten paces from the shore;' but he was wrong when he added that it was a 'sandy beach.' It was a sheer wall of rock which rose against the doomed passengers of the *Royal Charter*, and hurled them back, in all probability lifeless, into the raging sea. A very small narrow ledge at the base of this wall was the spot on which the few who were saved landed.

The work of destruction was complete and almost instantaneous. It was seven in the morning when she broke up. Those who were not killed by being dashed on the rocks, were carried down and killed in the *débris* of the wreck, and in the course of a very few minutes, four hundred and fifty-nine persons were numbered with the dead.

The news of the dreadful wreck spread quickly over the land, carrying the bitterest anguish into hundreds of homes; and, for many weeks afterwards, the road to the remote and scarcely known bay of Moelfra was crowded with visitors to the scene of the disaster; some of whom were attracted by idle curiosity, but, alas! many and many a one hurried along that dreary road with bursting heart and choking sobs, to gaze on the faces of the recovered corpses, and claim their dead.

A little church stands on the bleak coast of Anglesea, not much more than a mile from the scene of the wreck. To this the bodies were conveyed as they were washed ashore, and laid side by side, in their wet and torn garments, on the stone floor. It was a ghastly spectacle, the interior of that church. During those terrible weeks, a silent sermon was preached there such as is seldom addressed to man. In one place lay the body of a stout seaman, with the countenance flushed, as if still in life, and an expression of pain fixed upon it. Close to it lay the form of a woman, and beside her that of a little child. In another spot lay the remains of a man, so mangled as to be scarcely recognisable; and, not far from him, one whose countenance had been completely torn off. Some were contorted, as if they had died in agony; others lay with a peaceful expression, as if they had fallen asleep. But there they all lay in awful silence—the lady and the servant maid, the little child and the full-grown man, the passenger and the seaman, the muscular and the feeble;—some in the full glare of light that fell upon the pavement of the centre aisle, others in the shadow of the pews, and some in gloomy corners of the church. Yet those who went there to search for relations were, for the most part, but little affected -by the fearful sight. Intense anxiety and fear lest they should behold among them the well-remembered faces, absorbed all other emotions. The hurried, nervous glance, the gleam of hope as one after another of these ghastly faces passed under review, and the countenance sought for was not recognised; and the frequent groan of agony, the shriek of despair that resounded within those walls—these things will long dwell in the memory of those who witnessed them, and especially in the memory of that good man, the Rev. Mr. Hughes, the pastor of Llañallgo church, who, with his humane brother, was so kind and tender to the living, and so painstaking and gentle with the dead, at the time of the wreck of the *Royal Charter.*

## CHAPTER XV.

### THE GREAT EASTERN.

THE *Great Eastern* steam ship deserves to be regarded as the eighth wonder of the world, beyond all question. She is, at present, by far the largest vessel in the world, and is the most magnificent creation of naval architecture that was ever launched upon the sea.

Whether this monster ship will fully come up to the expectations of her projectors; whether her vast size will prove an advantage or a disadvantage; or whether her career will show to man that there is a limit to the dimensions of his structures, beyond which it is vain to attempt to pass,—remains yet to be seen. Hitherto, the *Great Eastern* has been attended with—under the circumstances —a fair measure of success. She has crossed the Atlantic and returned to us in safety several times ; and she has weathered, both in and out of harbour, some of the severest storms that ever blew.

The substance of the following account of this interesting ship has been gathered principally from the *Times*, the *Illustrated London News*, and from a pamphlet sold on board, by permission of the proprietors.

The *Great Eastern* was intended for the Indian and Australian route by the Cape of Good Hope. The result of large experience in steam navigation has proved that the size of the ship (when steam is used) must be in proportion

GREAT EASTERN.

to the length of the voyage. Mr. Brunel, the talented engineer to whose genius and perseverance this monster ship owes her existence, acting on this principle, calculated that—the voyage to Australia and back being 22,500 miles—a vessel of 22,500 tons burden (or a ton burden for every mile to be steamed), would require to be built capable of carrying fuel for the entire voyage; it being impossible, without incurring enormous expense, to procure coal for such a vessel at intermediate ports.

The Eastern Steam Navigation Company undertook the Herculean work; the total cost of construction was estimated at £804,522; Mr. Brunel prepared the designs; a spot of ground was chosen on the banks of the Thames, in the building yard of the company at Millwall, and the building was commenced, on the lines laid down by Mr. Scott Russell, on the 1st of May 1854.

Every minute detail of the arrangements and building of this wonder of the world is fraught with interest. The mere preparing of the ground to receive her enormous weight was calculated to fill the minds of men with astonishment. Her supports and scaffoldings, and the machinery by which she was ultimately launched, taxed the skill of her engineers even more than her construction. A very town of workshops, foundries, and forges, sprang into being round her hull, and as this rose, foot by foot, in all its gigantic proportions, the surrounding edifices dwindled down into insignificance, and the busy population of artificers clustered upon her like ants upon a prostrate monarch of the forest trees.

The hull of the *Great Eastern* is built entirely of iron, and is 680 feet in length, 83 feet in breadth, and 60 feet in height, from keel to deck. It is divided transversely into ten separate compartments of 60 feet each, rendered perfectly water-tight by bulkheads, having no openings whatever lower than the second deck; whilst two longitudinal walls of iron, 36 feet apart, traverse 350 feet of the length of the ship.

The mind will be better able to realize the magnitude of these dimensions, if we add that the *Great Eastern* is six times the size of the *Duke of Wellington* line-of-battle ship, that her length is more than three times the height of the Monument, while her breadth is equal to the width of Pall Mall, and a promenade round the deck affords a walk of more than a quarter of a mile.

There is no keel properly so called, but in its place a flat keel-plate of iron, about two feet wide and one inch thick, which runs the entire length from stem to stern. This is the base upon which all the rest is reared, plates and girders alike. The iron plates which form her planking are three-quarters of an inch thick. Up to the water-mark, the hull is constructed with an inner and outer skin, two feet ten inches apart, both skins being made of three-quarter inch plates, except at the bottom, where the plates are an inch thick; and between these, at intervals of six feet, run horizontal webs of iron plates, which bind the two skins together, and thus it may be said that the lower part of the hull is two feet ten inches thick.

This mode of construction adds materially to the safety of the vessel; for, in the event of a collision at sea, the outer skin might be pierced, while the inner might remain intact. This space may also at any time be filled with water, and thus ballast, to the amount of 2500 tons, be obtained.

Some idea of the magnitude and weight of the vessel

may be formed from the fact, that each iron plate weighs about the third of a ton; and is fastened with a hundred iron rivets. About thirty thousand of these plates have been used in her construction, and three million rivets. The fastening of these rivets was one among the many curious operations performed in course of building. The riveting men were arranged in gangs, each gang consisting of two riveters, one holder-up, and three boys. Two boys were stationed at the fire or portable forge, and one with the holder-up. This boy's duty was to receive the red-hot rivet with his pincers from the boy at the forge, and insert it in the hole destined for its reception, the point protruding about an inch. The holder-up immediately placed his heavy hammer against the head of the rivet and held it firmly there, while the two riveters assailed it in front with alternate blows, until the countersunk part of the hole was filled up, after which the protruding head was cut off smooth with the plate; the whole operation scarce occupying a minute. In riveting the double part of the ship, the holder-up and his boy were necessarily in the interior part of the tubes, and passed the whole day in the narrow space between (of two feet ten inches wide) in comparative darkness, having only the glimmer afforded by a single dip candle, and being immediately under the deafening blows of the riveters.

*The deck* of the *Great Eastern* is double, or cellular, after the plan of the Britannia Tubular Bridge. The upper deck runs flush and clear from stem to stern, and he who takes four turns up and down it from stem to stern walks upwards of a mile. The strength of this deck is so enormous that, if the ship were taken up by its two extremities with all its cargo, passengers, coals, and provisions on board, it would sustain the whole. The deck has been covered with teak planking, and has been planed and scrubbed to man-of-war whiteness. Not even a stray rope's end breaks the wonderful effect produced by its immense expanse. Her fleet of small boats (which are about the size of sailing cutters) hang at the davits, ten on each side. There are six masts and five funnels. The three centre square-rigged masts are of iron. They were made by Mr. Finch of Chepstow, and are the finest specimens of masts of the kind that were ever manufactured. Each is made of hollow-wrought iron in eight-feet lengths, strengthened inside by diaphragms of the same material. Between the joints, as they were bolted together, was placed a pad of vulcanized india-rubber, which gives a spring and bouyancy to the whole spar greater than wood, while at the same time it retains all the strength of the iron. The other masts are made of wood, and the canvas that can be spread is no less than 6500 square yards. On deck are four small steam winches or engines, each of which works a pair of cranes on both sides of the vessel; and with these 5000 tons of coals can be hoisted into the vessel in twenty-four hours.

*The engines* and boilers are of immense power and magnitude. There are both screw and paddle engines, the former being capable of working up to 6500 horse power, the latter to 5000; and the speed which has yet been attained is about 18 miles an hour, but it is expected that she will go much faster, and accomplish the voyage between England and Australia in from 33 to 36 days. There are 10 boilers and 112 furnaces. The paddle engines, which were made by Messrs. Scott, Russell, and Co., stand nearly 40 feet high. Each cylinder weighs about 28 tons, and each paddle-wheel is 58 feet in diameter, or considerably larger than the ring in Astley's Circus. The screw engines were manufactured by Messrs. Watt and Co. of Birmingham. They consist of four cylinders of 84 inches diameter, and 4 feet stroke. The screw propeller is 24 feet in diameter and 37 feet pitch; and the engine shaft is 160 feet long, or 12 feet longer than the height of the Duke of York's column. The paddles and screw, when working together at their highest pitch, will exert a force equal to 11,500 horse power, which is sufficient to drive all the cotton mills in Manchester! The consumption of coal to produce this force is estimated at about 250 tons per day. Besides these engines there are also several auxiliary engines for pumping water into the boilers, &c.

*The passenger accommodation* in the *Great Eastern* is very extensive, namely,—800 first-class, from 2000 to 4000 second-class, and about 1200 third-class passengers; or if troops alone were taken, it could accommodate 10,000 men.

*The saloons* are fitted up in the most elaborate and costly manner. The chief saloon is magnificently furnished. It is said that the mirrors, gilding, carpeting, and silk curtains for this apartment alone cost £3000. In the berths, of course, no attempt is made at costly decoration of this kind, though the fittings are good and sufficiently luxurious. The berths are arranged in three classes,—those for parties of six or eight, and these are large rooms; those for parties of four; and the rest in the usual style of double cabins. All are very roomy as cabins go—very lofty, well lit, and those on the outer sides exceedingly well ventilated. On the lower deck the berths are even larger, loftier, and more commodious than those on the upper. Both the berths and saloons here are in fact almost unnecessarily high, having very nearly 15 feet in the clear. The kitchens, pantries, and sculleries are all on the same extensive scale, and fitted with all the large culinary requisites of first-class hotels. The ice-house holds upwards of 100 tons of ice; and the lofty wine vaults—for such, in fact, they are—contain wine enough to form a good freight for an Oporto trader.

*Miscellanea.* In addition to the boats of the *Great Eastern* (twenty in number), she carries two *small screw steamers,* each 100 feet long, 16 feet broad, 120 tons burden, and 40 horse power, suspended aft of the paddle-poxes. These are raised and lowered by the auxiliary engines above referred to, and will be used for embarking and landing passengers.

As the captain's voice could not be heard half way to the bow, even with the aid of the ancient speaking-trumpet, that instrument is supplanted by *semaphore* signals by day, and *coloured lamps* by night; the *electric telegraph* is also used in connection with the engine-rooms. There are ten *anchors,* four of them being Trotman's patent, weighing seven tons each. The *cables* are each 400 fathoms long, and their united weight is 100 tons. The *tonnage* of the *Great Eastern* is 18,500 register, and 22,500 tons builders' measurement. *The Crew* at first consisted of 13 officers, 17 engineers, a sailing master, and a purser, 400 men, and two or three surgeons, all under the command of the late Captain W. Harrison (formerly of the Cunard's line).

*The launch* of this leviathan was a most formidable undertaking, and was accomplished by means of powerful hydraulic rams which propelled the vessel down the launching "ways." The ship rested on two gigantic cradles, and was forced sidewise down the inclined plane, until she floated on the river. By a complication of ingenious contrivances the great ship was regulated in her descent so as to proceed slowly and regularly down the ways. Several unsuccessful attempts were made to launch her, and several of the hydraulic rams broke down ere she floated on the bosom of Old Father Thames, and the cost of this operation alone is said to have been nearly £100,000.

*The trial of the engines,* both screw and paddle, took place for the first time on the 8th of August, 1859, when the completion of the vessel was celebrated by a banquet on board. The first movement of the gigantic cranks and cylinders of the paddle engines was made precisely at half-past one, when the great masses slowly rose and fell as noiselessly as the engines of a Greenwich boat, but exerting in their revolutions what seemed to be an almost irresistible power. There was no noise, no vibration, nor the slightest sign of heating, and the tremendous frame of ironwork sprang at once into life and motion, with as much ease as if every rod and crank had been worked for the last ten years.

*The trial trip* of the *Great Eastern* was an event that excited intense interest all over the kingdom. For the first time, she cast off her moorings on Wednesday morning (the 7th September), and reached the Nore on Thursday, where she anchored for the night before proceeding to sea. On Friday morning, at ten minutes past nine, she started on her first salt-water voyage. A conviction of the extreme steadiness of the vessel must speedily have seized every one on board. There was no perceptible motion of any kind. The giant ship was speedily surrounded by yachts, tugs, fishing smacks, and, indeed, by a representative of almost every kind of vessel which is prevalent at the Nore. These accompanied her as far on her way as their limited sailing powers would permit. Although there were sharp squalls and a chopping sea nearly all through the trip, not the slightest inconvenience was felt by any of the visitors, not even among the fairer portion of the passengers. The morning, which was rather fine at starting, suddenly became clouded, and the shifting squalls increased in violence. Though the squally state of the weather damped the pleasure of all on board, yet it afforded an opportunity of trying the properties of the ship, now under paddle as well as screw; and it was the wish of Mr. Scott Russell and all on board to meet a good gale of wind. At a moderate computation, the distance from the deck to the water could not be much less than 40 feet, while the vessel is nearly 700 feet long. This area would, of course, present an enormous surface to the force of the wind, and formed the subject of considerable discussion as to the effect it would have on her sea-going qualities. The ship was as stiff and steady as though she still remained on her cradles in the Isle of Dogs, and her course was as calm and true as though she were on a lake without a capful of wind.

It is said that at one portion of the voyage she steamed 19 miles an hour.

*The explosion.* All went well till the ship had passed Folkstone. About half-past five o'clock, while the majority of the passengers were on deck, and a few gentlemen only remained in the dining saloon, a tremendous explosion occurred, and in an instant showers of broken glass, and fragments of wood and iron, came crashing through the skylight. Those in the cabin rushed on deck. The ship was still pressing onward; at either end all was still and deserted, while in the centre all was smoke, fire, vapour, and confusion. The great funnel, of eight tons weight, had been shot up as if from a mortar, and fell on the deck broken in two pieces. The whole centre of the ship seemed to be only one vast chasm, and from it was belching up steam, dust, and something that looked like incipient conflagration. Captain Harrison acted nobly on this terrible occasion. He had been standing on the bridge overhead, looking into the binnacle, and the moment he heard the report, and whilst the destructive shower was still falling fast, he jumped upon the deck, and ordered an immediate descent to the ladies' saloon, in the firm conviction that they were all there as on the previous evening. But many of the men were panic-stricken, and had already shrunk away from the explosion. A foolish passenger had raised a cry of "The boats," and, assisted by some of the sailors, was madly attempting to let them down. In one moment all would have been lost, for the rush to the boats would have been general, and hundreds would have been drowned, whilst the noble ship would have been left to certain destruction. But the voice of the captain was heard like a trumpet, calling out, " Men, to your duty; officers, to your posts; give me a rope, and let six men follow me ! " The effect of this short address was electric. In an instant he had slid down the rope into the saloon, followed by his brave boatswain Hawkins, and six volunteers were not long wanted for the forlorn hope. One after another he dashed open the gilded panels, but the splendid apartment had, strange to say, only two inhabitants, his little daughter Edith, and her pet dog. It was the reward of his gallantry that his own child should be thus the one to be so providentially saved. But even then he did not for a moment lose his self-command. Snatching up the child, and with one glance seeing she was unharmed, he exclaimed, " Pass her along to the deck, there are more rooms to be searched." In this way did he move about rapidly, but coolly, and did not again return to the deck until he had satisfied himself that not a single woman was in the burning, steaming, suffocating chamber. His intimate friend, Mr. Trotman, who had followed him down almost immediately, found the poor lap-dog moaning under a heap of ruins, and was the means of restoring it to its little mistress.

The magnificent saloon was a mass of torn and shattered furniture, mirrors, and ,ornaments. Had the passengers adjourned to this apartment after dinner, instead of to the deck, the consequences would have been awful.

An eye-witness describes the scene of devastation as follows :—

"The mirrors which formed the covering of the funnel which had been the cause of so much mischief were literally smashed to atoms, and large fragments of the broken glass were hurled upon deck, a long distance aft of the paddle-wheels. The ornamental bronzed columns which supported the gilt cornices and elaborate ornamentation were either struck down or bent into the most fantastic shapes ; the flooring, consisting of three-inch planks, was upheaved in several places ; the gangways leading to the sleeping cabins at the sides were shot away ; the hand-rails were gone, and the elegant carpet concealed beneath a chaos of fragments of finery. The books on the shelves of the library remained unmoved, the piano was thrown on one side, and the floor presented huge upheaved and rent chasms, through which might be seen the still greater ruin in the lower cabin. Below the saloon, or drawing-room, is the saloon of the lower deck, which was, of course, traversed by the same funnel as the one above it. On each side of these spacious saloons were small staircases leading to blocks of sleeping cabins, scarcely one of which would have been without its two or more occupants a few hours later in the evening, They were now blown down like a house of cards. The furniture which they contained formed heaps of dislocated chairs, and wash-stands, and basins; the doors were off their hinges, the partitions were forced outward, the staircases leading to them had to be sought in the splinters and broken wood which lay in heaps in the lower saloon."

The unhappy men who were working in the stoke-holes and tending the furnaces were the sufferers by this catastrophe. Believing that one of the boilers had exploded, fears were entertained that the whole body of stokers and engineers attending the paddle engines were killed. Mr. Trotman went down the air-shaft communicating with the other boilers. Seeing by the light of the furnace a number of men moving about, he inquired if they were all right, and the response sent up from these lowest depths of the ship was, "All right at present, but we don't know how long." They were told to keep quiet, and stay where they were; that they could be of no service on deck, and all would be well in a few minutes. The gallant fellows remained by their fiery furnaces with resolute goodwill. In the case of the firemen tending the other set of boilers a very different scene was taking place. Ropes were thrown down, and one by one, wounded, bleeding, and staggering men were drawn up, their black, begrimed faces forming a ghastly contrast with scalded portions of their limbs and bodies. The men were taken aft to the hospital, and to the cabins, where mattresses and blankets were laid for them.

Two or three of these poor fellows walked up to the deck almost, if not quite, unassisted. Their aspect told its own tale, and none who had ever seen blown-up men before could fail to know at a glance that some had only two or three hours to live. Where not grimed by the smoke or ashes, the peculiar bright, soft whiteness of the face, hands, or breast, told at once that the skin, though unbroken, had in fact been boiled by the steam. One man walked along, and seemed quite unconscious that the flesh of his thighs (most probably by the ashes from the furnace) was burnt in deep holes. To some one who came to his assistance he said quietly, "I am all right. There are others worse than me; go and look after them." This poor man was the first to die. It was seen at once that but little hope existed for many, if not the majority of the sufferers, who were twelve in number. Most of them seemed very restless and almost, if not quite, delirious; but a few of those whose injuries were likely to be more immediately fatal remained quiet, half unconscious, or at most only asking to be covered up, as if they felt the cold. For these latter all knew that nothing whatever could be done, as, in fact, they were then dying.

The explosion had occurred in the double casing round the bottom of one of the funnels. We have not space to describe this minutely, and by the general reader the description, were it given, would scarce be understood; but it is well to remark that the piece of machinery which caused the deplorable accident had been previously condemned in strong terms by competent judges, and there is no doubt that the hot-water casing round the funnel ought never to have been there.

After the catastrophe the *Great Eastern* kept on her course as though nothing had happened, although the force of the explosion was sufficient to have sent any other ship to the bottom. The damage is estimated at £5000. She arrived at Portland on the 10th, and remained there for some time undergoing repairs. Afterwards she continued her trial trip to Holyhead, where she arrived on the 10th of October. The results of the trial, excepting, of course, the accident, were most satisfactory. Her speed under disadvantageous circumstances had been good, and her engines had worked admirably. Against a gale of head wind she went as steadily as if in harbour, but with the wind a-beam she rolled considerably. Altogether there was good reason to hope that the *Great Eastern* would fulfil the sanguine expectations of her warmest admirers.

The following account of the continuation of her trial trip from Portland to Holyhead, as gathered from the *Times*, is exceedingly interesting :—When steam was up and all ready for starting from Portland, the crew were sent forward to heave up the anchor. Eighty men sufficed to drag the *Great Eastern* up to and over her moorings. Bringing the anchor out of the ground, however, was not so easily managed; and it was not till all the musical resources known to sailors on such occasions were nearly exhausted that the tenacious gripe of Trotman's patent was released, when a slow drift with the tide showed that the great ship was again set free. In another minute, without shouting, confusion, or hurry of any kind, and with less noise than is made by a 100-ton coaster, a slight vibration through the ship, with a thin line of foam astern, showed that the screw engines were at work and the vessel once more under way. With such ease, with such perfect quietness and good order was everything accomplished, that the occasional cheering from the yachts and steamers was almost the first token given to those on board that the

trial trip had commenced.   At a quarter to four the "way"
on the vessel was rapid; her head went round like turning
a pleasure-boat, and so little sign was given of the ship
being under steam that it seemed rather as if the breakwater had got adrift and was slowly floating past, than that
the monster vessel was really cleaving the blue waves with
a force which, as yet, we have seen no wind or sea to resist
or check.   Directly the anchor was fished, Captain Harrison passed the word to steam ahead with both engines
easily, and the wheels began their revolutions, slowly at
first, but, nevertheless, making a track of foam upon the
water such as they never made on the first start from Dept-
ford to the Nore.   The accession of speed from working
the paddles was at first but slight—not from any want of
power, however, but simply from the fact that both engines
were ordered to work slowly, and though propelling the
great ship at something like eleven knots, were really scarcely
driving at indicated half-speed.

Quitting Portland, it was necessary to make rather a
round turn on leaving the breakwater, as right ahead on
the starboard bow was a small light-ship, looking like the
skeleton of a vessel, and marking the presence of a dangerous shoal, known by the most appropriate and significant
name of "The Shambles."   Inside this lay a long and turbid ridge of angry water, where the race of Portland ran,
and where a deep rolling swell, like the Bay of Biscay on a
reduced scale, kept tumbling and breaking into spray like
drifts of snow against the high, gaunt cliffs.   It, however,
required no actual watching of the low green mounds of
water, which seemed butting against the coast, to convince
all on board that the *Great Eastern* was at sea.   To the
infinite relief and comfort of all the passengers, the vessel

began to yield to reason, and to behave as much like another ship as she could consistently with her size. It would be too much to say she rolled at this time, for when the *Great Eastern* rolls, if ever she does roll, travellers may depend upon her accomplishing something in that peculiar style of ocean navigation quite in proportion to her bulk ; but one thing is certain—that she went from side to side sufficiently to show that she was susceptible of the motion of the water, and that if ever she steams across a beam sea, she is likely to move to it with a will, though slowly and easily.

Continuing for a considerable time under little more than half steam, the *Great Eastern* averaged more than thirteen knots (fifteen miles) an hour. The best guide to the rapidity of the ship's progress was the way in which she passed fast-sailing schooners and overhauled the steamers. At this time nearly all the swell had ceased, and the monster ship was rushing over what to her were the mimic waves, and leaving less wake upon the waters than is caused in the Thames by a Gravesend boat. The only peculiarity about her progress was the three distinct lines of frothy water which her screw and paddles made, and which, stretching out in the clear moonlight like a broad highway, seemed as if the *Great Eastern* had fulfilled her purpose, and really bridged the sea.

For a considerable part of the way the paddles were working easily, at from nine to ten, and the screw at from thirty-two to thirty-four revolutions per minute. It will give most readers a better idea of the tremendous nature of the size and speed of the engines which worked so easily when it is said that, at ten revolutions, the paddle-wheels dashed through the water at something like 1600 feet per minute, and the screw revolved at 2500. When accomplishing this, the consumption of fuel was at the rate of 250 tons a day for both engines, the indicated power being above 5000 horses —about 2000 horses for the paddles, and a little over 3500 for the screw. In order to secure her going at full speed, however, under such circumstances, the great ship should have been down by the stern at least eighteen inches more than she really was, for not less than a foot of the screw-blades was out of the water, and the slip or loss of power was of course very great. Off the coast of Cornwall, the swell caused her to roll very considerably as long as she was a-beam of the long swell.

Soon after this a small brig was seen right under the starboard bow. As usual with these small coasters, she was showing no light and keeping no look-out, and but for the anxious vigilance exercised on board the big ship, the brig would have been under the waves in two minutes more. Her escape was narrow enough, and nothing short of the instant stoppage of the engines and actually reversing the screw saved her from swift destruction. She drifted from under the starboard paddle within twenty yards—quite close enough to enable Captain Harrison to speak to her master, and to express a very strong opinion on his style of navigation and conduct generally.

Towards the close of the trip all the fore and aft sails were set. The look of her vast spread of canvas and the extraordinary effect it produced as one stood at the wheel-house and gazed beneath the long vista of brown sails stretched to the very utmost, and sending off the wind with the sustained roar of a volcano, was something almost indescribable. No mere description could convey a fair idea of the curious effect of the long unbroken avenue of masts, sails, and funnels,—like a whole street of steam-ships, if such a term is fairly applicable.

The rate of going throughout the whole trip was very satisfactory. Allowing for the want of trim on the part of the vessel, and consequent absence of immersion in both screw and paddles, it was calculated from this data by all the nautical authorities on board, that, in proper condition, the vessel might be depended on for eighteen miles an hour throughout a long voyage, and under steam alone. That, in a strong and favourable breeze she would at times accomplish · eighteen knots, or more than twenty-one miles an hour, there was no reason to doubt.

Among other tests to which the *Great Eastern* was subjected was the terrible storm of the 25th and 26th October. She lay at anchor in the harbour of Holyhead during that storm. So fierce was the gale that a large part of the break-water was destroyed, and several vessels went down inside the harbour, while some were driven on shore. For one hour the big ship was as near destruction as she is ever likely to be. Her salvation, under God, was due to the experience and energy of Captain Harrison and his officers. During the whole gale the captain was on the watch, sounding the lead to see if she dragged, and keeping the steam up to be in readiness to put to sea at a moment's notice. The gale roared and whistled through the rigging with indescribable fury. The captain, in trying to pass along the deck, was thrown down, and his waterproof coat was blown to ribbons. The cabin skylights were thrown open with a fearful crash, the glass broken, and deluges of rain and spray poured into the saloons. Two anchors were down, one seven tons, the other three, with eighty and sixty fathoms of chain respectively; but the ground was known to be bad and the lee shore rocky, while the waves came curling and writhing into the harbour, straining the cables to the utmost, and dashing against the rocks like avalanches of snow. The dash of these billows on the breakwater was like the roaring of artillery. All this time the red light at the end of the breakwater shone out cheerily in the midst of a turmoil of spray. At last masses of the timber-work and solid masonry gave way. The gale rose to its fiercest, and one huge billow came rolling in; it towered a hundred feet above the breakwater; it fell, and the red light was seen no more. The danger was now imminent. The cables could evidently bear no more, and the gale was increasing; so the screw was set going, but the wreck of timber from the breakwater fouled it and brought it to a dead lock. Then the wind veered round more to the north-east, sending a tremendous swell into the harbour, and the *Great Eastern* began to roll heavily. In this extremity the paddle-engines were set going, and the ship was brought up to her anchors, one of which was raised for the purpose of being dropped in a better position. At this moment the cable of the other anchor parted, and the great ship drifted swiftly toward what seemed certain destruction; but the heavy anchor was let go, and the engines turned on full speed. She swung round head to wind, and was brought up. This was the turning-point. The gale slowly abated, and the *Great Eastern* was saved, while all round her the shores and harbour were strewn with wrecks.

After the gale the *Great Eastern* started on her return trip to Southampton, which she reached in safety on the morning of the 3d November. In this, as in her previous experiences, the mighty ship was well tested, and her good and bad points in some degree proved. At the very outset the steam gear for aiding in lifting the anchors broke down, and one of the anchors refusing to let go, was broken in half. The condenser of the paddle engines seems to have been proved too small in this trip. For some time she went against a stiff head-wind and sea—which is now well known to be the great ship's forte—with perfect steadiness ; but on getting into the channel she *rolled* slowly but decidedly, as if bowing—acknowledging majestically the might of the Atlantic's genuine swell. Here, too, a wave actually over-topped her towering hull, and sent a mass of *green* water inboard ! But her roll was peculiarly *her own*, and wonderfully easy.

The vessel made eighteen knots an hour, she was under perfect command, even in narrow and intricate channels, and despite her varied mishaps and trials passed through this stormy period of her infancy with credit.

*Disaster to Great Eastern in September* 1861.—Having made three successful voyages to America, the *Great Eastern*, after all her troubles, was beginning to establish her reputation, to confirm the hopes of her friends and silence the cavils of her enemies, when the bad fortune that has been her portion from the cradle, once more overwhelmed her, and shook, if it did not altogether destroy, the confidence in her capabilities which the public had been beginning tardily to entertain.

There is nothing more difficult to ascertain than the true state of the case—with reference to culpability, accidental circumstance, inherent or incidental weakness, negligence, unavoidable risks, &c.,—in such a disaster as that which happened to the great ship in September of 1861. And nothing could be more unfair than to pass judgment on her without a full knowledge of the minute particulars, and, moreover, a pretty fair capacity to understand such details and their various relations. Before proceeding with the narrative of the event referred to, we may remark that while, on the one hand, it may be argued, with great plausibility, that her numerous disasters and misfortunes prove very clearly that she is unfitted for the navigation of the sea, it may, on the other hand, be argued with equal plausibility, that the very fact of her having come through such appalling trials unconquered, though buffetted, is strong presumptive evidence that she is eminently fitted for her work, and that, under ordinary circumstances and *proper* management, she would do it well. It is believed that any other vessel afloat would have been sunk had she been exposed to the same storm *under similar circumstances.* It must be borne in mind that although other vessels weathered the same storm successfully, they did not do so with their rudder and rudder-posts gone, their captains and part of their crews new to them, and their chain cables, cabin furniture, and other material, left as totally unsecured as if she had been a river steamer about to start on a few hours' trip.

We do not pretend to be an apologist for the ship; but we would deprecate the passing of a hasty judgment on a vessel which may, indeed, come at length to merit our condemnation, but which up to the present time is strictly entitled to our attentive regard and admiration.

On Tuesday the 10th of September the *Great Eastern* left Liverpool for America with 400 passengers and a large, though not a full, general cargo. Between 100 and 200 of the passengers occupied the berths in the principal cabins, the remainder of them occupied the intermediate and steerage cabins.

All went on prosperously until the Thursday, when, as

the ship was in full steam and sail, she encountered a terrific gale about 280 miles to the west of Cape Clear, and, in spite of the best seamanship, she failed to ride over the storm, which, with tremendous fury, swept away both her paddles. Simultaneously the top of the rudder-post, a bar of iron ten inches in diameter, was suddenly wrenched off, and her steering gear being also carried away, she broached to and lay like a huge log in the trough of the sea. From Thursday evening until two o'clock on Sunday, her bulwarks almost touching the water, she rolled about like a disabled hulk, the passengers and crew expecting that she would every moment go down. The working and rolling of the vessel, at one instant of dread, displaced and destroyed all the furniture of the cabin and saloons, and broke it to pieces, throwing the passengers pell mell about the cabin. Everything that occupied the upper deck was washed away, and a large part of the passengers' luggage was destroyed. Between twenty and thirty of those who were on board, including several ladies, had limbs and ribs fractured, with numerous cuts and bruises. One of the cow sheds, with two cows in it, was washed into the ladies' cabin, together with other things on board, and caused indescribable consternation and confusion.

On Sunday evening, after two days of terrible suspense, a temporary steering gear was fitted up, and the disabled vessel with her distressed crew made for Cork harbour, steaming with her screw at nine knots an hour. Her flag of distress was sighted at about three o'clock in the afternoon of Tuesday, off the Old Head of Kinsale, and H.M. ship *Advice* at once steamed out to her assistance and towed her to within a mile of the lighthouse off Cork Harbour by about nine o'clock.

Such is a general outline of this disaster—one which is

rendered all the more remarkable from the circumstance that the vessel had only been recently surveyed by the officers of the marine department of the Board of Trade, when new decks and other requirements were carried out and completed at a cost of £15,000.

The scene in the grand saloon, as described in detail by various passengers, was absolutely terrific. None of the furniture had been secured, and when the gale became violent and the rolling of the vessel increased, sideboards, tables, chairs, stools, crockery, sofas, and passengers were hurled with fearful violence from side to side in a promiscuous heap. When it is said that at each roll the top platform of the paddle-boxes dipped into the sea, any one who has seen the towering sides of the *Great Eastern* may form some conception of the angle of the decks, and the riot of unfastened articles that continued below during the greater part of the gale. The destruction was universal. The largest mirror in the grand saloon, which was about twelve feet high, was smashed to pieces by a gentleman going head foremost into it. Although much bruised and cut, strange to say he was not seriously injured. The chandeliers fell from the ceiling and the crashes they made in falling added to the general din. One of the other mirrors was smashed by a large stove. Some of the passengers escaping from the dining-room were dashed against the iron balconies which gave way with the pressure, and falling on the glass flooring at the sides dashed it to atoms. The noise and turmoil of destruction below, together with the howling of the tempest above and the dashing of spray over the decks whence it flowed in copious streams down into the cabins, formed a scene which cannot be fully conceived except by those who witnessed it.

On deck the confusion was equally great and destructive. Many of the boats were carried away ; the great chain cables rolled from side to side until they were actually polished bright by the friction, while they were a source of perpetual danger to the crew in the performance of their duties. The oil tanks broke loose, and after tumbling about for a time fell down through the upper hatchway. And the two cows that fell with their cowshed down into the ladies' cabin were killed by the violence of the shock. The chief cook was flung against one of the paddle-boxes, and having put out his hand to save himself, had his wrist sprained. He was then flung towards the other side, and coming against a stanchion in the way, had his leg fractured in three places. One lady had a rib fractured ; another her shoulder dislocated ; another her wrist. These are only specimens selected to show what the poor people were subjected to. It is said that there were twenty-two fractures altogether, among passengers and crew, besides innumerable cuts and bruises. The cabins were flooded to the depth of several feet, and broken articles of furniture floated about everywhere. The luggage in the luggage room, which had not been secured, was hurled about until trunks, boxes, valises, &c., striking against each other and against the sides of the compartment, were utterly destroyed,—the very leather of the trunks being torn into small shreds.

Throughout all this terrible scene the passengers behaved, with one or two exceptions, admirably. The ladies especially displayed great courage, remaining in accordance with the desires intimated to them, in their cabins, while the gentlemen did their best to keep order. On the Friday they appointed a sort of committee or police force, of upwards of twenty strong, who took the duty in turns of going round the vessel, keeping order, carrying information to, and re-assuring, the ladies and children. Four only of these, who were called directors, had the privilege of speaking to the captain during the storm, thus saving him from the annoyance of repeated and ceaseless questioning.

The crew also did their duty nobly. Captain Walker acted throughout with calmness, courage, and good judgment, and from the tenor of resolutions passed at an indignation meeting held by the passengers after their return into port, it would appear that they entirely exonerated him from any blame in reference to the disaster. The fitting up of temporary steering gear, which was begun on the Sunday when the storm moderated, was a work of great difficulty and danger. It was accomplished chiefly through the courage and cleverness of two men, John Carroll and Patrick Grant, who volunteered for it and were let down over the stern at the imminent risk of their lives ; and an American gentleman, Mr. Towle, a civil engineer, rendered great assistance in superintending and directing the work.

It was not until two o'clock on Sunday morning that the vessel got up steam in her screw boilers and steered for Cork Harbour. The whole of the iron work of both paddle wheels was carried entirely away. The ladder leading up to the larboard paddle-box was twisted in an extraordinary manner. The boats on the starboard side were all gone, and those on the other side were hanging loosely from their fastenings. Altogether the great ship presented a most melancholy spectacle as she was towed into port.

At the meeting of the passengers already referred to, the first resolution was expressive of their grateful acknowledgments to Almighty God for his kind care in protecting them during the storm, and bringing them in safety out of their danger. The second condemned the directors, and stated that "The *Great Eastern* was sent to sea thoroughly unprepared to face the storms which every one must expect to meet with in crossing the Atlantic ; and that, if it had not been for the extraordinary strength of the hull, and the skill which was manifested in the construction of the vessel and its engines, in all human probability every soul on board would have perished."

It has been said that if the ship had been more deeply laden she would have weathered the gale more easily. This, if true, is an argument in her favour. But in viewing the whole circumstances of this and previous disasters, and, indeed, the vessel's career from the launch to the present day we cannot avoid being deeply impressed with the fact that the *Great Eastern has not yet had fair play.* In her construction and general arrangements there have been some grave, and numerous more or less trivial errors. From first to last there has been a little pardonable, and a great deal of culpable, not to say gross, mismanagement; but the *Great Eastern* steam ship cannot yet, with justice, be pronounced a failure. It is possible that she may yet live to ride out many a wild Atlantic storm, and perchance become—who knows ?—the first of a race of ponderous giants who shall yet walk the deep,—to the utter confusion of timid croakers, and to the immense advantage of the world.

SHIP EMBEDDED IN ICEBERGS.

# CHAPTER XVI.

### DANGERS IN THE NORTHERN SEAS.

THE mysteries and the wonders of the polar regions were first made known to us by those adventurous mariners whose chief pursuit was the capture of the whale ; and the people who first prosecuted the whale-fishery as a commercial pursuit were undoubtedly the Frenchmen who dwelt on the shores of the Bay of Biscay in the twelfth century.

Those Frenchmen of the middle ages, however, attacked only such whales as frequented their own seas ; the English and the Dutch were the first who followed that finned giant called the " true whale " to his own peculiarly loved haunts in the frozen seas of the north, and there, amid perils such as other navigators had not even dreamed of, attacked and captured so many fish that the trade soon became, and has ever since continued, extremely lucrative.

It is not our purpose to record the history of the whale fishery. Passing from this preliminary reference to its commencement, we proceed to give a few anecdotes illustrative of the peculiar dangers to which those mariners are exposed who push their ships into the Northern Seas. The substance of the following paragraphs is gathered from an interesting account of the northern whale fishery in the well-known work entitled, "Polar Seas and Regions."

## DANGERS FROM ICE.

A furious storm assailed one of the whale-ships, which belonged to the Dutch, when near the edge of the Spitzbergen ice in the year 1639. Though the ship was violently agitated, the captain succeeded in steering her clear of the great bank and thought himself out of danger, when suddenly two immense icebergs appeared before him right in the course in which the wind was driving his vessel. An attempt was made to penetrate between the bergs, but the vessel was driven against one with a shock so terrible that it was immediately disabled and seemed about to sink.

By cutting away one of the masts, she was enabled to right; but as she continued to take in water rapidly, several of the boats were launched. These being instantly overcrowded, sank, and all in them perished. Those who remained found their condition becoming more and more desperate. The fore part of the vessel sank so deep in the water that it became almost impossible to stand on deck; while one of the masts broke, fell into the sea, and carried a number of the crew along with it, involving them in the fate of those who had gone before. At length the stern separated from the rest of the ship, and here again several men were lost. The

SHIP BETWEEN TWO ICEBERGS.

survivors still adhered to the shattered wreck, but one after another was washed off by the fury of the waves; half dead with cold, and unable to retain their grasp of the ropes and bulwarks, they dropped into the sea. The crew of eighty-six was thus speedily reduced to twenty-nine, when the ship suddenly changed its position, and assumed one in which they could more easily keep their footing. on board. Soon after this the sea calmed, and during the respite thus afforded some of the wretched men experienced an irresistible tendency to sleep—to some who gave way it proved the fatal sleep of extreme cold from which they never awoke. One man suggested the construction of a raft, which was accordingly framed with much difficulty, and contrary to the captain's advice. Happily no sooner was it launched than the waves swallowed it up. The remnant of the vessel encountered next night another severe gale ; and the sufferings of the crew from cold, and hunger, and burning thirst were so extreme that death in every form seemed now to have encompassed them. In the morning, however, a sail was descried ; their signals were understood, and twenty survivors were, after two days and two nights of extreme suffering and danger, restored to safety.

*The wreck of the Bleacher*, in 1670, is another instance of the dangers encountered among the ice by whale ships. This vessel,—commanded by Captain Pit—was during a gale driven against the ice with such violence that all her rigging was instantly dashed to pieces. Soon after the catastrophe twenty-nine of the crew quitted the ship, and leaping by the help of poles from one fragment of ice to another, contrived to reach the main field. The captain, with seven men, remained on board and endeavoured to open a passage ; but the ship soon struck again, when they were obliged to get into a boat and forsake her. The snow fell so fast and thick at first that they could scarcely see each other, but the weather cleared soon after, and they descried their comrades on the ice, who threw a whale line to them and dragged them to the same spot. Here they waited twelve hours, and then took to their boats and were most providentially saved, soon after, by a Dutch vessel.

Many hundreds of whale ships have been destroyed by the ice in every possible variety of manner, and many thousands of lives have been sacrificed, since the fishery began. Sometimes they are lost in the midst of furious storms; sometimes in beautiful calm weather by the closing of the ice and the crushing in of their sides. This latter disaster is called "nipping," and very few ships return from the polar seas without bearing the marks of having been nipped more or less severely.

A vessel was lying becalmed in the ice on one occasion. The captain was pacing the deck, when the steward summoned him to breakfast. He glanced round on the ice-laden sea before going down. All was calm, bright, and peaceful. The ship lay in a narrow channel of water between two immense fields of ice. Seeing nothing to alarm him the captain descended to the cabin, but five minutes had not elapsed when the ice closed gradually in—so gently as to be scarcely perceptible; but when the edges of the two vast fields touched the ship she was crushed together like an egg shell. The crew had barely time to rush on deck and leap out on the ice when the fields quietly separated, and the vessel sank between them. The whole thing was done in little more than ten minutes, and the crew were left without food on the floating ice. Fortunately another vessel was near and picked them up.

Something similar to this happened to the *Breadalbane* transport, a small vessel sent out in connection with one of the recent Franklin searching expeditions. The men had just time to leap upon the ice when her timber and beams were crushed together "as one would crush a box of lucifer matches in one's hand."

## THE DANGERS OF THE WHALE FISHERY.

Great though the perils encountered in the ice by whalers undoubtedly are, they are not equal to the risk run during the encounters with whales.

The whale is immensely powerful, and were it aware of its own strength man would not dare to attack it; but the Creator has seen fit to bestow upon the northern whale a timid and gentle disposition, so that it rather flies from, than courts attack. The sperm whale of the Southern Seas is much fiercer—hence the South Sea whale fishery is much more dangerous.

Sometimes, however, the northern whale exerts his utmost force in violent and convulsive struggles, and everything that comes into contact with him when thus enraged is destroyed in an instant.

One day, in the year 1807, the elder Mr. Scoresby was engaged in attacking a whale. The fish had been struck with a harpoon and had dived; soon it reappeared on the surface, but in such a violent state of agitation that they dared not for some time approach to throw a second harpoon. Mr. Scoresby courageously undertook to attack it in a boat alone, and was fortunate enough to strike another harpoon into it. Meanwhile the first boat had approached too close. The agonized whale brandished its tail in the air, and brought it down just over the bow on which the harpooneer was standing. The man had presence of mind enough to dive into the sea and scarcely had he done so when the tail came down like a thunder clap on the spot he had left and cut the boat entirely asunder. Happily all the others escaped injury and were picked up by another boat. The harpooneer returned to the surface, also unhurt.

When a whale is harpooned it usually darts away with incredible speed, dragging the line after it with such velocity that the mere friction of it against the head of the boat would set the wood on fire were not a man stationed to pour water upon it. One of the greatest and commonest risks run by whalemen is getting entangled in the line as it flies out, and having a limb torn off or being dragged into the sea and drowned. An accident of this kind happened to a sailor belonging to a Greenock ship. Happening to step into the centre of a coil of running rope his foot was instantly carried off, and he was obliged to have the lower part of his leg amputated.

On another occasion a harpooneer belonging to the *Henrietta*, had carelessly cast part of the line beneath his feet, when a sudden dart of the whale caused it to coil round his body. He had just time to cry out, " Clear away the line ! O dear ! " when he was almost cut in two, dragged overboard and never more seen.

A very terrible accident of this kind happened to a harpooneer belonging to Scoresby in the year 1822. It is thus described by that intrepid whaleman :—

" The whale they pursued led them into a vast shoal of the species. They were indeed so numerous that their blowing was incessant ; and they believed they could not have seen less than a hundred. Fearful of alarming them without striking any, they remained for some time motionless, watching for a favourable opportunity to commence an attack. One of them at last rose so near the boat of which William Carr was harpooneer, that he ventured to pull towards it, though it was meeting him, and afforded but an indifferent chance of success. He, however, fatally for himself, succeeded in harpooning it. The boat and fish passing each other with great rapidity after the stroke, the line was jerked out of its place, and, instead of " running " over the stern, was thrown over the gunwale ; its pressure in this unfavourable position so carreened the boat, that the side sank below the water, and it began to fill.

" In this emergency the harpooneer, who was a fine, active fellow, seized the bight of the line, and attempted to relieve the boat, by restoring it to its place ; but by some singular circumstance which could not be accounted for, a turn of the line flew over his arm, and in an instant dragged him overboard, and plunged him under water to rise no more ! So sudden was the accident that only one man, who had his eye upon him at the time, was aware of what had happened, so that, when the boat righted, which it immediately did, though half full of water, they all at once, on looking round at an exclamation from the man who had seen him launched overboard, inquired what had got Carr ! It is scarcely possible to imagine a death more awfully sudden and unexpected. The murderous bullet, when it makes its way through the air with a velocity that renders it invisible, and seems not to require a moment for its flight, rarely produces such instantaneous destruction. The velocity of the whale on its first descent is usually (as I have proved by experiment) about eight or nine miles per hour or thirteen to fifteen feet per second. Now, as this unfortunate man was occupied in adjusting the line at the very water's edge, where it must have been perfectly tight, in consequence of the obstruction to its running out of the boat, the interval between the fastening of the line about him and his disappearance could not have exceeded the third part of a second of time ; for

in one second only he must have been dragged to the depth
of ten or twelve feet !   The accident was indeed so instantaneous that he had not time for the least exclamation ;
and the person who witnessed his extraordinary removal,
observed that it was so exceedingly quick, that although his
eye was upon him at the instant, he could scarcely distinguish the object as it disappeared."

WHALE TOSSING A BOAT.

Sometimes a whale on being harpooned whirls his powerful tail, or "flukes" underneath a boat and sends it high
into the air, as represented in the above engraving.   One
would imagine that in such circumstances every man in the
boat would be killed or seriously injured.   Yet such is not
the case.   The crew are thrown violently into the water,

and a leg or an arm may be broken, but usually they swim about or cling to portions of the wreck until picked up by other boats.

A more common occurrence than the above is the boat being dragged under water by the whale when the line is all run out. In the year 1812, a boat's crew belonging to the *Resolution* harpooned a whale near the margin of a floe, or field of ice. Being supported by a second boat they felt much at their ease, there being scarcely any instance in which the assistance of a third boat was required in such circumstances. Soon, however, a signal was made for more line, and, as Mr. Scoresby was pushing towards them with his utmost speed, four oars—the signal of the greatest distress —were raised. The boat was now seen with its bows on a level with the water, while the harpooneer, from the friction of the line was enveloped in smoke. At length, when the relief was within a hundred yards, the crew were seen to throw their jackets on the nearest ice, and then leap into the sea ; after which the boat rose into the air, and, making a majestic curve, disappeared beneath the waves with all the line attached to it. The crew, however, were saved. A vigorous pursuit was immediately commenced ; and the whale being traced through narrow and intricate channels, among the ice, was discovered considerably to the eastward, when three harpoons were darted into him. The line of two other boats was then run out, when by an accidental entanglement, it broke, and the whale made off, carrying with it about four miles of rope, which, with the harpoons and the boat, were valued at £150 ! The daring whalemen were not to be thus robbed of their prey. They continued the pursuit ; again they came up with the fish and two more harpoons were struck into it. At last it became exhausted, the men plied their lances with effect, and the huge creature succumbed to its persevering enemies. Before it was finally secured it had drawn out no less than 10,440 yards, or about six miles, of line. Two miles of this and a boat were lost by the disengagement of a harpoon during the chase.

## WINTERING IN THE ICE.

Among other risks encountered by whale fishers, as well as by all who voyage in the polar seas, is that of being overtaken by winter and frozen in, or, as it is termed, set fast. Whalers, of course, dread this misfortune, both on account of the loss of time and their inadequate supply of provisions and necessaries, with which to encounter the rigours of so severe a climate. But those who go to those regions for the purposes of discovery, lay their account with having to spend one or more winters there, and make preparations accordingly. The records of the winter sojourn of discoverers in the realms of ice and prolonged night, form some of the most interesting chapters in Arctic history that ever were penned.

*The voyage of M'Clintock* in the *Fox*, is marked by one of the most singular instances on record of being set fast in the ice. Unlike most Arctic voyagers he was frozen in by immense fields of *unfixed* ice, in the centre of Baffin's Bay, and, although to all appearance the *Fox* lay embedded in the firm ice during the whole of a long winter, she was carried along with the whole field, slowly, imperceptibly, but steadily to the southward; and thus, lying still and apparently fixed, with her sails furled and her rigging frozen, the *Fox* performed a voyage—unfortunately in the wrong direction—of about 1385 miles! The following description will show what ships can encounter and come out of in safety.

The *Fox* was a small screw steam yacht, of one hundred and seven-seven tons, which was sent out by Lady Franklin to search for her husband's ships in the spring of 1857; Captain M'Clintock, R.N. commanding. The first part of the voyage was prosperous, but winter laid his icy hand on the little vessel in September, and on the 18th of that month they were frozen in completely in Baffin's Bay. Nevertheless, although all their plans had been thus prematurely blasted, and they were doomed to spend a long winter of absolute inutility, and in comparative peril and privation, the commander and his men faced their difficulties cheerfully, and preparations for wintering and sledge-travelling were carried on with unflagging energy. On the 24th, two bears were seen and chase was given, but without success. Games on the ice, skating, seal-shooting excursions, bear-hunting, and scientific observations filled up their time. Among other sources of amusement they had a beautiful hand organ. It had been presented by Prince Albert to the searching vessel bearing his name, which was sent out by Lady Franklin in 1851. The effect of this instrument on their Esquimaux interpreter was very amusing. He had never seen or heard of an organ before, and he regarded it with such awe and admiration, and seemed so entranced with delight as he turned the handle, that his shipmates felt quite envious !

As there was no hope of release from the ice till the following spring, the *Fox* was housed over and banked up with snow all round; when she assumed somewhat the appearance of the vessel represented in our illustration.

During the winter furious gales roared round their wooden

home out upon that frozen sea; but they had warm cabins, and heeded them not. When the weather was fine they

A BRIG SET FAST.

took long rambles over the ice, for the purpose of killing seals, as well as for the sake of health. A school was set on foot, which was immediately filled with zealous full-grown students of the three r's—reading, 'riting, and 'rithmetic. Scientific experiments were made with the pendulum, and an attempt made to discover the amount of azone in the air.

As winter advanced, the days shortened, until at last

perpetual night settled down upon the dreary sea. Out-door amusements were thus curtailed, and life began to grow very monotonous; yet it was relieved occasionally with such an event as the following:—

"There was a sudden call to arms to-night," writes M'Clintock; "whether sleeping, prosing, or schooling, every one flew out upon the ice on the instant, as if the magazine or the boiler was on the point of explosion. The alarm of 'a bear close to, fighting with the dogs,' was the cause. The luckless beast had approached to within twenty-five yards of the ship ere the quartermaster's eye detected his indistinct outline against the snow. So silently had he crept up that he was within ten yards of some of the dogs. A shout started them up, and they at once flew round the bear and embarrassed his retreat. In crossing some very thin ice he broke through, and there I found him surrounded by yelping dogs. Poor fellow! Hobson, Young, and Peter-sen, had each lodged a bullet in him; but these seemed only to increase his rage. He succeeded in getting out of the water, when, fearing harm to the numerous bystanders and dogs, or that he might escape, I fired, and luckily the bullet passed through his brain."

On the evening of the 28th of October, there occurred an unwonted and alarming disruption of the ice not two hundred yards from the vessel. The sound sometimes re-sembled the continued roar of distant surf; at other times, it was loud and harsh, as if trains of heavy waggons with ungreased axles were slowly labouring along. The sun took his final leave for the winter on the 1st November, and thenceforth they dwelt in constant lamp-light inboard, while, outside, they were dimly illuminated at times by the stars and moon, or by the aurora borealis. But very often these pale lights were completely quenched by stormy clouds and whirling drifts of snow.

In the midst of this scene of gloomy desolation the little community was visited by death. Scott, the engine-driver, received a fall which resulted in his death on the 4th of December. A hole was cut through the ice to the water, and his body was committed to the deep by his sorrowing comrades.

Thus the winter passed away, while the *Fox* lay unable to move from her icy bed, yet drifting all the time over miles and miles of ocean. Spring returned, and with it came daylight, and heat, and the hope of speedy deliverance; but with it also came the imminent dangers of disrupting ice. About the middle of April the ice began to break up. On the 24th, M'Clintock writes:—

"It is now ten o'clock; the long ocean swell already lifts its crest five feet above the hollow of the sea, causing its thick covering of icy fragments to dash against each other and against us with unpleasant violence. It is, however, very beautiful to look upon—the dear old familiar swell! it has long been a stranger to us, and is welcome in our solitude. A floe-piece near us, of one hundred yards in diameter, was speedily cracked so as to resemble a sort of labyrinth, or, still more, a field spider's web." Gradually the ice opened out, and the *Fox*, by aid of wind and steam, bored slowly but steadily out of the pack, receiving and returning many a sounding thump that caused her frame to shake, her bells to ring, and her crew to stagger. They were at last mercifully delivered from their dangerous position, having drifted down Baffin's Bay and Davis Straits 1194 geographical, or 1385 statute miles, during a sojourn of 242 days in the pack.

## THE TERROR NIPPED BY ICE.

During the voyage of the *Terror* in the Arctic seas in 1836 under Captain Back, that vessel received one of the severest nips on record.  It occurred on the 14th of September, within about four miles of Cape Comfort, and shows what rough usage ships can stand when properly prepared and strengthened for such navigation.

" A violent, agitative, landward motion pressed￢ all the surrounding ice into the utmost possible compactness, raised much of it into ponderous pointed heaps of twenty feet and upwards in height, and jammed the ship with perilous tightness between the nearest masses.  Not a pool of water was now to be seen; not a foot of shelter marred the terrors of the blast, and the hardy adventurers could look only to the interposition of Providence for deliverance and protection.  'None but those who have experienced it,' said their brave leader, 'can judge of the weariness of heart, the blank of feeling, the feverish sickliness of taste which get the better of the whole man under circumstances such as these.'

" The hapless ship was for many days drifted backward and forward along the coast and away from it, over a range of about thirty miles, just as the wind, or the current, or the tide directed.  The black frowning cliffs of Cape Comfort might have seemed to the most sluggish imagination to grin upon her in irony.  She lay in the grip of the ice-masses as helplessly as a kid does in the folds of a boa constrictor; and once, when she slipped from that grip, or was hurled into a change of position, she left her form as perfectly impressed behind her as if it had been struck in a die.  The many old Greenland seamen on board all declared that they had never before seen a ship which could have resisted such a pressure. The perils, too, were increasing; and at length, on the 24th of September, the officers unanimously expressed a conviction, founded on the experiences of the preceding thirty-four days, that all hope of making further progress that season toward Repulse Bay was gone.

"Captain Back now resolved to cut a dock in the only adjacent floe, which seemed sufficiently large and high to afford the ship fair protection. But on the very next day, by one of those extraordinary convulsions which are the last hope of the ice-bound Arctic voyager, the whole body of ice for leagues around got into general commotion, and burst into single masses; and commencing an impetuous rush to the west, tossed many blocks into heaps, ground others to powder, whirled all into a hurly burly, and bore away the ship like a feather toward the Frozen Strait. Nothing could be done by the crew but to await the issue; and when the storm subsided they found themselves midway between Cape Comfort and the entrance of the Frozen Strait, about three miles from the shore, without any prospect of either forcing their way into a harbour, or finding some little shelter in a floe. They were once more firmly beset, with the additional calamity of being so much tilted up that the stern of the ship lay seven and a half feet above the horizontal, and the bow was jammed downward on the masses ahead. 'This,' says Captain Back, 'ended a month of vexation, disappointment, and anxiety, to me personally more distressing and intolerable than the worst pressure of the worst evils which had befallen me in any other expedition.'"

## STRUCTURE OF ARCTIC SHIPS.

It may naturally occur to our reader's mind, that ships intended for such rough work as that just recorded, must be built in a much stronger fashion than ordinary vessels. Such is indeed the case. The hulls of ships intended for ice-laden seas, are either built expressly for their peculiar service or they are strengthened externally, as well as internally, to resist the rude shocks to which they are exposed. Usually a stout sheathing of oak, or other hard wood planks is fixed round the ship's bottom from the keel to within a few feet of the bulwarks, and beams are placed in such parts as are likely to be subjected to severe pressure. In the bow, especially, the timbers and beams, both outside and in, are so heavy and numerous that that part of the ship is almost solid.

The *Fox*, to which reference has already been made, was prepared for her cruise in the following manner. "The velvet hangings and splendid furniture, and everything not constituting part of a vessel's strengthening, were removed. The large skylights and capacious ladderways were reduced to limits more adapted to a Polar clime. The whole vessel was externally sheathed with stout planking, and internally fortified by strong cross beams, longitudinal beams, iron stanchions, and diagonal fastenings. The false keel was taken off; the slender brass propeller replaced by a massive iron one; the boiler taken out, altered, and enlarged. The sharp stern was cased in iron until it resembled a ponderous chisel set up edge-ways, and the rig was considerably altered."

### CHARGING THE ICE.

During the recent Franklin searching expeditions an instance of charging the ice occurred which is worth relating here. The expedition ships of 1850 were all beset in Melville Bay, and among them was a small vessel, the *Prince Albert*, which is said to have done marvellous deeds in the way of boring through the ice. One of her exploits is thus described in Mr. Snow's interesting journal:—

" As the wind was blowing right down upon the ice, and was pretty fresh, it was determined by Captain Forsyth boldly to try and break through the impediment by forcing the ship on it under a press of canvas. Accordingly, all sail was set, and the ship was steered direct for the narrowest and most broken part of the neck.

" As this was the first and only time the *Prince Albert* was made to come direct upon the ice to break it with the force she could derive from a press of sail, we were all anxious to see how she would stand it ; and right well did she bear the test. The two mates were aloft in the crow's nest * to con the·vessel. I was standing on the extreme point of her bow, and holding on by the fore-stay to direct her movements when immediately upon the ice ; and Captain Forsyth was by the side of the helmsman. Every man was at some particular station, and ready to perform anything that was instantly required of him. Cook and steward were also on deck, and throughout the ship an almost breathless anxiety prevailed ; for, it must be remembered, it was not a large and powerful ship, but a small and comparatively fragile one that was now about to try, of her own accord, and with her own strength, to break a piece of ice some feet thick, though not very broad. On either side of her were heavy floes and scone pieces ; and it required the greatest nicety

* The nest or sort of shelter, at the mast-head of whale ships, in which the man on the look out for whales sits.

in guiding her, that she might, in the strongest part—the bow—hit the precise spot where the neck was weakest, and not come upon any other part where she could do nothing but severely injure herself.

" On she came at the rate of full five miles per hour, gaining, as she proceeded, increased impetus, until she rushed towards it at the rate of at least eight miles in the hour. The distance from the neck was about a mile, and the breeze blew steadily upon it.   The weakest and narrowest part was that close to the starboard floe, and to that our eyes were all directed. .. ' Port, starboard ! so —o—steady ! ' was every now and then bawled out with stentorian lungs from aloft, and as energetically and powerfully repeated by the captain below to the man at the wheel.   Presently she came close to—she was almost upon it—a mistaken hail from aloft would have put her helm a-port, and sent her crushing upon the heavy floe.   I heard the order ' a-port ! ' and, before it had been repeated, shouted loudly, with the men around me, who also saw the mistake, 'starboard ! starboard ! hard a-starboard ! ' and the next instant, with a tremendous blow that for a moment made her rebound and tremble, she struck the ice in the exact point and caused it to rend apart in several fragments.   Ice-poles and boat-hooks were immediately in request; and myself and half a dozen men sprang instantly over the bows, working with hands, and feet, and with all our might, in removing the broken pieces by pushing them ahead of the vessel ; in which labour she herself materially aided us by her own power pressing upon them. In a moment or two it was effected ; and throwing ourselves aboard again like so many wild cats, we prepared for the next encounter.   This, however, proved nothing like the other.   The first blow sent the whole of it flying in all directions ; and the little *Prince*, as if in haughty disdain, passed through without once stopping, pushing aside the pieces as they came against her."

Since steam began to come into general use in navigation vessels bound for the Arctic seas have gradually begun to adopt it as an auxiliary force. Many of the whale ships now carry screw propellers, and are thus enabled to save much time and move about freely in calms, which in former years would have compelled them to remain for days at a time inactive. Ships are also enabled to act the part of battering rams more effectively than heretofore, and to force their way through " necks " of solid ice.

One of the steamers in connection with the searching expeditions of 1850, above referred to, made several desperate charges at the ice. The incident is thus briefly described by the same author from whom we have quoted the preceding account of the *Prince Albert :*—" We came to a heavy *nip*," says Mr. Snow, " and all the vessels had to be made fast to a floe until a passage could be cleared. The *Pioneer* (steamer), immediately on casting off the *Resolute's* tow-rope, was directed to dash at the impediment under full power. This she did boldly and fearlessly,—rushing, stem on, and fairly digging her bows into it in the most remarkable manner. Backing instantly astern, and then again going ahead, she performed the same manœuvre, fairly lifting herself up on end like a prancing war-horse. By this time the nip was too heavy to be so broken, though both steamers had previously cleared many similar impediments in that manner. It was now, however, necessary to resort to other means ; and, accordingly, parties from every ship were sent on the ice to assist in blowing it up and removing the fragments as they got loosened. The same plan as that, I believe, adopted in blasting rocks was here pursued. Powder was sunk to a certain depth, a slow match applied, and at a given signal ignited. Due time was allowed, and then the enormous masses would be seen in convulsive movement, as though shaken by a volcanic eruption, until piece upon piece was sent into the air and the larger bodies were completely rent into innumerable fragments. The steamers then darted forward, and with warps dragged out the immense blocks that had been thus dissevered."

## EXPLOITS OF DR. KANE.

Of all the navigators who have penetrated into the dark and dangerous regions of the Polar seas none have surpassed, and, with the exception, perhaps, of Sir John Franklin, none have equalled in daring and indomitable perseverance Dr. Kane, the American, who commanded the second expedition, sent out by Mr. Grinnell of New York to search for Franklin. One or two extracts from his intensely interesting journal of that voyage will strikingly exhibit some of the peculiar phases of the Arctic regions, and at the same time show what can be done by true heroism, and what was endured by the wood and iron of the little brig in which he sailed.

The name of Dr. Kane's vessel was the *Advance*. It was a brig of 144 tóns, a good sailer, strengthened for her peculiar work and fitted out with every requisite—but few luxuries—for a prolonged search in the Arctic seas. Spartanlike simplicity was the prominent feature of this expedition —simplicity of arrangements, simplicity (and brevity) of instructions, and simplicity of intentions. The leader and his officers were at once eminently scientific and thoroughly practical men. Here is their code of laws :—"We did not sail under the rules that govern our national ships ;" writes

Kane, " but we had our own regulations, well considered and announced beforehand, and rigidly adhered to afterwards through all the vicissitudes of the expedition. These included—first, absolute subordination to the officer in command, or his delegate ; second, abstinence from all intoxicating liquors, except when dispensed by special order ; third, the habitual disuse of profane language. We had no other laws."

It is worthy of special remark that the crew of this little vessel, although they used no strong drink whatever, underwent and overcame hardships more severe, and prolonged, perhaps, than any on record.

On the 30th of May 1853 the *Advance* left New York with a crew of eighteen picked men, including the commander, and proceeding to the head of Baffin's Bay entered the unknown seas beyond Smith's Sound. At the very outset they had a foretaste of their coming struggles. Fearing they should be set fast in the ice during a stiff breeze while heading towards Cape York, they endeavoured to make fast to a large iceberg, and after eight hours of heavy labour, warping, heaving and planting ice-anchors, they succeeded in effecting their object.

*A narrow escape* from sudden and overwhelming destruction was the result. " We had hardly a breathing spell," writes Dr. Kane, " before we were startled by a set of loud crackling sounds above us ; and small fragments of ice, not larger than a walnut began to dot the water like the first drops of a summer shower. The indications were too plain. We had barely time to cast off before the face of the berg fell in ruins, crashing like near artillery."

*Esquimaux dogs* are not pleasant companions, although undoubtedly they are most useful creatures in dragging

sledges for many hundreds of miles over the snow.  Dr.
Kane purposed continuing the search in native sledges after

THE ADVANCE ESCAPING FROM ICEBERGS.

the winter ice should set fast his brig, so he purchased more
than fifty dogs which he speaks of as "ravening wolves,"
and classes among his minor miseries.  To feed this canine
family was a matter of great difficulty.  Two bears lasted
the cormorants only eight days.  They were ready to eat

up everything that came in their way.   In order to provide
for them, a party set out with rifles to shoot walrus, of
which elephantine creatures there were many in the sea
around them.   But although they aimed well, the·hides of
the walrus were so thick that their " rifle-balls reverberated
from their sides like cork pellets from a pop-gun target,"
and they failed to get within harpoon range.   However, they
were somewhat consoled by the discovery of a dead narwhal
or sea-unicorn, which secured for them, in the doctor's words,
" at least six hundred pounds of good, fetid, wholesome
flesh !"   The horn of this unicorn was four feet long, of
beautiful ivory ; and his blubber or flesh yielded two barrels
of oil.   But this supply did not last them long, as we find
from the following passage, which occurs a few days later
in the journal :—

" More bother with these wretched dogs ?   Worse than
a street in Constantinople emptied upon our decks ; the
unruly, thieving, wild beast pack !   Not a bear's paw, or
Esquimaux cranium, or basket of mosses, or any specimen
whatever, can leave your hands for a moment without their
making a rush at it, and after a yelping scramble swallow-
ing it at a gulp.   I have seen them attempt a whole feather
bed, and here, this morning, one of my Karsuk brutes has
eaten up two entire birds' nests which I had just before
gathered from the rocks,—feathers, filth, pebbles and moss
—a peckful at least ! "

*A gale*, of the fiercest kind, arose one day, and well-nigh
wrecked them.   They had seen it coming, and were ready
with three good hawsers out ahead, fixed to a ledge of rocks
named God-send ledge, and everything was snug on board
the little brig.   But the gale proved fiercer than had been
anticipated.   On it came heavier and heavier.   Dr. Kane

had just turned in to warm and dry himself, after protracted watching and exposures, when he heard the sharp twanging snap of a cord.   Their six-inch hawser had parted, and they were swinging by the two others—the gale roaring like a lion to the southward.   Half a minute more, and "twang, twang!" went a second report, which by the shrillness of the ring was known instantly to be the whale-line.   They were now left swinging by only one hawser, but that one was good and strong, a "noble ten-inch manilla."   On hearing the snap of the whale-line Dr. Kane sprang up and was in the act of hurrying on his socks and seal-skin boots when M'Gary, one of the crew, descended the companion ladder, saying that he thought the hawser could not hold on much longer.   On reaching the deck the commander found the cable proving its excellence, and the crew, as they gathered round him, were loud in its praises.

"We could hear," writes the doctor, "its deep Eolian chant swelling through all the rattle of the running-gear and moaning of the shrouds.   It was the death-song !   The strands gave way with the noise of a shotted gun ; and in the smoke that followed their recoil we were dragged out by the wild ice at its mercy."

Instantly they were hurried away into the rushing drift, and it seemed as if nothing could be looked for but swift destruction.   But their course was not yet run.   There was work for them still to do, and the hand of the Almighty preserved them in this terrible crisis.   Ahead, in the direction in which they were being driven, heavy ice-tables were grinding up and clogging the passage. Out of this they must keep at all hazards.   There was but one course left, to drop the anchors ere they closed with the piling masses.   The heaviest anchor was let go with the desperate hope of wind-

ing the brig ; but there was no withstanding the ice-torrent
that followed them.　They had only time to fasten a spar
to the chain as a buoy and let her slip.　So went the best
bower !

They now drifted with the gale, scraping helplessly on a
lee of ice seldom less than thirty feet thick.　One upturned
mass rose above the gunwale, smashed in the bulwarks and
deposited half a ton of ice in a lump on the deck.　Soon a
new enemy appeared in sight ahead.　Just beyond the line
of the ice-floes against which they were alternately sliding and
thumping was a group of bergs.　They had no power to
avoid them.　To run upon them before the full power of
the howling storm would have proved as certain and instant
destruction as if they had been launched on solid rocks.
Their hopes were almost gone when a narrow passage was
observed between the bergs and the edge of the floe.　In a
moment they were in the midst of them, and then, to their
consternation, they found that the bergs were not at rest,
but bearing down on each other, and threatening to crush
the brig between them.　At the same time the wind failed,
from some inexplicable cause.　Just then a low mass of ice
drove past them ; an anchor was cast upon it as it passed,
and in the wake of this novel tug they were dragged past
the ice walls in safety.　But it was a close shave—so close
that the yards had to be braced to clear the bergs, and the
port quarter boat would have been crushed had they not
taken it from the davits.　Next moment they were under
the lee of a berg in comparatively open lead.　" Never,"
concludes Dr. Kane, " did heart-tired men acknowledge with
more gratitude their merciful deliverance from a wretched
death."

*A boat expedition* was undertaken, when they afterwards

found it impossible to advance further to the northward in
the brig.   It was termed the *Forlorn Hope.*   The men who

went in it were rigged out in Esquimaux habiliments—seal-
skin coats and boots with the hair left on—and with their
faces bearded and bronzed, and their hoods up, the sailors
looked so like Esquimaux that at a short distance no difference
could be discerned between them.   Into the minute details
of this interesting boat journey we cannot enter.   It was
rough and toilsome.   When they could advance no further
on account of ice the boat was abandoned and the journey
continued with a sledge.   Their usual night halts were upon
knolls of snow under the rocks, on one of which they were
caught by the rising tide, and, not being able to effect a re-

treat in time, had to stand in the water holding their sleeping gear in their arms until the tide fell. The skeletons of Musk oxen were found in various places along the coast, which was rocky and wild in the extreme. Protruding tongues of glaciers and wide chasms in the ice-belt were crossed with much difficulty ; and when, at last, they arrived at the places over which the sledge could not be dragged, the provisions and scientific instruments were strapped on the shoulders of the stoutest men, and the journey was continued on foot.

On their fifth day they discovered a noble river which was named the Mary Minturn, after the sister of Mr. Grinnell. Here they encamped and listened with delight to the unusual sound of running water ; and "here," writes Dr. Kane, "protected from the frost by the infiltration of the melted snows, and fostered by the reverberation of solar heat from the rocks, we met a flower growth, which, though drearily Arctic in its type, was rich in variety of colouring. Amid festuca and other tufted grasses, twinkled the purple lichens and the white star of the chickweed ; and, not without its pleasing associations, I recognised a solitary hesperis, the Arctic representative of the wall-flowers of home."

*Seal-hunting* became not only an amusement to Dr. Kane and his men, during their long sojourn of two winters in the Polar regions, but an absolute necessity. They were again and again reduced to the verge of starvation, and had it not been for the kind assistance rendered them several times by the Esquimaux, they must have perished.

One day Dr. Kane was nearly drowned while out after seals, with his Esquimaux interpreter Hans. The two hunters were dashing at a brisk gallop over the floes in their dog-sledge. Suddenly " Hans sang out at the top of

his voice," writes Kane, " ' Pusey ! Puseymut ! seal ! seal !'
At the same instant the dogs bounded forward, and as I
looked up I saw crowds of grey netsik—the rough or hispid
seal of the whalers—disporting in the open sea water.

" I had hardly welcomed the spectacle when I saw that
we had passed upon a new belt of ice that was obviously
unsafe.   To the right and left and front, was one great expanse of snow-flowered ice.   The nearest solid floe was a
mere lump, which stood like an island in the white level.
To turn was impossible ; we had to keep on our gait.   We
urged on the dogs with whip and voice, the ice rolling like
leather beneath the sledge runners.   It was more than a
mile to the lump of solid ice.   Fear gave the poor beasts
their utmost speed, and our voices were soon hushed to
silence.

" The suspense, unrelieved by action or effort, was intolerable.   We knew that there was no remedy but to reach the
floe, and that everything depended on our dogs and our
dogs alone.   A moment's check would plunge the whole
concern into the rapid tideway.   No presence of mind or
resource, bodily or mental, could avail us.   This desperate
race against fate could not last.   The rolling of the tough
salt-water ice terrified our dogs ; and when within fifty paces
of the floe they paused.   The left hand runner went through ;
our leader Toodlamick followed, and in one second the entire
left of the sledge was submerged.   My first thought was
to liberate the dogs.   I leaned forward to cut poor Tood's
traces, and the next minute was swimming in a little circle
of pasty ice and water alongside him.   Hans, dear good
fellow, drew near to help me, uttering piteous expressions
in broken English ; but I ordered him to throw himself on
his belly, with his hands and legs extended, and to make for

the island by cogging himself forward with his jack-knife.
In the meantime—a mere instant—I was floundering about
with sledge, dogs, and lines, in confused puddle around me.

"I succeeded in cutting poor Tood's lines and letting
him scramble to the ice, for the poor fellow was drowning me
with his piteous caresses, and made my way for the sledge;
but I found that it would not buoy me, and that I had no
resource but to try the circumference of the hole.   Around
this I paddled faithfully, the miserable ice always yielding
when my hopes of a lodgment were greatest.   During this
process I enlarged my circle of operations to a very uncomfortable diameter, and was beginning to feel weaker after
every effort.   Hans meanwhile had reached the firm ice
and was on his knees, like a good Moravian, praying incohe-
rently in English and Esquimaux.   At every fresh crushing
in of the ice he would ejaculate 'God!' and when I recommenced my paddling he recommenced his prayers.

"I was nearly gone.   My knife had been lost in cutting
out the dogs; and a spare one which I carried in my trousers'
pocket was so enveloped in wet skins that I could not reach
it.   I owed my extrication at last to a newly broken team
dog which was still fast to the sledge, and in struggling
carried one of the runners chock against the edge of the
circle.   All my previous attempts to use the sledge as a
bridge had failed, for it broke through to the much greater
injury of the ice.   I felt it was a last chance.   I threw
myself on my back, so as to lessen as much as possible my
weight, and placed the nape of my neck against the rim
or edge of the ice; then with caution slowly bent my leg,
and, placing the ball of my moccassined foot against the
sledge, I pressed steadily against the runner, listening to
the half yielding crunch of the ice beneath.

"Presently I felt that my head was pillowed by the ice, and that my wet fur jumper was sliding up the surface. Next came my shoulders; they were fairly on. One more decided push and I was launched on the ice and safe. I reached the ice floe, and was frictioned by Hans with frightful zeal. We saved all the dogs, but the sledge, kayack, tent, guns, snow-shoes, and everything besides were left behind."

## FIGHTS WITH POLAR BEARS.

The white bears of the frozen seas are both large and fierce, and almost all navigators in those regions have occasional encounters with them—in some cases prolonged and for a time doubtful, but usually terminating in the destruction of the bears.

There is a story related of one man who was out walking on the ice unarmed and at some little distance from his ship when he was met and chased by a bear. The sailor ran fast, but the bear ran faster, and no doubt the matter would have ended seriously had not the man accidentally dropped one of his mittens. The bear stopped to smell it, and then resumed the chase. The man observed the fact, and dropped another mitten—this time intentionally. Again the bear paused a moment, and the man gained a little distance. Thus by dropping one thing after another he reached his ship, where a volley of musket balls from his comrades arrested bruin's advance and sent him to the right about.

Esquimaux attack polar bears sometimes single-handed, and with no other weapon than a spear. They do not, however, attempt this unless compelled to it; but two natives never hesitate to attack and make sure of killing a bear. They proceed thus:—When the two men have advanced pretty near to the bear they separate and approach him in different directions so as to distract his attention ; then the one on his left side makes a feint with his spear ; bruin turns to defend himself and immediately receives a prick from the man on his right side.   With a growl of rage he turns to inflict summary vengeance on this enemy, but scarcely has he turned his eyes away when he receives a deadly thrust in the heart from the man on his left, and falls.   If the men are cool and courageous, as they usually are, there is very little danger attending this mode of attack, though the polar bear is terrifically powerful and more than a match for a dozen men if they did not use strategy in their assault.

Dr. Kane mentions a circumstance which shows the strength of this animal.   He had made a *cache*, or deposit of provisions, in the course of one of his journeys, but on returning to it found that the bears had discovered and broken it up.   " It had been built," says he, " with extreme care, of rocks which had been assembled by very heavy labour and adjusted with much aid from capstan-bars as levers.   The entire structure was, so far as our means permitted, most effective and resisting.   Yet these tigers of the ice seem scarcely to have encountered an obstacle.   Not a morsel of pemmican remained except in the iron cases, which, being round, with conical ends, defied both claws and teeth.   They had rolled and pawed them in every direction, tossing them about like footballs, although over eighty pounds in weight.   An alcohol-case, strongly iron-bound, was dashed into small fragments, and a tin can of liquor mashed and twisted almost into a ball.   The claws of the beast had perforated the metal, and torn it up as with a cold chisel.   They were too dainty for salt meats.   Ground coffee they had an evident relish for. Old canvas was a favourite for some reason or other; even our flag, which had been reared 'to take possession' of the waste, was gnawed down to the very staff. They had made a regular frolic of it; rolling our bread-barrels over the ice-foot and into the broken outside ice; and, unable to masticate our heavy india-rubber cloth, they had tied it up in unimaginable hard knots. M'Gary describes the whole area around the cache as marked by well-worn paths of these animals, and an adjacent slope of ice-covered rock, with an angle of 45°, was so worn and covered with their hair, as to suggest the idea that they had been amusing themselves by sliding down on their haunches—a performance, by the way, in which I afterwards caught them myself."

There is no doubt that polar bears are the reverse of nice in their tastes. It is said that a party of Arctic travellers once shot a bear, in the stomach of which they found, among other things, a quantity of raisins, tobacco, and sticking-plaster! No doubt this fellow had fallen in with a *cache* somewhere, and had made free with the doctor's, as well as the steward's stores.

Ever since man invaded the northern regions he has had to enter into contest with the polar bear. When the Dutch attempted to plant a settlement on the bleak and barren coasts of Spitzbergen so long ago as the year 1633, they met and battled with this formidable animal. One day seven sailors who wintered on that island turned out of their hut to repel a bear which seemed inclined to make more intimate acquaintance with their settlement than was agreeable. Two balls were lodged in his throat, and while he was endeavouring to pick these out with his claws the whole seven sailors rushed upon him with their lances. The bear dashed at one of them, tore the lance from his hand, and threw him on the ground ; but as the animal was about to destroy his victim another sailor struck and obliged him to quit his hold. Afterwards, however, though pursued by all the seven, he plunged into the sea and escaped.

From that time forward every northern navigator has had to tell of encounters, more or less successful, with those white monsters, which Dr. Kane has well styled the "tigers of the ice."

## FIGHTS WITH THE WALRUS.

If the Arctic bear may be styled the tiger, much more may the walrus be termed the elephant of the ice ; for that huge creature's resemblance to the elephant, in size as well as appearance, is very striking. Dr. Kane, whom we think more graphic in his descriptions than any other writer, says that the head of the walrus is not oval, like that of the seal ; on the contrary, the frontal bone is so covered as to present a steep descent to the eyes, and a square, blocked out aspect to the upper face. The muzzle is less protruding than the seal's, and the cheeks and lips are completely masked by heavy quill-like bristles. The tusks are sometimes seen nearly 30 inches long, and his body not less than 18 feet. When of this gigantic size his aspect is terrible ; and being possessed of a fierce and vindictive disposition he is truly a formidable foe.

Sometimes when attacked in boats the walrus, instead of shunning the fight, will collect in numbers and act on the offensive.

Morton, one of Dr. Kane's crew, went out on a walrus hunt with Myouk, an Esquimaux, and a party of his friends.

The ice was dangerous and thin, but the natives were bordering on starvation, so they pushed on to where they expected to find walrus.

"After a while Myouk became convinced, from signs or sounds or both,—for they were inappreciable by Morton—that the walrus were waiting for him in a small space of recently open water that was glazed over with a few days' growth of ice ; and, moving gently on, they soon heard the characteristic bellow of a bull awuk.   His vocalization was something between the mooing of a cow and the deepest baying of a mastiff ; very round and full, with its barks or detached notes repeated rather quickly seven to nine times in succession."   The party now formed in single file and approached the open pools, winding behind hummocks of ice as they went.   "When within half a mile of these the line broke and each man crawled towards a separate pool— Morton on his hands and knees following Myouk.   In a few minutes the walrus were in sight.   They were five in number, rising at intervals through the ice in a body, and breaking it up with an explosive puff that might have been heard for miles.   Two large grim looking males were conspicuous as the leaders of the group.

"Now for the marvel of the craft.   When the walrus is above water, the hunter is flat and motionless ; as he begins to sink, alert and ready for a spring.   The animal's head is hardly below the water line before every man is in a rapid run ; and again, as if by instinct, before the beast returns, all are motionless behind protecting knolls of ice.   They seem to know beforehand not only the time he will be absent, but the very spot at which he will reappear.   In this way, hiding and advancing by turns, Myouk, with Morton at his heels, has reached a plate of thin ice, hardly strong enough

to bear them, at the very brink of the water-pool the walrus are curvetting in.

"Myouk, till now phlegmatic, seems to awake with excitement.    His coil of walrus-hide, a well-trimmed line of many
fathoms length, is lying at his side.    He fixes one end of
it in an iron barb, and fastens this loosely by a socket upon
a shaft of unicorn's horn ; the other end is already looped.
It is the work of a moment.    He has grasped the harpoon ;
the water is in motion.    Puffing with pent-up respiration,
the walrus is within a couple of fathoms close before him.
Myouk rises slowly—his right arm thrown back, the left
flat at his side.    The walrus looks about him shaking the
water from his crest ; Myouk throws up his left arm, and the
animal, rising breast-high, fixes one look before he plunges.
It has cost him all that curiosity can cost ; the harpoon is
buried under his left flipper.

" Though the awuk is down in a moment, Myouk is running at desperate speed from the scene of his victory, paying off his coil freely, but clutching the end by its loop.  He
seizes as he runs a small stick of bone, rudely pointed with
iron, and by a sudden movement drives it into the ice.    To
this he secures his line, pressing it down close to the ice-
surface with his feet.

" Now comes the struggle.    The hole is lashed into mad
commotion with the struggles of the wounded beast ; the
line is drawn tight at one moment, the next relaxed.    The
hunter has not left his station.    There is a crash of the ice,
and rearing up through it are two walruses, not many yards
from where he stands.    One of them, the male, is excited,
and seemingly terrified ; the other, the female, collected
and vengeful.    Down they go again, after one grim sur-
vey of the field ; and on the instant Myouk has changed

his position, carrying his coil with him and fixing it anew.

" He has hardly fixed it before the pair have again risen, breaking up an area of ten feet diameter, about the very spot he has left. As they sink once more he again changes his place. And so the conflict goes on between address and force, till the victim, half exhausted, receives a second wound, and is played like a trout by the angler's reel.

" When wounded the walrus rises high out of the water, plunges heavily against the ice, and strives to raise himself with his fore flippers upon its surface. As it breaks under his weight, his countenance assumes a still more vindictive expression, his bark changes to a roar, and the foam pours out from his jaws till it froths his beard.

" Some idea may be formed of the ferocity of the walrus, from the fact that this battle which Morton witnessed, not without sharing some of its danger, lasted *four hours*—during which the animal rushed continually at the Esquimaux as they approached, tearing off great tables of ice with his tusks, and showing no indications of fear whatever. He received upwards of seventy lance wounds, Morton counted over sixty; and even then he remained hooked by his tusks to the ice, unable or unwilling to retire. His female fought in the same manner, but fled on receiving a lance wound.

" The Esquimaux seemed fully aware of the danger of venturing too near ; for at the first onset of the walrus they jumped back far enough to be clear of the broken ice. Morton described the last three hours as wearing, on both sides, the aspect of an unbroken and seemingly doubtful combat.

" The method of landing the beast upon the ice, too, showed a great deal of clever contrivance. They made two pair of incisions in the neck, where the hide is very thick, about six inches apart and parallel to each other, so as to form a couple of bands.   A line of cut hide, about a quarter of an inch in diameter, was passed under one of these bands and carried up on the ice to a firm stick well secured in the floe, where it went through a loop, and was then taken back to the animal, made to pass under the second band, and led off to the Esquimaux.   This formed a sort of 'double purchase,' the blubber so lubricating the cord as to admit of a free movement.   By this contrivance the beast, weighing some seven hundred pounds, was hauled up and butchered at leisure."

## ATMOSPHERIC PHENOMENA IN ARCTIC REGIONS.

No part of the globe presents such variety of singular and beautiful phenomena as the regions of ice around the poles.  The sudden and violent changes in temperature caused by the accumulation or dispersion of ice have a good deal to do with the phenomena referred to, but some of the singular appearances—especially those of the Aurora Borealis—have not yet been satisfactorily accounted for.   Philosophers say that electricity is the cause of the aurora, but having said this, they have dived their deepest into the subject, for electricity, like fire, is a mere name employed to indicate an agent with the substance of which we are unacquainted.

Whatever the cause, the effect of the aurora is indescribably splendid.   Its colour and coruscations are much more brilliant and lovely than they are in our more southern climes, and its light seems, though in a very small degree indeed, to make up for the long absence of the sun,

Another of the curious results of ice-influence on the atmosphere is refraction, which causes objects to appear as if floating in the air, and sometimes inverted. Thus ships are frequently seen in the sky upside down, as represented in our cut.

REFRACTION.

Scoresby, in his voyage of 1822, saw the rugged surface of the ice assume the forms of castles, obelisks, and spires, which, here and there, were so linked together as to present the appearance of an extensive city. At other times it resembled a forest of naked trees, and it scarcely required the aid of fancy to discover the forms of lions, bears, and other wild animals among them.

## CHAPTER XVII.

### THE ATLANTIC CABLE.

It is a trite mode of expressing inexpressible wonder at anything inexpressibly wonderful, to say, " Had we soberly asserted, fifty years ago, that so and so would have happened, we would have been regarded as a hopeless lunatic." Yet we cannot find a more forcible method of realizing the wonderful nature of the Atlantic telegraph than to call to life, in imagination, the last generation, tell it that we have actually held instantaneous communication with America by means of electricity, and watch the expression of unutterable amazement that would overspread that generation's visage, when it heard, understood, and *believed* the news !

It matters not that, for practical purposes, the Atlantic telegraph has proved, hitherto, a failure. It does not in the least detract from the great, stupendous consummation, that "the cable " is now lying,—like the great sea serpent, dead, drawn out, elongated, attenuated to the size of its original back-bone—rotting at the bottom of the sea. The cable *has* been laid; gushing words of liquid fire *have* passed, in a single moment, from land to land, through seas over which all the mariners of ancient days battled with such difficulty; the Atlantic telegraph is a *fait accompli*, and it needs not the gift of prophecy to tell that many years shall not pass away before we shall be sending messages at so much a word to our friends in the New World as we now do to those in the Old.

## LAYING THE ATLANTIC CABLE.[*]

The idea of uniting England and America by means of an electric telegraph, originated in America, and the attempt to accomplish this strange yet desirable union was made, in the summer of 1857, conjointly by the two countries, under the auspices of The Atlantic Telegraph Company.

Scientific explorations made in the bed of the Atlantic, by Lieutenant Maury, had proved that there is a submarine ledge or bank extending from Cape Clear in Ireland, to Cape Race in Newfoundland, varying from two to two and a half miles in depth. Along this bank it was resolved that the cable should be laid, and the time fixed for doing it was between the middle of July and the middle of August. A fleet of British and U.S. vessels were appointed for the work. It consisted of the U.S. steam frigate *Niagara,* and her H.M.S. *Agamemnon,* with six attendant vessels. The *Niagara* and *Agamemnon* were each to contain one half of the cable; they were to attach the ends to their respective shores and then steam off; meet in the middle of the Atlantic, and fasten the other ends together.

Some idea of the stupendous nature of the undertaking may be gathered from the following facts:—

The *Niagara* commenced shipping the cable from the factory at Birkenhead late in June, and a month elapsed before that part of the work was completed. The length of the entire cable was 2200 miles. The construction of the cable was—first a core, or *conductor,* composed of seven copper wires twisted tightly together; second, three coats of gutta-percha; third, six strands of yarn ; and, last, eighteen strands of iron wire. The cable was little more than half an inch in diameter, but it was so strong that six miles of it might be suspended in water without breaking, and so flexible that it could be tied in a knot round the arm without injury.  Its weight was 1860 pounds to the mile, which gives a weight of 4,092,000 pounds to the whole cable.

On the 4th of August the telegraph fleet assembled in Valentia Bay; the next evening the shore end of the cable was laid from the stern of the *Niagara* by a boat's crew of American sailors, in the presence of the Lord Lieutenant of Ireland, and an immense crowd of spectators.  On the 6th the expedition sailed, and in a few days returned, with the sad news that the cable had broken in deep water after 335 nautical miles of it had been laid.

The enthusiastic looked grave; the sceptical said, or looked, with the usual self satisfied smile, "I told you so," and the laying of the cable was postponed to another year. With an energy worthy of the cause, the Atlantic Telegraph Company prepared to repeat the attempt; the *Niagara* and *Agamemnon* were again placed at its disposal by their respective Governments, and they set sail in June 1858. The plan, however, had been changed.  The two vessels were to proceed to mid-ocean; there splice the ends of the cable, and, turning stern to stern, make for their respective shores.

Storm and disaster awaited them, and once more the fleet returned to port unsuccessful.  But the company was not to be defeated.  The vessels were once again sent out; they spliced the cable in mid-Atlantic, and, on the 28th of July 1858, began to "pay-out" the cable.

And now commenced days and nights of care and an-xiety on board these two ships as they steamed away from each other, paying out the delicate wire rope as carefully as if their lives depended on the issue ! And it is a strange thing to reflect that as the distance grew, and hundreds of miles of ocean lay between them, still that subtle current passed along the wire, and told the electricians on board each vessel that all was well. The minds of all—men of science, officers and crews of both ships—were on the stretch during the whole voyage. The grandeur and importance of the achievement if accomplished, the delicacy of the cable, its liability to accident, and the possibility of failure, kept every one in a state of constant anxiety, while those who had charge of the coil watched the index that told of *"continuity"* with intense and constant interest.

On the evidence of this continuity of the current everything depended. When the continuity was active, hearts were light and hopes high; when it became dull and uncertain, a load pressed on every bosom; if it should *cease*—despair !

Once and again this continuity did become defective, so much so that it was impossible to send a signal through the cable. Still it did not absolutely cease, so there was hope. For nearly two hours, at one time, there were none but blank faces on board, and it was whispered that "something was wrong," but the continuity returned, and although many a gallant tar knew not the meaning of the term, his heart beat freely again when the electricians translated it into the well-known words, "all's right again."

Then came the time when the change of the wire from one coil to another had to be made—from .the coil on the main-deck, for instance, to that on the deck below. It was a critical moment. Long before it had to be done, everything was prepared for it, and, more than an hour before, crowds of anxious men stood round the circles to watch the great event. The last coils of the circle began to pass out, and every one gazed with silent suspense ; only a few turns remained, and the order was given by the chief engineer to diminish speed, and the cable passed slowly out astern. The point was to pass the bight, or point of connection, safely out astern, and men stood ready to lift the cable at this part when it began to unwind. At last it reeled off, was sent safely overboard, and a murmur of applause greeted the event as the speed of the ship was again got up. Such incidents occurred several times in both vessels during the voyage. Once it was found that defective continuity was caused by the wire not being properly insulated at a particular spot, and the cable had to be cut and rejoined ; this was successfully accomplished, and the continuity returned in as strong force as ever.

But there were other causes of anxiety besides the risk of breaking the cable by accident or clumsy management in any of the delicate operations that had to be performed. The consumption of coal and diminishing of the cable's bulk lightened the ships so much that they rolled uneasily, and subjected the wire to heavy strains and jerks. The *Agamemnon*, too, experienced some very rough weather, though the voyage of the *Niagara* was comparatively quiet ; but the beautiful and ingenious apparatus for paying out the cable—the invention of Mr. Everett of the U.S. navy— worked so admirably that everything went well, and the crews at last began to entertain sanguine hopes that their work was really about to be accomplished triumphantly.

On the seventh day the *Niagara* sighted land, and the same evening entered Trinity Bay, Newfoundland. They were cheered by the signal "all's well" from the *Agamemnon*, which was now drawing near to the Irish coast. The

Americans landed their end of the cable on the 5th of August amid the cheers and rejoicing of the crews of their portion of the telegraphic fleet, and of the few persons who had long and anxiously awaited their appearance at the telegraph station. But it is a bleak, wild, uninhabited district on which the station stands, so there were no crowds assembled on the shore to witness the consummation of the great event, and welcome their new and interesting " connection " with lusty cheers.

The event was most appropriately celebrated by thanksgiving and prayer. Taking up his position on a pile of boards, " the officers and men standing round, amid shavings, stumps of trees, pieces of broken furniture, sheets of copper, telegraph batteries, little mounds of lime and mortar, branches of trees, huge boulders, and a long catalogue of other things equally incongruous, Captain Hudson, of the *Niagara*, said to those around him :—

" We have just accomplished a work which has attracted the attention and enlisted the interest of the whole world. That work has been performed not by ourselves ; there has been an Almighty hand over us and aiding us ; and, without the divine assistance thus extended to us, success was impossible. With this conviction firmly impressed upon our minds, it becomes our duty to acknowledge our indebtedness to that overruling Providence who holds the sea in the hollow of His hand. 'Not unto us, O Lord, not unto us, but to thy name be all the glory.' "

After these most appropriate remarks he then offered up the same prayer which was offered at the laying of the cable, with a few necessary alterations to suit the occasion.

The *Agamemnon* was equally successful in performing her part of the arduous task. The two ends of the cable having been attached to their respective telegraph apparatus, the work was completed, and a message was transmitted across the Atlantic from shore to shore.

The first message that winged its way through the deep, over the rocks, and sands, and mysterious caverns of ocean, was from the directors of the Atlantic Telegraph Company in England to the directors in America, and its purport was eminently appropriate to the occasion—on the 16th of August 1858 it left England, and the same day it rang throughout the whole Northern 'and Western states of America—"Glory to God in the highest; on earth peace, good-will toward men."

Immediately after, the Queen's message was telegraphed, but, owing to necessary repairs to the cable, it was interrupted in its course, and did not reach its destination in a complete form till the following day, (the 17th). It ran as follows:—

"The Queen desires to congratulate the President upon the successful completion of this great international work, in which the Queen has taken the greatest interest. The Queen is convinced the President will join her in fervently hoping that the electric cable which now connects Great Britain with the United States will prove an additional link between the two nations, whose friendship is founded on their common interest and reciprocal esteem. The Queen has much pleasure in thus directly communicating with the President, and in renewing to him her best wishes for the prosperity of the United States."

To this President Buchanan replied on the same day :—

"The President cordially reciprocates the congratulation of her Majesty, the Queen, on the success of this great international enterprise, accomplished by the science, skill, and indomitable energy of the two countries. It is a triumph more glorious, because far more useful, to mankind, than ever was won by conqueror on the field of battle. May the Atlantic Telegraph, under the blessing of Heaven, prove to be a bond of perpetual peace and friendship between the kindred nations, and an instrument designed by Providence to diffuse religion, civilization, liberty, and law throughout the world. In this view will not all the nations of Christendom spontaneously unite in the declaration, that it shall be for ever neutral, and that its communications shall be held sacred in passing to the place of their destination, even in the midst of hostilities?        JAMES BUCHANAN."

It may not, perhaps, be generally known that the - Atlantic Telegraph was in active operation for twenty-three days before it ceased to work and proved a failure. During that period 400 messages,—consisting of 4,359 words composed of 21,421 letters— were transmitted along the wires between the two countries, and there is little doubt that the success of the undertaking would have been complete had it not been for the faulty and careless manner in which the cable was constructed. But enough has been accomplished to show that the laying of an Atlantic Telegraph is both feasible and desirable.

We have merely selected a few of the most prominent and singular achievements that have of late years marked the progress of man, in connection with the ocean and with things pertaining thereto. Our space forbids us to touch upon, much less to enter into, the details of many naval structures and marine appliances, which are nevertheless deeply interesting and well worthy of our intelligent regard. The magnificent floating palaces that cross the Atlantic, summer and winter, week after week, with the regularity of clockwork; the splendid steam fleet of the Oriental and Peninsular Steam Company; the electric cables that connect England with France, Europe with Africa—the "west" with the "east," and render communication with distant parts of the world almost instantaneous; the diving-bells that enable men to wrest from the sea the treasures which for long, long years she has held in her firm grasp; and an innumerable host of kindred subjects, crowd upon our attention, and claim our regard. But *one* book cannot contain them all. We are constrained, most unwillingly, to come to a close and bid our reader farewell.

The great wide ocean is filled with and surrounded by subjects of the deepest interest to mankind. As it is the great reservoir into which all the turbid streams of earth flow, there to be purified and sweetened, so is it the scene to which poets, philosophers, scholars, and mechanists may turn, find congenial subjects of contemplation, and, if they will, have their minds and hearts purified and lifted up in reverent adoration of Him whose word tells us that—"They that go down to the sea in ships, that do business in the great waters; these see the works of the Lord and his wonders in the deep."